Lawbreaker

Also by Diana Palmer

Long, Tall Texans

Fearless
Heartless
Dangerous
Merciless
Courageous
Protector
Invincible
Defender
Undaunted
Unbridled
Unleashed
Notorious
The Loner

Wyoming Men

Wyoming Tough
Wyoming Fierce
Wyoming Bold
Wyoming Strong
Wyoming Rugged
Wyoming Brave
Wyoming Winter
Wyoming Legend
Wyoming Heart
Wyoming True
Wyoming Homecoming

For a complete list of books by Diana Palmer,
visit dianapalmer.com.

DIANA PALMER

Lawbreaker

CANARY STREET PRESS

CANARY
STREET
PRESS™

Recycling programs
for this product may
not exist in your area.

ISBN-13: 978-1-335-51311-3

Lawbreaker

Canary Street Press
22 Adelaide St. West, 41st Floor
Toronto, Ontario M5H 4E3, Canada
CanaryStPress.com

Printed in U.S.A.

To Clay and Lisa with love

Dear Reader,

I had more fun than you can imagine with Tony and Odalie. They spent the first book in my Everett family trilogy, *The Loner*, glaring at each other. But in this book...well, read it and see for yourself, LOL.

When I wrote *Heather's Song* back in the '80s (?!), I had only a handful of published titles. And honestly, I never dreamed I'd live to see over 206 of my novels published. It has been an honor and a privilege to have so many in print and to have such a large following of readers who have become like family to me. Since I lost Jim in 2021 and my German shepherd, Dietrich, in May of 2024, those close friendships have meant even more.

I have one more Everett hardcover to write, and that's John's story. I'm looking forward to it because of the very unusual pet and girlfriend who enter his life. You'll see what I mean later!

Thank you all for your kindness, your empathy, your friendship and your prayers throughout the last three difficult years of my life. Having all of you around has made it so much easier to get past the grief.

Much love, many thanks, big hugs and best wishes from your biggest fan,

Diana Palmer

1

Odalie Everett sat seemingly relaxed in her seat on Tony Garza's private jet, but inside she was a bundle of nerves. She and Tony had been adversaries since their first meeting, years ago. He mostly looked through her, and he could be bitingly sarcastic. It should have deterred her from thinking about him, but it didn't. He was gorgeous.

She watched him out of the corner of her eye as he lounged opposite her in a chair, sending text messages on his phone. He frightened most people who knew him. Tony had been a crime boss for a significant portion of his life in New Jersey. He had a reputation that sent chills down the backs of people who crossed him.

He didn't look like a man who made his living on the wrong side of the law. He was tall and husky and drop-dead gorgeous, with black eyes and wavy black hair, cut conventionally short. No beard or mustache. A big nose and big hands and feet. High cheekbones and a piercing stare that could go through people like a sliver of ice.

Not that Odalie wasn't gorgeous, too. She looked like her mother, Heather Everett, with long light blond hair and blue eyes in a lovely face. Besides that, she had a voice like an angel. She'd studied opera for years now, been in various local artists programs in her native Texas, been overseas to study with master coaches. Now she was living in New York, near the art gallery and museum where Tony made most of his money, studying with a famous local coach while she girded her nerve to apply to the Metropolitan Opera.

She'd never shared her stage fright with her mother, who was a former singer. Her family had sacrificed so much for Odalie already. She told herself that she could overcome it. But several therapists had been unable to help her break through the fear. And one doctor had warned her that the stress of performing daily onstage could eventually cause cardiac issues. It was the dream of her life, to sing at the Met. Or it had been, before Tony stormed on to the scene when Odalie's brother Tanner was in danger and almost killed for something he'd witnessed overseas.

Tanner's wife, Anastasia—Stasia in the family—worked for Tony. He'd discovered her phenomenal art skills, had put her through school so that she could work as an art restorer for him, and her paintings, almost lifelike, sold for a fortune in his gallery. Tony called her his adopted daughter. He'd been widowed years ago, his young wife having died of cancer, and he had no children. He looked after Stasia, pampered her and put up with her best friend, Odalie. He did the last thing reluctantly and with obvious bias. He'd barely spoken to Odalie in the past.

But during a visit to Texas, the one they were returning

to New York from now, something had happened in the Everetts' living room, where Tony and Odalie were looking at a delicately beautiful fairy statue created by Odalie's friend Maddie Lane Brannt. They'd looked at each other in a way that neither of them was comfortable with, and it had caused this sudden and violent silence between them.

Tony had said multiple times that he had only one use for women. Everybody knew he had a mistress in New York, where he had a huge estate on Long Island and a penthouse apartment in Manhattan near his art gallery. He'd also made it very clear that Odalie wasn't in the running. Too young, he said sarcastically, and too perfect.

It didn't help. She couldn't fight the feelings she'd developed for him. Knowing his background, the difference in their ages…nothing helped. He was striking, not only because he was handsome, but because of his manner. He was afraid of nothing on earth, and he never backed down. To a Texas girl, those were admirable traits. She came from a family of men who were comparable, her father, Cole Everett, being the foremost of them. She admired strength and character. Tony might be a hood, but he was elegant and highly principled. He didn't go after people he didn't like. Only the ones who harmed people close to him. But once provoked, his anger could be deadly. There were rumors that, like his friend former mob boss Marcus Carrera, he knew how to use a gun and had, in the past.

These days, though, he was gaining a reputation as a highly respected art dealer who never cheated his clients and made sure every piece he sold was thoroughly vetted, so no fakes passed through his hands. Not only that, he made sure that they were acquired legally, not obtained in some back alley by that most dastardly of archaeological bandits, the pothunter. Tony was legitimate. It was how he'd made his fortune.

Now, in addition to his old home in New Jersey, he had a mansion on an estate in the Hamptons and a fabulous penthouse apartment in Manhattan, the envy of many friends. The penthouse housed some of his most famous objets d'art and a housekeeper, Helene Murdock, who kept the place running when Tony was away. He also had men who served as bodyguards. The head of his security force was Big Ben, who'd been with him for years.

Ben, tall and husky like the boss, but a few years younger, sat in the back of the plane playing video games on a Nintendo Switch. He had whole setups in his rooms, both at the mansion in the Hamptons and at the New York apartment. But he had handheld games that he loved. He also had a big gun that rode in a holster under his jacket. Odalie had seen him practicing with it once, at the lake house Tony maintained on Long Island.

The residence was a sprawling yellow two-story house with a four-car garage, ten thousand square feet of floor space on an equestrian-zoned property, close to an airport and farmland, and only sixty miles from Manhattan. Perfect for a man who loved the ocean, which was close by, and horseback riding. There was a stable near the mansion where Tony could rent horses for guests. The home had several bedrooms with full baths, a swimming pool, a tennis court, and every amenity known to man. Odalie, who'd grown up on a similar property in Texas, felt quite at home there when she went to parties on the property with Stasia. She didn't want to. Tony made his disinterest so plain that she felt guilty just being there.

He also had a fabulous apartment in a high-rise in Manhattan, close to where his art gallery and museum were located.

He threw cocktail parties at the apartment and the gallery, hosting important events with some of the most famous names in Hollywood and sports, as well as people from New Jersey whom he'd done business with and old pals who seemed a bit twitchy in the rarefied company.

Odalie liked the New Jersey bunch best. She was used to being around cowboys, who would have been equally uncomfortable with the jet set, but Tony was careful to keep her away from anyone from his hometown of Trenton. She'd never understood why. Stasia said that was just Tony. But his hostility to Odalie had convinced her that it was very personal. He didn't want her near his old friends. What little she learned about them, she liked, but she was never allowed close enough to gossip with any of them.

Her oldest brother, Tanner, had recently been targeted by Phillip James, a former colleague, now head of a supersecret agency in the government. Tanner had witnessed a massacre of civilians, which James had been responsible for. Tanner had been the target of an assassination attempt by James to keep him from telling what he knew. However, the attempt had failed, and Tanner had disclosed what he knew of the massacre. He was waiting, and hoping, for a congressional hearing on the matter.

But there was one fly in the soup. There was a rumor that Phillip James had a powerful senator in his corner, one who could—and possibly would—stonewall the investigation. James also had influence on the Hill, and he could use it. If he did, if he managed to weasel out from under the charges somehow, it would put Tanner right back on the firing line. Odalie loved her older brother. He'd been alienated from the family for years because of his harsh treatment of Stasia, to whom he'd been married. Their relationship had recently been patched up and they'd remarried, to the delight of the family, who loved Stasia. She was Odalie's best friend, next to Maddie Brannt, who made the beautiful little fairy statues, one of which Tony had commissioned for his gallery.

That had been another difficult and broken relationship, Odalie's with Maddie. When they were in high school, Odalie had victimized the other girl and almost got her killed. It had resulted in charges and probation, but Odalie had managed to come through it almost unscathed. She'd persuaded Cort Brannt, who'd once been infatuated with her, to let her drive his Jaguar. In the process, she'd accidentally run over Maddie. Her recovery had been long and hard, and being needed by another human being had turned Odalie's life around. She'd taken charge of Maddie, called in specialists, paid all her medical bills. And in the process, they'd become friends. In fact, Maddie was the first real friend, except for Stasia, that Odalie had ever had. Odalie had conspired with Cort to find a buyer for Maddie's gorgeous little fairies, and now the other woman had a lucrative profession. She and Cort were very happy together and, in fact, expecting their first child. Odalie had already been asked to be the godmother, and that was a true honor.

"We're landing," Tony announced, barely glancing at her. "Ben and I will drop you off at your apartment on the way home."

"Oh, I could get a cab," she said at once and then flushed, because it sounded ungrateful.

He gave her a long, measuring look. "It's not out of our way. But suit yourself," he added in a biting tone.

She swallowed. Hard. He was intimidating with that level stare. "Then, if you don't mind…"

He just shrugged and averted his gaze back to his phone.

★ ★ ★

They stopped at the curb and Ben carried Odalie's suitcase to her apartment on the quiet street with trees and a nearby coffeehouse. It was like living outside the city, but in the city, in an updated one-story house with all modern conveniences. It was even pretty on the outside, with wrought iron banisters and a stone front, with long windows behind which elegant lacy white curtains fell to give their owner some privacy.

"Thanks, Ben," she said, smiling up at him.

"No problem. Listen," he added gently, "the boss has moods. Always has had. Don't let it upset you. He's got some little problems lately. Nothing big. But it makes him broody. It's not you or anything you done. Okay?"

The smile grew bigger. "Thanks," she said huskily. "It just seems like sometimes he hates me, you know?"

"A lot of people think that," he chuckled. "That stare. One guy said Tony could kill you with his eyes. I know just what he meant!"

"Me, too," she laughed. "Thanks again for bringing my bag. It gets heavy."

"I noticed. See you."

"See you."

She forced herself not to look toward the stretch limo, where Tony was sitting behind tinted windows. *Probably still glaring at me,* she thought as she unlocked her door and carried her bag inside.

Phillip James was almost purring as he spoke to the senator. "You don't want me to tell what I know about you," he spoke into the phone. "Now, do you?"

There was a grating pause. "No."

He almost laughed at the force with which the single word

was uttered. "I didn't think so." He drew in a breath. "So you'll tell them you can't dig up any evidence of wrongdoing."

"I'll tell them."

"I'm counting on you," James replied, and he hung up.

It was a relief. Tanner Everett had put him in a bad position. It was rotten luck that the man had so many damned scruples and that he'd actually protested the accidental killing of a few civilians. The operation hadn't been that important, and they'd been attacked by some members of a village. He hadn't paid much attention to where he was shooting. Automatic rifles weren't so easy to control in the heat of battle. Everett made him sound like a murderer. It wasn't as if a few ragged civilians would be missed in that mud-hut society. So some of the victims were children. What the hell. Stuff like that happened in firefights. Nobody got all up in arms about it. Well, most of his men didn't. Everett wasn't like the rest.

He'd tried to have the man killed in an overseas assignment. A handful of young agents had paid the price for that fumbled attempt, and now Everett had even more ammunition against him. But he couldn't really prove anything. James had covered his tracks in South America, just as he'd covered them in Iraq. And the senator he was blackmailing wouldn't dare go against him. One whiff of what James had in his office safe would cost the senator not only his well-paid career, but his reputation as well.

He leaned back in his desk chair, smiling to himself, and picked up his cell phone again. He dialed a number.

"Hi," he said. "How's things?"

"Hi, Dad" came the bright reply. "I'm just studying for exams," his son replied.

"Study hard," he told the boy. "I don't want to spend the rest of my life supporting you."

It was an old joke. They both laughed. James's wife had died years ago. It was just his son, Bob, and him at home now. Not that Bob was at home. He was taking classes at a nearby college, learning to be an architect. The boy had real talent. He could draw so well. If there was one chink in James's armor, it was his son. He'd do anything to keep the boy safe.

Over the years, there had been one or two attempts to get back at him through his child, but things had been quiet for several years now. He'd relaxed his scrutiny. Everett was the only real enemy he had at the moment, and that man wouldn't lower himself to attacking a soft target like James's son. It was one of the only things James admired about Everett. He only wished he'd known about the man's ironclad principles before he'd tagged him to go on that black ops job in Iraq. It had come back to bite him.

But now he had a senator, and a powerful one at that, in his back pocket, and Everett couldn't threaten him anymore. Life was good.

"You coming home this weekend?" James asked.

There was a slight hesitation. "Well, there's this party," his son began.

"Never mind. Have fun while you're still young," he replied, concealing his disappointment. After all, the kid was only nineteen. Let him enjoy college and all its perks.

"Thanks, Dad. Next weekend for sure," he added brightly.

"For sure. Take care. Love you," he added softly.

"Yeah. Talk to you soon." He hung up.

James sighed. Maybe he should have been a little firmer with the boy when he was younger. He lacked a lot of social graces, and he wasn't sentimental. But then, neither was Phillip James. Not at all.

★ ★ ★

Odalie was trying to hide her sadness while she took her voice lesson. She couldn't understand why she'd become so morose lately. Maybe it was nerves. Maybe it was her monthly that was making her melancholy.

Maybe it's Tony, she thought, and clamped down hard on the memory of that glare he'd given her before she got off the plane.

She hadn't even thanked him for the ride, she recalled with a grimace.

"Now, now, young woman. Less absentmindedness, more attention to the notes," her instructor chided with a smile.

"I'm sorry," she said at once and laughed. "I've just come from my home in Texas and I'm missing my family." It was a half-truth, but he seemed to accept it.

"At least you have a family to miss," he said gently. "I lost my wife twenty years ago and we had no children. If I could not teach, I would have no life at all. I love my work. Especially, I love finding talent such as yours to nourish."

"Thank you," she said sincerely. "You have no idea how happy I am to have found you to train me."

He just shrugged. "Your voice coach in Italy is an old acquaintance from my youth. I value his opinion."

"I'm afraid that I wasn't the best of pupils," she confessed. "I've changed a lot since I studied with him."

"So I've noticed," he said with a wicked grin, and she knew that he'd probably heard about her very snobbish behavior from his friend.

She'd left Italy in a huff because she didn't agree with her instructor's assessment of her vocal skills. It seemed like another life now, because she'd changed so much.

"I had a tragedy—or a near tragedy—in my life not too

many months ago," she told him. "It changed me as a person. I think sometimes the best lessons we learn are from the worst things that happen to us."

"I totally agree," he said. He smiled. "You are very easy to work with."

She laughed. "I wasn't in Italy, as I'm sure your friend told you. It seems like a lifetime ago," she added, shaking her head. "I've learned so much since then, and not just about ways to protect and project my voice," she added with a smile.

"That, I hope, will stand you in good stead when you finally muster enough nerve to audition for the Metropolitan Opera," he said firmly.

She grimaced. "I'll do it. But not just yet," she said.

He shook his head. "Well, as they say, the time will not be wasted as you train. But you must not wait too long."

"I won't," she promised.

"Excellent. Then, back to work!"

It was only a week later that Stasia called. "Hi," she said brightly. "How are you doing?"

Odalie sighed. It was Thursday and she had another boring, lonely weekend to look forward to. "I'm lonely and homesick," she confessed. "How are you?"

"Pregnant" came the smug reply.

Odalie laughed. "I know. I'm looking very forward to being an aunt in a few months."

"I'm looking forward to being a mom," Stasia said on a sigh. "It's like a dream, marrying Tanner all over again and living happily together. Not so long ago, that would have been a pipe dream. He's changed."

"So have I," Odalie confessed. "I still can't believe I was such a brat. You're not spoiling my nephew or niece, by the way, just so you know," she teased. "I'll be watching from the sidelines. I won't disturb you, but I'll advise, so be warned."

"No secret there." She hesitated. "Speaking of disturbing things…"

"Phillip James has surfaced again?" Odalie guessed worriedly.

"Nothing so dire. But there's going to be this huge house party at Tony's over the weekend at the Long Island mansion…"

"No!"

There was a pause. "I haven't even asked you yet," Stasia said, exasperated.

"It's still no," Odalie said shortly. "He glared at me or ignored me all the way home on the jet. My self-esteem can't survive a weekend of that."

"It can, and it will, because I'll be there, too," Stasia said gently. "We can share a room. I'll protect you from Tony."

"Why do I have to go?" came the plaintive reply.

"Because if you don't go, I can't go. Tanner's gone militant on me about the baby," she laughed. "He's afraid that I'll do things I shouldn't. I won't, but that's beside the point. He says if you go, it's okay if I go. And I need to go because Tony's trying to pry a Renoir out of the hands of an elderly gentleman who plans to leave it to his only son. The son thinks art treasures are ridiculous, and he says he's going to trash his father's collection when the old man dies."

"That's history!" Odalie exclaimed, horrified. "Would he really do that?"

"The boy has a very bad history of doing things just like that in the name of activism."

"What sort of activism trashes historic art?" Odalie asked.

"The sort that wants to wipe out history altogether and start over."

"But art is beautiful," Odalie said, from her heart. "It's the story of mankind in oils. It's a legacy from the past. To even speak of destroying such treasures is...is... I can't even think of the words!"

"Neither can I. So we have to go to Tony's place this weekend and talk the man into selling the collection to Tony."

Odalie ground her teeth together. "I guess I can stand a weekend around him, if I'm blindfolded and gagged." She paused. "Is his mistress coming?" she asked, trying not to sound as if it bothered her.

"No," Stasia said. "She doesn't really like the Long Island house because Tony always hires horses. She's deathly afraid of them."

Odalie gave a silent thanks for that small mercy. Tony's mistress was beautiful and even kind, Stasia told her once. She had a reputation for being snarky, but that was only when she was upset at something, and outbursts were rare. She sort of shared Tony and two other men. Why it didn't bother Tony was something Odalie, who'd never indulged, couldn't understand.

"Okay," she said.

Stasia hesitated to put into words what she was really thinking. Was Odalie jealous of Tony? There was so much antagonism there that she truly wondered if there wasn't a powerful emotion underneath it, and maybe even a mutual longing. Not that either of the two stubborn people would ever admit it. Not presently, anyway.

"I'm going to fly up Friday morning. Do you have a lesson then?" Stasia asked.

"No, my teacher has a doctor visit then." She laughed. "He says he spends three hours in the waiting room every time. But the doctor spends a lot of time with all his patients, including him, so he doesn't really mind. A lot of medicine these days

is supermarket-style. Get in, get out, don't talk, just listen."
Odalie sighed. "It's not like that back home. Our doctor always has time for us. Up here, I just go to quick-care places if I ever have to. And it was only once, for a migraine."

"Don't eat chocolate," Stasia said firmly. "Got that?"

Odalie hesitated. She grinned. "I might have a few chocolate-covered cherries Friday morning..."

"Don't you dare!" came the reply. "I'm not spending my weekend looking after you instead of persuading Tony's reluctant art collector!"

"I'd be okay in a few hours. I have medicine."

"Your migraines last for three days," Stasia replied knowledgeably, "and there goes my weekend."

"Spoilsport."

"There will be several handsome single men there," Stasia said slowly.

"I don't like men," Odalie said shortly. "I like music. Specifically, opera. I didn't study my whole life to give in to some man and be dangled like a participle."

Stasia burst out laughing. "Oh, my gosh, what a description!"

Odalie chuckled. "I'll copyright it first thing tomorrow."

"Anyway, no chocolate, no aged cheese, no red wine before Friday," Stasia added.

"Okay. I'll restrain myself."

"Good. I'll see you Friday, then."

"I'll be there. Give Tanner and the family my love, and tell them I miss everybody!"

There was a pause. "Even Earl?"

"No! No, I don't miss Earl!" she said, aghast. "Has Dad ever managed to show him what a bar of soap is for? At least it's winter and cowboys won't die if they get downwind of him!"

Stasia was laughing heartily. "I know. He's like a human skunk. Your dad has tried everything he knows. Nothing works. Earl has the same jeans and shirt he's been wearing for years, and not only will he not bathe, he won't wash his clothes. He says they'll just get dirty all over again!"

Odalie laughed, too. "We always have at least one oddball among the men. Dad gave him his own little cabin at least, so nobody has to live with the odor at night. He can't fire him. Earl knows more about the ranch and how it's managed than anybody alive, and there isn't any situation he can't handle. He's worth his weight in gold. If he'd just bathe."

"He needs a wife."

"She'd have to be without a sense of smell."

"Good point. Nose plugs?"

"Not likely. He's been a bachelor for his whole sixty years. I don't expect him to change anytime soon," Odalie said.

"Tony's got an eccentric guy like that," Stasia said. "Did you know that Big Ben knits?"

"What?!"

"Tony made him quit smoking, and he gets really nervous at night. So he got a book on how to knit and bought yarn and needles. He makes sweaters."

"I guess it's not so far-fetched," Odalie replied. "They say Marcus Carrera makes really good quilts and exhibits."

"He does. His casino on Paradise Island is called the Bow Tie because it's his favorite quilting pattern. He's won awards."

"So I heard. Amazing, considering what he used to do for a living," Odalie laughed.

"A lot of people from criminal backgrounds are moving into legitimate businesses. It's not that they give up who they are. They just adjust to a new way of making money. Carrera runs a casino. Tony deals in statuary and paintings. Not that I think he's given up any of his territory," she added. "He has underlings who carry on with the 'family' business back in New Jersey. But Tony's, shall we say, removed from the day-to-day operations."

"Once a crime boss, always a crime boss," Odalie said cuttingly.

"Tony's not your average boss," Stasia replied gently. "He cares a great deal for the people who work for him, and he treats them all equally. He has a kind heart."

"Which he keeps carefully tucked away so that nobody can see it. Except maybe you."

"Oh, so bitter," Stasia teased. "You need some company to cheer you up. I'll call you when I get in on Friday."

"You'll have to get a cab…" Odalie began apologetically, because she didn't have a car in New York.

"Big Ben will pick me up and bring me to your place, don't worry," Stasia said. "I'll see you then."

"Have a good trip," Odalie replied.

They hung up and she went back to her books on music theory. She hadn't wanted to go to the Long Island house, but now she was trapped. Well, at least she'd be with Stasia all the time, so maybe Tony wouldn't go for her throat in company. Maybe.

Tony was still brooding about that exchange of eyes with Odalie at Big Spur. He didn't want the woman around. He didn't know why. She was beautiful and talented. But she was too damned young, not street-smart, and she'd never been poor or operated outside the law.

No way in hell was he getting mixed up with a kid like her. She was what, twenty-three, twenty-four? Still years too young for a man of thirty-seven. Worse, she had no idea what his life was really like. He didn't want her to know. He didn't know why, either, and that made him mad, too.

He took a deep breath and stared out the window at the city below. It was convenient to live here, but he missed his garden. He'd had one at the house in New Jersey, but when his business interests centered in New York City, he bought this apartment to be close to the art gallery he owned. The house in Jersey had a cousin, an underboss, living in it now, taking care of business. Tony had a garden, still, but it was indoors on Long Island—his housekeeper called it "the jungle," but with affection. He grew orchids and exotic plants. The room had cushy chairs and grow lights and every comfort. Plus, a person could hide from guests in it. Tony did that, from time to time, when people started getting on his nerves. Most people couldn't understand why he loved it so. But then, only a gardener would.

His house on Long Island was huge and the grounds were beautiful. He loved it because it reminded him of where he'd grown up in New Jersey. Not the size and luxury, of course. But it felt like home. He'd spent a lot of time on his grandfather's farm in upstate New York, on the land. He really preferred it to the city, but he couldn't make money in some small backwater.

He was irritated because Stasia had insisted that he let her bring Odalie to the Long Island place for the weekend. He didn't want her there. Stasia, sure, she was going to help him convince Tom Bishop to sell him those exquisite old-world paintings. But Odalie? She'd just be in the way. Worse, she'd be in *his* way.

He couldn't take a whole weekend of her. He'd tried to talk Stasia out of it, but when she'd told him that Tanner wouldn't agree for her to come without Odalie—well, that

was it. He needed Stasia. He was no good at persuasion unless he used something that contained bullets. Stasia could do
it with words.

Odalie, for a whole weekend. He groaned out loud. How
was he going to bear it?!

2

Stasia rang the doorbell at Odalie's apartment just after breakfast on Friday. Odalie almost ran to open it, then laughed as they hugged.

"Thanks for bringing her, Ben," Odalie told him warmly.

"No sweat. I'll be back to pick you up about three. Boss doesn't like traffic snarls, so he leaves early when we go up to the house," Ben explained to her.

"He hates traffic," Stasia agreed. "But then, so do I. Thanks, Ben."

He shrugged. "See you later."

He put the two suitcases Stasia had brought in the living room and left.

"He's so nice," Odalie said. "I wish we could say that about his boss," she added with a venomous smile.

"Stop that," Stasia teased.

"Sorry." She studied her sister-in-law. "You're not even showing yet," she teased.

"You should see me try to fasten a skirt or a pair of pants" came the reply, and Stasia pulled up her sweater to show that her pants had the top button undone.

"Well, you're showing a little," she conceded. "Come on in. Have you had breakfast?"

"Yes, at the ranch, but I'd love coffee."

"I have decaf—it's okay," Odalie laughed when she noted the other woman's expression.

"Sorry. I'm still not used to things I shouldn't have," Stasia said.

"Dad says Mom drank a pot a day until she was pregnant with Tanner, and that the sudden stop almost killed her. They both still laugh about it—while they're chugging cappuccino."

Stasia laughed. "I love being around your family. I'm sort of short on relatives."

Odalie hugged her. "You have all of us. We're your family now."

Stasia fought tears.

"You stop that, or I'll start bawling, too." She shook her head as she made coffee. "Imagine, being stranded on Long Island all weekend with a barracuda, and all because I adore you and I'd do anything for you," she added with a meaningful glare.

"Tony's sweet."

"Like sauerkraut," Odalie agreed.

"Women love him," Stasia pointed out. "He's handsome, he's rich, he loves animals…"

"He kills people," Odalie continued.

"No, he doesn't," Stasia replied, chuckling. "Well, there were some rumors about him in the past. But he certainly doesn't do wet work now. He has the art gallery."

"Wet work?" Odalie asked, all at sea.

"When you live with an ex-mercenary, it rubs off," she confessed with a grin. "Wet work. Blood...?"

"Oh! Like in that book about 'painting houses,' that's really about killing people," Odalie replied and then bit her tongue, because she'd never meant to admit she wanted to know what Tony's former lifestyle had really been like.

But Stasia didn't say a word. She changed the subject to clothes instead.

"I've got this exquisite new dress," Odalie said, showing it to her. "It's a couture piece, but I fell in love with it, so there goes my allowance for the next three months." She sighed as she studied the gorgeous hand-painted sheath dress with its pink and silver and purple glittery highlights.

"It really is lovely. It will suit you," Stasia said. "I've got a new one, too, a black flare skirt with a glittery black-and-gold overlay and a draped bodice. Spent my allowance going forward on that, so I know what you mean!" she laughed. "Clothes are my weakness."

"For at least one more month," Odalie teased, nodding at her belly.

"Oh, they have couture for pregnant women, too" came the laughing reply. "I can still be at the forefront of fashion despite my lovely condition. Not that I love clothes more than your brother," she had to add. She sighed. "Dreams come true, you know?"

"For some people," Odalie agreed.

"You sing beautifully," her companion replied solemnly. "And you will sing at the Met one day. I've never doubted that. But you have to get over this stage fright and do the audition!"

"So my music teacher keeps saying," Odalie said.

"You've sung onstage in young artists' venues, you used to sing every Sunday in church—what's the difference?" her friend asked.

"Because this is going onstage and singing for professional people. I'm scared to death."

"Tanner has this great book. It's written by a former navy SEAL..."

"About how to do commando raids?" was the surprised reply.

"No. About how to use fear, instead of giving in to it. It's not about how to kill people. It's how to keep them from killing you in combat, if you get in a desperate situation. And I read it myself. It's full of useful tips."

"As if I'll ever be in a desperate situation," Odalie laughed.

"Well, it is a bit far-fetched. But it's still good information, even if it's never used for a life-and-death thing."

"Okay. Send me a link and I'll get a digital copy," Odalie agreed.

"I'll do that. You'll be surprised at how interesting it is."

Odalie sighed. "I guess I have been in one desperate situation, when I ran over Maddie." She grimaced.

Stasia remembered the other woman's agony after that tragic occurrence, when Odalie's now-friend Maddie Lane Brannt had run into the road chasing her pet rooster and Odalie had accidentally hit her while driving Cort Brannt's Jaguar. "You didn't mean to, though," Stasia pointed out. "And you stayed with her all through rehabilitation, paid all her medical bills and even got her a fantastic job making little fairy statues for collectors—including one for Tony's art gallery. She's incredibly rich now, even though the Brannts have that fabulous ranch, Skylance, right next to ours. She became rich when she married Cort Brannt." She sighed. "He was a dish. Not a patch on Tanner, however."

"Tanner really is gorgeous, even if he is my big brother," Odalie had to agree. "And you're forgetting that we shared the agony of thinking Tanner was dead when that James man tried to have him killed overseas."

"It was a horror of a situation. For all of us."

"That book on controlling fear would have come in very handy back then."

"Oh, would it!" Stasia sighed. "Well, let's get you packed for the weekend. My bags are ready," she teased, indicating them by the door in the living room, where Ben had left them.

"Let's see, I have a pair of jeans with no knees, and a black dress that covers me up from top to bottom..." Odalie began.

Stasia just looked at her.

She sighed. "Okay. I'll pack some couture things and I'll try very hard not to throw anything at your former boss."

"Current boss," Stasia teased. "I still work for him part-time, as long as I'm able. After the baby comes, I'll be making fewer trips to New York."

"I'll be making more to Texas," Odalie replied, beaming. "I'll be an aunt for the first time. I can't wait!"

"Neither can we. It's like my own personal fairy tale, with even the happy ending!"

"I hope I'll have one of those," Odalie said, "but with the Met at the end, not a man."

"Don't you want to get married and have kids?" Stasia asked seriously.

Odalie looked worried. "Well, I do and I don't." She glanced at her friend. "I've worked so hard at training to sing opera that everything else has taken a back seat to it. I loved having Cort Brannt serenading me and bringing me flowers, but I never really felt anything physical for him. He was just a friend. I felt bad that he had feelings for me that I couldn't return, but it just wasn't there."

"Like me with your poor younger brother, John," Stasia said sadly. "I've never felt worse than when I saw his face after Tanner came home wounded and I was taking care of him." She looked up. "John is a wonderful man. But I never felt that way about him. It's sad when it turns out like that."

"John is a survivor," Odalie said gently. "He's an Everett. He'll get through it and one day he'll find a woman who can love him back." She hesitated. "Of course, she'll need to love the smell of cow chips and the sight of cattle most all day, and conventions and auctions..."

They both laughed.

"If she loves him, she won't mind," Odalie added. "And maybe she'll even like cattle!"

Ben came to pick them up at three on the dot. He carried the suitcases out to the trunk of Tony's beautifully polished black stretch limo, and paused to open the back door to let the women get inside.

Odalie made sure that Stasia got in first so that she had to sit next to Tony, with Odalie on the outside by the other door.

Tony noticed that, and he started to ask her if she thought he had something contagious. But it wouldn't do to start a war with poor Stasia in the middle, especially in her condition.

"How are you?" Tony asked with a smile. "You don't even look pregnant!"

Stasia laughed. "You'd reconsider that remark if you could see me puking my guts out every morning and watch me go to bed with the chickens every night." She shook her head. "It's wonderful, but very incapacitating."

"You still look great," he said warmly. "How's my fairy statue coming?" he added.

"Maddie's putting on the last touches now," she told him. "She said by the end of the month, hopefully. She's puking her guts out and going to sleep with the chickens, too, you know," she laughed.

He chuckled deeply. "Maybe it's the water."

"Excuse me?"

"Next-door neighbors both pregnant at the same time," he explained.

"Oh!" She laughed. "Maybe it is. How's business?"

"Great. If we can land this deal, even greater," he said. He sighed. "Tom Bishop's son, Bob, wants to trash his art collection. Not sell it, not loan it, trash it. The kid's going to inherit about two billion dollars when his dad goes, and he said he hates the art because his dad spent more time adding to it than he ever spent with his kids. He blames his brother's death on the paintings."

"Why?" Stasia asked, aghast.

"Kid had appendicitis. Nobody was home except the kids because of an ice storm. Tom and his wife were stuck in town. Bob tried to call 911 but there had been a storm and all the phones were dead, and all the roads closed to traffic by ice. They live out in the boondocks in upstate Vermont." He shook his head. "The kid died. Tom and his wife grieved, of course, and nobody blamed Bob. But Bob never got over it. He felt responsible, but he blamed his dad even more. They hardly speak. This is why we've got to get those paintings away from Tom while there's time. He's in his late seventies, and he's got cancer. It's under control, but nobody knows for how long."

"That's so sad. About the cancer, and the child. But those paintings, Tony. They're like a history of Europe in oils!"

"I know," he said heavily.

Odalie, who'd gone to college on a music scholarship, but minored in art history, was intrigued. "What sort of paintings?" she asked, wondering aloud.

"Art history minor," Stasia told Tony, indicating Odalie.

He raised both eyebrows. He hadn't known about her interest in art. "One of them is a Renoir," he replied.

She whistled softly. "It would be a crime to throw away any art, but that should be a life sentence if he actually does it."

"I agree," he said, hating his interest in her. He didn't want to appreciate how very lovely she was, or how smart. He averted his eyes back to Stasia. It took some effort, but none of it showed on his poker face. "You'll have your work cut out to influence Tom," he told Stasia. "He loves Bob. He doesn't think his son's serious about trashing the paintings. But with two billion in his pocket, their monetary value wouldn't influence him."

"There are people who don't think art has any part in civilization," Odalie said.

"That would be the same people who are tearing down statues and gluing themselves to frames in museums," Stasia said, tongue-in-cheek.

Tony pursed his chiseled lips and his black eyes twinkled. "It would be interesting to see anybody try that in my gallery."

"I get cold chills just thinking about it," Stasia murmured without thinking.

"I don't kill people," he said indignantly.

"What? Oh!" Stasia burst out laughing. "I was thinking about the potential damage to the paintings, Tony."

He grimaced. "Sorry."

"I know you're touchy about the old days, you old bear," Stasia teased, smiling. "And you know me better than that."

"Of course I do," he said, relenting. He drew in a breath. "You never get away from the past, you know? It clings."

Odalie thought that was probably true if you'd whacked half a dozen people, which Tony had been rumored to do in the past. But she just smiled angelically and didn't say a word.

Tony saw that smile. It was more like a smirk. It bruised his ego. It shouldn't have. Why should he care about the opinion of a rich girl from Texas, after all? He ignored it.

"Who's coming this weekend?" Stasia asked.

It was an easy subject. He rattled off names, including one that he put some emphasis on. Burt Donalson.

"Oh, not him," Stasia groaned.

"I had to invite him," Tony protested. "He and Tom are best friends. He's driving Tom down to the house."

"We could have sent a car," she said.

"Sure, and he'd have found an excuse not to come. It will be okay. I'll put him out by the garage. Ben will keep an eye on him."

"Is his poor wife coming, too?" Stasia asked.

"No. She probably has had enough of him pursuing any pretty face he can find." He thought about Odalie's pretty face as he processed the thought, and he had a cold feeling in the pit of his stomach.

So did Stasia. She knew Burt from her time as a single woman. She'd finally had Tony have a word with him about being too forward. When Tony spoke, people listened. Burt was scared of him.

But Odalie was Burt's sort of target, a beautiful high-class woman. Odalie could handle herself, but she shouldn't be subjected to a predator like Burt for a whole weekend. Of course, it was possible that he'd pursue somebody else. Tony always had plenty of people staying at the estate when he went up there.

It would be crowded. So, maybe there wouldn't be trouble. She hoped so, especially when she'd had to coax Odalie into going with her.

The house on Long Island was a revelation to Odalie, who'd never seen it before. She caught her breath as it came into view past trees and a wrought iron fence with gates around the house proper.

"It's gorgeous," she exclaimed.

Tony almost ground his teeth. He'd wanted her to hate it, to live down to his opinion of her as an empty-headed rich girl.

"It's huge," Stasia said, noting that Tony didn't say a word. "It has about a dozen bedrooms all with private baths. There's an indoor heated Olympic swimming pool, a tennis court, a huge garage—Tony needs it for his classic cars," she added with a wry glance at her boss.

"Like Dad has," Odalie mused. "He has a 1960-something classic Jaguar convertible, the one with the teardrop-shaped headlights, that John keeps trying to sneak off the property. He's dying to drive it. Dad keeps hiding the keys," she added gleefully.

Tony gave in to curiosity. "Why doesn't he want your brother to drive it?" he asked.

"John just wrecked his second Jaguar," she explained.

"And he was lucky they make Jaguars with excellent safety features, to say nothing of air bags," Stasia added. "He walked away with scratches and bruises. But this time his insurance company made threats."

"Is he that bad a driver?" Tony chuckled, addressing Stasia.

"He's absent-minded," Odalie answered. "He was reaching for his cell phone in the pocket of the car door and took his eyes off the road. He went over a bridge into the river. Well, it's not a river this time of year, only when the rains come," she added.

"Okay, what was that?" he asked abruptly.

"A lot of our rivers don't have water certain times of the year," Odalie explained.

Tony, used to rivers that were full all the time, just stared.

"It's a Western thing," Odalie continued. "In Arizona, even in West Texas, it's way worse," she said.

He shook his head. "Every day, you learn something new."

Odalie's face revealed to her oldest friend that she was about to say something outrageous.

"Did your housekeeper come up already to supervise the cleaners and the other weekend hires?" Stasia said before Odalie could ask anything embarrassing.

"Yeah," Tony told her, leaning back in the comfortable seat. "It takes a lot of work to get ready for that many people. I always have the checks issued with bonuses for the workers."

"My parents do that for our workers when we have parties," Odalie mentioned, without meaning to. "It's a good thing to do. So many of them don't make much from the agencies they work for."

"My mother worked for one of those agencies, cleaning houses," Tony said with a faint bite in his voice. "But she very rarely got anything extra."

Which was probably why Tony paid people well, Odalie thought, and felt guilty for being so vicious to him half the time. She didn't know why she was antagonistic. Well, yes, she did. She found Tony very attractive. She loved to sit and look at him when he didn't notice. And she was still having uncomfortable flashbacks to that long, lingering look they'd shared at Big Spur while looking at the little fairy statue

Maddie Lane Brannt had made of Odalie. The moment had haunted her. She'd never felt such a sensation in her whole life.

"I guess your parents have always been rich," Tony mentioned to Odalie.

"Not really," she said. "When Dad was little, there wasn't much money. His grandfather and my grandmother's husband went into business together and started building the ranch. But it was Dad's idea to go into breeding purebred bulls and heifers. He's turned it into a prosperous business, and especially when he branched out into modern genetics and stuff. It didn't hurt that Mom had an amazing career as a singer and then started writing songs that won awards."

"She's a beautiful woman, too," Tony added.

"Yes, she is," Odalie said, smiling. "Dad loved her when they were teenagers. She loved him, too, but she fought him because he wanted to tell her what to do and how to live. She said she wasn't being owned by any man."

He chuckled.

"Cole would have walked all over her if she'd given in," Stasia remarked. "Heather often says that."

"Dad's forceful. But he's fair," Odalie added. She grinned. "He can still outride any cowboy on the place."

"I noticed," Tony said, having spent some time watching Cole when they were at the ranch not too long ago. "He's a tough guy."

"You have to be to control our cowboys," Odalie replied. "Talk about a wild bunch!"

"They get drunk occasionally," Stasia explained.

"And occasionally it takes a big fist in the right place to settle down the most belligerent of them," Odalie said gleefully.

"Sounds like home," Tony mused.

"I guess New York gets rough, too," Odalie conceded.

"New Jersey," he corrected. "I grew up on the backstreets." He clammed up. Some of those stories weren't fit for mixed company.

Odalie didn't say a word. She'd read about half of the book she'd mentioned to Stasia. She was beginning to get a picture of Tony's past life. Ironically, she felt sorry for him. A kid growing up in that sort of environment would have to be tough.

Stasia felt the tension in the car like a wound. So it was a good thing that they were pulling up at the front door.

Big Ben opened the back door and Odalie climbed out, followed by Stasia. Tony got out on the opposite side and stretched. Odalie, watching, almost groaned. He was so damned gorgeous!

She averted her eyes before he caught her staring. There, on the porch, Mrs. Murdock was standing, wearing a beautifully embroidered apron over her nice tan-and-white dress, her hair in a bun, her blue eyes twinkling behind the lenses of her glasses.

"Glory be, you made it alive! Big Ben drove all the way, then, did he?" she teased.

Tony made a face at her. "Show some respect, woman! I pay your wages," he roared.

She made a face back. "As good a cook as I am, I'd have a job five minutes after you fired me, and for more money!"

"Ha!"

Stasia was roaring with laughter. Odalie, watching, wasn't sure how to take what she was hearing.

"He makes threats," Mrs. Murdock told her. "I make threats. Pay it no mind. Come in! I have coffee. I expect you're all dying for it." She paused and glanced at Odalie. "I have spring water…"

"I love coffee," Odalie told her with a warm smile. "In fact, I live on it."

She relaxed. "All right, then! We've had a guest now and again with odd tastes in what to drink and eat..."

"Stop right there unless you want to be looking for work again," Tony threatened.

"Not my fault you brought her here," Mrs. Murdock said huffily. "Strange woman at that. Only wanted two leaves of lettuce with one radish on it, no dressing, and a bottle of fresh spring water. How in the world do you get fresh spring water...?"

"I said..." Tony began belligerently.

"Good thing she only lasted one day," Mrs. Murdock finished, unabashed. "I was searching out a source of hemlock leaves..."

"I said..." he repeated, louder.

"Oh, never mind," Mrs. Murdock sighed. "With my luck, poison would only have encouraged her anyway."

Tony threw up his hands.

The guests started arriving two hours later. Stasia had gone to the enormous room she and Odalie would share for the weekend to take a nap, and Odalie had gone right with her, unwilling to be left alone with Tony. He noticed that, and his even temper began to deteriorate.

"What are you going to wear?" Odalie asked Stasia while they were going through the closet, where a maid had hung their collection of garments.

"I thought this," Stasia said, indicating the long silk skirt with its pretty glittery blouse that matched.

"Lovely, especially with your coloring," Odalie replied, smiling. "But surely not with spike heels?"

Stasia shook her head. "Low stacked ones. I'm wobbly from time to time," she laughed. "What are you going to wear?"

"Is this too dressy?" Odalie asked, displaying the silk couture dress she'd shown her friend at her apartment.

"Not at all. It's lovely. We can dress down a little after tonight, but we want to make a good first impression," she added. "At least, I do," she teased.

Odalie slipped into the dress, which flattered her full figure, and then started to pin up her hair.

"No," Stasia said firmly. She took the clips away and the brush, and concocted a forties-ish hairstyle, with a wave in front and long, luxurious big curls that fell around Odalie's shoulders.

"I'll look odd," Odalie protested.

"You'll look unique," she replied. "It's gorgeous, so hush. I'm wearing mine the same way. We'll be twins," she teased.

"In that case, okay. I didn't want to stand out."

Stasia eyed her, taking in her elegant carriage, her lovely face with just the lightest touch of makeup, her pretty hairdo and the couture dress she was wearing with spiked heels that matched. "Wow," she said. "You'll have men following you around like puppy dogs."

Odalie made a face. "The last thing I want," she scoffed.

"Doesn't matter what you want," her friend teased. "You're a knockout."

"You look lovely. Pregnancy makes you radiant," Odalie said with a smile.

"I feel radiant. Well, we should go down."

Odalie made a face. "Is this trip really necessary?"

Stasia took her arm. "Yes."

The hall was full of people. Tony was standing there with a male guest, but when he noticed the two women coming down the winding staircase, he turned. His black eyes landed on Odalie. She was a vision, so beautiful that his stomach clenched.

He felt his heart drop with every step she took. She was the most exquisite woman he'd ever seen in his life. He ached to wrap her up tight and kiss her until she couldn't stand. His teeth ground together. But that was a thought he had to kill, and at once. He didn't dare touch her. She had a career in sight that she'd worked all her life for. Besides, what did a guy like him have to offer a young woman like that?

Odalie was stifling similar thoughts. Tony in a tux was a sight to make the most sophisticated woman drool, much less Odalie. His olive skin contrasted with the spotless white shirt he was wearing with the tux and black tie, which made him look even more handsome than he ordinarily did. His tall, husky, muscular body was also the stuff of dreams. Add that to his wavy black hair with just a few silver threads and those black eyes, and he was a delight to anybody's eyes.

She lowered her eyes to the steps because she was staring at him. That would never do. He didn't like her and couldn't have made it any more obvious. He tolerated her for Stasia's sake, but that was all he did, and she'd better remember it. Tony had a mistress. Everybody knew. She wondered if the woman wanted to come tonight, or if he let her mingle with his highbrow guests. She fought down jealousy. She'd never met the other woman. Stasia said she was beautiful and very sweet, that she wasn't catty or mean or unkind. Stasia also said that the woman had men besides Tony. That was still a puzzle. Tony looked the possessive sort.

Well, that kind of lifestyle was a mystery to Odalie. She tried not to think about it. She didn't like to imagine Tony with other women.

"Big crowd," Stasia told Tony with a grin.

He chuckled and bent to kiss her cheek. "Just my style," he teased. "You look lovely."

"Thanks," Stasia replied, smiling up at him.

"This the adopted daughter you tell everybody about?" the man with Tony asked, staring at Stasia. "What a dish!"

The man was tall and athletic, with too many teeth, a smile that was just short of arrogant, and a face that was pleasant but not pleasant enough to attract any but a truly desperate woman.

Stasia just stared at him, unsmiling.

It was so unlike her that Odalie's eyes widened.

"Yes," Tony said shortly. "You need to sample those cakes Mrs. Murdock made, Burt," he added curtly. "Over on the canapé table."

So that was the infamous Burt Donalson, Odalie thought. He looked like what he was, a slick predator who thought he was God's gift to women.

"You can't banish me without formal introductions, Tony, not after I drove Tom all this way," he added, nodding toward an elderly man in a tux standing at the drink table demanding something nonalcoholic.

Tony had to grit his teeth at the way Burt was already looking at Odalie. But it was a party and he had to be nice. No good thinking about where his bullets were...

"This is Stasia Everett," he introduced, "my adopted daughter. She's married to an ex-merc, and she's pregnant, so hands off," he added coldly.

"Who, me? I'm married, you know, Tony," Burt said in a sleazy tone.

"Yeah, I know. Do you?" Tony shot back.

But the man had industrial-strength skin, and it showed. "And this is?" he asked Odalie.

"Stasia's sister-in-law, Odalie," he replied curtly.

"So nice to meet you," Burt said and moved a step closer.

Odalie moved a step back, smiling politely. "Nice to meet you, Mr. Donalson," she said in a hostess-type voice. "Oh, look, isn't your friend motioning to you?" she asked, looking over his shoulder.

In fact, Tom actually was, and emphatically. It was a stroke of luck.

"So he is. I'll talk to you later, then," he told Odalie, and smiled at her warmly before caressing her with his eyes. He left with obvious reluctance.

Her smile was beginning to hurt. The minute he turned his back, it left her.

"Nice manners," Tony remarked without wanting to.

"My mother raised me that way," she said. "Sadly, there's never a latigo handy when you really want one!"

"A what?" Tony asked.

"Sorry," she apologized. "It's a long strap on a saddle, attached to the pommel, that you use to adjust the cinch," she explained. She grinned. "Or, in Spanish, if the accent is on the first syllable of *luchador*, which also means *latigo* without the accent, it's a Mexican wrestler." She wiggled both eyebrows.

He raised both eyebrows. "What would you know about wrestling?" he asked unexpectedly.

"Are you kidding?" she asked. "*Monday Night Raw*? The Rock? Nature Boy Ric Flair? The Undertaker? Vince McMahon…?"

Tony was almost gasping.

Odalie gave him an exasperated look. "I grew up watching wrestling with my brothers. I got my first broken bone trying to take John down into a leg lock!"

"Well, I'll be damned," Tony said slowly.

"You might be, but what does that have to do with wrestling?" Odalie asked pertly.

3

"He's a fanatic," Stasia answered for Tony. "He never misses *Monday Night Raw*. He's watched every WrestleMania since the first one. He has all the guys in to watch it with him every year. If there's a wrestling move, he knows it."

"Wow," Odalie said, and her eyes brightened.

Tony was glowering. "I'm not a fanatic," he told Stasia. "I watch it once in a while. That's all."

"Oops," Stasia said, realizing that he didn't want that information shared with Odalie. "Sorry."

He shrugged it off. His eyes went back to Burt Donalson. "I have to talk to Tom," he said and walked off.

"I would never have figured him for a wrestling fan," Odalie said as they melted into the crowd in the living room.

"He really is a fanatic, whatever he says," Stasia chuckled. "He's got framed autographed photos in his study."

"I don't like that Donalson man," Odalie said shortly.

"No woman likes him, except, apparently, his wife," Stasia replied. "If things get too hot for you, go sit in the Jungle Room."

"The what?"

"Let me show you."

Stasia led her to the very back of the house, to a large ornately carved wooden door. She opened it into South America. At least, that was what it looked like.

"Oh, my goodness," Odalie exclaimed as words failed her. "It's just heaven!"

And it was, to a gardener, or even just to a woman who loved flowers. The room was filled with vegetation. Vines, plants, lit tables filled with blooming orchids of every color in the rainbow, tropical plants, even a few potted trees. And in the midst of it, comfortable chairs and even a hanging rope swing.

"I've died and gone to heaven," Odalie murmured as they wandered through it.

"Burt wouldn't come in here to save his life," Stasia said.

"Oh? Why?"

"Are you afraid of snakes?" Stasia asked.

"You know I'm not. Why?"

"Because of Rudolf."

She frowned. "Rudolf?"

Stasia pointed. There, in the exposed very smooth rafters, hung a huge yellow and white snake with red eyes.

"He's lovely!" Odalie exclaimed. "John used to have one. We'd chase one of the ranch hands with him when we were kids. We got in so much trouble!"

Stasia grinned. "Burt's afraid of snakes. He doesn't like Rudolf."

"Well, I like Rudolf. Hello, you sweet boy!" She reached up and stroked his head. He just looked at her.

"If I tell Tony, he'll faint," Stasia laughed. "He can't get any woman he knows to come in here, not even Mrs. Murdock. He has to hire a firm to come and take care of Rudolf during the week. Even the maids won't clean the place."

Odalie shook her head. "Wimps," she muttered. "And don't you dare tell Tony," she added firmly, with a glance. "I don't share intel with the enemy."

"Now you sound like my husband," Stasia remarked, and chuckled.

Odalie just laughed.

Despite her incredible good looks and approachable demeanor, Odalie was shy. She could act when she was in a group, even be the life of the party with family and close friends. But among strangers, she was uncomfortable. Especially in an artsy crowd like this. Her background in art history might have opened doors, but she was too shy to walk up to people she didn't know and try to butt in on their conversation.

Which was sad, because it made her the perfect target for Burt Donalson, who'd been keeping her under surveillance covertly ever since the guests had arrived.

"And here she is, the belle of the ball," he said, smiling like a lizard while nursing a highball. "Aren't you a knockout!"

Odalie turned and looked at him without smiling. Without speaking.

"Oh, don't go all Roman goddess on me, honey," he said, displaying perfect white teeth. "I know all the tricks women play."

Odalie cocked her head and studied him. "You're married, I believe, Mr. Donalson?" she asked pleasantly.

"So what?" He shrugged. "It's an open marriage. We do what we please. It's a great time to be alive. No rules." He moved a step closer. "Why don't we go outside and look at the flowers?"

"How would you see them in the dark?" she asked.

"We could light up the night together," he said suggestively, dropping his gaze to her breasts.

She felt her skin crawl. But it wasn't politic to insult one of Tony's guests in Tony's home.

"I need a refill," she said, displaying her empty glass, which had held only ginger ale.

"I can fill it for you," he said. "What is that, Manhattan iced tea?"

"Ginger ale," she corrected.

"At your age?" he asked, aghast.

"Mr. Donalson, I'm working toward an audition at the Met. I don't drink. I don't go out at night when it's cool because it might damage my throat. I also don't get involved with men. Ever."

"Aww, poor Tony," he said sarcastically. "Does he know?"

She straightened. "I said that I don't get involved with men, Mr. Donalson," she repeated and this time in a clipped tone that held no trace of a drawl. "Any men. Married or unmarried. I have a career."

He let out a snort and looked her up and down insolently. "On second thought, I'd rather pile in bed with a call girl. At least she wouldn't freeze me to death, honey."

"Water finds its own level, doesn't it?" she asked pleasantly.

He stared at her. "Huh?"

"She means," a dark-haired, dark-eyed girl just out of her

teens interjected, "that a call girl's about your style. Honey," she drawled, and gave him a look of such distaste that he bristled.

"I must be welcome somewhere in this house," he muttered, glaring at both women before he turned away and went to the drink table.

"Thanks," Odalie said gently and with a smile. "I didn't want to insult one of Mr. Garza's guests, but that man was so overbearing!"

"He's a weasel," the younger woman said, glaring after him. The smile returned. "I'm Connie."

"I'm Odalie" came the reply.

"Come on over here with us. We're good at repelling the Donalsons of the world."

"Shouldn't you be in there—" Odalie indicated the stuffed living room "—with the arts people?"

"You're joking, right?" Connie laughed. "We don't fit with Tony's uptown friends. We're the outlaw bunch from Jersey."

"Oh!" Odalie said, and the smile grew broader. "Big Ben says you're the best people on earth."

"Well!" Connie led her to a sofa where a white-haired woman and an older dark-haired woman were sitting. "This is Mama. That's my sister, Julie."

"Nice to meet you," Odalie replied, and perched on the edge of an easy chair. "I'm Odalie. I came with my sister-in-law. She works for Mr. Garza."

"She means Tony," Connie chuckled, her dark eyes twinkling as she informed the other two women, who laughed. "Nobody calls him Mr. Garza."

"Yes, but you're in a whole other category. You're his friends. I'm a pest."

Eyebrows rose.

Odalie colored. "I mean, I get included in stuff because

my sister-in-law works for him." She shrugged. "He doesn't like me."

"Why?" Connie asked, aghast.

"I haven't the faintest idea," Odalie said.

Connie was looking at the other woman, who was really gorgeous, with a startled expression. "But you're beautiful! And Tony says you have the voice of an angel when you sing."

Odalie blushed further. "He does?" she asked, pitifully elated from that one grain of praise she'd never heard from him.

The women were exchanging knowing looks, but they gave nothing away. "Yeah," Connie added. "He says you want to sing at the Met. That true?"

Odalie nodded. "I've worked at it my whole life," she said. "I'm scared to death to audition, though."

"Tony loves opera," the other woman told her. "Our great-great-grandfather sang opera in the old country, in Italy. He was famous. In those days, opera stars were treated like sports stars are today in this country."

"No wonder he loves opera" was the warm reply from Odalie.

"Did any of your people sing opera?" Connie asked.

"Not opera, no. But my mother was a recording artist before she married my dad," Odalie said. "She writes songs. The singing group Desperado recorded two of them, and both won Grammys."

Connie's lower jaw fell. "Your mother is Heather Everett?"

"Yes!"

"What a small world!" Connie exclaimed and hugged her warmly. "Desperado is my favorite rock group. One of those songs is 'Moon Sailing.' I loved it so much that I wrote your mom a fan letter. She even answered it!"

Odalie hugged her back, laughing. "Mom answers every letter she gets. She's flattered by them."

"Some talent," Connie said, the other two nodding.

"She pampers Big Ben when we go down to the ranch," Odalie said. "She cooks lasagna just for him."

"He's a big softy," the older woman said.

"Yes, he is," Odalie replied. "He's really good at his job, too."

The women stared at her for a minute.

Odalie frowned. "He's good at taking care of Mr. Garza," she added.

"Oh!" Connie slapped her forehead. "Sorry, my mind was elsewhere."

"Are you related to Mr. Garza?" Odalie asked.

"First cousin," Connie said. "Mama's mother and his mother were sisters, like me and Julie."

"What the hell are you doing hiding in here?" Tony thundered from the doorway.

Odalie jumped because she hadn't heard him coming. The other three women just laughed.

"We were busy saving our future opera star here from that lizard-lipped houseguest of yours," Connie told him.

Tony's face tautened. "Why?"

"He was putting the make on her," Connie said. "She was very much the lady, although she did tell him that water found its own level." She smiled sweetly.

The other women laughed. Tony didn't. His black eyes swept to Odalie, searching out any trace of upset. It was well concealed, but it was there. The thought of Donalson even touching her made him wince. He hated having Burt near her. He'd have something to say to the guy about that later, after he'd convinced Tom to turn loose of that Renoir and the other famous paintings he owned. He was having some success even this early into the weekend.

Odalie didn't know what to say. Tony was glaring at her. She averted her eyes, feeling miserable. Tony had such a low opinion of her. He probably thought she'd encouraged the disgusting man.

His black eyes slid over her exquisite figure in that beautiful dress. She was gorgeous. Any man could be forgiven for trying his luck. But Donalson...!

"If he goes near her again, you come get me," Tony said curtly. "I'll settle his hash for him!"

"Oh, no, please, not on my account," Odalie said at once. "If he's driving the other man, the one with the paintings, it could cause you to lose them."

He was surprised at her reply. It bothered him that he liked having her concerned for him. But he couldn't afford to let it show.

"It won't," he said. "I thought you three were headed home tonight."

"We are," Connie said. "I don't want to go, but Mama's sister is coming. We thought it would be quicker to drive up and get her than to wait for her to try and figure out how to get out of the airport," she added on a laugh.

Tony smiled. "I know. Tell Aunt Lucia I love her. You could bring her back by here," he added.

"Sorry. It will be midnight before we get home anyway."

"Okay. No pressure. But you come back the next time I throw a big party, got that?"

"You bet," Connie said. "We should leave," she told the other women, who got up, and all of them hugged Tony.

"Thanks for coming. Even if you barely stayed long enough to warm a sofa cushion," he added shortly.

"We'll stay longer next time." Connie turned to Odalie and hugged her. "You come down to Jersey and see us sometime," she added. "We got lots of room. It's a big house. We'll feed you up," she added, noting the other woman's slender figure. "You need some bulking up to sing opera properly," she chuckled with a wicked smile.

Odalie laughed, too, and hugged Connie again. "Thanks."

They went out the door and Tony turned to Odalie. "Stasia's lying down," he said quietly. "She's having morning sickness at night. You can come in to the party with us or go see about her."

She knew which one he was thinking about. "I'll go see about her," she said quietly.

He glanced at the empty glass in her hand. "Need a refill?"

"I'll get it on the way. It's just ginger ale."

His black eyes twinkled. "Ginger ale."

"I can't drink," she confessed.

"It's a bad habit." He indicated the ice-touched whiskey in his squat crystal glass. "Better not to ever start."

She nodded.

"If Donalson bothers you again, come get me," he said.

She felt bubbles in her stomach. She was certain he didn't mean it the way she was thinking it, but it made her warm all over. "Okay," she said.

"I mean it."

"I'll just stay out of his way," she said.

"I don't want him bothering you," he said. He hesitated. "Stasia would never forgive me."

That stung, but she just smiled.

He cocked his head, looking down at her. "Connie and her sister have some rough edges," he began.

She gave him a long look. "So do our cowboys on the ranch, but they're part of our family and they're treated that way."

He smiled, and it was a genuine one. "I keep forgetting that you weren't city bred."

"I like people," she said. "I just...have a hard time mixing with them."

"Especially this crowd?" he mused, nodding toward the living room. "Just between us, so do I. I've got a few rough edges myself."

"It doesn't show," she blurted out.

He searched her eyes until she felt her toes curling. She cleared her throat. "I'd better go see about Stasia," she said, almost dropping the glass. She glanced up at him. "I like your family," she added, and moved quickly away.

It was almost funny. He'd kept her away from the Jersey bunch for fear she might insult them, since they weren't highbrow or used to high society. But she'd been treating them like family when he went looking for her. It made him feel good. And because it did, he crushed those feelings flat. He wasn't going to even think about why he felt compelled to do it. She was off limits. He intended to keep her that way.

He turned and went back into the living room.

The first person he ran into was Burt Donalson.

"That girl of yours is a real snob, isn't she?" he asked unpleasantly.

"I don't have a girl," Tony said with a stabbing glare. "She's Stasia's sister-in-law. And if you want trouble," he added, lowering his voice to a dangerous rumble, "keep pestering her."

Donalson felt his blood freeze. He knew Tony. And he knew a threat when he was presented with one. "Well, sure," he said quickly. "I knew that. She doesn't mix well, does she?"

"This isn't her sort of crowd. She sings opera."

"I see."

"You'd better," Tony replied, and he smiled. The smile sent Burt to the drink table for a refill. A big one.

Stasia was drowsy from the medicine she took for morning sickness, but she was cheerful despite that.

"Tony said you were sick," Odalie said softly and sat down beside her friend. "Can I help?"

"No, sweetheart, it goes with the turf," she sighed. She grinned. "But pay attention. You may need to know these things one day."

"Fat chance. I'm going to sing opera, not get married." She was assured.

"You never know. And the first lesson is that morning sickness very often comes at night!" Stasia laughed.

"Is that in the books?"

"Not that I've read so far," Stasia sighed. "The fatigue and sleepiness are just as distracting. But being pregnant, that's…" She sighed again and smiled. "That's awesome!"

Odalie just smiled. "I'll take your word for it. Want something to drink?"

"Some ginger ale would be lovely," she said. "Isn't that what you've got?"

Odalie nodded. "I'll go get you some. Oh, Tony's family was downstairs," she added. "They're really nice."

Both eyebrows went up. "Well! He's kept you away every time they've come to visit."

"I noticed," Odalie said with a sigh. "I guess he thought I'd be snobby. As if!" She rolled her eyes. "Our cowboys are rough and tough, but I'd never be ashamed of any of them. Not even Earl," she added, shaking her head.

"Earl won't bathe," Stasia recalled.

"Not until the boys get tired of holding their noses and throw him into one of the ponds," she laughed.

"Oh, the rural life. City people don't know what they're missing!"

"Tell me about it. I'll be back as soon as I can. I'm sort of trying to avoid that Donalson man," she said, making a face as she got to her feet.

"Tell Tony."

"Tony knows." She sighed. "But he can't be everywhere."

"Stick to the Jersey crowd."

"I would, but they left to pick up somebody at the airport."

"Aunt Lucia," Stasia said knowingly. She laughed. "She's a card. She can get lost in a store and need directions to find the way out. She's a character, though. You'd love her. Are they going to bring her by here?"

"They said not. It will be late when they get home."

Stasia sighed. "That's because Aunt Lucia feels safer at La-Guardia Airport, because it's smaller, so they have to drive up from Jersey to get her." She laughed. "She's eccentric. Well, maybe I'll see her next time."

"I'll get you that ginger ale," Odalie said, and went out the door.

Donalson was nowhere in sight when she got downstairs, but another man saw her, and his eyes lit up. He made a bee-line for her, where she was refilling her own glass and filling one for Stasia, with crushed ice as well.

"Hello, gorgeous person," the man said with a long sigh. "How are things in Mount Olympus?"

Odalie stood with wide eyes and the bottle of ginger ale suspended in midair while she stared at the man in stunned surprise.

He wasn't handsome. His face was too angular. But he was tall and well-built. He had kind dark eyes and a nice smile and nice hands.

"I'm Rudy," he said. "Who are you?"

"Odalie," she replied quietly.

"Pretty name," he remarked and sipped champagne from a flute. "Did you come with somebody?"

"Yes," she said and didn't elaborate. She smiled faintly. "And I have to get back. I'm expected."

"All right, then. Here for the weekend?" he asked hopefully.

"I don't know."

"Ah, well. If Mount Olympus reclaims you, I will mourn. Farewell, sweet sprite."

She blinked. He was laying it on thick. She nodded and turned around. Right into Burt Donalson.

"Hello, stuck-up," he said with a faint sneer. He glared at the man behind her. "You propping up the drink cart and hunting big game?" he asked sarcastically.

The other man pursed his lips. "What do you think?" he asked, not retreating an inch.

They squared off. Tony saw the building confrontation; the two men were business rivals, and not any business he wanted Odalie to be part of.

He moved into view.

"You two planning a tug-of-war or something?" he asked in a voice that turned them both around smartly.

It reminded Odalie of two young bulls suddenly confronted by an older, bigger one. They retreated.

"Excuse me," she said, red-faced, and took off with her drinks.

When she was out of sight up the staircase, Tony turned to the two men. "This is a party," he said in a soft, chilling tone. His black eyes were making threats. "My guests aren't game to be hunting. That clear?"

"Can't blame a man for looking," Rudy said, lifting his glass of champagne in a salute. "She's a goddess!"

"She's got her nose so far in the air, she'll drown in the first rainstorm..." Donalson began.

Tony moved one step closer.

Donalson took a long, slow breath. He cleared his throat. "I see a man I need to talk to," he said quickly, looking past Tony.

"Then you'd better talk to him. Hadn't you?" Tony asked.

Donalson nodded and went quickly out of the area.

Rudy chuckled. "I don't think I've ever seen him move that fast."

"Maybe once, but he had a gun pointed at him at the time," Tony replied, glaring after the man. "In fact, if I knew where I could find a bullet real quick..."

"Now, now, that isn't prudent," Rudy told him. His expression changed. "You've got a problem in Jersey," he said under his breath. "We need to talk."

Tony's black eyes narrowed. He nodded. "Let's go into my study."

Stasia was overly grateful for the cold drink. But her friend was looking odd. "What happened downstairs?"

Odalie groaned. "I attracted some odd man making weird remarks, and then that Donalson man came up and they squared off. Tony broke it up and I ran for my life."

"What man?"

"He said his name was Rudy. I didn't hear the other part."

"That guy," Stasia said quietly. "He's with a group back in New Jersey that I can't tell you about. He's a friend of Tony's.

In a bad situation, he's the sort of man you want backing you up," she added. "I've never seen him back down. He and Tony have been friends for a long time. He used to wrestle professionally. Now he works for Tony."

"A wrestler?" she exclaimed. "But he hasn't got muscles as big as cantaloupes…"

"He can press two hundred pounds without even breaking into a sweat," Stasia laughed. "It isn't obvious, but he's very strong."

"He was nice."

"How was he weird?"

"He asked about the weather in Mount Olympus," Odalie replied on a laugh.

Stasia looked at her with warm eyes. "You do look very regal," she pointed out. "And you're beautiful, like your mother."

"Stop that."

"I mean it. I'm not exaggerating, either." She sipped more of the fizzy liquid. "This is great for an upset tummy."

"I thought it might be. I love it, even when I'm not sick."

"I'm sorry we're not sharing a room, but Tony had a lot of guests show up and the double rooms went to couples. But at least we're just down the hall from each other."

"Please tell me that Donalson man isn't down the hall," Odalie groaned.

"Listen, if he gives you any trouble, you go find Tony."

"I can't do that," Odalie said. "Tony's trying to get those paintings from Donalson's boss. I can't interfere with that. The paintings have such a history," she added.

"Tony wouldn't care," Stasia said. "He doesn't like people

preying on each other. Well, not these days, anyway," she added with a chuckle.

"I'll just stay out of his way," she said. "It shouldn't be that hard!"

But it was. On the way to her room, she saw Donalson come out of a room only two doors down from the one she was supposed to occupy. So instead of going to her room, she darted down the stairs.

Donalson had seen her, and he was coming down as well. She looked around for Tony, but he was nowhere in sight. She didn't know any of the other guests. Where to go, she agonized. Then she remembered. The Jungle Room!

She turned the corner and opened the door to it just as Donalson approached. But as soon as she went inside, he cursed loudly and went back to the bar.

Odalie felt like a deer in hunting season. She was miserable. If this was just the first day, what were the next two going to be like? She could see herself moving in to the Jungle Room with provisions and a tent and a pith helmet for the duration. She laughed. It was a silly thought.

She walked over to Rudolf, who was now curled up next to a potted tree. She reached down and stroked his big head. "Hello, sweetie," she said softly, smiling. "I'm so happy to see you. It's nice to have at least one friend here."

The hanging rope swing was just a few steps away. She kicked off her shoes, climbed into it and curled up. It had been a long week, and a really long day. She was tired. She closed her eyes, just for a few seconds. And fell asleep.

Tony stopped by Stasia's room on his way to bed to check on her.

She smiled. "Hi."

"Your light was on," he said with a returned smile. "I thought you'd still be awake. Need anything?"

She shook her head. "No, thanks. I'm fine. Odalie brought me some ginger ale and it helped settle my stomach."

"Where is she?"

"Gone to bed, I think," she replied.

He frowned. "I just remembered something. Donalson's room is two doors down from hers." His jaw set. "He's moving." He called Mrs. Murdock on his cell phone and gave her new instructions. He hung up. "It's a smaller room than the one he's in," he said with a cold smile. "And the toilet stopped working today—it will need a plumber. He'll have to knock on old Morris's door to use his."

"Morris is deaf."

He pursed his lips and his black eyes twinkled. "Exactly."

She laughed.

"I'll check on your sister-in-law. Just in case," he added.

"Thanks. She was really upset, but she didn't want you to know," she replied. "She said if she caused trouble, you might lose the opportunity to get that Renoir and its companions."

His face softened, just a bit. "Nice."

"She's not the enemy, Tony," she added.

He gave her a long look. "That's what you think. Sleep tight. If you need anything, ring that bell. We've got six temporary maids working in round-the-clock shifts. Nobody will lack anything, even at two in the morning."

"Nice to know. Maybe Donalson won't be able to harass Odalie."

"I can guarantee he won't," Tony said. "Not on my turf. Night."

"Good night."

He went down the hall to Odalie's room. The light was

still on. He frowned and knocked on the door. There was no answer. He knocked again and opened the door. The bed was still made, her suitcase hadn't been opened where it had been placed on its stand. Nothing was disturbed, and the bathroom door was open. She wasn't in there.

Scowling, he closed the door as footsteps sounded behind him. He turned at once, his senses honed from years of living in dangerous circumstances.

Donalson came down the hall. "Looking for Goldilocks, huh? Well, you won't find her there. You may not find her," he added cheerfully. "She went into the room with that snake. Maybe he'll eat her," he added with malice.

As he was speaking, Mrs. Murdock came down the hall with the wife of one of the guests.

"Tony, I hear we're moving. How kind of you!" she said, smiling at him.

"Yes, into this room." Tony indicated it.

"Hey, that's my room," Donalson said belligerently.

"I'm sure you won't mind switching with the Mannings, Burt," Tony said easily. "They're cramped into a twin bed and he's eaten up with arthritis, something we overlooked when we made room assignments."

"It's so sweet of you to do this, Mr. Donalson," Mrs. Manning said with a gentle smile. "Old age has its drawbacks."

Now caught between Tony's malicious smile and Mrs. Manning's genuine one, Donalson gave in. "Sure," he told the woman. "No problem. No problem at all." He'd think of some way to get to that blonde filly, he told himself, Tony or no Tony. He wanted payback. No woman was going to get away with snubbing him!

"I'll help you pack, Mr. Donalson," Mrs. Murdock said with a smile. "Glad to help."

Both of them went into the room. Tony turned on his heel and went down the staircase. If Odalie saw Rudolf, she might be on the floor passed out, or worse...

4

She was curled up in the jungle swing, in her beautiful silk couture dress. It shimmered like fairy dust in the lights, all pink and purple and silver. Her shoes were off. Her head was pillowed on one hand on the arm of the swing. She was asleep. She looked like any man's vision of the perfect woman.

Her beauty wasn't blatant, but it was stunning. Her mouth was like a perfect bow, soft and pretty and palest pink in a complexion that seemed to be aided by nothing more than a light dusting of powder. Her eyes were closed, graced by long blond eyelashes that curled and contained no messy mascara or shadow, and the eyelashes were real. Her cheekbones were high, slightly flushed from sleep, not from any artifice. Her fingers were long, tipped by silver glitter nail polish on a pink background. She had pretty hands. He recalled that she played the piano. So did he, but he'd never shared that skill with her. Nor another that he kept secret even from Stasia. He was very private about some facets of his life.

This was intoxicating. He never had the luxury of just looking at her, because he didn't want her, or anyone, to see how fascinating he really found her. He was too old for her, too much of a bad influence. Their backgrounds were incompatible. But she was like a fairy, lying there in the quietness of the room. His eyes drifted down to her breasts. They weren't large. They were small, but firm and perfectly shaped. He ached looking at them. Her hips were wide. He thought about babies and hated himself for it. He was sterile. He could never have a child. Her legs were long and elegant, outlined under the dress that fell almost to her ankles when she walked.

She was a picture that would linger in his mind until he died, and he knew it. If only, he thought sadly. If only.

She stirred and grimaced, as if she was feeling the discomfort of such a position. He wondered how long she'd been in the swing. He looked around. There was Rudolf, curled up by the potted palm.

Had she seen his pet? he wondered.

Her eyes opened. When he turned back around, those beautiful pale blue eyes looked straight into his black ones, but vacantly, as if she wasn't quite awake.

"Hello," she said softly.

"Hello," he replied, his voice as quiet as hers.

"I fell asleep."

"I noticed."

She drew in a breath and stretched as much as she could, pulling the dress tight around the luscious curves of her body. Tony felt himself go tense all over, and he fought the sensation.

"What are you doing in here?" he asked as she started to uncurl herself and lower her hose-clad feet to the floor.

"I was escaping," she blurted out, and flushed, because she hadn't meant to tell him.

He drew in an angry breath. "Donalson. Well, I moved him downstairs, so you won't be running into him in the hall anymore."

"You did?" she asked, and helpless delight flickered in her eyes.

He averted his. "The Mannings needed a double bed. He's got arthritis. Donalson switched with them." He didn't want her to think it was concern for her that had prompted the change.

"Oh. Of course," she said at once. She felt around for her shoes. They'd scattered.

Tony saw her looking and went to pick them up where they'd been shifted several feet away.

"Does Rudolf like shoes?" she asked whimsically, smiling at the big reptile. "I'm afraid mine won't fit you, old dear," she told the snake. "You'd need a snake sock." She laughed.

It was like hearing wind chimes. He loved the sound and grew somber, fighting his desire.

"Here," he said, going on one knee. He slid her feet into the high heels one at a time, and the feel of her skin against his fingers, even through the nylon, sent shivers of pleasure down his spine.

She was vibrating all over at that touch. His hands were big and lean and beautifully masculine. She loved the way they felt on her skin. She wondered helplessly how they'd feel higher up. She forced herself to stop thinking about it. "Thanks," she said. Despite her best efforts, she was flushed, and her heart was going like an overwound clock.

Tony knew that, but he pretended not to see it. He stood

up and gave her a hand to hold on to to pull herself out of the swing.

She came up close to him, too close. She could feel the warm strength of his body, smell the spicy, clean scent of him. She didn't want to move. He still had her hand, and she tingled all over at just its touch. She wanted to move closer. She wanted to feel him against her, all the way up and down. She wanted his hands to go around her, his arms to go around her. She wanted…him.

He was feeling the same sensations. The room was quiet. Too quiet. He could hear his own heart beating. He could hear her quick breaths. God, she was beautiful, and that body was like something out of a fantasy. She was the most gorgeous woman he'd seen in his life, and he couldn't, didn't dare, even touch her. It would lead to catastrophe. He had to get a grip on his fraying emotions. Ridiculous. He could face down armed men without a hair out of place, but this young woman turned his knees to jelly and made him ache.

He let go of her hand and moved back. "You knew Rudolf's name," he said after a long, tense silence.

It broke the tension. "Yes," she said, with a breathy laugh. "Stasia introduced us. He's gorgeous!"

His eyebrows arched. "You aren't afraid of snakes?"

She shook her head, her pale blue eyes twinkling. "John, my brother John, had an albino python when I was just about eight years old. He and I would take the snake out to the barn and chase poor old Billy Tanner with it. He was terrified of snakes! Dad caught us, and we had to give up video games for two weeks as punishment."

"Video games. Snakes." He shook his head. His black eyes twinkled. "You're not what I used to think you were when Stasia brought you up to visit. I thought you were a snob."

"Me?" she exclaimed.

His eyes narrowed in thought. "You don't mix well, do you? You're an introvert, and you're shy. It makes you look stuck-up. But Connie's wild about you." He chuckled. "She called me from the airport. She's got a brother, Angel, and he's single. She said she wanted to bring Angel up to meet you because you'd be the most wonderful sister-in-law in the family."

"Oh," she exclaimed, beaming. "That's the nicest thing anybody's said about me in ages!"

"Not so much," he replied, smiling. "Angel's no pinup boy. He's got scars and an accent thicker than yours, and he's a semipro wrestler."

"I love wrestlers," she said. "I watch movies that the Rock is in, and I never missed *Monday Night Raw* when he was in the ring."

"Damn!" he burst out. "You weren't joking? You really like wrestling?"

She grimaced. "Well, there's nothing wrong with liking wrestling," she said defensively, even while remembering that he loved it. "Lots of women do. I thought Eddie Guerrero was a dish, and I bawled when he died. I loved the Hardy Boyz and Lita and Triple H…"

He was still trying to contain his surprise. "You like wrestling," he repeated. He chuckled. He'd have to tell her about Big Ben's background one day. "And those are my personal favorites. Especially the Rock. I've got all his movies. But my favorite is *Moana*."

Her whole face lit up. "Mine, too, but I love it just as much for the music. The score is beautiful."

He nodded. This was terrible. They loved the same things. He was getting in over his head and they hadn't been talking more than ten minutes. He shook his head, as if to clear it.

"I was afraid Rudolf would scare you to death," he said after a minute.

"I like snakes," she said simply.

He just shook his head. "You are the oddest damned woman I've ever known," he said slowly.

"I come from an odd family," she pointed out.

"No, you don't," he replied. "Your people are down-to-earth and perfectly normal." He studied her. "I'll bet you were spoiled rotten in school by every teacher you had."

Thinking about school broke her heart. She'd been so mean to poor Maddie Brannt when they were in the same class. It had taken a near-tragic wreck that she'd caused to patch up years of torment she'd given the woman, who was now her best friend next to Stasia.

"You closed up," he said. "What did I say?"

"It wasn't that. I was a bad girl in high school," she confessed, looking at the spotless white shirt over his broad, muscular chest under his jacket. "I almost went to jail once."

"You?" he exclaimed.

She looked up at him. "You never really know people," she said. "I mean, you can be around them for years and talk and go places together, but you don't really know them. People hide the dark places so that they don't show."

He grew more somber as she spoke. His black eyes narrowed and grew sad. "Yes, they do," he replied quietly.

One big hand was toying with a button on his jacket, and she frowned, looking at it.

"What is it?" he asked.

"I wanted to ask, but it seems a little, well, personal," she began, nodding toward the very obvious scar on the back of his hand.

He drew in a breath. "I was in a gang when I was fourteen," he said, his eyes with a faraway look in them. "There was a rival gang. I got careless, and they caught me out. Took me to a warehouse that was deserted. It was where they hung out. The gang leader smiled and said they were going to give me a nice tattoo before they killed me, so everybody would know who did it."

He studied the scar. "This was their sign. He carved it into my hand with a knife. Then he put the knife against my throat and told me to say my prayers, if I did that sort of thing."

She was listening intently, her breath suspended, hiding horror at what could have been.

"There was a rattle at the door that diverted him, just long enough."

"What happened?" she asked when he didn't continue.

He searched her pale, innocent eyes. This wasn't a story he could share. "He got a lesson in manners and went home on a stretcher, so to speak. His gang broke up."

"You could afford to have the scar removed. But you didn't," she said softly.

He nodded, his face somber. "I kept it because it reminds me to never get careless, never puff myself up with false pride. I thought I was one tough guy, invincible. I wasn't. It was a life lesson I never forgot. This—" he indicated the scar "—is a talisman, of sorts."

"I'm glad he didn't kill you," she said with simple honesty. "But how did you get away?"

"I had a gang, too," he replied with a smile. "My guys were a little tougher than his. My best friend missed me and guessed what had happened. They came after me. That's all. But there's always somebody bigger, stronger, smarter, more dangerous. That's why you never let your guard down, with anybody. You can be sold out by the best friend you ever had."

"I guess that's true," she said sadly.

His eyes were ancient as they met hers. "It is. Did you ever read about the former head of the criminal organization in Chicago, what they call the Outfit?"

She nodded. "I have this book about painting houses, except it doesn't have anything to do with painting houses..."

He scowled. "You read that stuff?"

"I read everything," she said simply, smiling. "I like true crime stories and mystery novels, that sort of thing."

He was fascinated by her and trying very hard not to betray himself. "There's a story in that book about how one of the leaders died. Remember it?"

She nodded. "They said his best friend killed him. That was true?"

"It's like this," he told her. "People who get high up in those circles are suspicious of everybody. Nobody outside can get close enough for a hit. So you pick a close friend and you say either you do him, or we do you and him, and he's still dead." He shrugged. "That's how it works."

Her lips fell apart. "I thought it was just a story."

He searched her eyes until his body began to ache. He pried his away. "No."

"Goodness."

He glanced at his watch. "It's late."

"Yes." She turned to Rudolf and bent to pat him on the head. "Thanks for sharing your space with me, sweet boy," she said gently.

The big snake just looked at her with his big red eyes, but he moved restlessly and blinked at her.

"Somebody told you that Donalson hates snakes, I guess," he mused.

She chuckled as she stood up. "Yes. I couldn't get by him

to go back upstairs because he was heading right for me. So I thought about Rudolf and I came in here."

"I warned him..."

She moved a step closer. "Don't do anything because of me," she said softly, meeting his black eyes. "I minored in art history in college. I don't want to be the cause of priceless paintings being destroyed. I'll just keep away from him. Honest."

He cocked an eyebrow. "Donalson won't have that protection any longer. I not only got Tom to promise them to me, we set a price and I had an attorney downstairs go get his notary seal and notarize it for me and two witnesses to sign it. I wired half the money to his account, with the rest on delivery. All tied up with a bow. So Donalson is now fair game."

Her eyes twinkled. "Listen, Lita used to do this incredible toss by jumping off the ropes, wrapping her legs around a wrestler's neck and throwing him...!"

"I don't have ropes, you can't jump in that dress and Donalson would get slime all over you."

She laughed. "Excuses, excuses."

He drew in a long sigh and smiled at her. She was a breath of spring in his lonely life. If only she was older, less honest, less...everything.

"I've rented horses for tomorrow," he said. "I know some pretty trails around the property. Not all the guests ride, but several do. Want to come?"

"I'd love to, but it depends on Stasia. I don't think she'll be able to, and I did come to keep her company and look after her. I promised my brother. He said to keep my cell phone where I could get to it, and not let her go anywhere alone." Her face became solemn. "He said that James man who almost killed him is hopping mad and looking for revenge, that

Stasia was a soft target and that's the kind of attack that would come, if there was one." Her eyes were cold. "He said that was the kind of man James really was. Big with a gun in his hand. An ostrich unarmed."

"The world's full of those," Tony told her.

She nodded. She looked at him with helpless appreciation. His face was leonine, broad and tanned, with a chiseled mouth and long nose and square jaw. His hair was black as night and wavy, with a few silver threads. There were some small scars on his face. He was so handsome that he made her senses come alive. Just standing close to him made her hungry for something she didn't really understand.

"Stop that," he muttered.

Her pale blue eyes widened, and she gaped at him. "I beg your pardon?"

His eyes narrowed. He bent just enough that his eyes pierced straight into hers. "I don't start things I can't finish," he said, emphasizing every word. "And don't pretend that you don't know exactly what I mean."

Her heart stopped and then ran away. She stepped back. Her eyes were now throwing sparks at him. "I was not... I didn't... I never have...!" She grasped for the right words to express her frustration.

"I know you never have," he said flatly. "But if you plan to, don't look in my direction. Maybe nobody told you, but I keep a mistress. I don't need any imported talent. Capisce?" he added in a tone that dripped icicles.

Her lips trembled. It embarrassed her that he saw through her so easily. There she stood, quivering with anger and embarrassment and rage and no way to express it. Her hands clenched at her sides.

"Come on," he said imperturbably, pausing to pat Rudolf on the head. "I'll walk you up, in case Donalson's still around."

She would almost rather face Donalson than have this conceited man go anywhere with her. But she was intimidated by Donalson, and she couldn't admit it, or turn down Tony's offer.

She brushed past him and opened the door.

Donalson was at the drink table. He spotted her and took a step in her direction until he saw Tony come out after her.

Tony saw that. He looked at the man and smiled. The smile sent Donalson to a nearby whiskey bottle.

Odalie noticed it and stifled a laugh.

He heard it. "He's a piece of work," he muttered.

She went up the staircase ahead of him, still bubbling with indignation complicated by her amusement at Donalson.

"Concrete overshoes..." she muttered to herself.

"Concrete galoshes," he corrected. "If you plan to off somebody, at least learn the terminology."

"Snob," she said under her breath.

"Amateur," he muttered back.

She went ahead of him to her room, opened the door and turned to him. "Thank you for saving me. I think." She didn't look at him.

She was almost trembling with pent-up emotion. He looked at her mouth and wanted to throw his head back and rage at life for putting her off-limits. He could have made a banquet of her soft mouth. Just thinking about how it would feel under the crush of his made him go rigid.

She didn't dare look up at him. She knew he could already see everything she felt. She didn't have the experience to hide her hunger. It was humiliating to have him know it.

"Lock your door tonight."

"I always lock my door," she said. Then she added absently, "I hate earthworms."

He blinked. "Are we having the same conversation?"

That tricked her into lifting her eyes. "Earthworms. When I graduated from high school, I had a little too much to drink at my graduation party and spilled a pitcher of lemonade on my brother John. He swore vengeance. So I had a shower and put on my gown and turned out the lights. Then I screamed so loud that everybody in the house, including my parents, came running."

His eyebrows arched in a simple nonverbal question.

"John had gone to a bait shop and bought every container of worms in the place. He washed off the dirt, dried them a little, and put the whole kit and caboodle in my bed under the sheets. I didn't know it until I climbed in." She smiled sheepishly. "In the dark."

He started chuckling and then laughed out loud until his stomach hurt. He could picture it. "My God, what a thing to do," he blurted out.

"Oh, I got even," she said. "I went hunting. I found ten bullfrogs around the stream behind the house, and I put them in his bed two nights later."

"What did he do?"

"He stood outside my door waving a white flag he'd made out of his old baseball bat and a white undershirt."

He shook his head. "I could have sworn your family was normal."

"Parts of it are," she confessed. "John and me...not quite." She studied him. "Didn't you ever put something in your family's bed?"

He smiled sadly. "After my grandparents died, my father was never home. I only had my mother. She was the sweetest woman I ever knew. Nobody would have thought of doing anything like that to her. And my wife…" His face closed up. "She was like Mama. She never hurt a soul in her little life."

She grimaced. "Sorry. I shouldn't have mentioned…"

"It was a long time ago," he interrupted. He smiled musingly. "Do I look that sensitive to you?"

She searched his eyes and shook her head, very slowly. "I think it would take a bomb to dent you."

"Dead right. Good night."

She nodded. "Thanks again."

He stared down at her with conflicting emotions, aching all over. The bed was visible in the background. She was beautiful. She wanted him, he knew it. He could…!

He cleared his throat. "Good night," he said again.

While she was working through an equal set of milling emotions, the door down the hall opened and elderly Mrs. Manning came out, holding a vase of flowers. She saw Tony and Odalie and winced as she approached them.

"Oh, I hope I'm not interrupting," she began quickly.

"No, you aren't," Tony replied with a smile. "I was escorting Miss Everett to her room."

"I had sort of a problem downstairs," Odalie began, flustered.

"That Donalson man, I guess," Mrs. Manning said, and her eyes flashed. "If he were my son, I would thump him so hard that he'd be unbuttoning his shirt to eat!"

They both laughed. She looked so sweet and innocent.

She handed Tony the roses. "I'm really sorry, but my husband has asthma and although these smell so delicious…!" Her voice trailed away.

He took the vase. "No problem," he said gently. He handed the roses to Odalie.

They were gorgeous. The bouquet had yellow and white roses, baby's breath, and several other varieties of blooms including tulips. "They're glorious," Odalie exclaimed, burying her nose in them.

"Consider them yours," Tony said, and he smiled at her.

That smile made her toes curl up in her shoes. She smiled back, shyly. "Thank you. Good night, then," she said, including both of them, then she went into her room and closed the door.

Tony walked Mrs. Manning back to the room she now shared with her husband. She turned to him, glancing around. "I suppose you know that Donalson has ties to New York?" she said with meaning. Her eyes were like gray steel.

"I do know," he replied. "Steps are being taken."

"Of which I know nothing," she said with an icy smile. "But certain people, including my husband, will be grateful. There may be retribution, however."

"If it comes, it comes," Tony said easily. "I've got everybody covered who might be in danger."

"There's another complication. In DC," she added quietly.

"Known and attended to," he said. He smiled. "But thank your husband for the heads-up. I've had some issues with New York in the past. I'd hoped that we'd settled whatever differences existed."

"There's always a newcomer trying to spread his wings. You know that. This one has aspirations, but he's foolish and he talks too much." She cocked her head. "There are so many ways to deal with these little problems. I'm certain you'll have no worries there."

He chuckled. "None at all. I'll just run my business and wait for the problem to come to me. They always do," he added on a sigh.

"Be careful that they don't come to the wrong person." She

indicated Odalie's closed door. "She looks like an angel," she said softly. "What does she do?"

"She's a soprano, trying for the Met soon." There was faint but unmistakable pride in his voice.

"Is she good?" she asked.

"I've never heard better," he said flatly. "She sang 'Un bel dì,' and I actually felt pins in my throat." He shook his head. "She has an incredible talent."

"Does she come from musical people?"

"Her mother is Heather Everett. She used to perform onstage, but she just writes songs these days. Two of hers were performed by Desperado, and won Grammy Awards."

"My!" she exclaimed. She smiled secretly. "About the Met—I might have a word with a friend of mine."

He smiled back. "I'd be grateful. Her sister-in-law is trying to prod her into an audition. She's afraid she won't be accepted, so she's delaying it."

"We can do something about that, when the time comes. I'll let you know."

"Martha, are you ever going to stop jabbering and come to bed? You'll wear Tony's ear out," her husband called through the open door, but affectionately.

"I'm coming, Teddy, honest," she called back, laughing. She smiled up at Tony. "Well, good night. Sorry about the flowers."

"They went to a person who loves them. They'll be happy," he teased.

She reached up and kissed his jaw. "Take care."

"You two do the same."

He went back downstairs. Big Ben was standing near the drink table, not drinking, but looking around constantly. He had two burly security men with him here, unobtrusive, but watchful.

Ben's eyebrows rose. "Something, boss?" he asked under his breath.

"Something." Tony nodded. "Let's step outside."

The night air was cool. Stars were out in a clear sky, diamonds on a black canvas. Tony stuck his hands in his pockets. "We've got another possible intrusion from the New York bunch on our turf in Jersey."

"Did you talk to Mr. Manning about it?"

He shook his head. "I talked to Martha. Teddy's gone to bed."

"Teddy can handle it."

He shrugged. "Maybe." Tony was deep in thought.

Big Ben's eyes narrowed. It wasn't like the boss to be absent-minded. "Something bothering you?" Ben asked.

"Donalson," he said through his teeth. "He's getting too aggressive with Stasia's sister-in-law. She wouldn't admit it to me, but she's spooked."

"You backed him down."

"Yeah. But he's the sort of vermin that doesn't pay attention." His chin lifted as he turned his head toward Ben. "I want him gone. I got a signed contract for the paintings from his boss, so I'm going to suggest that they leave in the morning. You get Donalson to one side before that and tell him what it is. Just in case he has any ideas about getting even with her afterward. You know what a sneaky son of a toad he is."

"I do. And he's got an apartment in town not far from hers that he uses when he comes down from Vermont to do business," Ben reminded him.

"Tell him he's already had more leeway than I'm used to giving. There won't be any more warnings."

"I'll tell him." He paused. "Miss Everett is a sweet woman. She doesn't deserve to be treated like that. He was following her down the staircase when she went into Rudolf's turf." He chuckled. "Most women won't even go in there. She wasn't scared?"

Tony grinned. "She likes snakes. And wrestling."

"Really!"

Tony nodded. "Odd woman."

"But beautiful."

Tony shrugged. "Beauty is relative. I'll take brains and talent over that."

"She's got both."

"Yeah." His face tautened. "She'll end up with some rich guy in Texas when she's tired of singing. If that ever happens."

"She sings good, does she?"

"Like angels do," Tony said quietly. "I've heard sopranos all my life. I've never heard one with a voice like hers. Clear as a summer day, every word enunciated, every pause perfect and she never flats a note."

"Maybe we can go hear her at the Met one day."

"Maybe."

"When do you want me to talk to the weasel?"

"Wait until morning. Oh, and keep an eye on Rudy, will you? He and Donalson almost came to blows earlier. I don't want him involved in anything right now. Don't let him give Donalson an excuse to take him to court."

"I'll do my best, boss, but Rudy's a hothead."

"Yeah. But we need him not to be, at least for the time being," Tony replied. He looked up. "No sign of rain. I'm glad the weatherman got it wrong this time. I'm taking my guests horseback riding in the morning."

"Not all of them, I'll bet," Ben chuckled. "Miss Stasia is

going to be too sick to go, and Teddy and Martha don't like horses."

"It will be a small group," Tony agreed. "One more thing. Put somebody on Miss Everett's apartment, will you?" he added.

"Because of Donalson?"

"Her brother's worried that the James man in DC is looking for revenge and lining up soft targets. Stasia will be safe up here and at home, but Odalie doesn't have protection at her apartment. Right now, she's the most available soft target because Tanner Everett is her brother."

"I'll get somebody good," Ben agreed.

"Get two guys, split shifts."

"Sure."

Tony sighed. "Connie likes her."

Ben's eyes widened as they started back into the house. "Connie doesn't like other women."

"Yeah." Tony smiled to himself. "I know."

5

Stasia was much better in the morning. She sat at the big dining room table picking at eggs and toast and smiling as she and Odalie talked about Maddie Brannt's little fairy figures. Maddie had just finished the one she did for Tony and had sent her a photo of it in a text message. They were both enthusing over it at their end of the table.

Tony was sitting across from the Mannings while the owner of the Renoir was smiling from ear to ear.

"I'm happy that you'll have the paintings," Tom told Tony. "My son has no appreciation for art history. I hate to give up the paintings, but I'm not likely to be around for too many more years, even with chemo and radiation. And besides that, you never know at my age what tomorrow might bring. Even a light stroke would give my boy the opportunity to get rid of my collection. He's got so much money that their value doesn't even enter into his attitude."

"It's a shame," Tony said, sipping coffee. "You raised him better than that."

"Yes, I did. Burt, please stop glaring at Tony's other guests," he added with a curt glance at his driver.

Burt let out a huffy breath and stopped glaring in Odalie's direction.

"You're not Mr. America, and at any rate, she's obviously not interested," the older man said firmly. "Besides all that, you're married!"

"God help your wife," Tony added, and the look he gave Donalson was molten.

"She's a snob," Donalson muttered. "I wouldn't touch her with a pole."

Both of the other men knew that was sour grapes. Tony was fuming, but he tried not to make a scene. "When are you going?" he asked the Renoir's owner.

The older man wiped his mouth with a napkin. "Right now, in fact," he replied surprisingly, and with a smile. "Burt, go get our bags and bring them out, please. I'd like to get home before dark."

Donalson looked disappointed but he shrugged. "Okay." He got up and went after the luggage.

"I'm sorry for the way he's behaved," the older man told Tony sincerely. "If I could have found another driver, I would have."

"It's all right. I kept him honest."

"That poor young woman," he said, glancing at Odalie down the long table. "So beautiful. I imagine looks like that can be a curse from time to time."

Tony frowned. "A curse?"

He nodded. "Unwanted attention. I'm sure she's had her share of it."

"I suppose she has," Tony replied thoughtfully.

The old man got to his feet as Donalson came out with two suitcases. Tom shook hands with Tony. "I'll have the paintings boxed up and shipped directly to the gallery first thing Monday morning, overnight express and insured," he promised.

"I'll wire the other half of the money as soon as they arrive."

"Take care of them. They were my most prized possessions."

"They'll be mine now, and I'll make sure they have the best of homes."

He nodded. "Take care."

"You do the same."

He walked out with them. After Donalson put the old man in the car, Tony halted him at the hood. "Just so you know," he said pleasantly, but in a voice that chilled, "Miss Everett will have twenty-four-hour protection at her apartment in the city from now on. And anyone who even attempts to harass her..." He let his voice trail off. He cocked his head. "I may be the boss, but I haven't lost any skills. You remember Bud Davies?" he added very quietly.

Donaldson lost two shades of color. He swallowed. Hard. "Oh, yeah."

"I never make threats. You get me?" he added in a voice that dripped ice.

Donalson felt his blood freezing. "Yeah, Tony, I get you, I get you."

"Good." He stepped back.

Donalson took off like a bullet, eased his friend into the car and spun gravel getting out of the driveway. Tony didn't move until the car was out of sight.

The horses were beautiful. Odalie chose a spirited black mare, laughing as the animal pranced. Stasia had insisted that she go. Stasia, meanwhile, was going to keep the Mannings company.

"That's Lady," Tony told her as he moved up beside her on a big bay horse. "She's a little jumpy."

"I don't mind. I'm usually a little jumpy myself," she said, her face flushed with pleasure, her blond hair in a long braid. She was wearing a blue sweater with jeans and boots. She looked good enough to eat.

"I imagine you grew up on a horse," Tony commented.

"I did. Dad put me on a pony when I was three and taught me to ride. I used to do barrel racing. I love to ride."

"So do I," he said.

"But with you, it was draft horses, I'll bet."

His eyebrows went up.

"You said you used to visit your grandfather on a farm in upstate New York," she reminded him. "And that he had draft horses."

He chuckled. "I'd forgotten that I told you that. Yes."

"I love big horses. John's built like you, big and husky, so it takes a big mount. He likes that Belgian Dad keeps in the stable."

"It's a pretty mare," he recalled.

"She has a little age on her now, but she's still John's favorite." She glanced at him while two other couples and the single man, Rudy, got on their own mounts just outside the stable. "Thanks."

"What for?"

"Sending that Donalson man off," she said.

"His boss was ready to leave," he said easily. "Since he drives him, he had to go along. He won't be missed," he added coldly. "He was after one of the maids late last night, too," he told her. "She was in tears."

"If I'd had access to an iron skillet, and you didn't need his boss to sell you those paintings, he'd have been in tears," she said with some heat, her pale blue eyes sparking.

He glanced at her and chuckled.

She made a face. "Sorry."

"Don't apologize. If he ever comes back—and don't hold your breath—I'll buy you an iron skillet."

She grinned. "Thanks."

"Are we ready to go? If you need any pointers," Rudy told Odalie with a grin, "I'll be glad to provide them. I go riding down in Jersey on a friend's farm."

Odalie gave him an amused look.

Before she could answer, Tony rode closer. "Her parents own one of the biggest ranches in Texas and she used to do rodeo," he informed the other man.

Rudy sighed. "Well, boy, is my face red!"

"Serves you right," Tony muttered. "How about keeping an eye on the Daly couple? She's afraid of horses."

"Sure thing," Rudy said at once, nodding politely at Odalie. It became clear at once that Odalie was spoken for, whether she or Tony knew it or not.

Odalie was in the dark. She thought Tony was just being nice, helping her ward off unwanted attention.

"That was kind of you," she said as they started out the gate toward the wooded trail. "He's a nice man, but I'm really not interested."

"No problem. Stasia wouldn't like it if I let you be harassed. By any man."

Her heart dropped with disappointment, but she forced a smile. "Thanks."

The trail was a long one, but it was cool and pleasant, with blooming trees and shrubs all along it. There was a small stream across the dirt trail and Tony pulled up at it to let the horses water.

They got off and let the horses drink.

"It's beautiful here," Odalie said to Tony while the other guests wandered downstream. "One doesn't think of places like this in New York."

"Why not?" he asked.

"Well, for some reason, we think if we're in New York, it's a big city." She shrugged. "We don't think of open places with streams and lots of trees."

He chuckled. "We tend to think of Texas as big guys in cowboy hats and boots riding horses."

Her eyes twinkled. "These days, it's mostly bib caps and four-wheelers to help with roundup. Only the really big ranches do it the old-timey way."

"That's news."

"Dad's ranch is one of the exceptions," she agreed, because it was done the old way on Big Spur. "It's huge. We pack out a chuck wagon when roundup's in swing, because it's so much area to cover. The men set up temporary corrals and tilt trays all over for branding and tagging and vaccinations."

"You ever go out with them?"

"We all used to," she said. "On a ranch, everybody works. If you have company on a weekend, they work, too," she laughed.

"What a life," he teased.

"I loved it. I never minded getting down and dirty when we had to."

"And you look like you never touched dirt," he pointed out.

"I fell in a mudhole during one roundup. When I walked in the door, my own mother didn't recognize me. It took forever to shower it off."

He smiled. "I fell in an equally clingy substance, but it wasn't mud. One of the cows had functioned, and I tripped. I thought my grandfather would laugh himself to death."

She smiled back. "You must have loved him a lot."

"I did. He didn't have much, he and my grandmother, but they loved each other a lot."

"My parents are like that. You almost never see one without the other, even at their ages. They said my grandparents on both sides were like that, too. Happy marriages run in my family. Or they did, until Stasia and Tanner split up." She glanced at him. "Luckily, that's no longer the case. They're both very happy."

"I noticed," he said. "Stasia's beaming."

"Yes. She's taking no chances. They want the baby very much."

"I'd have liked kids," Tony said, his eyes faraway. "But we never had any. Some men can't produce them," he added, and his voice was cold.

She started to speak, but he'd already turned away. "Better get moving," he called to the others. "There's a cloud coming up."

And there was; a big, blue one, heralding a possible nor'easter. They came at the most unexpected times. At the most unwelcome ones, too.

When they got back to the house, the weather channel was blaring out. People needed to batten down or head for the mainland; it was going to be a bad storm.

"I'll drop you and Stasia off at your apartment," Tony told the women. "Get your stuff together while I arrange to get the rest of my guests to the airport."

"Will do," Stasia said, drawing a disappointed Odalie along

with her. "You and Tony were getting along so well," Stasia said sadly as they packed. "I'm really sorry."

"It's okay," Odalie said on a sigh. "He'd already warned me off."

"What?!"

"I guess I was wearing my heart on my sleeve. He said he had a mistress and he didn't start things he couldn't finish," she replied. "So going home is not a bad thing. In fact," she added before Stasia could speak, "I think I'd like to go spend a couple of weeks at home. I need a break."

Stasia just smiled. Things were looking up, although Odalie might not think so. If Tony had to pull out his long-unvisited mistress to ward off her sister-in-law, something was truly in the works, even if Tony was fighting it tooth and nail. It gave her hope.

"That would be great," Stasia said. "We can pick up Tony's fairy from Maddie Brannt and you can take it home with you when you go back to New York."

"She did a really wonderful job on it. But Tony will never sell it," she added. "He'll tuck it away somewhere at home. I'd bet on it."

Stasia chuckled. "So would I. It might be a good idea to commission Maddie to do one of some pretty girl instead, one that he can display."

"I'll ask her," Odalie said. "But you'd better clear it with Tony first, right?"

"Right. I'll do that."

It was a quick trip back to the city with the cloud on their tail all the way.

"This is going to be some storm," Odalie said on a sigh. "We got caught up in Dallas in a hotel at a cattlemen's convention once. The whole building shook every time it thundered, and the lightning was so nonstop that it looked like daylight. Until then, I thought our storms in Big Spur were really bad."

"We're not that far south of Dallas, but the weather doesn't seem to reach us as much," Stasia agreed. "Storms anywhere in the plains are bad, though."

"There have been some terrible ones in recent years," Odalie sighed. "I don't like storms that hurt people and change lives, but I love storms," she added softly, smiling to herself.

"Of course you do. You like wrestling and snakes and... earthworms," Tony said.

Stasia burst out laughing while Odalie flushed. "Oh, do I remember hearing that story!" she chuckled. "Odalie and John got into more trouble, trying to one-up each other. We won't even go into the spider incident," she added with a wicked smile at Odalie.

"Well, I didn't know he was afraid of spiders," she argued. "Honestly, he never even told Dad, he was so afraid of being made fun of. Dad didn't like weakness in those days," she explained. "We were expected to toughen up and do what needed to be done."

"Which is why, when you were twelve, Dad gave you a handful of rubber bands..."

"We should really forget that," Odalie said, and flushed even more.

"But..."

"No butts." She flushed more. "Just...drop it, okay?"

Stasia laughed. "Okay. If you say so."

"Am I missing something here?" Tony teased.

"Not a thing. Honest. Just a misunderstood episode that

we should never, ever repeat in mixed company!" Odalie told her sister-in-law firmly.

"Come on," Tony teased. "Tell it."

"If you do, I'll present you with your very own hive of hornets the very minute you're not pregnant anymore!" Odalie promised.

Stasia chuckled helplessly. "All right, but you're stifling my creativity."

Odalie glanced at him. "That's what Mama used to say to all of us when we interrupted her piano lessons. She never knew how we used it on each other."

"We were too soft. Heather isn't somebody you mock, even in private," Stasia agreed. "She's all heart."

"She really is," Odalie agreed. "I hated disappointing Dad when I was small, but it was worse when I disappointed Mama. She cried. I couldn't take it."

"It was that way with me, with Mama," Tony agreed. "I'd do anything to make the tears stop, and I mean anything." He grimaced. "I even went to mass with her when I was home, to make up for one thing I did that shamed her."

"That was nice of you," Stasia said. "Especially considering that you avoid church like the plague usually."

"I'm getting older," he said. "I think about things more now than I used to."

"Older. Pshaw!" Stasia chided. "You aren't even in your prime."

"I'm headed for an oil barrel. No joke," he added with a grin at Stasia.

Odalie stared at him. "What's an oil barrel?"

"Don't tell her," Stasia said abruptly. "Really."

Tony's eyebrows lifted but he didn't add to his allusion.

He glanced out the window. "Storm's going the other way. Lucky for us. Nobody's even got an umbrella."

"We could get Big Ben to pull up a tree and use it as an umbrella," Stasia said, loud enough for Ben to hear.

"For shame!" Big Ben called through the lowered glass partition. "I never hurt trees! They have a spirit!"

"His dad is Cheyenne," Tony told them. "They're the original earth stewards. They did a better job than we're doing, for sure."

"I love you, Big Ben," Odalie called to him. "I love trees, too!"

"Fanatics," Tony scoffed.

"Says the man who plants trees in the national forests for any of his people who die," Stasia replied blandly.

"Look. We're here," Tony said to divert her.

"I'll take Odalie's suitcases in," Ben said, and went to get them out of the trunk.

"It was a lovely break. Thanks, Tony," Stasia said. "Odalie's going to the ranch next week. Can you send somebody with her?" she added innocently, just in case.

"Sure. I'll go myself. I've got to go over to San Antonio to talk to a guy and then down to Jacobsville to talk to a friend of a friend."

"No, don't go to so much trouble just for me," Odalie protested, flushing. "I can get Dad to come up and take me back…"

"Tony has to go anyway—he just said so. Dad's up to his ears in cattle woes right now."

"If it wasn't convenient, I'd say so," he told Odalie with a bite in his tone.

Odalie sighed. She couldn't fight them both. "Okay. Thanks," she added, smiling without meeting Tony's eyes.

"Oops," Stasia said suddenly. "I have to get inside. Tell Tony about the fairy... Oh, gosh, I hope I make it!" she exclaimed, and moved quickly from the car across the sidewalk to the apartment's front door. "And don't leave without me!" she called back. "I have to be at the airport in an hour to meet the plane Dad's sending for me! Leave my bag in the car. It's all I need!" And she vanished into Odalie's apartment.

"What about the fairy?" Tony asked while Stasia was inside.

She looked up at him, trying to fight the attraction she felt and failing hopelessly. "Stasia says that you'll tuck the fairy Maddie's making for you up on a shelf somewhere and you won't sell it. So Stasia said to ask Maddie to do one that you can sell..."

He sighed. "Well, she's right. The little things are precious." He shrugged. "Maybe it's a good idea to get her to do another one." He glanced down at her. "She could do another one of you."

"She's already done one. Maybe one of Stasia."

"No good. Tanner would buy it immediately."

"Nice point. Well, how about getting her to do one of Heather?"

"Your dad would buy it."

She grimaced.

"Don't you have some art history books?" he asked. "Stasia told me about them."

"Yes, I do, and I gave Maddie a set of her own while she was recuperating from her back injury."

"Then get her to pick a subject from one of the books, something with no ties to any of us," he suggested.

"That's a good idea."

"Yeah."

"Well, thanks for the weekend."

"Some weekend, with Donalson stalking you like a doe in the forest," he scoffed.

She drew in a breath. "It's something I never got used to," she confessed. "None of the boys I liked in school ever liked me. Of course, I was a stuck-up little snob in those days. Nobody really liked me." She looked out at the city beyond the backstreet with a sigh. "Now it's almost the same, except the wrong men like me too much and in the wrong way. They think because I come from wealth and I'm not bad looking that I know my way around bedrooms."

"Which you don't."

That surprised her into looking up.

"You don't think it shows?" he asked, his voice husky and deep and soft like velvet. "I know the other kind all too well. You've got class. It shows." He smiled. "I'll bet you sang in the church choir back home."

She flushed. "So much for being sophisticated."

"You don't need sophistication. You have style and grace and principles. That's more than enough, even in the city."

She was surprised by the remarks. They made her feel as if she had champagne in her veins.

He realized that, at once. He shrugged. "What I said before, however, still goes. You're attractive, but I've already got…"

"…a mistress," she finished for him, with a weary smile. "I know. I'm not your type."

"No." It hurt him to say it. He turned away. "How does Monday sound, to go home? About three o'clock?"

"Midafternoon is fine."

"Three o'clock. A.m.," he emphasized.

"In the morning?!" she exclaimed. "That's a myth," she said, her lower lip protruding. "There's no such thing as three in the morning!"

He chuckled. "Oh, yes, there is. Don't worry. If you aren't awake, I'll send Big Ben over with a large bucket. He'll pour water on you until you get up."

"He'll get a red toaster up alongside his head, too, the minute I can slosh my way into the kitchen to get it!" she promised, her blue eyes sparking.

"Hey!"

They both turned to look. Stasia was standing not five feet away, both hands on her hips. "Finally, you've noticed me! I said, the weather channel's on and they say the storm is headed this way! We need to get to the airport before it hits!"

He glared at Odalie, who glared back.

"I'll see you Monday at three." He turned and helped an impatient Stasia into the car gently, after she hugged Odalie half to death. He got into the car beside her. Ben closed the door.

"He's bluffing," Ben whispered out loud to Odalie.

The back window buzzed down. "Hell, no, he's not bluffing! You don't wake up, I'll prove it to you!" The window buzzed back up.

Odalie glared at the car and thought of giving him a one-finger salute, then shocked herself because she even thought of it. "I'll be awake," she told Ben. "But not because he made threats," she muttered to herself. She muttered all the way into the apartment, even after the car had driven away.

She stumbled around in the apartment, half asleep, already missing Stasia's company, tossing a few more clothes into a still-packed suitcase. She had a few things at home, mostly jeans and T-shirts and boots and jackets. She didn't need to pack much, but she always packed more than she thought she'd need.

She'd meant to call Tony's bluff, but she'd often heard Stasia say that he never bluffed. He made promises, and he kept them. She pictured herself in her thin gown, drenched in cold water. It was enough to get her out of bed after only three hours' sleep.

It was two thirty. She still had on a long lined lemon silk nightgown that fell to her ankles, with spaghetti straps and a square bodice trimmed with lace. It had a peignoir, but she never wore it in the apartment. Stasia had given it to her as a birthday present, and she loved it. Her long blond hair was down to her waist in back, neatly combed and as silky as the gown. She had no makeup on, but why bother? Tony had already said he wasn't interested, so why should she...

The doorbell rang. Surely it wouldn't be Big Ben at this hour...?

She opened the door without thinking and looked straight into Tony Garza's black eyes, but only for a second. His gaze fell to the gown, and he almost choked on emotion. She was exquisite like that. A painter would have loved her for a subject. No makeup, her long, beautiful hair loose, barefoot, in palest yellow silk and lace. It was a picture he'd never get out of his mind.

She hadn't thought about what she was wearing until she noticed him looking pointedly away from her.

"Oh, gosh, I didn't think...sorry!" She turned and ran for her bedroom, then closed the door behind her.

While she was climbing quickly into her clothes, Tony noted the already-packed bags. He went outside and motioned to Big Ben, who took them to the trunk of the limo.

Tony was still cursing himself five minutes later when she reappeared in a pair of beige palazzo pants with a silky tan blouse, her hair up in a complicated knot and a long open beige sweater over it all, with beige heeled sandals and a gold-buckled belt for accessories. No jewelry except a pair of yellow gold studs. She looked good enough to eat.

"Going on the runway?" he asked, just to show her he wasn't impressed.

She glared at him. "Nobody goes on a runway at three a.m. And you said three, not two thirty," she added hotly.

He pursed his lips. "You were awake. Sadly."

Her eyes widened. "I know where I can find a big red toaster if anybody even tries to pour water on me!"

"Too late. You're dressed. Any other bags?" he asked.

She wanted to throw something. All this pent-up anguished passion and no way to let it out. She wondered what he'd do if she tried that primal-screaming thing that had been popular years ago.

"No," she said. "No other luggage."

He turned to look at her. "No makeup bag?"

She gave him a droll look. "I'm going home. To a ranch? Where cowboys are? What do I need makeup for?"

He studied her pretty face. "Nothing that I can see." He smiled slowly. "Most women look like hell without all that paint."

It was a compliment, but she wasn't taking the bait. She didn't answer him.

"If you're ready, let's go. Everything turned off?"

"Yes. I double-checked."

They went out and she locked her door. She heard an odd noise, but it was gone seconds later. Apparently, Tony hadn't noticed. But then, he was almost at the car.

He let her slide in first, and he slid in beside her as Ben closed the door.

She put her purse on the floorboard and rubbed at her eyes.

"Sleepy baby," he teased.

"I'm not sleepy. My eyes are."

He chuckled. But he pulled out his cell phone and stayed occupied all the way to the airport.

It was a short flight. Odalie had long since learned to take a motion sickness pill before she got on a plane. She sat in her seat playing mahjong on her cell phone the whole way, with an occasional dip into solitaire.

Tony glanced at her. "You ever win that?" he asked, indicating the solitaire app.

"Not often. But it's still fun."

"Not when you lose a bundle on a card you don't get dealt," he said philosophically.

She smiled. "You should ask John about poker."

"Your brother? Why?"

"Just ask him sometime."

He gave her a curious glance and went back to his app.

Tanner was waiting for them at her father's airstrip. She ran into his arms to be hugged and hugged some more.

"How's Stasia?" she asked at once.

"Blooming. She really enjoyed the trip. Hi, Tony. Nice of you to hand deliver our parcel," he teased, shaking hands.

"Least I could do. She had a rough couple of days at my place on Long Island. She'll tell you about it." He checked his watch. "I've got an appointment to make. Let me know when you want to come home. I'm down this way every other week. I'll fetch you."

"Thanks," she said.

"Find a reason to come along weekend after next," Tanner suggested. "We'll be getting the yearlings ready to go to market. It's an experience. Plus, we have a celebratory barbeque."

"Barbeque!" Big Ben enthused.

"See what you did?" Tony asked Tanner with a mocking glare. "Now I'll have to bring him. You can't get past a grill if it's got barbeque, but he's crazy about the way you make it."

"The way Dolores makes it," Ben replied, and wiggled his eyebrows.

"I'll tell her you said that," Tanner teased.

Ben just grinned.

"So, we'll see you weekend after next. You going to talk to Mrs. Brannt about the fairy?"

"Yes, I am," Odalie promised.

"Good. I'll see you."

He turned and walked up the ramp into the plane without a backward glance.

Odalie stared at it with a poignant look she wasn't aware of.

Tanner threw his arm around her and turned her toward the Lincoln he drove. "Come tell me all about the weekend at Tony's."

"Okay," she agreed, and forced herself not to watch the plane take off without her.

6

Tony was quiet all the way back to Jersey and then to the limo at the airport and on to the contact's motel room. He couldn't forget the look on Odalie's face as he'd turned to leave. He'd pulled out all the stops, thrown his longtime mistress at her, insinuated that she wasn't his type, done everything he could think of to discourage her.

But that one long look had hit him right in the heart. She was attracted to him. With her impeccable background, it should have been some handsome young man with a bright future and wealth like hers behind him. It shouldn't be a hoodlum feeling his years, putting her in constant danger from the enemies he had, past and present. He was dying for her, and he didn't dare touch her. It wouldn't take much to start that brush fire. Only a tiny spark. He had to be ever so vigilant.

"We're here, boss," Ben interrupted his thoughts.

"So we are."

There was a light in the second-story motel room where they'd been asked to meet a contact.

"Lucky for us that this guy knew the right bar to hit to find a contact," Tony chuckled. "And that Rudy was having a whiskey sour when he started asking questions. I swear to God, some people have the craziest damned ideas about how we work things," he added, shaking his head.

Ben checked his .45 and holstered it, then spoke to two contacts who'd arrived much earlier and had the room staked out.

"We ready?" Tony asked, checking his own weapon before he stuck it back in the pancake holster behind his back.

"Ready."

"I wonder if there's something about government offices that drains brain cells," he muttered as Ben came around the car to open his door, looking around constantly.

Unknown to the target inside, he had his own men down here, concealed and ready for any surprises. There was even one on the stairs, who nodded, then jerked his head toward a nearby door. The signal meant everything was okay, no danger from any quarter. Of course there was always danger. Tony didn't even trust his own men. Except for Ben, who'd proved many times that he was in Tony's corner no matter what.

But that only meant that he was safe until one of the other really big bosses decided he'd done something unforgivable and called a vote on whether or not Tony would be hit. In which case Ben would be sent to off him. It was the way things were done, as he'd told Odalie. Only somebody close could get close enough for a hit. Hate it though Ben might, it would be his life or his and Tony's lives, and the hit would still get made. Better not to think too much about that, he decided. It was the here and now he had to deal with, not the future. Besides that, Teddy liked him. Teddy was about as high up as it got.

He knocked on the door, the knock Rudy had shared with the contact when he'd shared the location for the meet. The door opened. The man inside, young, nervous, wearing a suit off the rack, quickly slid his pistol back into its holster, fumbling a little. "Sorry," he told Tony as he invited him in with Big Ben. "I'm twitchy."

"We're all twitchy. What do you know," Tony asked, "about a sting in my territory?"

"Don't know exactly where the aggravation began," he told Tony. "Except that it's coming from New York. Sal the Penny got hit in his own living room in front of his family. That's not how we do things. This new generation came up on video games. They like gore."

"I remember Sal. He was one of Dad's pals."

"Yeah. Well, the cops are on it. No matter who you are, murder is murder. If they catch him, he'll be a guest of Uncle Sam until his hair turns silver."

"Maybe not that long," Tony said deliberately. "Sal had friends."

"He had a lot. Plus the trouble is coming from a punk kid."

"What?"

The contact laughed, a little too loudly. "No joke, a kid barely twenty years old. His dad was a made man. He learned it from the floor up and he likes it. He's not greedy—he just wants what he thinks should be his," he added.

"He won't like what he gets," Tony said simply. "The big guys like our friend in upstate New York don't like noise. It draws attention from the feds." He leaned forward, his dark eyes steady and piercing. "Anybody who puts a hit in my territory is asking for trouble."

The younger man swallowed and averted his eyes. "Sure, sure, and that's why I asked to meet you, to tell you about this. The kid needs to be taken out before he brings down the heat on all of us."

Tony was still staring at him. "Where do we find this kid? And what sort of backup are we talking about?"

The younger man brightened. "I've got the data, I mean, the lowdown, right...right here." He fumbled an envelope out of his pocket and laughed as it tangled. "Uh, you did a job with the feds not so long ago, didn't you, and they saved your bacon? I heard about it."

"Yeah," Tony said, his voice going soft, "they did. I owe them for that. But I told them up front, I don't sell out my people, even if I die for it."

"That's how we all feel. Nobody wants a rat for a pal."

Tony looked through some typed sheets that contained two grainy photographs, three names—one in boldface—and an address in Newark. "Your guys got somebody on this?"

"Oh, yeah. We...we got a guy out of Quebec."

Tony's eyebrows went up.

"He's a veteran of many hits," he told Tony. "And he hasn't got one blemish on his record. Not one. That tell you how good he is?"

"It tells me a lot."

"He's got no family, no close friends. He works for the money."

"That's not enough. Not for that job."

"He likes it," the other guy said quietly and with distaste.

Tony drew in a long breath. "Well, I guess nobody likes a fresh kid threatening to bring down the cops, either, do they?" He leaned back in his chair. "You sure you want to do this?" he asked suddenly.

"I told you. We've got it all managed, no real outside talent, just the guy from Quebec. And no rats."

"Didn't they say the *Titanic* was unsinkable?" Tony asked. There was a nervous laugh.

"So you've got a target, you've got talent—what am I here for, exactly?" Tony asked.

The young man brightened. "Intel," he said. He flushed a little. "I mean, the facts, the setup, how we take the guy out."

Tony raised a black eyebrow. "The cleaner does that."

He hesitated. "No, I mean, he'll come when he's asked, but we need advice from a pro," he emphasized with a pearly smile, "about the best way to put the hit on this upstart! If you could just tell us, me, how you usually go about these things…?"

Tony leaned back in his chair, just staring at the man.

"You're not getting cold feet, are you?" the younger man asked.

Tony didn't blink. "Cold as the grave, in fact."

"Wh-what do you mean?" the man asked, looking very twitchy at the moment.

"I owe a guy a favor," Tony said. "Sorry. Nothing personal. Just business."

Before he could say another word, the door opened and two older guys in suits walked in. The guy at the table tried to pull his gun, but the older men were quicker.

Tony got up and looked down at the man with utter contempt. "Sal the Penny is in Minnesota visiting his grandson," he said. "The closest you've ever been to us was when you showed up uninvited to a birthday party at a local restaurant and tried to fit in." He smiled coldly at the man's surprise. Rudy had been thorough. "You've never even fired that piece you carry on your hip. Plus," he added, the smile fading, "you're wearing a wire, you son of a bitch."

The man colored. He struggled in Ben's grasp and stammered, trying to think up a way to save himself.

"Don't worry about it. We'll handle the wire when we get him out of here," one of the guys told him with a cold smile.

"Hey, listen here. This is my bust!" the young man argued. "I called you and told you where to come. You're on my side!"

"How's that?" one of the older suited men asked.

"You're on my side!" The younger man was almost hysterical now.

One of the newcomers glanced at Tony. "We'll take care of this package for you, Tony, no worries."

"Make sure there's not a trail leading back here," Tony said quietly.

The man was breathing like a steam engine, his eyes going from Tony to the guys in suits. "But...but...these are feds, and you're talking right in front of them!"

Tony cocked his head. "They tell you they were feds?" he asked. He turned to the men. "You know what to do. And you know who's behind this. Make sure he knows what he's sticking his nose into."

"We'll get the message to him." The taller man in the suit clapped handcuffs on the squirrelly man squirming for release.

"But you're supposed to be feds!" he exclaimed. "I'm wearing a wire for you, to catch him in the act of ordering a hit!" He was almost screaming, nodding frantically toward Tony.

"The feds aren't the only guys who hang around bars looking for customers who want to off relatives," Tony told him. "You just learned a lesson. Too bad you won't get to apply it."

He nodded at the men in suits.

"This isn't how it's supposed to go!" the man sobbed.

Tony glared at him. "You really think you can get at us that easily?" he asked, and the softness of his voice chilled. "We're more powerful than you know, in darker places than you'll ever look. Even underground, we can reciprocate harm. You aligned yourself with a man who's already digging himself a grave. He has more blood on his hands than you even know. He'll pay for it. After you do."

"I don't know anybody, I don't know anybody. I was just told to set you up and get you out of the way!"

"With a couple of feds in a location out in the sticks, toting a gun that's never been fired, an operative in a cheap brand-new suit and shoes?" Tony scoffed. "I made you the minute I walked in the door." He cocked his head. "And the underboss who set up this meeting for you works for me," he added softly, "not your vindictive pal in DC!"

"Please, I just did what I was told to do!" the man whimpered.

"That was the Gestapo's excuse. Did it work for them?"

"Please!"

He was still wailing until they put him out. He was trussed up nicely, bagged and tossed into the back of a sedan. Ready for delivery.

"Now that we've taken care of business, let's get back to the airport and head down to Jacobsville, Texas," Tony said as he got in the car. "My other adopted daughter is visiting her sister, with the new little girl. I can't wait to see them!"

"What about that package we left back there?"

Tony chuckled. "They'll deliver it to the right office in DC. That will be an interesting story to tell one day," he said simply, and he leaned back in his seat with his eyes closed. "Some guys watch way too many old movies and television shows."

"You got that right," Ben agreed.

★ ★ ★

Odalie was delighted with her own brand-new goddaughter at the Big Spur near Branntville, Texas. The child was a delight to hold. She fell in love with her at first sight.

"You'll spoil her rotten," Maddie Brannt accused with glee as she watched Penelope gurgle up at her godmother.

"She's just adorable," Odalie said. "I can't decide which one of you she favors yet."

"She'll look like her daddy," Maddie said, still madly in love with Cort, her husband.

"I think her eyes will be more like yours," Odalie replied, "except the shape is what I'm talking about, not the color." She looked up. "When you're up to it, Tony wants you to take a picture out of one of the art books I gave you and make him a fairy of it. We all agreed that he's never going to put the one of him in any gallery," she added with a grin.

Maddie laughed. "Actually, I figured that out for myself. I picked one of the fantasy paintings and made a little red-headed fairy with big blue eyes. She doesn't look like anyone we know, so she'll be easy to let go of. I'm just thrilled that Tony's willing to exhibit my babies in his gallery. The cattle business is having some issues lately."

"Tell me about it," Odalie agreed. "Dad's having problems, too. If the government would just get its fingers out of the cattle business…"

"…and doctors' offices and everything else that it regulates, and oversees, and taxes to death, people might find a way to pay their bills!"

"Two kindred spirits," Odalie laughed.

"Rural people don't think like city people," Maddie said simply. "I actually heard one woman in an interview say that we didn't need ranchers to provide meat or farmers to provide vegetables because we had, and I quote her, supermarkets!"

"Don't they know that food is only in supermarkets because of farmers and ranchers?"

"I think they'd decided that we shouldn't have either, that we should all eat bugs and be happy."

"I don't know about you, but I'm pretty tired of having billionaires make rules and laws and designate even the food we eat. We don't even have a voice anymore."

"Time to get out and vote," Maddie said. "It's the only thing that might save us now."

"God is the only thing that can save us," Odalie replied with a smile. "But so many people don't believe these days. It makes me sad."

"That's their problem," Maddie replied on a sigh. "But eternity is forever. It's something to consider. If they're sure there's nothing after death, they'd better be right."

"Amen."

"Now, down to business. Let me put our Penny down for her nap and I'll show you my newest fairy!"

Odalie laughed. "I can't wait!"

But when they got into the studio that Cord Brannt had built for her inside the Skylance ranch, there were two fairies. One was redheaded and blue-eyed. The other was a dead ringer for Odalie.

"But you already did one of me," Odalie protested.

"This one's for the gallery," Maddie said, and smiled, not giving away the fact that it had been commissioned by Stasia. It had a purpose that Odalie wasn't supposed to know about.

"Oh. Well, okay," Odalie said reluctantly. She smiled. "She looks just like me, except that I don't often wear lacy white gowns to bed, and I almost never wear my hair down." She thought of Tony's eyes on her the day she was in the gown with her hair loose, and her heart ran wild. She bit down hard on the memory. "This one's lovely," she added softly.

"I'm glad you like it. Is Tony coming down anytime soon? I want to show both of them to him."

Her heart jumped. "Yes, the end of next week," she replied.

"Great! I can give them to him then."

"Sounds good," Odalie said, and missed the mischievous look on her friend's face.

She spent the time before Tony's visit practicing her scales in the soundproof room her mother used for a studio, with the door closed. Heather accompanied her on piano when Odalie practiced the arias that she would choose from to try out for the Metropolitan Opera with.

It hadn't escaped anyone's notice that she kept putting off the audition. When queried, she had all sorts of excuses. She couldn't tell them why she was so reluctant to do it. It was what she'd trained for her whole life. It was almost in her grasp. But she hesitated. The threat of nightly performances in front of hundreds of people terrified her. She had honestly tried to work around it. She just wasn't sure enough that she wanted to live with that fear for the rest of her life.

The end of the second week came, bringing with it good weather and the last day of the most grueling thing ranchers had to do, next to roundup in the spring and fall—moving bulls to summer pasture and getting culls ready to ship.

Tempers were short. Cowboys got into fights. Others threatened to quit. And on and on.

Cole came into the dining room covered in dust and sporting a furious scowl.

"Who quit?" Heather asked, and then she noticed his knuckles. "And did he quit before or after you hit him?" she asked belligerently.

Before he could come up with a good answer, a truck pulled up outside. Voices came from the porch, and then Tony and Ben came in the door, Ben carrying two travel bags and a big suitcase.

"Hello!" Heather greeted them with a big smile. "You're early."

Tony raised his brows, trying not to look at Odalie, who was dressed in jeans and a revealing T-shirt with her hair in a ponytail. "Who got slugged?" he asked, having noted Cole's fists at once.

"Larry," Cole said, giving the name the sound of a snake hissing.

Heather rolled her eyes. "What did he say this time?"

"That I should have been a dictator, because I could give Mussolini pointers," he replied curtly.

Tony hid a smile. So did Heather.

Cole threw up his hands. "Well, somebody had to take charge. It's my ranch, you know. I own it," he raged. "Two of the cowboys, including Larry, were so drunk they could hardly stand up, and Dan threatened to let Larry use a branding iron on one of my cattle dogs because it was barking too much!!"

"Now, honey," Heather began, "I'm sure he wasn't thinking…"

Tony's face had gone from amused to icy. "I'd have slugged him, too," he muttered.

Cole pointed to Tony.

Heather just let out a long sigh.

"If he didn't quit, you should fire him," Odalie said darkly.

Cole pointed to her, too.

Heather sat down.

"And Dan, too," Odalie added.

"I did," Cole replied. He glared at Heather. "At least my baby backs up her dad."

Odalie laughed. "Don't. She already thinks it's us against John and Tanner."

"Yes, I do, because it always is," Heather shot back. "You two…!"

"We have company," Cole said with affectionate amusement. "Be nice."

"Tony's not company—he's family," Heather replied.

Tony's face had the oddest expression. He averted his eyes. Odalie had heard a lot about Tony from Stasia, who said that Tony's homelife had been pure hell. It obviously touched him that Heather considered him part of her family.

"Suits me," Cole said. "He can come help with the bull roundup."

"Oh, no, you don't," Odalie began.

"And you, too," he added.

She let out an exasperated sigh. "Dad!"

"Anybody who's here during work hours is free labor," Cole said with a grin. "Look it up. It's in the bylaws of the cattlemen's association, somewhere." He clapped his hands. "So get changed," he told Tony and Ben. "You'll do," he told Odalie. "Outside in ten minutes." He avoided Heather's poisonous gaze and barreled out the door.

"He's joking, right?" Ben asked, wide-eyed.

"He's not," Odalie said apologetically. She clapped him on one broad shoulder. "It's okay—he'll put you to watching for the cattle trucks or counting heads or something." She added under her breath, "I hope."

Tony just laughed.

He had jeans and boots and a straw hat on, with a blue checked shirt that was all too revealing of the muscles in his chest and the thick mat of hair over his breastbone. Odalie deliberately didn't look at him except for a quick glance as they rode out to the pasture where the culls were being readied for shipping and a selection of new calves Cole had bought at auction the day before were being processed.

"There's flies," Ben muttered, swatting at them as he rode not on a horse, like Tony and Odalie, but in the bed of a pickup truck.

"Oh, those aren't flies. Those——" she indicated a black mass of flying insects as they arrived at the portable processing fences and tilt trays "——are flies!"

"If they spook you, just shoot them," Tony advised easily as he swung out of the saddle.

Odalie jumped down with ease and they both went to help at the tilt trays where the new calves were being processed.

It was dirty, sweaty work, but not nearly as bad as roundup, Heather had told Tony. Then, there were swarms of volunteers. In cattle country, neighbors turned out to help with what was a big-time enterprise on a ranch the size of Cole's. Of course, he and his own men were ready and willing to help the neighbors when they were doing their own roundups.

"Isn't it awful?" Odalie asked Tony with a grin. She wiped away sweat from her forehead and loosened hair from her ponytail. "I love it!"

He laughed at the picture she made. Lovely in couture clothes, incredible in evening wear, she was just as pretty in stained jeans and shirts and with no makeup on. No wonder Connie had been so impressed with her, he thought, and with a sense of pride. Odd, feeling proud of a woman he could

never have. He didn't think about that too long. It led to a
place he wasn't going. Ever.

They finished just as night was falling. Everybody ran for
the showers and thank goodness it was a many-bedroom house,
each bedroom with its own bath. Then a late supper, and off
to bed. Nobody wanted to sit on the porch and talk. Not after
that exertion!

The next day, there was going to be a barbeque for the
treaty sale Cole had scheduled for some of his young bulls
and a few heifers ready to be bred. He did private sales for
these rather than use the auction house, which he did use for
his yearling calf crops.

Odalie, in a summery yellow-print cotton dress with puffy
sleeves and a demure neckline, went up the hill to see about a
kitten one of the hands had found. Tony went with her. They
hadn't said much to each other, but there was a companion-
able silence between them. No arguing. For the moment.

They looked around in the sparse trees beside the path that
the riders used when they rode out to tend cattle, but there
was no kitten in sight.

"It's probably looking for a cool space," Tony suggested.

She avoided looking at him. He was still wearing jeans,
but with an emerald green designer pullover shirt today, and
he looked good enough to eat.

"There are no cool spaces," she groaned, wiping a hand
over her forehead.

"There might be one or two up in Iceland," he sighed.

She glanced at him and laughed. "Poor Ben! He really
hates flies, doesn't he?" she asked with twinkling blue eyes.

She was a picture. He hated her for the beauty that was

making him miserable, for that exquisite body that haunted his dreams. "He's a city boy," he said.

"But he likes Mercedes," she laughed. "And she's not a city girl."

He turned and glared at her, out of sorts because he was more attracted to her than ever and he was fighting it tooth and nail. "Maybe so, but he's not the sort of man to settle for life in the sticks any more than I am."

"I was just making a comment…"

His black eyes narrowed. "And if you think wearing pretty clothes and flirting will get you anywhere with me, think again."

Her temper flared. "Oh, how will I go on?" she said with mock sorrow. "As if what I wear has anything to do with you!"

He smiled coldly. "Don't you think it shows, Texas cowgirl?" he asked in a slow, sensuous tone, his eyes eating her from head to foot, so that she was almost shaking with hunger. "You'd die to have me."

"I wish I had a rope!" she said, infuriated. "I'd tie you to a tree and let the coyotes eat you, you, you, you hoodlum!" She threw the words back at him with smarting pride. She hadn't even deliberately tried to entice him!

She turned and stomped off the trail toward the ranch house.

"Stop!" he said tersely.

She did, because he'd never spoken to her in that tone of voice before, and she knew it had nothing to do with their argument.

"Stand still. Close your eyes." He was giving orders very quietly. "Don't jump when you hear the shot. Do you understand? Nod, don't speak."

She swallowed, hard, and nodded, even as she heard the telltale sound of frying bacon near her feet. She knew what would happen next if he missed. Cowboys died from rattle-snake bites, even in modern times. And even if she lived, it would mean the hospital and days of agony, perhaps loss of muscle tissue or even a limb. The venom was potent.

She waited for the shot. When it came, she only flinched a little. Two shots, one after another, quick and loud, so close together that they merged.

"He's dead," he said.

She opened her eyes. Shaking, she turned and ran into Tony's arms, pressing hard against him, shaking all over. She couldn't stop. All her life she'd been terrified of rattlesnakes. One had lived with them in Texas, because they were part of the landscape. That didn't make it easy.

Tears rolled down her cheeks as he held her close, so close, as if he could only breathe through her.

His face was buried in the hair at her throat. She felt it there, felt his lips against her.

"God, that was close!" he groaned.

"I'm…so…scared of them," she whispered, even her voice shaking. "Thank you. Thank you…!" She held him even closer.

He didn't protest, and he should have. The floral scent of her worked its way into his nostrils while he fought the most intense desire he'd ever felt for a woman.

"It didn't strike you?" he asked urgently.

"It didn't have time." She was still shaking. She couldn't stop. But she felt Tony's quick heartbeat under her ear, smelled the clean scent of him, overlain with spicy cologne. She felt his body hard and powerful against her own and felt safe, as she'd never felt safe before. She wanted to stay there forever. She wanted him to bend and take her mouth under his, to feel those chiseled lips pushing hers apart, devouring and insistent against her own. It was ridiculous. He didn't want her. He'd said so, often. But hope died hard. Very hard.

He felt himself weakening. He'd been terrified that he wouldn't shoot in time, that the snake would strike before he could pull the trigger. She might have been dead, mutilated, horribly mangled. He was so relieved that he'd forgotten all the reasons why he should never touch her. In fact, he wanted to touch her. Now, more than ever. His hands moved on her back, slowly pulling her even closer.

But before he could follow up on that involuntary movement, Cole and Ben were headed toward them. Cole, on horseback, reached them first as Ben ran up the hill more slowly.

"What happened?" Cole asked after he'd flown off the horse.

Tony nodded toward the snake, a long way from where they were standing.

Cole frowned. "Hell of a shot, Tony," he noted as he kissed his daughter's hair. "Sweetheart, you okay?"

She pulled back reluctantly and hugged her dad. "I'm okay. I hate rattlesnakes."

"We all hate them," Cole said. "You didn't see it?"

She shook her head. "They blend. If it hadn't been for Tony…"

Tony was reloading his .38. He made a face. "Sorry. I should have told you that I always carry. Old habit."

Cole swept back his overshirt, displaying a .45 Ruger Vaquero double action pistol in a tooled leather holster. "We all carry around here. Never know if there will be a snake or a rabid animal that has to be put down, or even one of our animals that's injured too badly to save." He cocked his head as Tony finished reloading and put the two wasted shells in his pocket and the pistol in the pancake holster behind his back. "You don't carry an automatic?" he added.

Tony shook his head. "I had an auto fail on me at the worst possible time," he replied. "If it hadn't been for Ben—" he indicated the bodyguard who was just joining them "—we wouldn't be having this conversation."

"Well, I'm not giving up my Glock," Ben announced.

"I don't remember asking you to," Tony chuckled.

"What happened?" Ben asked, wincing when he saw the tears on Odalie's face.

"Snake," Tony replied. "No big deal. And nobody's blaming you, capisce?"

Which led to a spate of Italian that neither Cole nor Odalie could understand and that sounded like a family scene from a *Due South* episode.

Cole started laughing.

"What?" Tony asked, diverted.

"You two. You sound like a scene I remember from a show called *Due South*. There was this Italian family…"

Tony started laughing. So did Ben.

"Oh, God, that show," Tony chuckled. "It's just like that," he told them. "Just like that, when we all get together. Connie, Odalie met her at my house on Long Island, and the others, the cousins, we get together on the holidays and it's one argument after another." He shook his head. "I guess it's just how Italian families are."

"We should take him to see Great-Aunt Ophelia at Christmas," Cole told Odalie.

She laughed with him. "It's a riot. She and her sister, Gracie, had four children between them, and the kids had kids. So now that makes sixteen grandchildren, about thirty great-grandchildren, five great-great-grandchildren…"

"Six," Cole interrupted. "You forgot Margie's new baby."

"Sorry, six great-great-grandchildren. So Ophelia and Gracie are rich beyond the dreams of avarice and they're very old and all the kids and other descendants think they should get part of the estate. Then Gracie and Ophelia get into it and talk about changing their wills." She shook her head. "Pure theater."

"Almost makes me wish I'd been a foundling," Cole sighed.

"Liar." Odalie smiled at him.

He just shrugged.

Ben was standing over the snake. "You shoot him from there?" he asked Tony.

Tony nodded.

"Not bad," Ben mused.

"Not bad at all," Cole agreed. "You shoot straight."

Tony just nodded again. It meant his life if he didn't, and it had, a time or two.

"They stop doing this eventually?" Ben asked, with a mock shiver.

"What?" Cole asked.

"Wriggling like that?"

"Just until the sun goes down," Cole assured him. "It's natural."

"Oh, like with a guy when you—"

"Is anybody else hungry?" Tony asked, deliberately interrupting his unthinking bodyguard. "I'm starved."

"So are the rest of us," Cole agreed with a chuckle. "Bull roundup is hard work, not to mention branding and vetting for that new lot of calves I bought at auction. And thanks for the help. Even though it did involve some arm-twisting."

"Not much, and I enjoyed it," Tony said easily. He glanced at Cole. "Don't you do ear tag now, instead of branding?"

"Ear tags fall off. They can even be pulled off when a cow

gets her head tangled in a tree limb or something. We mostly use them for ID. But heated brands last. We still have rustlers, you know. Except now they do it in sixteen-wheelers instead of box canyons," he chuckled.

"Which is why freeze brands don't work, either," Odalie chuckled. "They shed along with the animal's coat."

Tony was watching her involuntarily. He'd been frightened for her when the snake had started rattling. Not that he was ever going to admit it.

"You sure you're okay?" he asked Odalie, his eyes betraying only a hint of the turmoil inside him. She was beautiful.

"I'm fine. Thanks." She smiled wanly.

"Di niente," he said.

"Cos' è?" she replied without thinking.

Tony stared at her without speaking. She blushed. "Capisce?" he asked.

"Capisco un po'," she replied. "And that's about all I know," she confessed, "although when I studied in Italy, I picked up a few words. Very few. When I sing operas in Italian, I just memorize the sounds."

Tony just smiled at her.

Later, Cort Brannt brought over two little fairy statues that his wife had done for Tony's gallery.

"She'll overnight them to the gallery when you get back to New York," Cort said, placing them from a layered box onto the cleared dining room table. "But she wanted you to see them."

Tony was amazed. He picked up the redheaded one and smiled. "This one is really pretty," he said. "Almost ethereal. Your wife is talented."

"Very," Cort said with a sigh. "I'm proud of her."

Obviously. But Odalie didn't say it. She was just as proud of Maddie.

Then Tony noticed the other statue. He put down the redhead and picked up the delicate little blonde in her white gown with her long pale blond hair trailing behind her as she held a butterfly on the tip of one finger. She was smiling.

"How does she do this?" Tony asked, shocked. "I can hardly see the faces here, but she's got every detail perfect."

"It's a mystery to me as well," Cort replied. "She's amazing."

Tony was still staring at the little statue. It was Odalie. He knew it. He wasn't about to acknowledge it. But he was also certain that this statue would never be placed in the position of available art in his lifetime. It would be kept at his apartment, or his house, under lock and key. It was the most beautiful little creature he'd ever seen, except for its real-life counterpart talking to Cort while Tony admired his new possession.

"What's this about a snake?" Cort was asking.

"A rattlesnake," Odalie said. "We were looking for a stray kitten. We never found it, but I found the snake. Tony killed it. He shot it. Two shots, at distance, dead center in its head."

He turned. They were all smiling at him.

He just stood there, trying to think of something to say.

Heather, divining the scene, walked in and hugged Cort, breaking the spell.

7

Tony managed to drag his eyes away from Odalie, but it had been another close call in a veritable buffet of them.

She was feeling something similar. It was obvious that he found her attractive, but he did everything in his power to push her away. She reminded herself that he had a mistress, and that he wasn't a forever-after sort of man. That wasn't going to change. It was something she had to accept.

She'd noticed the way he looked at the statuette Maddie had made. There had been something in his expression, in the way he turned the pretty thing in his big, beautiful lean hands that made her heart do loops. But he was never going to give in to the interest she was certain he felt. He wanted no part of her in his life. Well, he was a bachelor. No, a widower. He'd talked about his wife, about how much he'd cared for her. Was he still grieving for her, and he thought getting involved with someone else was like being unfaithful to her memory?

But he had a mistress, she reminded herself again. Even as she thought it, her face tautened. She hated the thought of some other woman in Tony's arms, being held the way he held her when he'd killed the snake. That had been real hunger, mutual hunger, just before Cole and Ben had run up to them.

It hadn't lasted, that feeling. He was talking to Heather about the statuette, showing it to her and laughing with delight.

"It's very pretty," Heather told Maddie. "Like the baby…!" She held out her arms and Maddie put Penny in them.

Heather cooed into the little face watching hers with such intensity. She kissed the little forehead.

"Do they always look at you like that?" Tony wondered as he looked at the baby over Heather's shoulder. "I mean, it's like she understands everything she hears!"

"Who knows?" Heather asked. She turned and handed the baby to Tony, showing him how to hold her so that her little head was supported. He chuckled, reminding her that his goddaughter down in Jacobsville was about the same age. He was getting used to holding babies.

It was like a scene out of a movie. Big, husky Tony holding the tiny little girl, his whole face glowing with delight, his eyes luminous as he looked down at her and talked to her. And she laughed up at him, little gurgles of happiness bubbling up and escaping her tiny body.

"Look at that!" Tony said, enthralled.

Nobody noticed Maddie, with a smartphone, taking pictures of the two of them. Later, one would find its way into Odalie's smartphone.

"I always wanted kids," Tony said as he reluctantly handed the baby back to Heather. "But we couldn't have them."

"You're still young," Heather pointed out with a grin.

"Not so very," he replied solemnly and with a wistful smile. He glanced at Maddie. "She's a beauty," he told her, and grinned at Cort, who joined them. "You two did good."

"She did most of the work," Cort said with dry humor, and they all laughed.

"You really love kids, don't you?" Heather asked Tony as they all went to the table, where places were set with plates and napkins, utensils and glasses as the cowboys started dishing up food.

"I do," he replied. "It was one of our greatest sorrows that we couldn't have any. My wife had cancer. It took her a long time to die." His face hardened. "I was suicidal right after it happened. We were both in our early twenties. I thought we'd have years and years together."

She turned to him. "You can't live in yesterday."

He drew in a breath and smiled down at her. "I keep hearing that."

"On a different note, thank you for saving my daughter's life," she replied solemnly. "We have to deal with those stupid rattlesnakes every single year. There's no way to get them all."

"God made butterflies and he made rattlesnakes." He shrugged. "We make do."

She smiled. "Yes."

He glanced at Odalie, who was talking to the leader of the local band that was playing while the ranch hands and their families stood around and listened. "She gets along with everybody, doesn't she?"

"Most people. She wasn't always like this. She's changed a lot in the past two or three years. Good changes."

"Growing up hurts," he said from a wealth of bad memories.

"I know you have cousins," she said gently. "But nobody closer?"

He shrugged. "Friends, mostly, except for Connie and her family in Jersey." He laughed. "She loved your daughter at first glance. And she doesn't like most people." He looked down at her. "My background is rough. So is Connie's. I didn't really have the measure of your daughter at first. She's classy. So... I sort of kept my people away from her."

"She's not like that. Not snobby. None of our kids are." She grinned. "Cole and I came up hard, too. Ranching isn't everybody's cup of tea. You might have noticed the thing about free labor...? Anybody who shows up here at regular roundup or bull roundup or any other labor-intensive time gets impressed, as in pirate ships?"

He burst out laughing. "Well!"

"Get Cole to tell you about the government inspector who turned up one year. It's a doozy."

"We can talk all day without mentioning the feds," he said in a mock low tone.

"Right! Got you. Sorry." She grinned.

He grinned back.

Odalie, glancing at them, thought how well Tony fit in here. It was as if he'd been born on a ranch. He was comfortable with most everybody. With the notable exception of herself. Ah, well, she thought, she was young and there was time. She hoped.

Heaping plates of food were carried from the serving line. Odalie, for all her slenderness, could eat with the best of them. Tony watched her put away enough beef to feed a family of three.

She saw him watching her and grinned. "I'm still a growing girl," she pointed out. "God forbid I should get skinny and weak, so I wouldn't have to help throw calves when Dad brings home another lot of them!" she added in a loud voice so her father, nearby, would hear her.

He raised a fork. "You live here, you work here!"

"Communist!" somebody yelled.

"That will give you two weeks of mucking out the stables!" Cole called back.

A white napkin was raised in the air and waved back and forth.

"Good enough for you," Cole said, and went back to eating.

Tony was chuckling. "Never a dull moment around here," he mused.

"We'd get dull if we just talked about heritability traits," Odalie mused.

"You hush about that," Cole called to her. "That's family secrets!"

"Is it really?" she chided. "You told that reporter from the cattle magazine all about it just last week!"

"He promised me that he wouldn't breathe a word of it."

Odalie rolled her eyes. "John, did he promise that?" she asked her brother.

"I can't say," John chuckled, glancing at his dad.

"Why not?"

"He found my worm bed," he said, pointing his fork at his father.

Everybody burst out laughing. Tony was remembering what Odalie had told him, about John washing a bucket of earthworms clean and dumping them in her bed before she got in it.

"They should have given you a medal for that," Tony told him. "That's original thinking."

"I know where a lot of worms are," Odalie told Tony with a frown.

He raised his hand. "I take it back. Sorry," he told John. "I'm scared of worms."

"Like fun," Odalie laughed.

"No, really," he protested. "My grandad used to feed them coffee grounds. Anything that will eat coffee grounds has got to be dangerous!"

Odalie laughed softly and dug into her dessert.

Later, there was dancing. There was Big Ben on the dance platform they'd put up, holding pretty little Mercedes and doing a pretty good box step. Odalie danced with two of the visiting ranchers who were here for Cole's purebred heifers, but didn't enjoy it. Her feet were hurting in the pretty new shoes she'd worn for the barbeque, and both ranchers were heavy on their feet and pretty uncoordinated.

She ended up back at the drink table reaching for ginger ale.

"You look washed-out," John noted as he and Tony got refills of coffee.

"You try dancing with cattlemen who spend their lives with bulls," she muttered. "My feet are killing me!"

She kicked off her shoes and sighed. "Oh, that feels good!"

"You'll get cuts," John said.

She made a face at him as she put ice in a glass. "You wear those shoes for a few minutes and tell me that."

"Not me. I look awful in high heels."

"You look awful when you're not in high heels," she retorted.

"Worms!" he said. She smacked him in the stomach playfully. It was like hitting a wall.

"Can't dent me," he teased. "I'm made of good Everett steel."

"Is she always that mean to you?" Tony asked John.

"Only when she's here," he agreed. "We never fight when she's in New York." He grinned.

Odalie started to hit him again when one of Cole's cowboys, a new one with red hair and a big smile, caught Odalie's hand and tugged her toward the dance floor.

"No, Ray," she pleaded. "Look, my poor feet have blisters. I can't dance!"

"It was a fair bet," he reminded her. "And I won."

She made a face at him and sighed. "Okay. But if I collapse on the dance floor, it's going to be your fault, and I'll tell Maude!"

"Oh, God forbid!" he groaned as he led her toward the dance floor.

"Who's Maude?" Tony asked John, not pleased to find Odalie in some other man's arms.

John noted the older man's expression and hid a smile. "Ray's wife," he said, and watched Tony visibly relax.

"Oh."

"Ray bet her that she couldn't throw a calf. So she tried and got knocked over. Ray threw the calf and won the bet. Hence—" he nodded toward the dance floor "—that."

Tony watched her with a rapt expression, unguarded for those few seconds. "She can sing, she can dance and she looks like a fairy," he murmured. "But no boyfriend."

"Singing has been her life from the time she was in grammar school," John told him. "I tried a lot of things before I realized that Dad had to leave Big Spur to somebody and it was probably going to be me." He shrugged his broad shoulders and smiled. "It's not a bad life. I love animals, and I know everybody in a ten-mile radius. I could have landed worse."

Tony sipped coffee. "I hated it when my grandfather died and the farm got sold. My grandmother never got over it. She died a couple of years after he did. I guess I was too much of a city boy to settle in the sticks, but I loved summers on the farm."

"Dad said every shot you put in that rattler hit dead center in its head, and from a distance," John remarked.

"In my line of work—my former line of work," he amended, "a gun was a necessity. I learned to shoot straight when I was a kid. It's saved my life a few times." He glanced at John. "They made all these movies about the old-timey gunfighters being so fast. Fast is nothing unless you can hit what you aim at. The shooter who takes his time and aims well doesn't die."

John sighed. "I'm no good with guns. Dad despairs of me. Tanner can shoot anything. So can my sister. I'm the odd one out," he chuckled.

He noticed that John, like himself, was drinking coffee. "No beer?" Tony mused, nodding at John's coffee cup.

"I don't have a head for alcohol," John confessed. "It's better not to drink if you can't handle it. I mean, one little glass of wine and I'm wasted."

Tony laughed. "I can put away a fifth of bourbon and keep going. But drinking is a bad habit, and I'm not the person I used to be." His dark eyes twinkled. "Well," he corrected, "not so much, anyway. I mostly stick to coffee now."

"I like latte," John replied. "I bought this little coffee machine that uses pods so I can make my own. It's a long drive to a coffee shop from here," he added ruefully.

"I get the beans and grind my own coffee," Tony chuckled. "I'm a fanatic about good coffee."

"Coffee is one of the major food groups," Odalie added as she joined them. "You sadist," she told Ray. "My big toe will never be the same. I'm telling Maude!"

"Please don't," Ray pleaded. "She'll banish me to the laundry room, and I'll be washing diapers until my hands wrinkle up and fall off!"

"Well, all right," Odalie conceded. "I wouldn't wish that on you. Honest." She grinned at him. "And you're not a bad dancer, compared to a goose."

He made a face at her. "Was she always like this?" he asked John.

"Oh, no," John said at once, with a mischievous look at his sister. "She was worse!"

"Worms!" Odalie threatened.

John put down his coffee. "Ray, let's go look at Dad's new bull and get out of the range of fire," he said quickly, taking Ray by the arm. He shot Odalie a grin and they left.

Tony was still amused. He shook his head, looking at her pretty little feet. "No stockings?" he asked, wondering.

"I was hoping nobody would notice," she confessed, noting that her skirt was ankle length. "It's too hot for hose!"

"I never wear them myself," Tony replied deadpan.

She laughed. The idea of Tony in pantyhose was hilarious. "Connie would have a field day talking about that!"

He chuckled.

"Why aren't you dancing?" Heather asked as she joined them. "Just look, only two couples on the dance floor. Those poor boys in the band look so miserable. They're playing this lovely music and everybody's too busy eating to enjoy it!"

"We can fix that." Tony put down his coffee and took Odalie by the arm.

"My feet..." she complained.

"You're the one who wanted to go barefoot," he pointed out.

"My shoes are worse than bare feet."

He glanced at her as they reached the dance floor. "Then why did you buy them?"

"They're the latest style," she replied sadly.

"Style is individual. Buy what looks good on you. Don't be a lackey to the fashion houses." He took her by the waist and pulled her closer as the band broke into a cha-cha. "I think I remember that you know how to do this?" he teased.

"Do I!"

She followed his quick steps exactly, loving his hand around hers, his big hand at her waist. She laughed. It was another moment out of time. She felt joy well up in her like a fountain. Her face was luminous with it.

Tony saw her reaction and felt it all the way to his feet. She was magic on a dance floor. He was surprised all over again at how easily they moved together.

"Feet still hurt?" he asked as the band finished the song.

She flexed them. "Just sore. My own fault. Stupid shoes."

He sighed and pulled her close as a sentimental slow tune began to lift from the band. He did a complicated box step, which she followed with ease. She smiled and closed her eyes as they moved around the floor.

"You aren't looking where you're going," he chided softly.

"That's your job," she pointed out. "You're leading."

"So I am."

He turned her and every step seemed to bring them closer together. She was fighting her own reflexes the whole time, trying not to give herself away.

"Can I ask you something?" she said after a minute.

"Sure. What?"

She drew away just enough to see his face. "Why don't you carry an automatic, like Ben does?"

He smiled. "When I was fourteen, I got into a shoot-out with some gang members trying to take over one of our venues," he said simply. "I was carrying an auto, because everybody had one. It was just the way we did things." He turned her again. "So this fresh kid comes at me, firing the whole time. I took off the safety and shot back. And the damned gun jammed."

"Oh, gosh," she said, lost in his memory with him. She could picture it. "What did you do?!"

"I threw the damned pistol to the ground and went straight at him. Old advice from my people. You run at a man with a gun, and away from a man with a knife. I was quicker than he was."

"And you were fourteen?" she asked, shocked.

He nodded. His face tautened. "I've lived a hard life. It's left me with some rough edges. Very rough."

She studied his handsome face. "It doesn't show."

"You don't see the scars?" he asked on a dry laugh, because there were some scars. They didn't disfigure him, but they were obviously knife cuts.

"That's not what I meant, Tony," she said softly. "I mean, your rough edges don't show in company. You're very sophisticated with people at the gallery. You're a lot better at mixing than I am." Her eyes fell to his broad chest. "I'm painfully shy."

"No, you aren't," he argued.

"Oh, not with people I know," she protested softly. "But with strangers. I bluff by smiling and telling them my name and asking for theirs. Well, mostly. Not with that Donalson man, at your house on Long Island," she added, averting her face.

"He was lucky to leave in the same shape he arrived," he said darkly. "He was very lucky."

"He isn't somebody who might try to, well, try to get back at you for protecting me from him, is he?" she asked, and the worry was on her face, in her pretty blue eyes.

He got lost in them. "If he tried, he'd regret it for the rest of his life," he said in a quiet, deep tone that chilled. His eyes swept over her face, slowly, intensely. "He was lucky that he left the house intact." His voice deepened. "Nobody touches you."

Her heart turned over in her chest and she flushed. She couldn't even answer him. She felt that same, strange joy bubble up inside her. She tried to keep her ragged breathing from showing with a little laugh. "Well, thanks," she said huskily.

He smiled slowly. "You're Stasia's best friend," he added. "That makes you family."

Her joy leaked out. Her heart felt heavier. She kept smiling anyway. It would never do to start crying in the middle of the dance floor.

He scowled. "Where is Stasia?" he added.

"She went with Tanner to a cattleman's workshop up in Montana," she said. "They'll be back in a few days. And yes, the doctor said it was okay. Plus, Tanner took two of our men with him who were feds before they came to work here. He's cautious. He thinks Phillip James isn't through with him."

"That's what I think," Tony agreed. He didn't tell her about his meeting at the motel. He knew who was behind that attempt to entrap him. But he wasn't sharing it. Not with her.

If Tanner had been home, however, he'd have shared that information. "Feet still hurt?"

She shook her head and smiled. He smiled back as they moved around the dance floor with a growing number of couples.

From the trestle tables under the tent, Cole and Heather watched them dance.

"Don't they remind you of us, when we were that age?" Heather sighed.

Cole leaned over and kissed her warmly. "They do. Except that Tony is fighting it tooth and nail."

"Why, do you think?" she asked.

"Well, if I were guessing, I'd say that he was fighting a losing battle," he said softly. "Just like I was, all those years ago."

She smiled and brushed her fingers against his cheek. "They've been good years."

"The best of my life," he said softly.

"And mine," she agreed.

Odalie glanced at her parents and smiled. "They're like two halves of a whole," she remarked. "We've envied them all our lives. It seems that so many marriages end in divorce these days."

"They do," Tony agreed.

She sighed as they moved lazily to the music. "Despite all the hard work, I'd rather live on a ranch than any place on earth. I love it here."

"It's quite a place," he agreed. He chuckled. "Does your dad really put all his guests to work?"

"If they show up during roundup in the spring and fall, yes," she said. She chuckled. "It happened to a congressman who stopped by to chat, and even a doctor who wanted dad to sponsor a benefit for the hospital."

"Good grief!"

"Well, word does get around, you know," she said with a laugh. "So now, it's pretty much confined to relatives and friends who don't protest too much."

He grinned. "It's hard work. But it's fun, too."

"I've always thought so."

He looked down at her with a faint smile. "When I first saw you, in New York, I couldn't picture you in anything that wasn't couture. Certainly not in jeans, throwing calves."

"Appearances can be deceptive," she pointed out.

"Damned right."

She closed her eyes and let her senses fill with Tony's closeness. The cologne he wore, the warm strength of his body, the feel of his big hand holding hers, all combined to wrap her in a cocoon of sensation. She never wanted the music to end.

He was feeling something similar and grinding his teeth. All those reasons why this was a bad idea swarmed around his mind like flies around honey. His hand contracted on hers.

"I'm not getting involved with you," he said flatly, out of the blue.

"Suits me," she said with feigned laziness. "I'm not getting involved with you, either."

"Okay," he murmured on a deep breath. "Just so you know."

"Right back at you, big man," she murmured.

He tuned in to the soft music that was playing and put tomorrow out of his mind. She smelled of flowers, and she felt like sweet heaven in his arms. At the moment, that was all that mattered.

Sunday was spent recuperating from Saturday. Monday, Tony directed Ben to pick up his and Odalie's suitcases, and they headed out to the airfield in a ranch pickup driven by John.

"Skeet season starts in two weeks," John told his sister as Ben started loading up the plane. "You'll miss it. Again."

She grimaced. "I haven't put in any practice this past year," she sighed. "Too much work on my voice. Maybe when I get some free time." She went on tiptoe and kissed his cheek. "You go shooting for me. Win some medals."

"I haven't won any yet," he lamented. "Tanner might go, though. But he said it's not as much fun as it was when you and he went on the circuit together."

"That was years ago," she sighed. "I don't really have the fire for it anymore. And Tanner's not likely to leave Stasia alone so much, with the baby coming. Practice becomes obsessive." She hugged him. "Take care of yourself."

"You do the same."

She climbed aboard the plane.

Tony hesitated, waiting until she was out of earshot before he turned to John. "Phillip James is on the prowl," he said quietly. "He's probing for weaknesses. Don't let your guard down here, and make sure that Tanner doesn't let his down, either, not for a second. If we can get him indicted, it's a capital crime, and I've already robbed him of a congressman he was blackmailing to stop the investigation." He didn't mention the setup attempt by one of James's operatives. He could tell Tanner about that later.

"I'll keep up our end. Please, take care of Odalie," he added quietly. "She's impulsive. It would kill us if anything happened to her."

"I know that. She'll be safe," he replied. "I've got two good men on twelve-hour shifts keeping her under surveillance, at home and anyplace else she goes. If Stasia comes up, make sure I know when. I'll put on more people."

"Thanks, Tony."

He shrugged. "Stasia's the only adoptive family I've got outside Connie and her family, and my other adopted daughter in Jacobsville," he said with a smile. "That means I have to take care of her relatives, too," he chuckled.

"We'll do our best as well," John said. "We have two exfeds who work here, and Tanner has three on his place. They were all working as mercs when they were hired, so they're pretty good."

He nodded. "Just don't lose focus," Tony said. "There are more things going on than I can tell you about right now."

"We won't. Thanks, for all you do for Stasia and my sister."

"It's no trouble."

"Have a safe flight."

Tony grinned. "Thanks."

On the plane, Odalie wanted to ask what Tony and John had been discussing so intently, but she was suddenly shy of him. She buried herself in her solitaire app while Tony busied himself with business on his laptop.

It was raining when they landed in New York at JFK. Odalie hadn't packed a raincoat or an umbrella, so Ben had to run her down the sidewalk to her apartment and then run back with her luggage.

"Thanks, Ben!" she said at the door.

"No worries. Keep your door locked," he added.

"You bet. See you!"

He ran back to the limo, folding the umbrella as he got to the driver's side. Odalie closed the door and didn't let herself look at the vehicle pulling away from the curb.

The past few days had been sweet. At least she had memories, she thought, even if Tony kept warning her off. She didn't have time for men, anyway, she told herself. She had a career ahead of her. That was where her head needed to be now, not on some man—regardless of how attractive he was. It was just that fear of the stage, all the time, eating at her confidence. She turned toward the kitchen to make coffee and put it out of her mind.

8

Three weeks passed, during which Odalie spent time on voice lessons and wandering aimlessly around the shopping district, looking for bargains that she never bought.

Ballet season was over, but there were occasional performances outside the season and one of her favorites was playing now at Lincoln Center: *Swan Lake*, by New York City Ballet, along with two other ballets choreographed by the late Balanchine. She bought a ticket online and had a limo come to take her to the Met, where it was playing. A lot of people didn't dress for such occasions, but many did. Odalie loved to.

She had a gold lamé dress, very extravagant, strappy and elegant, which she wore with high-heeled gold sandals and a gold-sprinkled shawl. Her hair was up in a coiffure that dripped curls around her ears, where diamond earrings sparkled, matching the diamond necklace she wore and the diamond watch on one wrist. She looked young and beautiful, and she drew eyes all the way down the aisle.

She didn't pay attention to the frankly admiring stares she was getting from men as she went to her seat and settled in. At least, not until a familiar face loomed up beside her.

"As I live and breathe," a familiar voice intoned. "The goddess Diana herself!"

She glanced up into the dancing eyes of the man she'd met at Tony's last party on Long Island.

"Miss Everett, I believe?" he added with a warm smile.

She smiled back. "Yes. Rudy, wasn't it...?"

He nodded. He was wearing a dark suit with a red tie and handkerchief. He looked very cosmopolitan. "You like ballet?"

She nodded back. "All the arts."

"Me, too. But I think ballet is the most graceful... Excuse me," he said, moving back to let the couple with seats in Odalie's row slide past her with apologies. She smiled and moved her skirts aside, oblivious to a pair of angry black eyes pinning her from the back of the theater.

"The seat next to me is vacant," he said. "Why don't you come and sit with me?"

She hesitated. "I don't know..."

"It's not a hanging offense," he whispered at her ear with a chuckle.

She shook her head and laughed softly. He was incorrigible. She hadn't forgotten that he'd saved her from the overbearing man at Tony's Long Island house. "I guess it would be okay," she said.

"If anything's said, I'll take the blame, no worries," he replied easily, and escorted her out of her seat and over to the one next to his. Actually, it had been for his date, but the woman had come down with a virus and couldn't use her ticket. He'd never been happier about being stood up.

In the dress circle, Tony was livid. He hadn't known that Odalie was coming to this performance, although Rudy had alerted him that he'd be here so they could talk later without arousing too much interest.

"You're very quiet tonight," Mauve, his mistress, muttered. "And I bought a new dress just to impress you!" She was staring at Odalie, who was letting a man help her out of her seat. "Would you look at that gown?" she asked on a sigh. "What a beautiful couture piece! I think I'll go tomorrow and see if they can make one for me."

He had to choke back his thoughts. It didn't matter how attractive Mauve was, she would never hold a candle to Odalie in her couture.

"Isn't she beautiful?" Mauve was whispering. "That man she's with looks familiar. Doesn't he work for you?"

"He works with me," he said, and in a tone that didn't invite further comment.

"What's the difference?" she murmured. She looked at her program. "I hate ballet. Why are we here? There was a fashion show at the Red Mill this afternoon. You could have taken me to that instead."

He was only half listening. His eyes were on Odalie's laughing face. He didn't like her palling around with Rudy, who was ten degrees off-center and on the outs with Tony's people at the moment because of a bad error in judgment. It was one of the reasons they were meeting tonight. Rudy was a loose cannon. He didn't want the man around Odalie.

He'd had his guys deliver the so-called colleague from the

motel to the appropriate office in DC during lunch hours week before last, where he was left tied to a chair.

To say that Phillip James had been upset was an under-statement.

"What the hell did you do?" he asked his idiot operative.

"They made me," the man muttered as he was set free. "And I don't know how! I was playing it perfectly!"

"I almost had him," he muttered, "except for your stupid foul-up!"

"He knew all about the guy who was supposedly whacked," the man said shortly. "And the guys I hired turned out to be his guys."

"We could get him for kidnapping," James murmured.

"How?" his operative asked curtly. "They didn't abduct me. Well, not at gunpoint. And there were no witnesses when I got tied up in here!"

"He's like an eel," James said, smoldering. "Just when you think you've got him dead to rights, he slithers right out of your grasp." He glared at the man he'd untied. "All right, get back to work on those amendments I want changed. And not a word about this assignment."

"I'm not stupid," the man said. "I don't want to go to jail."

"See that you remember that!"

"Sure. Sure."

Phillip James stared after him until the door closed. Then he picked up one of his burner phones and called his son.

"How's it going?" he asked.

His son yawned. "Fine. What time is it?"

He frowned. "Didn't you have a class today?"

"Yeah, but it was just social studies. I wasn't in the mood."

He ground his teeth together. It was costing him a small

fortune to keep his son in school. He'd hoped for a better attitude about his studies.

"I can always retake the course if I have to, Dad," he added. "It's no big deal. I went to this great party last night. We didn't get home until after four."

"Oh." He took a breath. "I thought you said there were some underworld types at that bar where you and your buddies hang out," he added.

"Yeah. They're always talking about stuff they get into. They've got some really hot girls they hang out with, too."

It didn't occur to him that real underworld types wouldn't be advertising it at a public venue.

"I see," he murmured, his mind still on the fiasco his employee had unleashed. Now Garza knew he was trying to pin some stuff on him. It wasn't going to help his situation.

"I'm going back to sleep. Talk to you later, Dad."

"Are you coming home this weekend?" he asked.

"Maybe next weekend. There's this great party…"

"I see," he said again.

"Bye." The boy hung up.

James sat down heavily in his chair. It had been one lousy day.

The ballet was gorgeous. Rudy tried to put his arm around Odalie, but she removed it with a blithe smile and he got the idea.

Tony, watching from rows behind them, was doing a slow burn while his mistress played solitaire on her smartphone—minus the sound effects that he'd had to remind her to turn off before they were barbequed by the patrons around them. Glares didn't slow her down. She didn't even notice.

He wondered why he'd even had this idea. He loved the

ballet, but he usually went during the season. It was just that Balanchine's choreography was his favorite, and he'd looked forward to this. He hadn't realized that Odalie would be here, although he knew she loved the ballet. Stasia had told him once that *Swan Lake* was one of her favorites.

He was glad that he'd come now. He'd have a chance to tell Rudy to keep his eyes off Odalie. He'd find some logical excuse that wouldn't sound as if he was burning with jealousy.

At least she could see through Rudy. It had made him feel good when she removed Rudy's arm from her shoulders. She wasn't attracted to the man. Not that it mattered to him. He was only protecting his own turf. Rudy didn't need to mix himself up in the Everetts' situations. He was an outsider, and he was going to remain one.

He tried to picture Rudy on Cole's ranch trying to keep up with the cowboys during any sort of roundup.

Rudy was a city boy from the floor up. He'd never fit in. Tony, on the other hand, had fit in very well. He liked Odalie's relatives.

Beside him, Mauve was yawning pointedly. He groaned inwardly. This had turned into an ordeal.

Ben drove Tony and Mauve to a coffee shop down the street from the Met while Tony waited for Rudy to join them. He'd remarked pointedly in a text that he'd expect him as soon as he got out of the building.

Rudy came sauntering up as soon as Tony had ordered their cappuccinos. He paused and ordered one for himself with a pastry before joining them at the table.

"Hi, Rudy," Mauve drawled. "That was a gorgeous girl you had with you."

"Thanks," Rudy said, intercepting Tony's quick and covert shake of the head.

"Ben, take Mauve home and come back for me," Tony told his driver.

"Sure thing, boss," he said.

"But I haven't finished my coffee..." Mauve protested.

"You can have another one next time we go out," he promised.

Ben was already hustling her out the door to the limo.

"Well, that's one way to get rid of a date," Rudy chuckled as Ben drove off.

"Works every time. What did you hear?" he asked.

"James called his son. He was upset that the kid took another boy's brags for one of our guys."

"As if we'd go out and advertise who we are," Tony sighed, sipping cappuccino.

"He decided that he couldn't afford to prosecute us for kidnapping."

"Good thing."

"But he hasn't given up on your adopted daughter's family," Rudy added quietly. "He called another subordinate in after he hung up with his kid. He's sending somebody up here to see what he can dig up about Odalie's schedule."

That caused Tony's dark brows to meet in the middle.

"He thinks she's his best soft target," Rudy added. "The rest of the family, down in Texas, is too well protected. And he doesn't seem aware that you've got Odalie covered."

"I haven't advertised it," he replied, with a pointed look at the other man.

"I haven't said a word about it," Rudy said defensively.

"Good. Don't. If he makes a play for her, we've got all the bases covered."

"There was a guy watching from the shadows when I saw

her walk out to the car tonight," he added. "Not one of ours, either. Too young and too obvious."

"Judging by the goon he sent to set up the scheme on me, he isn't too wise about how we work."

"He needs to watch a few more old movies, I guess," Rudy chuckled.

"He's about fifty years behind the times and doesn't seem to realize it," Tony agreed. "Unless," he added, "he's trying to throw us off the scent by acting stupid."

"Could be."

Tony finished his drink. "I want you to go see Teddy. Tell him what's going on and ask what he wants to do about it."

"I thought you already had."

Tony shook his head. "I don't like to involve him until things get really hot." He met Rudy's eyes. "He won't like having James hit on Odalie. Civilians aren't part of this."

"I know. He gets nervous if his people start hitting on outsiders. Especially ones with rich parents." He frowned. "Are her people that well-to-do?"

Tony nodded. "Not only that, her father's a power in regional politics."

"Ouch. Not the guy to make an enemy of."

"Plus, his son's got the goods on James. He could put him away for good."

"No wonder he's trying to get at you."

"So far, it's just hints." He met Rudy's eyes. "If he tries anything on Odalie, it will be the last thing he ever does."

The threat in those black eyes was enough to make Rudy's insides churn. "Private stock, is that it?" he asked very quietly.

The eyes narrowed. "That isn't your business. At least, it isn't as long as you keep your hands off her," he added in a soft, menacing tone.

Rudy put both hands up, palms out. "I was just helping her get the shawl off her shoulders, honest," he said at once. "She's gorgeous, but I like living."

"Good. Consider that keeping her at arm's length will guarantee that for you."

"You bet, Tony!" He finished his coffee and got up. "I'll phone you when I talk to Teddy."

Tony handed him a slip of paper with a number on it, plus a spare burner phone, already activated. "No slipups," he cautioned.

"You bet!"

He watched the younger man head down the sidewalk, his dark eyes narrow and assessing.

Back in her apartment, Odalie had changed into sweatpants and a soft T-shirt for sleeping. The ballet had been wonderful. But she had this odd feeling that she'd been watched in the theater. That was silly. Tony had assured her once that he had all the bases covered. She had nothing to worry about from Phillip James.

Just the same, it was an odd feeling.

It had been a surprise to run into Rudy. She knew he was one of Tony's people, but she had no idea why he'd been at the ballet all by himself. She had wondered if Tony might be there as well, but there had been no indication of his presence. As if he'd want to be around her, anyway, she thought with resignation.

Tony avoided her like the plague whenever he could. There were occasions, like when the snake had almost bitten her, or when they'd been on the dance floor at the ranch, when he seemed to care about her a little. But those occasions were quickly covered up. He'd made his position clear. Odalie wasn't his type.

That was just as well. She wanted a career in opera. It was why she'd remained heart-whole all these years. So just as well not to start anything. Except that her stupid hormones all went wild when Tony was anywhere around, and her stupid stomach started churning every time she pictured a stage.

Now that Stasia was staying close to home, there wasn't much opportunity for interaction with Tony in New York. That was a blessing and a curse, she supposed.

She still wondered why Rudy was at the ballet. He didn't seem the sort of man to appreciate it. But that wasn't her business.

She was on her way back to her apartment a few days later, by way of a high-ticket department store, when she ran into Tony's cousin Connie from New Jersey.

"Odalie?" she exclaimed, laughing as she hugged her. "What an incredible coincidence!"

Odalie hugged her back. "I know! What are you doing in New York?"

"I came up with Angel to do some shopping. I told you about Angel—this is him," she said at once, pulling a muscular man in his late twenties toward Odalie. "Angel, this is Odalie that I was telling you about. She had the run-in with that Donalson reptile at the Long Island house. Remember what I said?"

"Yeah." Angel had jet-black hair and dark eyes and olive skin. He wasn't handsome, but he was very masculine without being overbearing about it. "Hi," he said.

Odalie smiled back. "Hi."

"She's from Texas," Connie added with a grin.

Angel smiled slowly. "Oh, yeah? Well, where's your big hat and your boots?" he teased.

"In my closet at the ranch," she returned, laughing. She eyed him. "Where are your tights?"

His eyebrows arched.

"I heard you used to wrestle," she persisted.

He chuckled. "Yeah, I did. One tombstone too many and I had to give it up," he added.

She knew what a tombstone was—another wrestler picked you up and dropped you on your head. The taller the wrestler, the farther the drop. "Ouch," she said.

"Ouch is right. Now I do less strenuous things," he added.

"Come have lunch with us," Connie said. "I had to get Mama a new coat. She got that stupid virus and lost thirty pounds, so nothing fits. And she had to have just the right coat from the right store…!" She rolled her eyes.

Odalie laughed. "Did you find it?"

"Yeah. I had them send it. I hate carrying things on a plane. We didn't bring the car this time. What's your fancy? Italian, Indian, uptown, downtown…?" Connie probed.

"Sushi," Odalie said with big eyes.

"Fish bait?" Angel exclaimed.

"You stop that," Connie said, and hit him. "Listen, he once almost closed a Japanese sushi shop because he ordered so much to-go stuff. He loves it." She wrinkled her nose. "Me, too," she laughed.

"And we know where the best sushi is," Angel added.

"Okay!" Odalie replied, laughing.

They did, in fact, and Angel spoke Japanese, something that fascinated Odalie, who loved languages but drew the line at trying to learn most of them.

"I was stationed in Okinawa," Angel told her as they

worked their way through a platter of freshly made sushi. "I loved the people, and the language."

"I'll bet you stood out," Odalie teased, noting his height.

"I did."

"My brother John drew crowds everywhere we went on our last trip to Osaka," Odalie noted. "He's even taller than you, and he never goes anywhere without the boots and the Stetson."

"Wow," Angel chuckled.

"Don't you have another brother?" Connie asked.

She nodded. "Tanner. He had some real trouble not so long ago. Tony helped us get him out of it."

"Out of some of it," Angel murmured. "Not all. The guy causing the trouble is still looking for ways to make more."

"Rudy will settle that, when he's let loose," Connie said.

"Rudy, who was at the party on Long Island?" Odalie asked. "He was at the ballet with me last week."

"Rudy, at a ballet?" Angel asked, with eyes like saucers.

Odalie frowned. "Doesn't he like ballet?"

"No. He hates all that stuff. If he was there, Tony sent him."

Connie was giving her brother a glare that would have stopped traffic.

"Rudy works for Tony," Connie said. "But he does like some classy stuff. Just occasionally."

"I wondered," Odalie said, missing the expressions on her companions' faces. "I mean, it was like the expression my brothers wear if we drag them to a fashion show," she added on a chuckle.

"Exactly," Connie said. She swallowed a sip of hot tea. "Wasn't Tony there, too?"

Odalie blinked. "No. Well, I mean, I didn't see him."

"He likes ballet, and he's crazy about opera," Connie said. "Me, I like hard rock and heavy metal."

Odalie laughed. "Me, too," she confessed.

"And that would be because your mom writes songs for Desperado," Connie teased.

"Say what?" Angel asked.

"Her mom composes," Connie told him. "She won Grammys for two of her songs that Desperado recorded."

"That's my favorite band!" Angel remarked. "And your mom composes for them? Wow!"

Odalie grinned. "Mom used to be a recording artist, too, but then she married my dad and gave it up."

"That's some background," Angel mused. "Cowboys and heavy metal."

"I told you she was unique," Connie teased. She finished her tea. "We're coming back up next weekend for the musical on Broadway," she said and named it. "We've got tickets. Want to go with us?"

Odalie hesitated.

"Now, it's not nice to be a musical snob," Connie teased. "Just because you favor opera doesn't mean you should turn up your nose at a nice musical, and it's even got cowboys in it."

Odalie burst out laughing. "Well, I guess you're right. I would like to come," she added, noting Angel's warm smile.

Connie, sensing comradeship, smiled to herself. She'd gotten some firm vibrations from her cousin Tony about Odalie. He was fighting tooth and nail not to get attached to her. Angel here might be the straw that broke the camel's back. He wasn't exactly Odalie's type. But Tony was.

"So, Saturday night?" Connie prodded.

Odalie smiled. "Saturday night."

They exchanged cell phone numbers and Odalie went home by herself. She liked Angel. He really wasn't her type, but he was a lot of fun and she'd recognized him when he told her his stage name from when he'd wrestled. They had enough in common that they could get along. After all, Tony had warned her off. It wouldn't hurt to show him that she wasn't sitting alone on the shelf pining for him.

Rudy sat back on the sofa while Tony spoke to him about Teddy's instructions. The James man was getting a little too nosy about their operation in his quest to put down Tanner Everett. Teddy had been unsettled by vague threats and he was ready to take action.

"We're limited in what we can do," Tony reminded him as he leaned back against his big oak desk with his hands in his pockets. "We don't want to draw any unwanted attention. On the other hand, we need to shut him down before he becomes a problem."

"That's what Teddy said," Rudy replied.

"Why did you switch Odalie's seat?" he asked abruptly.

Rudy blinked. The question had startled him. "She was all by herself. I didn't think it was a good idea under the circumstances," he added. "She shouldn't be out on the town without protection."

"I've got two guys on twelve-hour shifts," Tony pointed out, "with nothing to do except follow her around."

"I know that, but neither one of them was in the theater." Tony glowered at him.

"And this weekend, they won't even be needed. Well, not for Saturday night, at least," Rudy murmured.

Tony scowled. "Why not?"

"Don't you ever talk to your relatives?" he replied. "Connie and Angel are taking her out to a Broadway show Saturday."

Tony was so still that he seemed not even to be breathing for a few seconds. "Excuse me?"

"Connie and Angel are taking her to see the revival of that cowboy musical."

"When the hell did she meet Angel?" Tony asked abruptly.

"He and Connie came up to buy Francesca a new coat. They ran into Odalie and the three of them practically ate out a sushi restaurant."

"She likes sushi?" he asked blankly.

"Apparently."

Tony's eyes narrowed. "Angel is out of her league," he said shortly. "He's got his fingers in too many rackets."

"She isn't marrying him, for Pete's sake, Tony," Rudy reminded him. "They're just going to the theater, and Connie's going with them."

Before Rudy finished getting the words out, Tony was punching in numbers on his cell phone. It rang two, three times.

"Connie?" he asked abruptly.

"Yeah. Hi, coz!"

"Hi, yourself. What's this about you and Angel taking Odalie to Broadway?"

"Now, Tony, it's just a date..."

"I thought it was just a threesome," he said curtly.

"Oh, it was, but you see, I mean, I can't actually go..."

"Neither can Angel," he said at once. "You get me? You call him off it right now, right this minute, or I'll make your worst nightmares seem like Saturday at the amusement park!"

Connie's breath caught. "Now, Tony..."

"Now nothing! You hear me?"

She let out a breath. "But she likes him," she muttered. "And he likes her. They got along like a house on fire!"

"She's going to be an opera star," Tony shot back. "She is no way going to get mixed up in any sleazy business with Angel! You know what he's into—I don't have to tell you why it's a bad idea. She's got enough problems with that idiot who's after her older brother. I'm not letting you put her in the line of fire with Angel!"

"But she's nice and I like her. Angel's not bad…"

"Angel is bad," he corrected. "And shame on you for shoving them together!"

"She'd make the nicest in-law," she argued.

"She wouldn't. I mean it. If I see Angel within a city block of her apartment, I'm coming down there. And I'll tell Odalie he's seeing someone already."

She groaned. "Oh, all right! I'll call and tell her something came up. It will break her heart! She likes Angel!"

"I like Angel, too, as long as he's in Jersey. And you keep him there!"

"All right, spoilsport," she muttered. "I love you anyway."

"Yeah. Me, too. Stop interfering in things you don't know about."

"Angel is going to be very disappointed."

"I'll send him a sweepstakes card. He'll get over it. Now, goodbye!"

He hung up in the middle of her next word.

Rudy pursed his lips. "So, she liked Angel, huh?"

Tony glared at him.

Rudy got to his feet. "Well, I guess that puts your two-man detail back on the job." He paused. "I could take her to see the show on Broadway…?"

Tony's eyes started to glitter.

Rudy threw up his hands. "I'm going, I'm going. I'll be in touch."

Tony glared at him all the way out the door.

9

Connie was all apologies when she called Odalie the next morning to cancel the Broadway-show date.

"Angel and I were really looking forward to it," she wailed, "but we just can't make it. I'm so sorry!"

"It's okay. Really," Odalie assured her. She hadn't been enthusiastic about the evening out anyway. "Another time, maybe."

"Another time," Connie agreed. "Angel says he's really sorry to miss it."

"He's nice," Odalie replied.

Nice. Connie heard that note in the other woman's voice and drew a wistful sigh. She'd hoped Angel had made an impression, but it didn't sound as if he had. She'd hoped to have Odalie in the family one day. Now, thanks to Tony, that wasn't going to be possible. She almost told Odalie why she'd been forced to cancel the date, but she was too wary of Tony's temper to do it.

It was odd, the way he tried to keep everybody away from Odalie. If Connie and the others hadn't shown up at the Long Island party, they'd probably never have met Odalie. Tony didn't seem to want any of his people around her. And she was so nice. It didn't make sense.

But then, Tony played his hand close to his chest. She just accepted that he had some reason for not wanting Odalie around the Jersey family.

Odalie had no idea that Tony had nixed her date with Angel. She hadn't seen him since he'd made it very clear that he knew how she felt and he didn't want her interest. It was a good thing that Stasia had stayed in Texas, because now Odalie wouldn't be dragged to any more of Tony's parties. Not that she wanted to go anyway. She had her singing lessons to carry on.

But there was a small party at the art gallery the next weekend, and Stasia flew up from Texas for it. Odalie tried to opt out. It didn't work.

"Tony won't want me there," Odalie protested as she put the finishing touches on her face. She was wearing a beautiful black cocktail dress with puff sleeves and a deep V neckline. She wore rubies with it—drippy earrings in yellow gold with a matching necklace and bracelet. She left her hair long and loose around her shoulders.

"You look gorgeous," Stasia said. "Men will follow you everywhere," she added teasingly.

"Heavens, I hope not," she replied with a mock shiver. "Every time I go to one of these parties, some drunk immediately becomes a homing pigeon and I'm stuck with him until he passes out."

"Not at Tony's party," Stasia assured.

She sighed. "I don't want to go," she muttered. "He treats me like a fatal virus."

"I don't believe that for a second," Stasia replied.

She looked at Stasia. "I was going to go to a Broadway show with Connie and Angel, but she called to cancel it. I liked Angel, too."

Stasia pursed her lips. "Angel is a little rough for polite company," she said.

"He was an absolute gentleman," Odalie protested. "Between the three of us, we almost wiped out the inventory at a Japanese restaurant eating sushi," she added, laughing.

"I'm glad you had fun. But Angel isn't supposed to be around us. Tony will have a long talk with him if he finds out."

She glared at herself in the mirror. "I don't understand why," she said.

"Good. Let's keep it that way," Stasia said just as there was a knock on the door.

Ben was standing there, looking around as he spoke. "You two ready to go?" he asked.

"Yes, we are," Stasia said, smiling at him.

Odalie picked up her purse and they climbed in the limo.

"Is the place already crowded?" Stasia asked Ben.

"To the eaves," he replied as he started the engine. "And he's not happy about Angel taking our future opera star to any Broadway shows."

"What?" Odalie asked, stunned.

"Boss will explain it to you," he replied. "It's complicated."

And he raised the window that cut off the passenger area from the driver.

Odalie let out a long sigh. "It will be my fault, somehow," she predicted.

"Tony isn't mad," Stasia assured her. "He really does have a bad temper, but it only shows itself when people he cares about are threatened."

"He'd feed me to a shark in a heartbeat and assure the authorities that the poor creature was starving and he was doing something for the ecology."

"I can just picture Tony dangling you over a shark pit," Stasia laughed, "but he'd never really do it."

"You think?" She shook her head. "At least the art gallery isn't near the ocean!"

Stasia just laughed again.

Ben let them out at the entrance and went to park the car. The two women found a path through the guests, and there were many, to find Tony at the buffet table.

"And I thought you said you never fed people during these shows," Stasia teased him.

Tony was wearing a tux with a red handkerchief in his breast pocket. Under it, his shirt was carelessly unbuttoned, with no tie, showing a glimpse of the thick black hair on his broad chest.

"I think what I said," Tony replied with amusement as he hugged her gently, "is that I never fed people to lions. And I said it because you were eating half the table all by yourself."

"I'm a growing girl," she teased, indicating the swelling of her stomach that accommodated the baby growing there.

"Boy or girl?" he asked.

She lifted her chin. "Surprise," she countered and then grinned. "We don't even know ourselves. We like the mystery."

He just shook his head. "To each his own," he replied, his eyes approving of the simple sheath dress she was wearing. "You look nice," he said softly, pointedly ignoring Odalie in her couture finery.

"Thanks," Stasia said reluctantly.

There was a small band playing bluesy tunes and a few couples were on what passed for the dance floor, the room temporarily empty and waiting for a new exhibit. "Nice band," Stasia remarked.

"Yeah. One of them is a cousin of Connie." He said that deliberately, with a glare in Odalie's direction.

"Connie must have a lot of cousins," Odalie said. "But her brother is really cute."

"You don't need to get mixed up with Angel," he said curtly.

Odalie was getting odd messages in her head. "You told them not to take me to the show," she said suddenly.

His face tautened. "Yeah. So what?"

She started to shoot back, but Stasia got in the way. "Where is Maddie Brannt's exhibit?" she asked Tony. "I'd really like to see that."

"So would I," Odalie added.

"Follow me." He started walking, then paused long enough to grab a glass of champagne off the tray of a server. He offered some to the women, but Stasia didn't dare drink, and Odalie couldn't handle liquor.

"Shades of prohibition," Tony chuckled, shaking his head as they moved along.

"I can get drunk off the fumes of alcohol," Odalie remarked. "So I don't drink."

"And I'm pregnant, so I can't drink alcohol," Stasia added. "The baby wouldn't like it. He'd tell me so with a kick that a football player would envy," she said, rubbing her stomach and laughing.

He laughed. "That's a good omen," he teased.

It was, but Stasia didn't say it out loud.

Tony stopped at a cabinet in the front window of the gallery. And there, in all her glory, was the redheaded fairy that Maddie Brannt had done for Tony. It didn't look like any of the women he knew, which was the only reason it hadn't joined his private collection.

"I remember that one," Odalie remarked, smiling. "It was in one of the books I gave Maddie. I have a copy, too."

"The artist did a great job," Tony said. "But a statuette is perfect in every way so that you see the person, or the fairy, in all the angles."

"Yes, you do," Stasia agreed. "Maddie is incredibly gifted."

"So are you," Odalie said with real warmth. "Your paintings capture everything."

"They do, but the woman who painted that portrait of Tony over his mantel at home, she was fantastic."

"My adopted daughter in Jacobsville did that one," Tony said. "It was true to life, and she'd never seen me. She did it from photos and really good insight."

"Oh, there's Mr. Naguchi," Stasia said. "I need to double-check with him about next month's exhibit here!"

"I could handle that, but I'd rather you did. You're not as hotheaded and stubborn as I am," Tony chuckled.

"I practice diplomacy with words," she said in a loud whisper. "I don't need a gun to do it!"

"Spoilsport," he shot back.

Odalie was nibbling on a small plate of crudités with a few drops of dressing. She liked raw veggies, but she was tired and sleepy. Tony was speaking to a gorgeous brunette, completely ignoring Odalie.

Well, she thought, two can play at that game. She walked away from the buffet table toward the band. She wondered which of the musicians was Connie's cousin. Most of the band members had dark hair and eyes. She was looking for a man who looked Italian. But they all looked Italian.

A man she didn't know asked her to dance. He was bad at it. Her feet felt like open wounds because he kept stepping on them. He apologized. It didn't help.

The dance ended and she was just starting to go the other way when Tony caught her by the upper arm and pulled her along with him to his office. He brought her inside and closed the door behind them.

"Why did you come?" he asked shortly. "My secretary sent out the invitations and I'm damned sure you weren't sent one."

She felt her face flaming. "Stasia wanted me to come with her," she said. "She didn't tell me about any invitation."

He glared down at her. "I have to put up with you occasionally, but you don't need to show up every time I have an exhibit, regardless of whether Stasia comes or not."

She ground her teeth together to stop from saying what she'd have liked to say. "I won't be here long. Stasia said we'd leave by nine o'clock. She tires easily."

Her calm tone was at odds with her heartbeat, which had gone wild from the moment she spotted him. Even now, it was shaking the thin fabric of her bodice.

"Then watch the clock," he said shortly.

"Angel was nice," she muttered, glaring at him.

"Yeah, he's nice. He's also engaged to the daughter of a friend of mine," he added. "I would hate being put in the position of telling him that his son is going around with another woman."

"We had sushi," she said, flabbergasted. "Sushi! Dead fish with three people. No romantic interlude, no rendezvous!"

He was in the wrong and he knew it. But he wasn't going to let her go around with anyone who had his hand all over the rackets. Angel did.

She just looked at him. Glowered at him. "If you're through telling me who to date, I'll ask Ben to drive me home. Or I can walk." She smiled icily.

"For two bits, I'd let you walk," he muttered.

That hurt, as it was meant to. She turned around and ended up on the dance floor, where Stasia was dancing with one of the guests.

"Tony, can you still do that box step?" she teased.

"Of course I can!"

"Odalie, make him prove it," Stasia challenged. "Go on!"

Tony glared at her. She glared back. But they were going to cause gossip if he walked away. He caught her around the waist and pulled her close. His head was already swelling. He felt joy well up in him like light from the sun as he brought her so close that he could feel her heart beating wildly against him.

This was a tragedy in the making, he thought furiously. She smelled of spring flowers. That dress she was wearing left her back bare to the waist, and his big hand was resting there, feeling her warm flesh. He ached all over, and there was no relief. He didn't dare let her stay around him. It was too dangerous, in many ways. But it was sheer heaven to hold her, to rock her in his arms, just to dance with her.

Odalie felt the same sensations, but she was certain that Tony was hating this. She could feel his posture go stiff. He was only dancing with her to spare any gossip if he refused. But he didn't have to do it for long. The band wound down and stopped.

Tony and Odalie were at the end of the room, temporarily alone. Her hand had slid from his vest into the opening where his muscular chest was visible, thick with black hair. Involuntarily, her hand rested there, and she was feeling safe and happy as sensation overwhelmed her. His arm was still around her, keeping her close. She let her hand move on his chest, slowly, along the line of his collarbone, while he fought for sanity.

He wasn't going to get mixed up with a woman who was too young, too naive, too everything! He had to get away from her. Now!

He dragged her hand away from his chest. "Stop trying to touch me," he said in a gruff undertone, watching her face. "It's disgusting to me! I don't want you. Got that?" he asked with pure venom in his tone. "Now, go home and stop finding excuses to come here and make my life miserable!"

She felt the words all through her body. She hadn't wanted to come. Stasia had insisted. Until now, she'd had at least the illusion that Tony might like her one day. But he'd taken away every wisp of hope she'd ever had. He thought she was disgusting. She almost laughed at that. Considering the men she'd refused all these years, she knew she wasn't disgusting. But to him, perhaps she was.

She shrugged and drew in a breath. "Sorry I offended you," she said quietly. "I'll see myself out."

His hands balled at his sides as he watched her walk away with quiet dignity. He'd gone too far this time. He was sorry he'd opened his mouth. She'd never forgive him for what he'd just said. He could have smoothed it over, surely. It was cruel, doing it this way. But he had to keep her at arm's length. He couldn't afford to get attached to her or let her become attached to him. She was destined for a career in opera.

In fact, she didn't know it yet, but Teddy and his wife had pulled some strings for her on her private audition that was upcoming in November. She'd find out about it later. She certainly had the talent. She'd sweated it out from spring until now, working with voice teachers, to avoid the competitions. Better to apply singly and in a private audition, she had told herself when she applied. Hopefully it would be less nerve-racking than the regional competitions. And these private auditions were held at the Met itself.

Tony had gone into his office and closed the door after he'd chased Odalie away. Stasia knocked on the door and went in when he called to her. She wasn't smiling. "Did you just say something to Odalie?" she asked. "She said she had to leave." She hesitated. "She was crying, Tony."

He ground his teeth together and averted his eyes. "We had a little disagreement," he lied.

"You told her to leave, that she hadn't even been invited. How is that a disagreement?" she asked gently.

He took a deep breath and turned around. "I'm almost thirty-eight years old," he said curtly. "You know my background. She wants a career."

Stasia didn't dare tell him what she was thinking. He'd already confirmed it, in a roundabout way. "What does your age have to do with her career?" she asked.

He wouldn't look at her. "She's got a crush on me," he said stiffly. "I'm not about to take advantage of it. She can't see the roadblocks, but I can."

Stasia hurt for him. She could only imagine why he'd hurt

Odalie, and it had to be because he also had feelings for her and he didn't think there was a future for them. He had a past that he couldn't hide. Besides, any woman he was serious about was a weakness he didn't need. Or want. Of course, Stasia saw right through him.

"Nice story," she said. "I could write one almost as good."

He glared at her from black eyes.

She just smiled at him. "Don't worry. I won't sell you out."

"That would be a nice first," he muttered, jamming his hands deeper into his pockets. "I've been sold out my whole life."

"Some of the people who let you down are dead. Most of them, in fact. And you still have people in your life who'd die for you. Ben, for one."

He grimaced. "I suppose so." He stared at the bookcase in his office. It was overflowing. He needed to put some in boxes he guessed. His eyes went back to Stasia. "I'll apologize the next time I see her," he bit off. His conscience was already stinging. "She was crying?" he asked, and felt as if he'd pulled the wings off a butterfly.

"Yes." She hesitated. "I could count on the fingers of one hand the times I've ever seen Odalie Everett cry," she added solemnly.

He drew in a long breath, wincing inside. He'd been brutal. "There are things going on that you don't know about. That I can't let you know about. But the fewer people I have around me, the safer they are." He turned around. "You could tell her that when you go home."

"I could. But I won't," Stasia said. "You've got a problem that you created. You'll have to solve it on your own."

He glared at her.

"The stare won't work, either. I have one just like it that I'm married to."

"Damn," he said softly. "Oh, all right. I have to be near the apartment tomorrow around lunchtime. I could apologize over coffee."

She laughed. Tony was incorrigible. "Okay. I'll pave the way for you. But you're still going to have to smooth it over."

"I'll work on it," he said.

"I'll hold you to that."

Odalie was still crying when Stasia came in. She hugged her friend and rocked her, making soothing sounds until the tears finally ended.

"I disgust him, he said," she sobbed, wiping away tears.

In a pig's eye, Stasia thought, but she didn't say it. And Tony should have been flogged for telling her sister-in-law such a blatant lie.

"I should just go home," Odalie said heavily. "I don't think I'm cut out for a career in a big city."

"That doesn't sound like you," her friend pointed out. "And you haven't been sleeping well. Go to bed and don't think about it. Problems solve themselves if we wait patiently."

"How about if we wait impatiently?" Odalie asked.

"Go to bed anyway," she replied with a smile. "Sleep well."

"You, too," she said, knowing that she'd lie awake all night with Tony's heart-crushing words ricocheting in her mind.

The next morning, she was on her way out the door with her coffee in a travel mug when she noticed a solitary man across the street, staring out toward the traffic in the distance.

Luckily, her taxi pulled up before he spotted her. She jumped into the cab, and they sped away before Tony could get to her. She didn't want anything to do with him ever again. If it took her years, she was going to pry him out of her heart.

The voice lesson went very well. Her voice teacher advised her to go by the Met and speak to a certain man backstage. It sounded odd, but she did as he said and made a stop at the complex on her way home.

Mr. Perkins was the manager, and he already knew about Odalie's talent and her reluctance to participate in the regional competition. He'd also heard the recording that her voice teacher had made, and he was impressed. He gave her a date for the private audition, and she agreed with tears in her eyes and many expressions of joy.

Now all she had to do was show up and sing. Surely she could do that. She'd have to get used to looking out at a much bigger audience when she sang in an opera. She'd been afraid of it from the very beginning, when she'd performed in other venues. The tension was back again as she faced the new challenge. She could do it, she told herself. She could do it. Maybe.

The cab pulled up in front of her apartment. She paid the driver and thanked him and started to open the door. And there was Tony, sitting on the steps. It had been almost two hours since she'd walked out the door.

She couldn't face him. Not yet. She moved away from the door and told the cab driver to go around the corner without stopping. Then she walked into a small bookstore near her apartment and bought a book she really didn't want, just to kill time. Maybe he'd be gone when she got back.

It was clouding up two hours later. It looked as if a storm might be on the way. The wind was rising, and the heat was blatant.

As she turned the corner, there was Tony, all at once, tall, dark and raving mad.

"You saw me sitting there," he accused angrily, pointing at the steps. "And you had the cab driver go right by me!"

She drew in a breath. She was hurting inside and out, and her temper, usually nicely buried, stood up and blew flames at him. "You!" she accused. "You think I can't wait to see you, after what you said to me?" she raged. "What do you think you are, some pinup male model that I can't keep my hands off of?! I slipped! I wasn't trying to seduce you in front of a crowd of art patrons! What kind of a stupid idiot do you think I am?!"

Tears of pure rage were running down her cheeks.

"You don't have any idea what I think of you!" he raged back.

"And I don't care anyway!" She turned on her heel, unlocked her door and slammed it shut behind her.

Tony stood there with the door in his face. He was smoldering inside, so full of rage and passion and fury and desire that he could barely get his breath. She was the most maddening damned woman he'd ever known in his life. He wished he'd never met her. She was driving him nuts!

He boiled over all at once. He threw open the door and slammed it shut behind him.

"You get out of my apartment!" she sobbed. "You...you hoodlum!"

"You don't even know how to insult people," he grumbled, making a beeline for her.

"I do so! I can...!"

"You can what?" he asked, his voice husky.

Before she could come up with an answer, he had her up in his arms. His mouth hit hers like a storm, sudden and hard and insistent. And delicious. Maddening. Expert. Drowning her in pleasures she'd never experienced in her whole life.

She should protest. She should hit him. Or something. But his mouth softened almost at once on her lips, gently insistent, caressing, hungry.

Months of suppression hadn't helped his humor. He'd ached for her since his first sight of her, and this was like a feast following a prolonged fast. He waited for her to slap him, push him away, protest.

She did nothing of the sort. She was as hungry as he was. Her arms met around his neck, and she pushed up against his mouth, inviting something even more insistent than before. And when he obliged her, she moaned, a soft, sweet piercing sound that brought his blood up so hard, he thought he'd choke on his own desire.

"*Bella mia,*" he whispered deeply, his voice rough, his big, beautiful hands sliding all over her back, caressing and slow and arousing while his mouth devoured hers. He wouldn't have stopped if a gun had been pointed at him. This was feast after famine, ecstasy beyond ecstasy. Locked in each other's arms, they gave in to the passion that had been denied for so long.

Her mouth opened under his and she made a wild little sound as his became more demanding, as his arms folded her so close that she could feel his heart beating.

Tears were running down her cheeks, but not from anger or hurt. She was crying because it was the first real, passionate kiss she'd ever shared with a man. The child of overprotective parents, with two vigilant big brothers and a town full of kindly gossips who would have told on her for any amorous adventures, she was as innocent as Tony's first wife.

He'd always suspected that, long before she was in his arms

and proving to him how unsophisticated she was. He loved it. He smiled against her mouth, and his own gentled again, cherishing the softness of lips that were experiencing something totally new.

Finally, he was able to lift his head. He looked down into drowned blue eyes, drowsy with passion, wide and searching on his face.

"This," he whispered, "is a very bad idea."

She nodded slowly.

"You are going to get in over your head very soon."

She nodded again.

"Your parents are going to lock you up and never let you out of the house again."

She nodded.

He let out an exasperated breath. "Are you hearing me? I'm telling you what's going to happen, and you're just nodding your head!"

"Couldn't we go back before the lecturing part to the kissing part?" she asked, her eyes dropping to his mouth.

"Oh, God," he groaned as she tugged at his neck.

There was no way he was going to resist her. He'd always known that he couldn't. That's why he'd worked at keeping her away. Now it was too late. This was all his fault. It was going to blow up in both their faces.

But that would happen tomorrow or the next day or next week sometime. For right now, right here, she was his girl, and he was going to make the most of something he'd have died for.

She tasted of flowers and candy and innocence. He was getting drunk from the taste of her. Her arms locked around his neck as he lifted her even closer, his mouth hard and insistent on hers. And just as he was about to do something much worse than just kiss her, a key sounded in the lock and the door swung open.

They jumped apart guiltily. Odalie tugged down her blouse and Tony moved back two steps.

Stasia walked in to total silence and stopped suddenly with her eyes wide open. "So that's what the bodyguards were snickering about outside," she murmured with a quickly hidden grin.

"Snickering about what?" Tony asked gruffly. "I told you I was coming over here to apologize."

"It looks as if you apologized with a broom," she replied, with a speaking glance at the disarray of Odalie's blouse and hair and makeup.

"Not nice," he said. "And after all I did for you, too. For shame."

She just chuckled as she laid her purse on a side table. "I've been shopping for the baby," she said, dangling a designer bag.

"And you'll want to show it to your sister-in-law. Count me out. I don't do baby things," he said, turning toward the door. He hesitated. "I'll make lasagna if you two want to come over for supper tonight."

"If you're cooking lasagna, I'm coming," Stasia said.

He turned at the door. Dark, soft eyes slid to Odalie's flushed face and quickly away. "Fine. You can bring your friend here with you, if you want to." He grinned at both of them and went out the door.

"That man!" Stasia sighed, exasperated. "Honestly! Did he really apologize?"

Odalie looked stunned. She nodded.

"Well, I'm shocked. I mean, he does usually convey an apology, but not in real words. Did he use real words?"

Odalie swallowed. She could still taste Tony on her lips,

and she was breathless, still trying to make sense of what had happened. "He used a few words."

"And a few something else?" a delighted Stasia persisted.

Odalie turned beet red. "I have to get into something comfortable," she blurted, heading for her bedroom. "Be right back." She went into her room and closed the door.

Stasia pursed her lips and tried not to laugh. Things were definitely heating up. And it wasn't because of the weather.

10

Odalie stared at herself in the mirror, trying to understand what had just happened. It was amazing that Tony had kissed her, especially after he'd spent so much time denying that he even felt attracted to her. But that hadn't been any teasing kiss. It had been half desperation and half passion, and it surpassed her wildest dreams of what a kiss should feel like. The man was amazing.

Well, of course, he'd been married, and there was a woman in his life already. So certainly, he knew his way around women. She caught her breath remembering the expertise in the long, slow kisses that had almost singed her.

But was it just lust on his part? Was he honorable enough to try and keep away from her, because it was just lust that he felt? She wished she knew more about men. She wasn't close to anybody except Stasia and Maddie, and she could hardly ask them any of her burning questions. Maybe, she thought, there was information online somewhere on male behavior. Surely there was. She'd have to find it. But not today. She and Stasia were going over to Tony's for supper. And the way he'd smiled at her as he left! Just the memory of it left her breathless. There had been such wicked delight in that smile.

She sighed at her reflection. Then she blinked. She had to change clothes and go back and make lunch for herself and Stasia. She could daydream later, when they got home after supper.

As long as Stasia didn't know what was going on. This was private and personal, so personal that she didn't want to share it with anyone just yet. She wanted to live in her dreams without being reminded that Tony was dangerous and the world was bigger than Big Spur, Texas, for a cowgirl in couture in the big city.

She and Tony had been adversaries for a long time. He'd glared at her every time he saw her when she went to parties at the art gallery with Stasia. He'd started fights, he'd been insulting. But let some other man threaten her, in any way, and Tony was suddenly right there, glaring at somebody besides her.

She'd been certain that it was pure antagonism, that he hated her. But the man who'd kissed her a few minutes ago hadn't been an adversary. She still felt faint just remembering the utter hunger in those hard kisses. That hadn't been an assault, or taunting, or anything of the sort. That had been pure, unadulterated passion.

She was anxious about how it would be when they went to Tony's apartment. Would he be back in his shell, antagonistic again? Would they start all over from square one, like after the barbeque at her parents' ranch when they'd danced and hunger had spawned between the two of them?

She didn't want to think about backtracking. She put her hair up and went to the kitchen.

"Tony wasn't growling at you, was he?" Stasia asked. "He's not really a bear. Well, he can be, if he needs to. But he bluffs occasionally."

"He wasn't mean." She hesitated. "He was at first. He was yelling, and I started crying…" She swallowed and paused to sip coffee.

"And…?" Stasia prodded. "Why was he yelling?"

"He was sitting on the steps when I came home from my voice lesson," she said quietly. "I told the cab to drive on around the corner and then I sat in the bookshop for an hour." She glanced at her friend's face. "Well, I didn't want to face him. I knew he'd be angry. I hoped he'd just give up and go home."

"Anybody who knows Tony could tell you that he'd still be there in the morning if he had something to say to you."

"I found that out." She put down her cup. "He was fighting mad when I got out of the cab. He saw me go past the apartment and around the corner. He knew I was dodging him. So he yelled and I yelled and then I went into my apartment and slammed the door."

"And Tony went right in behind you and slammed the door himself." Stasia chuckled at her friend's expression. "I know Tony very well," she added. "You may run from a fight, but he never will."

"I found that out, too." Odalie took a long breath. "So we…discussed it," she lied, not looking at Stasia's face. "And we sort of worked it out."

"Sort of?"

"Sort of." No way was she admitting what had actually happened.

Not that Stasia couldn't guess from their guilty expressions and her sister-in-law's rumpled appearance. But she was kind enough not to point that out.

"Anyway, we've arrived at a truce," Odalie announced with a fake smile. "How's the salad?" she asked.

It was a diversion. But Stasia let her get away with it.

The apartment was lit up like a Christmas tree when they got there. Mrs. Murdock was fussing around with table settings while Tony took the lasagna out of the oven. He was wearing an apron that had a shark with a fork standing in front of a grill on it, over slacks and a sports shirt. Odalie thought how appropriate it was, and smothered a laugh.

"Lasagna," he said. "Made properly, the way my mama used to make it," he added, sliding off his oven mitts. "Garlic bread's already on the table. Hey, Ben—" he raised his voice toward the living room, from where video game music was booming "—food!"

The music went off at once and Ben appeared in the doorway. "Food! The only thing worth giving up *Halo Infinite* for!"

"You and your video games," Tony said, shaking his head.

"Well, a man has to have a few vices," he protested.

"We could list yours, if we had enough paper," Tony suggested.

Ben answered in Italian, followed by Tony answering in Italian, followed by a lot of arm waving.

"Enough!" Mrs. Murdock muttered. "Everybody sit down, right now!"

It was hilarious how fast everybody did. Even Tony, after

he seated Stasia. Odalie seated herself, too shy to wait for him to do it.

"Mrs. Murdock has you intimidated," Stasia teased Tony. "Admit it."

"Of course I'd admit it! She carries a Ka-Bar around in that apron pocket. I've seen it!" he added.

"Wuss," Mrs. Murdock huffed. "I can use it, too, so you just mind your manners."

While she was in the kitchen, bringing in the fruit salad, Stasia turned to Tony and asked, "Does she, really?"

"She does!" Ben answered for him, lowering his voice. "One of our guys came back from overseas with his National Guard unit. He gave it to her. It's her treasure," he added with bright eyes.

"Yeah, we think she's smitten," Tony added on a chuckle. "He's her age."

"An officer, too," Ben added.

"I hear you in here talking about me," Mrs. Murdock teased.

"We were only remarking how dangerous you were," Tony said.

"Yes, I fit right in," she agreed, putting down the salad. "I have a rosebush that you'd look lovely under, Tony, my dear," she purred.

He held up both hands. "I'd look awful under a rosebush. How about something more in keeping with my image. Deadly nightshade…?" he suggested.

She made a face at him and everybody laughed.

"At least you two have finally learned not to try and sneak off into the kitchen at meals," Stasia said with pointed looks at Ben and Mrs. Murdock.

"Am I missing something?" Odalie asked.

Stasia chuckled. "The first time I had supper here with Tony, I asked him where those two had gone. He led me to the kitchen and pointed. They were sitting at the kitchen table with food halfway to their mouths."

"So, what did you do?" Odalie asked, because she already knew the answer.

"I picked up my plate and sat down with them."

"Well, in our defense, we knew you came from wealthy people in Texas," Mrs. Murdock began.

"Wealthy people on a ranch in Texas," Stasia added, sipping coffee. She grinned at Odalie. "They never pulled that stunt again."

Everybody laughed.

"This is really good," Odalie remarked as she savored a bite of Tony's home-cooked lasagna.

"Thanks," he said, smiling at her and letting his glance linger just a bit too long for politeness. "It's the ricotta cheese. You need to add enough."

"And it helps if you can cook," Mrs. Murdock added, with a really vicious glance at Ben.

"Hey, I protect the boss," Ben grumbled. "Nobody said I should learn to cook, too."

"What did you do?" Odalie asked him.

"I made scrambled eggs." He glared at Tony, who glared back.

"Scrambled eggs." Tony nodded as he finished a bite of lasagna. "With raw whites, burned yolks, a tablespoon of eggshell and no seasoning."

"Everybody was sick!" Ben defended himself. "I was only trying to help."

"I called my cousin who owns the restaurant, and he loaned us a cook," Tony said.

"And *he*—" Mrs. Murdock pointed at Ben without looking in his direction "—was never allowed in my kitchen ever again."

"Some thanks I get for trying to be helpful," he muttered.

"We thanked you," Tony responded.

"They locked me out of the apartment for half a day!" Ben retorted, glaring from one to the other. "People laughed at me, sitting in the damned hall on the floor!"

"One guy snickered," Tony translated. "And he was one of ours."

"Well, it hurt my feelings."

"He doesn't have any," Tony said helpfully. "He was tombstoned in the wrestling ring so many times that only about ten of his brain cells are left."

"Don't you listen to them, Ben," Odalie said soothingly. "I used to love watching you on *Monday Night Raw!*"

"You did?" Ben asked, wide-eyed.

"I did. I have an autographed picture of you back home in my room," she added. "Dad took me to a match in Dallas. You were signing photos, so I got one."

"Well." Ben brightened. He smiled at her.

"He can write?" Mrs. Murdock asked Tony in mock astonishment.

"Don't look at me—I didn't know, either," Tony replied.

Ben picked up the container of salad dressing and looked narrow eyed from one of them to the other.

Tony and Mrs. Murdock looked at each other, sighed, got to their feet together and waved their napkins in defeat.

Ben beamed.

After supper, they sat over cups of coffee in the living room with its comfortable stuffed sofas and chairs.

"Tony, you've never shown Odalie the orchids, have you?" Stasia asked.

"Orchids?" Odalie asked, wide-eyed.

"Orchids," her sister-in-law replied, smiling. "He has some beautiful rare ones. Even rarer than the ones in the Jungle Room on Long Island."

"But aren't they really hard to keep?" Odalie asked.

"Very," he said, getting to his feet. "I have light tables with automatic waterers. But I still mist them myself every day. The rare ones tend to be temperamental."

"He was going to put in a terrarium and bring Rudolf over here from the Long Island house to live. Until the revolt, that is."

"Revolt?" Odalie asked as she stood up.

"Mrs. Murdock and Ben and both bodyguards stopped him at the door on the way out," Stasia said. "It was them or the snake. So poor Rudolf is stuck on Long Island."

"Poor baby," Odalie sighed. "I'll bet he gets lonely."

"Our neighbor's teenage son comes over to check on him every day," Tony said. "I think the kid's in love with him. I came home one day to find him watching old DVDs of Ben's wrestling tours with Rudolf sitting in his lap. Actually, partially in his lap. He's too big to be a lap snake," he chuckled.

"Orchids," Stasia prompted. "Thataway." She pointed toward the hall.

"I think we can find it, thanks," Tony said, tongue in cheek. He motioned to Odalie, who followed him down the hall with her heart doing the hula.

"You like orchids?" he asked as he opened a door.

"I love them, but I killed one by not taking care of it properly, so I wasn't going to try again. It was so beautiful!"

"What kind was it?" he asked when they were in the room with the door closed.

"It was an orchid," she repeated.

He sighed, feasting his eyes on her unconscious beauty. "There are a lot of different types. If you don't know how to take care of them, phalaenopsis are the safest. They do well with just light from a window and careful watering. These—" he indicated tall shelves on which many trays of orchids rested under lamps "—are more complicated. They need this sort of setup."

"Oh, my." She moved closer, catching her breath. There was every color in the rainbow, even spotted ones, all in glorious bloom. Shelf after shelf of them. "I've never seen anything so gorgeous!"

He explained the different species and how they grew in the wild and how they were propagated.

"It must take a lot of work," she remarked, turning to look up at him. Her heart flipped as she met his soft, dark eyes.

He nodded. He moved a step closer, so that he was close enough to feel her breath at his throat. His hands went into her hair, pulling out the pins that held up her complicated hairdo. She stood very still, not protesting. The feel of his big hands was seductive. So was the silence of the room, with only the sound of her own heartbeat loud in her ears.

He put the pins on a shelf and ran his fingers through her long, wavy pale blond hair, loving its silkiness and the faint perfume that drifted up into his nostrils. His hands framed her face and tilted it up to his. "This is a still a very bad idea," he whispered, his voice husky and deep as velvet as he bent to her mouth.

She was beyond words. Her hands flattened on his broad

chest. Then, remembering what he'd said to her the day before, they hesitated.

"I lied," he whispered. He was wearing a white silk shirt with nothing under it. Her hands sank onto the smooth surface. Under it she felt thick, curling hair like a cushion over hard, warm muscle. "It was make you mad or reach for you. I was still trying, at that point, to remain sane."

"And...did you? Remain sane?" she whispered at his lips.

"Hell, no," he breathed into her mouth just as his settled ever so slowly onto her soft, open lips. "Nothing of the sort."

His arms were around her now, half lifting her into his body. It was warm and hard muscled, and she felt enveloped, safe, cherished. His hands smoothed over her back, up and down, creating little waves of feeling that made her tingle all over.

Her breasts pushed into his chest, soft and firm as her arms reached up around his neck. She'd been kissed before. But Tony was a whole new experience. Her dates had been mostly boys, and then men, her own age. Even in a sophisticated age, many of them were as innocent as she was. Tony was in a class by himself.

He cherished her mouth, as if they were kissing for the very first time, as if the earlier kiss had never happened. He'd dreaded this, because he knew she was going to become the worst addiction of his entire life.

He drew back a breath and looked down into her sultry half-closed pale blue eyes. "At this point, you should be trying to get out of the room."

"Why?" she murmured, tugging at his neck to coax his mouth back down.

"Because it's going to end badly."

"Right now, you mean?" she whispered, her eyes on his firm, chiseled mouth.

"Eventually."

"There's only today," she said quietly. "Yesterday is a memory. Tomorrow is a dream."

"You should write poetry."

She sighed. Her fingers touched his mouth with wonder. "I never used to like kissing," she whispered.

He raised an eyebrow, suddenly jealous. "You did that a lot, did you?"

She shook her head. "I told you, I didn't like it. Besides, I'd already decided to sing opera. I didn't want to get involved with anybody."

"Well, kid, you're involved now. And you may wish you hadn't been."

"Yesterday is a memory, tomorrow is…" she began with a mischievous smile.

He covered the words with his mouth and his arms tightened. He moved and his mouth was suddenly hard and insistent.

She went under in a drugged haze, holding on for dear life while her body suddenly got its first taste of real passion and started demanding more.

He felt her gasp when the sensation began to affect her. It was affecting him as well. He felt his own body hardening, swelling. He moved back a whisper, just enough to keep her from finding out how involved he already was. Before she could question it, his mouth grew even more insistent, twisting sensually on her lips, teasing her mouth open to a deeper and far more intimate kiss than she'd ever had.

She stiffened just a little. He almost missed it. His own senses were swimming in heat. He'd had women since his early teens. This was different. Different even from the relationship he'd had with his late wife. No woman had ever aroused him so quickly and so completely. It was only physical, of course, he told himself.

He lifted his head and looked into shocked eyes. So much for other men, he thought with shameful pride. He could have bet real money on her reactions before now.

His thumb rubbed over her soft mouth, arousing her all over again. She felt swollen. She felt a heat and swelling that she'd never felt in her life. She was drowning in sensation.

"Odalie," he whispered in a moment of something almost like panic.

Those pale blue eyes lit up like candles in a dark room.

"What?" he asked, diverted.

"That's the first time I remember you calling me by my name," she said unsteadily.

"Is it?" He frowned. He touched the hair at her cheeks, moving it away.

She nodded.

He cupped her face in his hands and bent again, lightly brushing his mouth over hers in the quiet room. His heart was going like a fast watch. So was hers. He almost groaned out loud. If he didn't get her out of here soon, he'd never be able to let go. She had no idea what she was doing to him, either.

The sudden knock on the door stunned both of them.

"Dessert!" Stasia called. "Hurry up or it will melt. Mrs. Murdock made homemade vanilla ice cream."

"Be right there," Tony called. He hoped his voice sounded normal. Probably it didn't.

He looked down at his wrinkled shirt and her wrinkled blouse and her disheveled hair. "Oh, boy," he sighed. "Are we going to raise eyebrows!"

"Eyebrows?" She was still floating.

"Like to take a guess at how you look?" he asked wryly.

"How I look…" She let him move her gently away and her eyes went from his rumpled shirt to her own. "Oh!"

He nodded. He chuckled. It was funny. He'd never cared how he looked after a few casual moments with a woman. Not before. But what was between them was new and private. He didn't want people speculating. Not even people he considered family.

He tucked his shirt back in and handed her the hairpins he'd removed.

She gave him an astonished look. "What am I supposed to do with these, pick a lock?" she asked.

"Put your hair up."

She glowered at him. "Without a brush and a mirror?"

He gathered up her hair, piled it on top of her head and started putting in hairpins. After a minute he stopped and raised both eyebrows. He handed her the rest of the pins. "Hell with it," he muttered. "The fan messed us up, got that?"

She looked around. "What fan?"

"I'll close the door quick when we go through it," he said, imperturbable. "They'll never know."

Of course they knew. But they were kind enough not to tease or make fun of the condition of their friends.

Tony sent Stasia and Ben out to the limo while he paused in the doorway with Odalie, who wanted to leave as little as he wanted to let her.

He brushed back stray wisps of her pretty hair. "I have to go downtown for a meeting in the morning. When's your next voice lesson?"

"Not until next week," she said. "My instructor is going out of town."

He smiled slowly. "Okay. How about lunch? I should be free by eleven or so."

"Lunch." She grinned at him with her heart racing. "Okay."

He touched the tip of her nose. "I'd kiss you good-night, but too many people are trying not to look."

"I left my glasses on the back porch," Mrs. Murdock called. "Can't see a thing."

"You don't wear glasses," he pointed out as she sailed past them into the kitchen.

"Complaints, complaints, and here I'm doing my best to portray an ostrich!"

"Thank you, Mrs. Murdock," Odalie called after her.

"You're welcome, dear, any time."

He glared after Murdock and turned back to Odalie. "I'll text you when I'm on the way." He hesitated and frowned. "I don't have your cell number."

She dug out her phone and handed it to him. He dug his out of his pocket and handed it to her.

They put their respective numbers into each other's phone and handed them back.

"Okay, then. Sleep tight," he said softly.

She smiled up at him. "You, too. Night."

"Good night."

She turned and started to walk away. She heard him say something, so she stopped and turned. "What?"

He was just looking at her and smiling. "Angel," he said softly. "If there are angels, and I'm sure there are, you look like one."

She smiled back, radiant, and walked on to the car.

"I'm not going to ask a single question," Stasia promised

when they were back in Odalie's apartment. "So you don't need to think up excuses for your hair looking like birds built a nest in it."

"All my hairpins fell out at once," Odalie said, tongue in cheek. "I have no idea how it happened. Magnetic storm? Poltergeists? It's a puzzlement!"

Stasia just laughed.

She tried to sleep but it was impossible. Her stubborn mind went over and over again that passionate interlude among the orchids in Tony's office. It was a new experience to be lonely for someone. Not since a crush on a boy in grammar school had she felt anything remotely like it.

She tossed and turned, looking at the clock occasionally, only to repeat the exercise over and over.

It was one o'clock in the morning when her cell phone buzzed. She stared at it in her bedside table.

She didn't know anybody who would be up this late back home unless it was an emergency. But when she pulled it out, there was no voicemail. There was a text. She stared at it in disbelief and managed not to laugh out loud.

It was from Tony.

Are you as wide awake as I am?

She lay back in the bed, reading the bright display in the darkness of the room. She typed back.

Of course.

There was a Lol. And then a pause. Then the phone rang. She answered it.

"I think the hands on my clock are stuck. They aren't moving."

"I have the same problem," she said.

"Where do you want to eat tomorrow?" he asked.

She thought for a minute. "Sushi?"

There was another laugh. "My favorite. Next to Italian," he added.

"Except they don't have dessert at the sushi place."

"We can have dessert anywhere you like."

Her heart was racing. She felt on fire with a renewed joy of life. It was an exhilaration she'd never known. New, exciting. Dangerous. Tony wasn't a forever-after sort of guy.

"French pastry," she said finally.

"Bigot," he said. "Italians invented dessert."

"Okay. Italian pastry." She laughed softly.

"Better."

"Don't you have a meeting in the morning?"

"Yeah. But I can't sleep. I'll send Ben. You can come over and sing me a lullaby. That might do it."

"There would be a scandal. Stasia would miss me."

Another laugh. "Okay. Better not, then. See you in the morning."

"See you."

"Sleep good."

"Ha, ha."

He sent an emoji of rolling eyes.

She sent him a kiss before she thought it might be too much, too soon.

But he sent one back. The phone went quiet.

She stared at the screen with her breath caught in her throat. She wondered if he could possibly be as excited about what was happening to them as she was. He'd fought it for ages, but now he seemed resigned to getting involved with her.

She wasn't sure how it would end, but she knew she was too weak to try and cut it off before there were complications. In the end, she put the phone away and pulled the covers up and closed her eyes, hoping for the best. Amazingly, she was asleep in seconds.

The next morning, Stasia slept late while Odalie riffled through her closet for what seemed forever, looking for just the right thing to wear on her date with Tony. Because that's what it was. A date. The first date that had ever really mattered to her.

She pulled out a pretty long-sleeved beige dress that clung to her waist and flared out into a skirt. She paired it with a wide belt and suede boots.

The car was outside right on time. Ben grinned at her as he opened the door and let her slide in beside Tony.

He was wearing a suit with a blue striped tie and a matching handkerchief in his vest pocket. He looked expensive and handsome.

They smiled at each other.

"I love sushi," she remarked.

"Me, too."

"Have you ever been to Japan?" she asked, wanting to know.

He nodded. "Just once. It was great. But the trip over..." He groaned. "I thought I'd go crazy cooped up for that long."

"I know what you mean. I can never sleep on long flights."

"Alcohol helps," he teased. "But there's never enough to knock me out, no matter how far I have to go."

"Have you ever gone down to the Caribbean?" she wondered, lost in his dark eyes. It took a few seconds for her to remember what Stasia had told her, that Tony had been accused of a murder he didn't commit, and he'd stayed in the Bahamas with Marcus Carrera, another big name in deadly men. She flushed. "Sorry. I forgot."

He reached for her hand and locked his big fingers in her long, soft ones. "It was a bad time. One of my adopted daughter's in-laws helped me clear myself. Hell of a thing, to be framed for a murder I never committed. I got lucky. The vicious little jump-up who thought he'd take over my territory made an enemy of the biggest man upstate. Big mistake."

The feel of his fingers in between hers made her heart jump. She was trying to concentrate, though. "What happened to him?" she asked.

He leaned toward her, his cheek sliding gently against hers. "Bad things," he whispered, and his lips brushed her ear. He chuckled deeply at her soft gasp.

He drew back just as Ben pulled up to the curb. "Lunch," he announced.

He opened the door for Tony and Odalie and helped them into the Japanese restaurant. They were greeted and led to a booth near the window. Odalie slid in, and Tony slid right in beside her, close enough that his leg was against hers. The waitress handed her a menu with a smile before she put one in Tony's hands and then in Ben's.

"Would you like hot tea?" she added.

"Please," Odalie said. "Green tea."

"Same," Tony replied.

"Me, too," Ben added.

The waitress grinned and went to get it.

Odalie barely looked at the menu.

"What?" Tony asked.

"Miso soup and ebi," she said with a grin. "It's my favorite. Lots and lots of ebi."

"Shrimp." Tony rolled his eyes. "You have to try it all. You might like different things."

"I tried different things," she assured him. "That's why I want shrimp. Because I tried the other things." She made a face. "I ended up with sashimi instead of sushi." She closed her eyes and gave a mock shiver. "Some fish," she whispered, "absolutely must be served cooked!"

"Wimp," he teased, and his dark eyes sparkled as they met hers.

Her breath caught in her throat just looking at him. He was so handsome.

He was thinking the same thing about her. She was a true beauty, inside and out. It was useless to try and backtrack now, no matter how it ended. At least he'd have sweet memories. In the meantime, he could try to keep his enemies away from her.

One of his enemies, in fact, was fuming. He'd just been warned by the senator he thought was in his back pocket that a full investigation was being initiated into the massacre in Iraq.

"It's ancient history," Phillip James snarled. "Nobody cares anymore!"

The senator just smiled. "One of the victims had a relative who lives in New York City. He's a United States marshal."

James went pale for a few seconds, until he remembered that he had reasons to know that important people in Justice would back him up. They wouldn't want to. But they'd do it. So he smiled, too.

"I'm not frightened," he told the senator. He laughed softly. "So there's no evidence to convict you. But—" he toyed with a paper on his desk "—you have a daughter who's involved in some very bad things, don't you?" he added, lifting his eyes suddenly to catch the senator's.

The senator's breath left him in a rush. That was totally unexpected.

"Call off your dogs," James told him coldly. "Or else."

The senator didn't have a comeback. He didn't speak. He just turned and walked out of the room.

James smiled to himself. It was very important to have something on as many people as possible. He'd learned that from a former boss who'd been in Justice for many years. Everybody smart had backup information that could hurt somebody important. If you were ever up against the wall, it would save you.

He'd be all right now. But there was one loose cannon he still had a grudge against. Tanner Everett. He'd tried to off the guy, even sacrificed two agents to do it, and had failed. Everett's wife was pregnant, but she was untouchable. Damned Tony Garza had her covered like tar paper with some of the most dangerous mob guys James had ever heard of. Everett's people were on a ranch that was crawling with ex-feds and mercs. No way he could get to them.

He groaned. He wanted to make Everett pay for the hell he'd been through. He was out of danger now and ready for some major payback. He had to find somebody that Everett cared about, a family member, somebody close, so he could pay the man back for all his misery. That it was a result of his own behavior was something he'd never consider. He didn't make mistakes—other people did. He was important, and ruthless, and ready for some payback.

While he was thinking about vengeance, his cell phone rang. He answered it, smiling when he saw the number. "Hey," he said softly. "How's things?"

"Okay," his son said lazily. "I found a new hangout. There's this bar near school. Some really cool guys come in, and they're good at pool. One of them's teaching me and Ralphie."

"Not bad guys...?"

"Oh, for God's sake, Dad, I know how to spot gangsters," he laughed. "No, these are blue-collar guys. One's a plumber, one's an electrician. They work together. They come in after work to blow off steam. They're cool."

Blue-collar. He didn't like his son associating with the wrong people. He almost said so, but he didn't want to start a fight. He and his son weren't as close as he'd like, and he was reluctant to alienate him. He'd always given in, given the kid anything he wanted, to try and make up for losing his mom when he was little. He still gave him anything he wanted. The boy was his whole heart—in fact, the only weakness he had. Fortunately, none of his enemies knew about the kid; he'd kept him in a famous school up north, out of DC. He didn't even have his last name. Well, that was because he'd changed his last name just after the Iraq thing. It was providential right now, too, because it gave the kid an extra layer of protection.

He laughed. "Okay, then. You just watch your back, okay?"

"Sure, Dad. Hey, can you wire me a few bucks? I'm running short again. And I guess I'll have to repeat remedial algebra..."

"What, again?"

"Well, the professor didn't like me," the kid said icily.

James sighed. "Okay, sorry, sorry. Sure, I'll wire some money to your bank. And it's okay about the algebra. Some people have trouble with math."

"Sure. I'll talk to you later, then. Bye."

"You not coming home for the weekend?" he asked quickly.

"It's not a good time," the boy said hesitantly. "Besides, I'm getting good at pool, and they have competitions at the bar..."

James nodded to himself. "Well, have a good weekend, then."

"Yeah. Bye."

He hung up. Sometimes, he felt the kid only liked him for money. Certainly the boy wasn't as fond of him as he was of his son. But that was life. He went back to his desk.

11

After lunch, Ben drove Tony and Odalie to the Italian restaurant owned by Tony's cousin. There were tables outside because it was a glorious fall day, with the first golden and red tinges appearing on the maples on both sides of the quiet street, and leaves dancing on the pavement in the chilly wind.

Tony ordered dessert and vanilla cappuccinos, because he knew that Odalie loved it. So did he. Ben just ordered black coffee.

They were halfway through dessert when a tall, attractive man with an olive complexion and dark hair and eyes joined them and sat down at the table.

Tony chuckled. "You slumming?" he asked.

The other man grinned. "I have a weakness for espresso," he said. "But latte isn't bad. Your cousin makes a good cup of coffee."

"I think so, too." He glanced at Odalie and smiled tenderly.

"This is Dane Hunter," he told her. "An old…acquaintance," he said, choosing his words.

"Cough…the heat…cough," Ben joked.

Odalie glanced around at the amused faces.

"He's a US marshal," Tony told her with a grin. "But we forgave him after he saved my life."

"Nice to meet you, Mr. Hunter," Odalie said, and smiled.

He cocked his head and smiled back. "And you, Miss Everett," he said politely.

She was surprised. It showed.

"We keep tabs on him. Just to make sure nobody rubs him out," he added with a wisp of a smile as he nodded toward Tony.

"And he appreciates it, too," Tony replied, laughing. He waited until Hunter's drink was served before he spoke. "What?" he asked.

"Miss Everett's brother Tanner sent a photograph of a certain nasty incident in the Middle East to a senator he thought would help him with an investigation. Your guy James found out. Now he's hot for revenge," he said under his breath. "He's made certain threats. Make sure your soft targets are covered."

"I always do," Tony said. He cocked his head. "He had a senator in his pocket, but I removed the incriminating article."

"Won't help," Hunter said as he sipped latte.

"Why?" Tony wanted to know.

He looked up. "Senator's got a daughter," he said. "And you don't want to know what she's got her little fingers in."

Tony cursed under his breath.

"We have options. We're trying to wait him out while we examine them." He looked at Odalie. "Your sister-in-law is pregnant. James wants to hurt your oldest brother. He's mad to do it. Your father has protections around the ranch, I'm told..."

"Dad has two ex-feds on his payroll, and Eb Scott, who runs the counterterrorism school in Jacobsville, Texas, loaned him two mercs just back from overseas duty. They're covered."

"How about you?" Hunter asked, and the concern was obvious.

"Two men, twelve-hour shifts," Tony said easily. "Plus extra men if we need them."

Odalie stared at him, eyes wide.

He glanced at her and smiled. "What? You think I'd let you walk around unprotected?"

She flushed and then laughed.

"Were there any other eyewitnesses who might be willing to testify?" Hunter asked Tony.

"A contact of mine with one of the letter agencies says one of James's own agents was in Iraq when the murders happened. He's tried to quit the agency, but James has something on him, too."

"Damn!" Hunter finished his latte. "He's like a poisonous snake," he muttered. "Just when you think he's cornered, he slithers under a rock or bites somebody."

"Blackmail is very effective," Tony said.

"Yes. I noticed." He picked up his receipt and looked at Tony. "You've got my number. If you hear anything..."

"Sure," Tony said. "I'll put out a few feelers."

"I wish I had your connections," he sighed.

"No," Tony said, and he didn't smile. "You don't."

Hunter sighed. "See you around."

The minute he was out of sight, Tony punched in numbers on his phone. "I've been hobnobbing with the heat," he told whoever he was calling. He chuckled. "Yeah, I figured it would be going the rounds already." He paused. "No. He says the senator has a member of his family with deadly secrets, so he's not willing to apply pressure. Not yet, at least. Yeah. Okay. I will. Thanks." He hung up.

"Teddy?" Ben asked.

Tony nodded. He drew in a sharp breath. "Well, back to square one and more backup."

"No problem," Ben said. "I'll line up the troops."

When they were back in the car, Odalie slid closer to Tony. "Can I ask?" she said.

He picked her up and cradled her against him, lounging back on the seat. "I was talking to a fed," he explained. "If you do that, and you don't tell the appropriate people, it can bring down unwanted attention on you."

She just nodded. "But you're all right, now?" she asked, all eyes.

He smiled slowly, looking into her eyes. "I'm all right." He bent and kissed the top of her head. "I have to stop by the gallery. You can come with me."

She smiled, cradled against his jacket. "Okay."

He smoothed over her long silky blond hair. His heartbeat was audible at her ear, strong and fast. She closed her eyes. "Coffee and dessert was lovely."

"I like cappuccino."

"Hmm. Me, too."

He cuddled her close and sighed as she melted into him. "Hey, Ben, drive around the backstreets for a little while, okay? Give us time to digest lunch."

"You bet, boss!"

Tony smoothed his big hand over Odalie's soft hair. "Sleepy?"

She nodded.

He kissed the top of her head again. "Go to sleep. We're in no hurry."

She smiled and curled into his body, her cheek against his soft shirt under the jacket, her hand flat on the hard, strong beat of his heart.

Phillip James called Brock Peters into his office and closed the door.

He was fuming. He handed the man an unsealed card. "Look at that!"

It was a sympathy card. Peters would love to have laughed out loud at the sheer brass it took, but he didn't dare. His boss was bombed out on drugs half the time. You never knew which way he'd jump if he was upset.

"He's taunting me! You see that? He's taunting me!"

"You had it sent to the lab yet?"

"Of course I did, you think I'm stupid?" he raged. "No prints, nothing that could lead us back to Garza, but I know it's him!"

"It's just a card…"

"It's a taunt!" He slammed the card down on the desk. "I never should have sent that stupid kid to take on Garza. He didn't know what he was talking about. You don't just walk into those places and do business."

"I guess that kid watched too many old gangster movies."

"Yes, and now Garza knows it was me behind it!"

"What can he do, huh?" Peters asked. "Listen, boss, what can he do? He thought he had the senator in the clear, but we found out about his daughter, so he's right back in your pocket. Garza's got nothing."

"Everett." He almost spat the name. "He knows. He sent a photograph he got from God knows where to the senator and

asked him to call for an investigation. If I didn't have something good on the old man..."

"Lucky you did," Brock replied.

James was almost spitting with fury. "I should have made
sure Everett was taken out. I should have gone myself to South
America. What a mess!" He paced. "And now that ranch is
guarded like Fort Knox. No way can I get to Everett." He
whirled. "But those two women are in and out of the city—
his wife and his sister." He smiled coldly. "I want one of them.
Doesn't matter which. We'll take her and keep her and torture
her. Let him find the body. Yes." His eyes gleamed. "That
will show him! I'll pay him back for the misery he's caused
me!" He sat down behind his desk. "If I can't kill him, I can
take away something he loves!"

"Boss, his dad is rich and he's a big name in politics. He
could hurt you. He would, if you hurt his family."

"He runs cattle," he said. "What can he do to me?"

"His son could do a lot if he can get the intelligence committee on this."

"He hasn't, so far, because he hasn't got my connections."
His eyes narrowed. "I want revenge. My career has suffered.
I almost lost my job, my pension, because of his accusations.
He has no proof! It's his word against mine." He looked at
Peters. "You'd never sell me out, would you?"

"Never," Peters said firmly. "We started out together. We'll
finish together."

James stared at him for a long time. Finally, he relaxed. "All
right. We'll finish together. Find out how many bodyguards
those women have and how they're deployed."

"Garza considers Everett's wife like an adopted child."

He frowned. Tony Garza was dangerous. He was mostly
respectable these days, but still... He shrugged. "The sister,

then. They said Everett was very fond of his baby sister. That will hurt him if we take her."

"Tony…"

"Garza hates her," he interrupted. "He won't make trouble. He doesn't care. Get some men on it."

"Okay, boss." Peters went out into the hall and caught his breath. It was getting harder to deal with James's outbursts. Revenge was dangerous. If he killed Everett's sister, he'd bring down the heat on himself and on everybody in the top-secret agency. But James was so high, he didn't know, didn't care. And Peters was going to be left holding the bag, whatever happened.

He recalled how excited he and Phillip James had been when they were accepted as senior CIA agents and given their badges. It had been the high point of both their lives. From grammar school they'd been buddies. Peters had been best man at James's wedding. He'd been at the christening of James's son.

Then, so suddenly, James had succumbed to pressure and power and money and drugs. Almost overnight, he'd changed from the idealistic young man Peters knew to this raging, wild husk of a man who wanted nothing but power, power, more power.

Peters didn't want to go to prison for what James was authorizing. But if he tried to get out, he'd be dead. No way would he survive the attempt. He was in it for life now. It was not the future he'd planned for himself. Not at all.

Odalie had gone to the art gallery with Tony and admired his collection while he talked business in his office. She marveled at the many fine pieces he'd acquired and authenticated and then sold.

He came back out smiling. He shook hands with the man he'd come here to meet and walked him to the door. Then he went back to Odalie and caught her by the hand. "Enough business," he said, eyes sparkling. "Let's go somewhere and dance."

"Dance?"

He grinned. "How about the Latin club?"

She knew the one he meant. She'd gone there with Stasia a few times. "I love it there."

"Me, too. I'll get Ben."

They ate and drank and danced until late. Odalie was sleepy. Ben drove them back to her apartment. Tony walked her to her door and went inside with her. Stasia had left New York that afternoon, so they were alone.

She started to turn on the light, but he prevented her.

"We don't need the light," he whispered, and brought her close.

He kissed her softly, slowly, lifting her against his body until she moaned. Then he brought her close, close, in his arms, and his mouth opened on hers in a slow, rough heat of passion.

He drew back, finally, groaning, and buried his hot face in her throat. "How have I lived without that?" he whispered.

"You were so busy telling me what a pest I was," she teased.

"Trying to ward it off," he murmured. He drew in a long breath and lifted his head. He searched her eyes. "I thought I'd be sorry." He smiled gently. "I'm not sorry." He bent and kissed her quickly, roughly. "Keep your door locked and put on the chain latches, okay? Call me if you hear anything. Promise me."

"I promise."

He kissed her one last time. "I'll call you in the morning."

She smiled. "See you."

He went out and she locked the door behind him, almost floating in the aftermath of such joy that she felt weightless. She wanted to call him back, to prolong this. But they had all the time in the world. There was no reason to rush it. She wanted to savor the newness of Tony in her arms, like an expensive, delicious wine.

Early in the morning, in the wee hours, she thought she heard something outside her window. She knew Tony had men watching her, though, so she didn't panic. That was probably what it was.

That was what she thought until the doorknob rattled on the back door. It had a dead bolt and a thick chain latch. No way was somebody going to get inside. But it spooked her.

She picked up her cell phone and punched in Tony's number. It wasn't even daylight.

"What is it?" he asked abruptly.

"Somebody rattled the doorknob. Do you have anybody here...?"

"Hold on." He cut her off. A minute later he came back on. "That's not any of my people. Is he still there?" His voice was curt, urgent.

She listened. "I don't hear anything right now."

"I'm on my way."

He hung up.

Not five minutes later, he and Ben and another man pulled up at the curb. She heard running footsteps, followed by more running footsteps.

"Odalie, are you all right?" he asked, banging on the front door.

She opened it. "Tony, I..."

He backed her into the apartment, closed the door and bent

to her mouth, lifting her against him. "Oh, baby, I've never been so scared," he breathed into her mouth. His voice was just faintly unsteady as he kissed her hungrily.

He wrapped her up against him, only vaguely aware of some soft, silky fabric under his hands. After a minute, he realized that what he was feeling was silk, and that there was nothing under it...

He groaned out loud as he lifted his head and looked down at her in the pink silk gown with its low-cut lacy bodice that revealed more than it concealed, and spaghetti straps that did nothing to hide soft tanned shoulders under long silky blond hair.

She felt the impact of his eyes like a hot brand and almost shivered with delight. She felt her body tauten and swell. He was staring at her bodice, his breath coming in soft, rough expulsions.

She had no defense at all. She was so hungry for him.

He reached down to her knees and slid his hands under the gown. They were warm and strong and rough on her bare skin as they moved slowly, tenderly, up to her rib cage.

"This is where we start getting in over our heads," he said in a husky, velvety soft tone.

Her lips parted on a tiny gasp as his thumbs teased at the underside of her firm breasts.

"Your skin is like velvet," he whispered.

She arched her back almost imperceptibly, trying to tempt his hands to move up. *Just a little more*, she thought, twisting slowly. *Just...a...little!*

He knew what she was doing, and why. He loved that innocence that was all his, open and warm and welcoming. He couldn't see the obstacles anymore. He was already drowning in her.

"This what you want?" he whispered, watching her eyes

half close, and his fingers moved up and touched her, traced the hard nipples pushing against the lace.

She made a sound, a high-pitched little moan, that drove him over the edge.

"Baby…" he breathed into her mouth as his own settled slowly, tenderly, over it. His hands possessed her, slow and warm and insistent. She arched her body to urge them closer and moaned again, shivering.

He picked her up, his mouth still on hers, and laid her down on the sofa. His big body settled on hers in the silence of the room and he groaned, too, as her long legs parted to admit his, her mouth open and hungry for his.

She could smell the spicy, sexy cologne he wore, with its faint whiff of cigar smoke. She could taste coffee on his hard mouth. Her hands went up into his thick, cool wavy hair and tangled there, holding his face down to hers. One of her legs rubbed slowly against his. He shifted, and she felt the contours of his body changing.

His head lifted and he looked into her shocked eyes. He actually chuckled. "I'm a man," he whispered. "This is how we work. Temptation brings noticeable…inflations."

She gurgled with sudden laughter. They were intimate, and it wasn't frightening or embarrassing, it was fun.

He grinned. "So, you learned something new." He stared at her breasts, more visible in the position she was in. He bent his head, and his mouth smoothed over just their pretty pink tops, where the fabric dipped just enough.

She caught her breath.

"So many new things," he teased. He lifted his head. "But we'd better get up and look dignified."

"Why?" she moaned, holding on.

"Ben."

She blinked.. "Ben?"

"Coming in the door…?"

She cried out softly. "Oh, damn, where's my bathrobe…!"

She tore out of his arms and ran for her bedroom while Tony roared with laughter.

Ben, oblivious to what he'd interrupted, stared at Tony with raised eyebrows. "What?" he asked.

Tony was buttoning his shirt. He looked rumpled and happy. Happier than Ben had seen him in years and years.

"We couldn't catch the guy," Ben continued. "But one of our boys got a look at his car. We'll have something soon."

"It will lead back to James," Tony said. He shrugged. "We can deal with him, when the time comes."

"Yeah."

Odalie, hair combed and thick bathrobe buttoned to the neck and barefoot, came back into the living room, trying to look unaffected. "Did you see who it was?" she asked Ben.

He shook his head. "But one of the boys got some clues. We'll find him. Don't you worry."

"We won't. She's coming home with us."

"What?" Ben and Odalie chorused.

"Listen," Tony said, and he wasn't smiling as he turned to Odalie, "somebody got past my guy and almost broke in. You're not safe here. Not now."

Odalie was quick. "Is something going on that I don't know about?"

He nodded.

"Something bad," she guessed.

He nodded again. "So pack some stuff and get dressed. Nobody touches you," he added in a tone that made her toes curl.

She just smiled. "Okay, Tony."

She went to pack. Ben tried to muffle a laugh.

Tony turned and looked at him. "You don't know anything. You haven't seen anything. You're blind, and deaf."

"How can I drive in such a condition?" Ben asked reasonably.

"I'll buy you one of those self-driving cars."

"I'll quit first," Ben said, outraged. "What's the fun in even having a car that drives itself?"

"It would cut down on drunk drivers," Tony suggested.

"I can see them now, putting Jack Daniel's in the gas tank…"

Tony just laughed.

Tony had planned for Mrs. Murdock to be a chaperone, but when he got to the apartment, he found a quickly scribbled note taped to his favorite chair.

"Mom had a heart attack in Wichita," she wrote. "Must leave at once. Will call when I know something." It was signed "Helene," which was Murdock's first name.

"Damn," Tony said. "Her mother is all she's got left of family."

"I'll find out her mother's address and send a bouquet," Ben said.

"Do that, and make sure she's got access to the best cardiologist available. Price is no object."

"I'll do that, too," Ben said, and went into the study and closed the door.

"Ben is handy," Odalie said.

"Very."

"I'm so sorry about Mrs. Murdock's mother! Is she very old?"

"She just turned sixty," Tony said. "Not old enough for social security, and she works as a housekeeper, just like Helene."

"That's rough. Anything heart related is expensive," she

added. "One of our wranglers had to have valve surgery. The bill was awful. Of course, Dad has the best insurance he can get for all our hands."

He smiled. "Your father has a caring nature."

"I know. But it really doesn't show," she laughed. "He scares people."

He framed her face in his hands and kissed her gently. "He wears a Ruger Vaquero in a holster. Of course he scares people."

"Yes, well, he does that without a gun, mostly," she replied with a grin.

He kissed the tip of her nose. "So do I," he said, and he wasn't kidding. "We have two guest rooms. You can choose."

"The smallest," she said. "I don't need a lot of room. There's just me and a few clothes."

He chuckled. "It's a good thing, to travel light."

"Daddy used to take us all camping. We learned not to overpack."

"I never got to go camping. I'll bet it's fun."

"Great fun. I had a wonderful childhood."

"Courtesy of terrific parents," he replied, and bad memories were in his eyes.

She moved close, her hands flattening on his chest. "We move on, because we have to. Most often, the future is better than the past."

His eyes softened as he looked at her. He smiled gently. "Yeah. Well, sometimes we get lucky. Really lucky."

She wrinkled her nose at him and smiled. "Where's my room?"

She was comfortably moved in shortly and sent to bed, because it was late. She'd rarely felt as safe in her life as she did with Tony. She stopped looking ahead. She was going to live for the moment and not one minute further.

A loud knock on her door woke her. "Is it morning already?" she protested. "I just went to sleep."

Tony stood over her, grinning. "Biscuits, scrambled eggs, ham and bacon and hot strong coffee," he offered.

"Ooh, I'll be right there!" she said.

He chuckled and went back out, closing the door.

She dressed in comfortable sweats and joined the men at the table, barefoot and with her long hair in a ponytail. And no makeup.

Tony's eyes widened. "That's how you dress at home?"

"Yes," she said, surprised.

He frowned.

She gave him a droll look. "I'm eating breakfast, not going to a fashion show." She cocked her head. "I brought nice stuff with me. For later."

"Oh." He brightened.

She grinned at Ben, who chuckled, too.

"This is really good," she told Tony. "I can make biscuits, but mine aren't this good."

"What do you put in them?"

"Olive oil."

He stopped with a biscuit halfway to his mouth. "Excuse me?"

"Olive oil," she said. "Medical studies show that people who live around the Mediterranean don't have the heart issues that we have. They figured out it's because of the olive oil that's in most people's diets there."

"Well, I'll be."

"So Mom decided that it was healthier for Dad to have it because he erupts pretty often."

"Erupts."

"Like you," she said, and grinned at him.

He chuckled. "Well, I usually cook with olive oil. But I put lard in my biscuits. That's how my mama made biscuits."

"Lard." She sighed. "Well, it makes them taste super good."

"I know it's not supposed to be good for you. I just put it in biscuits. Otherwise, olive oil and nothing fried."

She grinned. "Me, too."

"But I love a steak."

"I love steaks, too. But I'd eat fish every meal if I lived on the ocean. I love seafood."

"He fishes," Ben said with disgust. "Nasty habit."

"Hey, some of my cousins are still fishermen back in Sicily," Tony replied. "Bigot."

"I am not. I'm just fastidious," Ben huffed, indicating his nice suit and spotless white shirt.

"Me, too, but I still love to fish," Tony replied.

"It's one of my favorite things," Odalie said, surprising both men. "But I can't really use a spinning rod or flies and stuff like that. I use a cane pole with a hook, line and sinker. Last time I went with Daddy, I caught three more fish than he did," she said, chuckling. "He was really snarfed."

"What does he use?" Ben asked.

"A spinning reel. He's good at casting, but in any case you don't get tangled line with a spinning reel."

"No, you don't," Tony replied. "But you're talking about little fish. I like to go after the big ones."

She stared at him. "Big ones?"

"Marlin," he said, his dark eyes glittering with delight. "But also tuna. Grouper. Red snapper. Those kinds of fish."

"Deep-sea fishing!" she exclaimed. "Daddy and John and

I went out on a fishing boat on the Texas coast and caught all sorts of fish to take back home with us. Gosh, was Mom mad."

"Why?"

"Well, John and Daddy and I like catching fish," she confessed. "But we hate cleaning them. So when we got the cooler home, we put it in the kitchen and ran for our lives. Mom spent a whole afternoon cleaning fish." She sighed. "And then she fed us pancakes for supper."

Tony burst out laughing. "What did she do with the fish?"

"She froze them. Every single one. And they didn't get cooked for a month!"

Now Ben was laughing, too.

"Well, I don't mind cleaning fish. So I'll take you with me one day and we'll see what we can catch."

She just smiled at him, her heart vulnerable and filling her soft eyes. He smiled back. Ben, watching, was happy for them. He just hoped they weren't headed for tragedy. His man was still trying to backtrack Odalie's prowler, but he had a hunch it would lead them right to DC and Phillip James. If they weren't very careful, they could lose Odalie in a very bad way. Considering the way his boss was looking at her, that might be the one thing that could bring him down.

Tony had to meet someone at the art gallery. Odalie dressed up in a sexy red pantsuit and high heels, also red, with her hair in an upswept hairdo. She looked so gorgeous when she joined Tony in the living room that he just stood and stared.

She'd never really cared about her looks before, but it made her proud that Tony liked them so much. She beamed, which only made her more beautiful.

"Wow," he said. "Now I understand why they say blondes look good in red."

"Thanks."

He bent and kissed her nose. "Lipstick," he muttered, staring at the bright red lipstick that matched her outfit.

"I only wear it when I go out," she whispered. "I don't like it, either."

He pursed his chiseled lips and grinned at her. "Later, I could help you take it off."

Her heart jumped and she laughed. "Okay," she said, and flushed a little.

"Angel, you are the light in the darkness," he said, and for a few seconds, he was solemn.

"Me?"

"You." He traced around her mouth. "And nobody is going to hurt you. Not ever."

She smiled slowly. She didn't have to speak. He saw everything she felt in her eyes.

They were almost to the gallery when she mentioned her upcoming audition. "I knew they were going to start arranging them, but I got called over to the Met by a friend of my voice coach and he gave me a day and time. I'm so nervous."

"You'll do fine, honey," he said, hating his resentment. He didn't want to lose her to a career when he'd just found her. But he couldn't bear to stand in her way. "That's great."

It actually wasn't, but she didn't want to say so. She'd been in therapy for years. Her parents thought it was because of the incident with the law when she was in high school. It wasn't. She was terrified of being on the stage. Yes, she wanted to sing at the Met. She'd trained for it, sacrificed for it, hungered for it for years.

But when it came right down to it, she knew in her heart that she was never going to be able to manage going out on stage night after night after night. It never improved, despite the therapy. She sang, and then she ran to the bathroom to throw up. Afterward, it took tranquilizers to bring her back from her terrified state. She'd never told anybody. It was one of many secrets she kept to herself.

"Didn't you go to the regional auditions?" he asked, because he knew about opera stars and their early days.

She forced a smile. "I missed the audition," she lied, "so I went about it in an easier way. I have an agent. I had her ask for an audition." She smiled. "I have to send a tape of myself singing and do a few other things. I cut a few corners," she lied.

He just smiled, not telling her he'd helped arrange the solo audition. "When do you audition?"

"Next month," she said.

He relaxed. A lot could happen in a month. A whole lot. He reached for her hand and held it all the way into the art gallery.

12

When they got through with the art gallery, Tony took her to the sushi place and they all ate their fill, including Ben. Then they went by Tony's cousin's restaurant for a pastry.

"Didn't I tell you Italian food is the best?" Tony teased her as she finished her cake and ice cream.

"It's out of this world!" she agreed.

"Mario makes his own ice cream," he added as he finished the last of his own dessert and reached for the strong espresso he liked.

Odalie sipped cappuccino and sighed. "It's so nice here," she said, looking around as the wind blew leaves down from the little trees all along the sidewalk. "I love New York," she added softly, smiling, with her eyes closed as the wind stirred her hair.

Tony, looking at her, felt his heart clench. She was a country girl, but she was just as much at home in the city. Even with his family from Jersey. She wasn't stuck-up or snobbish or heartless, as some beautiful women were. Just looking at her made him ache. He questioned the wisdom of keeping her at home with him, but he really had no choice. He couldn't risk her life. Phillip James was on drugs and unpredictable, desperate for vengeance. Odalie would be a nice target. But not on Tony's watch.

"Listen," he told Ben, "you put on all the extra security you need. We don't want any slipups."

"You got it, boss," he agreed.

Oblivious, because they spoke in Italian, Odalie kept sipping cappuccino.

They were both in the mood for something light at supper, so they made big salads with homemade bread.

"I didn't know you could make bread," Tony sighed with delight as he wolfed down the second of two buttered rolls. "And you made them with olive oil!"

She laughed. "Yes. You don't really notice the taste because it's so light, and it's good for you. Well, the butter probably isn't, but you just can't eat homemade rolls without butter!"

"Absolutely!" Tony agreed at once. Ben, still grabbing rolls, just nodded.

Odalie grinned from ear to ear. Nothing more welcome to a cook than men who couldn't stop eating her food.

Later, Ben went to bed, leaving the boss and Odalie in the living room watching a movie.

"I love *Guardians of the Galaxy 3*," Odalie said when it finished, wiping tears, "but I cried as much as I laughed on this one."

"It was great, wasn't it?" He got up and stretched lazily,

pulling her up with him after he cut off the TV. "You need some sleep and so do I. I've got meetings tomorrow with my board of directors."

"You have a board of directors?" she asked, surprised.

"Necessary evil," he replied on a sigh. "But I handpicked two of them." He grinned. "Those two keep the others tied up in knots so I can get things done."

She laughed.

He bent and kissed her gently. "That's not all I'd like to do," he whispered, "but Ben sleeps light. So go to bed and dream about me."

"Okay," she whispered back. "If you'll promise to dream about me, too."

He didn't smile. He looked at her with such hunger that it was blatant. "Honey," he said softly, "I've dreamed about you since the day I met you. And fought it every inch of the way."

"Why?"

He sighed. "Lots and lots of reasons. We could name them all. It wouldn't help."

She reached up on tiptoe and kissed his chin. He drew her close, wrapped her up in his arms and kissed her until her mouth was sore and she was aching all over. He had to fight to turn her loose. His dark eyes were blazing with hunger as he looked down into drowned, drugged blue eyes that adored him.

"This will not end well," he bit the words out, feeling his body harden to painful levels.

She touched his cheek gently, her eyes full of drowsy passion. "There's only today," she whispered, smiling.

His heart jumped. He had to force himself to let her go. It wasn't easy.

He nodded slowly. "Okay. One day at a time."

She smiled. "Exactly."

"Good night."

"Good night, Tony." She started toward her room, but turned and just looked at him, still aching.

"Go. Now," he said in a rough undertone.

She shrugged faintly and flushed a little. "Okay. I'm going." She gave him a last longing look and went into her bedroom and closed the door.

But she didn't, couldn't, sleep. Her body, awakened to passion and eager for experience with the man she was crazy about, was driving her wild. She'd never felt such a raging hunger for anyone. She tossed and turned in her pink silk gown. Every time her breasts rubbed against the fabric, they swelled. She ached. She moaned softly. It was the most agonizing night she'd ever endured.

Doors opened and there were voices. Then a door closed and locked. She wondered what was happening. But it wouldn't do to go out and ask, not in her present condition. She turned some more and arched her back like a cat asking to be stroked. *Tony*, she thought with anguish, *oh, Tony!*

Even as she thought about him, the door opened slowly. She lay in the light from the hall, one leg raised, the gown sliding down to her hips, her breasts pointed and half-revealed as the gown dipped.

Tony was wearing nothing but pajama bottoms. His chest was broad and bare, thick with curling black hair. He looked like every woman's secret dream, handsome and virile and muscular without it looking vulgar. And she'd never wanted anything as much in her life as she wanted Tony in her arms at that moment.

She arched, helpless, and moaned softly.

"Oh, God," he groaned. He'd gotten up because Ben had a call about the prowler and was going out. But Tony hadn't been able to get past her doorway on his way back to bed. He was in agony from wanting her. And he'd been positive that he wasn't the only one. Now he was even more positive. He knew this was going to end badly, but a man had only so much self-restraint. He took a deep breath.

Then he closed the door...

Ben sat at a table in an all-night bar waiting for a contact. He had a beer but avoided hard liquor. He needed his wits about him.

Finally, his contact showed up. "Hey, Ben, how's it going?" Rudy asked as he took a seat and ordered a beer of his own.

"Badly," Ben said.

"Yeah. I noticed." Rudy waited until he was served before he spoke. "The irritation is coming from a political place, and you know which one."

"Boss will be wild when he knows."

"You need to put on more people," Rudy said under his breath. "He can't get to her family, too much protection. He wouldn't dare risk trying to get around Tony's people at her apartment..."

"But that's exactly what he did," Ben informed him, and outlined what had happened.

Rudy grimaced. "So what's he doing about it?"

"She's moved in with us."

Rudy sighed. "Okay. That's one worry out of the way. But you make sure she's trailed everywhere. She's the best soft target of all, and we may not see it coming."

"I know that. Thanks," he added with a smile.

"We're all in this together, one way or another," Rudy said

easily. "Boss may get hot at me from time to time, but we're family, just the same."

"All of us," Ben agreed. He looked at his watch and grimaced. "No use going back home to bed," he said with a sigh. "I guess I'll go round up my boys and give out assignments. If you hear anything…?"

He nodded. "You bet."

Odalie felt his approach, actually felt it in the darkness of the room. She moaned as he stood over her, barely visible in a trickle of light from outside the window.

"You'd better be sure," he whispered. "I don't want to stop. I want you too much. And that isn't all. It's like eating potato chips. Once will never be enough." He was relieved that he'd mentioned he couldn't have kids on their lunch date. It would stop her getting ideas about the future.

She sat up and let the straps slip off her shoulders, the gown falling to her waist. In the faint light, her skin had the sheen of silk.

He actually groaned. He stopped talking. His pajama bottoms hit the floor. He sat down beside her, and his mouth all but swallowed one small, perfect breast. She made a sound that drove him mad.

She arched under his mouth, so enthralled that she couldn't even speak. Her nails bit into his shoulders as he moved against her, onto her, his mouth insatiable on her breasts, her belly and, finally, her silky thighs.

She was so wild for him that when she felt the first hard thrust, she didn't even try to draw back. She lifted up to him, helping him remove the last little barrier that kept them apart. She couldn't have felt pain at that point. Desire rode her so high that all she could think of was relief.

Tony had been with women since he was fourteen. He knew exactly what to do and when to do it to bring a woman to ecstasy. As he drove into her, he recalled some of those women and thought how they couldn't hold a candle to this one, to her sweetness, her beauty, her spunk. And she was his. All…his!

He heard her cry out and shudder under him. The first time, he thought while he could. The first time, and she was climaxing!

He wanted to speak, but he was dying for her. He drove harder, faster, hearing her cry out again and again and shudder as he satisfied her over and over again. And, finally, he satisfied himself, in a last shuddering drive as far into her as he could get. The sudden burst of pleasure made him cry out, something he'd never done in his life, and then he was shuddering, just as she had, caught in a maelstrom of fulfillment that excelled his wildest dreams of passion.

She held him while he endured it, kissed everywhere she could reach, lifted into him to prolong his pleasure. Tears were running down her cheeks, tears of absolute joy.

Finally, he collapsed on her, gasping for breath, his heart hammering so hard that it shook her. He was damp with sweat, shivering.

"Oh, Tony," she whispered, clinging.

He wrapped her up in his arms, holding her close. He was still shaking. "I never felt anything like that in my whole life," he whispered.

"Me, neither," she whispered back.

He laughed softly. "I noticed." He kissed her tenderly. "You climaxed. Your first time. I was so proud, I wanted to crow."

"Really?" she asked, still shy with him.

"Really." He rolled onto his back and held her at his side,

enjoying the feel of her bare breasts against his rib cage. "My God, I thought I was going to die!"

"It isn't always like that, for a man?"

"Not for me. Not ever." He drew in a long breath. "I wanted to take longer with you, but it's been a long dry spell. I needed you, so much."

She frowned. "Long dry spell?"

He drew in a breath and curled her hair around one big hand. "For the past year, I haven't had a woman."

Her heart jumped. "But...but they say you have a mistress...?"

"I couldn't touch her." He drew her closer and bent to kiss her gently. "I wanted you every time I looked at you, for the past year. I was terrified that I might do something about it. And," he added ruefully, "I finally did."

"Don't sound so regretful," she said.

"I can't help it. You and I are very different."

"Yes. I just noticed all the differences...ouch!"

They both laughed. He'd pinched her lightly.

"Not those differences. The big ones. Background."

"I don't care about your background."

"One day, you might," he said.

"Pessimist," she chided. "There's no tomorrow. There's only today. Only right now. Right here..."

She smoothed her bare leg over both of his and moved sinuously against him, sighing. "Potato chips," she whispered, her voice vibrant with rekindling desire.

He rolled her over. "I'll show you potato chips," he teased, and his mouth slowly covered hers.

He took longer. He moved with maddening slowness. He had her crying out, begging for relief, and still it didn't come.

Finally, he eased himself up against the head of the bed and pulled her over him, onto him, and moved her a little roughly on his body. He groaned as he increased the pressure and the pace.

"Tony!" she cried out, frightened as the spiral began, climbing up and up and up to heights she hadn't experienced their first time.

"Feel me," he whispered roughly. "Feel me deep in your body. As deep as I can get. That's why...we're doing it...like this. I want...all of you!"

His voice broke as passion overwhelmed them both. She shuddered as the wave hit her, so strong and volatile that she almost couldn't take it. Under her, his muscles spasmed, too, in the heat of a passion so high that she thought she might die of it.

He turned her over suddenly and drove into her. What she'd thought was the culmination was only a plateau. He pushed her up a new one, and she cried out so loudly that he covered her mouth with his to muffle the sound. It was the most exciting few minutes of his life. Of hers, too. She hadn't dreamed that her body was capable of so much pleasure. Almost too much. She sobbed as she finally came down to earth again, held tight in his arms.

"Did I hurt you?" he asked at once. "Baby, I'm sorry...!"

"I'm not hurt," she sobbed against his chest. "It was so sweet, so sweet, and it only lasted for a few seconds!"

"Yes." He relaxed a little, smoothing her over his body with both hands. "What a night!"

She kissed his shoulder. "Oh, yes." She sighed. "I'm so sleepy..."

She fell asleep in his arms.

She woke the next morning with very sore places and vivid memories of the night before.

She was in her bed, alone, and totally nude. While she was recalling what they'd done, the door opened and Tony came in, wearing his pajamas and carrying a mug of black coffee.

He grinned when she flushed. He put the coffee down and pulled off the covers, pulling her back when she tried to dive under them.

"No way," he teased, pulling her across his lap to study every soft inch of her. "We're together now. There's nothing to be embarrassed about."

She searched his dark eyes. They held such tenderness that they made her feel warm all over. She was in awe of him.

He touched her soft breasts, watching them peak, watching her arch up to his touch helplessly.

"You are the sweetest candy I've ever had," he whispered, bending to kiss a hard nipple.

She moaned and tugged at his head, protesting when he tried to lift it again.

"No, honey," he said softly. "It would hurt you now. I was too greedy last night."

She understood at once what he meant. She grimaced. "I am sort of...sore," she confessed.

"Me, too."

Her eyebrows arched. "Men get sore?"

He gave her a sideways glance. "We both have tender spots. Too much rubbing...?"

"Stop!" She put her hand over his mouth, flushing.

He chuckled. "You're sweet to tease." The smile faded as he looked at her. "What if I can't turn you loose?"

She cocked her head. "Why? Do you want to?" she asked and looked wounded.

"No!" he said at once. He drew in a breath. "Never mind. There's only today." He smiled and put her back under the covers and handed her the mug of coffee. "Ben will be back later. But that's okay. For a few days, at least, we're walking wounded."

"Damn," she muttered.

He grinned wider. "We'll heal."

She wiggled her eyebrows. "Something to look forward to." She frowned. "But Ben sleeps in and I..." She recalled her wild cries of the night before and flushed.

"Yes, and you make noise. A lot of noise." He bent and kissed her, hard. "I love it when you make noise," he added gruffly, his eyes dark and intent. "I feel ten feet tall when you do that, and I know that it's because of what I'm doing to you."

"I never knew," she said softly. "Never dreamed it would be like that."

He brushed back her hair. "It would never, never, be like that with any other man. Ever. Never." He studied her. "Honest. You'd break out in green warts. All over."

She smiled from ear to ear. "Okay."

He chuckled.

"On the other hand," she replied, "if you sleep with another woman, parts might fall off...?"

"Damn, woman, that's below the belt!" he roared.

She grinned. "Isn't it, though?"

He got up. "I'm losing this war. I have to get dressed and go to work. You can sleep in. And there are two guys outside the door who make gorillas look wimpy."

She smiled. "Okay. But you have to be careful, too," she added quietly.

He warmed at the emotion in those soft words. "I'll be careful. See you later, pretty girl."

She just sighed, smiling as he left the room.

★ ★ ★

But later, after a bath, she worried about what she'd done. Her parents had been strict and had told her there were ancient taboos about sleeping with a man to whom you weren't married. She hadn't wanted to stop, though. She loved Tony so much…

She sat down heavily on the bed and caught her breath. She loved Tony. Incredible that, until right now, she hadn't realized that.

Her mind went back to her first sight of Tony, when he'd come to the ranch to see Stasia about a painting he'd seen at the local art gallery. He'd been immediately hostile. She'd wondered why at the time. Now she understood. He'd wanted her even that first day, but he'd held her at bay with sarcasm and insults and avoidance.

Honestly, she'd been equally antagonistic. But she'd adored him almost at once. He was the stuff of dreams, big and handsome and afraid of nothing on earth. She loved a man who wasn't intimidated by the pressure to soften his image to satisfy some ethereal ideal of what modern men should be. He was tough, but he was also tender. Not a man who'd ever hurt a woman or threaten her in any way.

He hadn't liked her, but when she'd been airsick on that trip to the ranch back home, he'd picked her up and cradled her in his arms until she slept. He'd been nurturing, although reluctantly, from the beginning.

He was a tough guy, but never mean. That was a far cry from a man who thought being rough with a woman was the way to behave. He didn't talk much about his father, but she'd gathered that he was physically abusive to Tony when he was a boy—probably to his mother as well. Tony had loved his mother. Odalie was curious about his family, about all of it. The ones she'd met so far were really good people.

They ate in the next night, with leftover rolls and steak and mashed potatoes.

"You're as good as my Mrs. Murdock in the kitchen," Tony said as he finished his meal.

She laughed. "Thanks. But I'm not quite in her class yet!"

"Almost." He grinned.

"There's pie for dessert. I peeked." Ben laughed when they stared at him.

"Let's save it for later," Tony said. "I'm too full for dessert right now. We can watch a movie."

"I got a new game," Ben protested.

"Well, go play it, then," he said. "But first, what did you find out from Rudy?"

"Just what we suspected. The guy took a powder. We can't find him. But we've got feelers out," he added.

Tony sighed. "We know the trail will lead back to DC."

"Of course," Ben replied. "Where else?"

"I'll have to go home eventually," Odalie pointed out. "And I have that audition date just before Thanksgiving…" She thought suddenly and sadly that she'd go home for Thanksgiving, as she did every year. Tony wouldn't be there. He probably went to New Jersey to have the traditional meal with his family.

"Hey, what's wrong?" Tony asked, watching her face. "Don't you want to sing at the Met?" he added, trying to tease but feeling miserable for reasons he wasn't sure about. Her whole life had been dedicated to singing there, and she had a unique talent. He should be encouraging her, not thinking of reasons for her to postpone the audition—which was what he was doing, to his shame.

"Oh, I was just thinking about Thanksgiving. On the ranch." She lowered her eyes to her coffee cup. They were sad.

Tony felt that sadness. "Mrs. Murdock goes home to her family for Thanksgiving and Christmas," Tony said surprisingly. "He—" he pointed at Ben "—goes back to Jersey to spend it with his dad."

She lifted her eyes to his. "Where do you go?" she asked.

He shrugged. "To a restaurant, usually. The family down in Jersey gets together, but I have issues with a few of them, so I try to avoid the conflicts…"

"You could come home with me," she interrupted and then flushed at her own rush of enthusiasm.

He smiled slowly. "I could? Wouldn't your folks mind?"

"Oh, no, of course they wouldn't!" she said. Her eyes were wide with hope.

He studied her flushed face with delight. "I'd like that," he said, his voice deep and husky.

"My dad's flying out to Oregon to have Thanksgiving with my brother and his wife," Ben said with a long, sad sigh. "So I guess I'll have dinner out somewhere, alone, all by myself, with no company, at a table by myself…"

"Oh, for heaven's sake, you can come, too!" Odalie burst out laughing. "Mercedes would love it! And she cooks this enormous meal with all sorts of breads and vegetables and meats…!"

Ben beamed. "That would be nice!"

"So that's settled," Tony said. "You'll have to call your folks in time to warn them," he added with twinkling eyes.

"They won't mind. Honest they won't. Just don't upset John," she added with a mischievous grin.

He frowned. "John?"

"Worms?" she added with raised eyebrows.

Ben and Tony both chuckled.

They found an action movie about commandos to watch, with Odalie curled up beside Tony on the sofa, her cheek resting on his broad chest over the silky shirt he was wearing.

It felt so good to be close to him, to feel his strength and warmth against her. She couldn't bear to think ahead even one day. Tony had become her whole world.

When the movie went off, he turned off the television and dimmed the lights. The fireplace was blazing with gas logs. In the semidarkness of the room, it was comforting.

"I love gas logs," she said, closing her eyes. "It's like having an open fireplace but without the work."

He chuckled. "Yes, it is."

"What was your mother like?" she asked softly.

He sighed and pulled her closer. "She was a lot like yours," he replied. "She was a sweet, gentle little woman. She'd married my father because, well, because that's mostly how things were done. You married into other families to connect them to yours. But she got a bad bargain. My father had a gunpowder temper and no real conscience that we could ever find. He beat her up for nothing. He'd make up a reason if he didn't have one."

She looked up at him. His face was like stone. "I'm sorry. I didn't mean to bring back bad memories."

He shrugged. "We live with the past. It never goes away. Luckily, he wasn't home much. He had his hands in several of the rackets. He hung out with a couple of his guys in a local bar most of the time. He didn't come around much after I hit my growth spurt," he added with faint satisfaction.

"Why?"

"He drew back his fist and hit my mother when I just walked in the door. I beat the hell out of him. He was barely able to crawl out to his car. I told him what would happen if he ever touched her again. By then, I had a reputation of my own." He looked down at her with dark, cold eyes that chilled. "I never bluff."

"You came out of it well, though," she said, searching his eyes.

Both eyebrows went up. He stared at her.

"You have your own business. You're an entrepreneur. You're cultured, you have the respect of people around you and you can afford to live the way you please." She leaned her head back against his shoulder and smiled. "I imagine your father could never say that."

He laughed shortly. "No. I guess he couldn't."

Her eyes went to the portrait of him over the mantel and she adored it. "I've never seen a painting that was so alive," she said. "It's like a synopsis of your life."

"You think so?"

"The cross on your watch fob." She pointed at it.

"My mother's," he said. "She wore it all her life. I keep it on my pocket watch. I don't wear it much these days, just on very special occasions."

"She'd like that, I think."

He nodded. "She would. She prayed for me every day. She was so afraid I'd end up like my old man. It was a real possibility at the time," he added.

"Doing bad things like your dad?" she asked.

He shook his head and looked down at her. "Being found in the trunk of a car down by the docks."

13

Odalie wasn't quick enough to disguise her sudden intake of breath.

He smoothed back a strand of her long blond hair. "Nobody grieved much at my house," he confessed. "It turns out that he got greedy and was pulling some dough off the top before he turned in his take." He kissed her nose. "The big guys don't tolerate that without a really good reason. My dad didn't have one. Just greed. And he'd insulted one of the lieutenants who took orders from the big boss down in Jersey."

"It's all very complicated."

He smiled. "You have no idea." He stared at her. "And you won't. One of the cardinal rules is that you don't discuss business with family members who aren't involved in it."

"Did your mother know what he did?"

"She didn't. Not for sure. When the cops came to get him now and then, she was always quick to say that she was a housewife and knew nothing about how Jackie did business or even who he did it with."

"Did it work?"

"It did. The cops were local boys who grew up in the neighborhood. They knew her family. They knew her. She almost married one of the cops. Big Irish guy with a red nose and a wild sense of humor. We all liked him."

"Past tense?" she asked, fishing.

He shrugged. "He was pulling over a speeding car. Got out to give a ticket and dropped dead of a heart attack right at the driver's side door."

"Oh, gosh!"

"My mother grieved. She said she wished she'd married him when he asked. For a long time, I was as much a victim as she was. It's hard on kids, having a violent parent. He liked drugs, too, and that made it worse."

"I guess I had it pretty good, growing up."

"Your family is terrific," he said. "My grandparents were like your parents. They were good people. They had nothing to do with anything outside the law. Maybe if I'd been left with them, I'd have turned out better."

"There's nothing wrong with you," she said indignantly.

He studied her curiously. "You can't have been around Stasia all this time without knowing something about my past."

"Of course not."

He scowled. "And it doesn't bother you?"

"It does," she confessed. "Because I kept hearing about the death threats against you."

He was fascinated. "I meant the things I've done."

She searched his eyes. "I worried about what might happen to you," she said simply, and flushed when he kept staring.

"Even though you just tolerated me while all that business was going on, when you were in danger."

"I tolerated you because I could have eaten you like candy, even then," he said gruffly.

Her heart raced. He drew her up closer and bent to her mouth, then kissed her slowly, insistently, his lips demanding but tender, nurturing. Her hand slid up to his hard cheek and rested there while she drowned in joy.

He lifted his head, his breath a little quick. "You missed those first steps with boys and went in headfirst with me," he said huskily. "I hope you don't regret it."

She shook her head slowly, searching his face with eyes that adored it. "No way."

"One day…" he began.

She put her fingers over his sensual mouth and smiled. "There isn't any 'one day,'" she pointed out. "There's today. Right now."

He chuckled softly and kissed her again. "Okay. That's the way we'll play it."

She curled up against him. She'd never been so happy in her whole life.

His big hand tangled softly in her hair. He felt the same way. His life had been empty until now. He'd had women in it, he'd made lots of money. But there hadn't been this incredible joy, this feeling of warmth that burst inside him. Women had never had such an effect on him. He'd loved his first wife, but even that experience hadn't had this intensity. Everything felt new and bright and shiny.

He glanced at the thin gold watch on his wrist. "I have to make a couple of phone calls and then I'm going to turn in." He got up and pulled her up and kissed her to within an inch of her life.

When he let go, she was breathless and her were eyes were so bright with joy that they almost blinded him.

He smiled slowly. He loved her reaction to him. "What would you like to do on the weekend?" he asked. "Ballet? Broadway show? Opera?"

"Anything," she whispered, her eyes riveted to his. "As long as we go together."

His heart jumped. He'd been so careful to keep her at arm's length, but now he was really in over his head. There was no way out. And he didn't care. He was happier than he'd ever been.

He sighed. "Okay. We'll decide in the morning."

"Have you heard from Mrs. Murdock?"

He nodded. "She called earlier, when I was answering calls in the office," he said. "They're still running tests and talking to specialists." He touched her soft mouth. "It's just as well. I'm not ready for you to leave."

She grinned.

He bent and kissed her nose. "Go to sleep."

"You, too."

He let her go. "We'll go walking in the park in the morning, how about that? Unless you'd rather go shopping?"

She shook her head. "Walking is nice, especially on days when it's just a little nippy and the leaves are turning. I love this time of year!" She sighed. "The only thing I love more is when the Christmas decorations go up. I love to see the bright colors everywhere, and the big Christmas tree over the ice-skating rink. The holidays back home are lovely, but New York is flashy. I adore it!"

He laughed as he watched her face. She was always so enthusiastic about things that pleased her. She made him feel as if he had champagne in his veins.

It was an odd sensation. He didn't pay a lot of attention to it, of course. They could live for the moment, just for a week or two. But reality would soon come to invade the new and exciting relationship they were enjoying. He knew, as she didn't, that there was no future for an ingenue with a man like him. Everything was against them. But he was going to enjoy her as long as he could. Later, when he was alone again, he'd have memories as sweet as candy canes.

The park was gorgeous. The maple trees were just starting to show a little color here and there. Before too much longer, they'd be decked out in yellow and orange leaves, bright as paint splashed on canvas. The wind was just nippy enough to be pleasant without chilling bones inside overcoats.

"I used to hear about New York City when I was little. I thought all of New York State was one big city."

He chuckled. "A lot of people think like that."

"Yes," she agreed, nuzzling close to let a faster walker go by. "People used to say it was unfriendly, too, but it's not. Once you're here for a while, you get to know the people who live around you. It's like a lot of little neighborhoods put together."

"It is." He had her hand in his while they walked. It felt good just to be with her.

She glanced up at him with loving eyes, which she tried to hide. "I really hate to bring it up. But what about Phillip James?"

He stopped and turned to her with a long sigh. "I suppose I can tell you. He's one of those annoying variables that you have to add into every equation," he said after a minute. "Right now, we're playing politics with him. I have an acquaintance who sits on the intelligence committee. He was going to schedule a hearing and I had him protected from blackmail attempts by James to stop it. But he's got a daughter with problems." He smiled sadly. "It's amazing how many people can be blackmailed."

"He can't be responsible for what his child does. Can he?" Then she remembered her own time with the law and how her poor parents stood to be prosecuted with her while both sides tried to find a compromise.

"He can," he replied. "In politics, you never know what sort of scandal can cost you your position. When you're a congressman, you're even more vulnerable, especially if your constituents are conservatives. His are."

"Is he a good person?"

He shrugged. "He keeps his word, and he doesn't take kickbacks. That makes him a good person, in my book. But he had his hand in a particularly nasty pie when I saved your older brother from James and convinced him to help. I managed to get rid of the evidence that would have convicted him back then, but his daughter put him right back on the firing line." He studied her pretty face. "We give hostages to fate when we love." He laughed shortly. "Funny. A politician said that, back in the sixties. It's still true today."

"Isn't there any way to get him before a judge?" she asked.

"I'm looking for one. It takes time."

She sighed as she looked up at him, her eyes soft with feeling, her face faintly flushed from the cool wind and excitement at being near him.

"You'll ruin me," he said suddenly, taking her by the waist and pulling her gently closer.

"How?" she wondered aloud.

"The way you look at me," he said, his eyes falling to her soft mouth. "You make me feel taller."

She laughed. "Can I help it if you're gorgeous?"

"You're the gorgeous one," he said, smiling. "Everywhere we go, you turn heads. Good thing I'm not the jealous type." Actually he was, but he hoped it didn't show. It was never a good idea to let a woman know how she affected you.

She let her eyes fall so he wouldn't see the disappointment in them. "Yes," she said.

He looked over her head. "What about that audition at the Met?"

Her heart jumped and ran away. She felt panic from the toes upward. Everybody thought it was just the audition that made her jittery, that kept her awake nights. Nobody but Stasia knew the truth. She'd kept it hidden even from her mother, all this time. It was why she hadn't gone the traditional route to the Met, with competition at the district level and then at the Met itself. Instead, she had an agent to present her, along with the requisite materials that included an unaugmented tape of herself singing two arias.

It was easy to sing in a studio. Even to sing in the choir. Or to sing in competition at smaller venues.

But it took a whole different kind of attitude to get up in front of hundreds of opera fans who knew the works letter by letter and impress them. It took guts to face reviewers who wouldn't take into consideration a small-town girl's hidden fears. It took even more guts to do that night after night after night, in some of the biggest cities on earth. Because it might mean a trip overseas to sing in operas there as well as just at the Met in New York.

"You're so quiet," Tony said. "What's wrong?"

She forced a smile to her lips. "Nothing. I was just thinking about the audition, and my voice lessons."

"Listen, you sing like an angel," he said softly. "There's no question of getting picked to sing at Lincoln Center, you hear me? You'll be turning down venues. I've never heard a voice like yours, and I know opera."

She sighed as she met his dark, warm eyes. "I'm just being jumpy, that's all," she confessed.

"Stop being jumpy. How about a cappuccino and a panino?"

"A panini?" she corrected.

He made a face. "Panino is singular. Panini is plural. Both mean a sandwich."

"Oh!" She learned operas in Italian by rote memorization. Her ability with languages was another sticking point. She had trouble with even the most basic grammar. She studied hard, but her mind wasn't tuned to foreign tongues.

"So. You learned some new Italian. We'll get coffee and a sandwich. Singular. Not plural."

She laughed with pure delight. He was so much fun to be with. She adored him and hoped it didn't show. He liked her in bed, but he was no different away from it. She was head over heels, but Tony was used to women, and he didn't react the same way Odalie did. He was fond of her, of course, but what she wanted was something wilder, deeper, eternal. She felt that way. He didn't.

There was a song about love. It expressed the certainty that you couldn't make somebody love you. As she stared into Tony's dark eyes, she felt an emptiness that all earth's oceans couldn't fill.

"Now you look all sad," he chided.

"I'm just hungry," she said lightly. It was true. She was hungry for something other than food, however. "And I'd love a sandwich, singular, with a coffee." She grinned.

He turned her around and they started back down the path.

"I'd love to go to the park in warm weather," she said. "And maybe feed the ducks."

He sipped cappuccino. "We'll put that on the agenda," he said easily.

Her heart jumped and she smiled. That sounded hopeful. Summer was a long way away. He was looking forward. It gave her hope.

"Not too long until Christmas," he mused. "What would you like Santa to bring you? Diamonds? Pearls? A Ferrari?"

She stared at him and just smiled. "I already have diamonds and pearls and a very fast red Jaguar." She cocked her head and studied him. "I'd like more days like this with you. That's all." She ducked her head and sipped coffee so that he wouldn't see that she really wasn't teasing.

He chuckled. "Okay," he replied. He was trying not to look as pleased as he was. Her feelings for him were blatant. They made him feel as if he could conquer the world.

She peered at him over her cup. He looked...different somehow. Younger. More carefree. Gone was the somber, antagonistic man she'd known for so long.

She grinned. "Okay, then."

"You never answered me about the rest of the weekend," he said. "Opera? Ballet? Broadway?"

"You choose," she said. "I love all those things." She made a face. "Broadway, not so much, though. Really, I'm not big on musicals."

His eyebrows arched. "You're serious?"

She nodded.

"Why?"

She made a face. "It's frivolous music."

He burst out laughing.

"Well, it is." She defended herself. "Opera is exquisite. It's like angels singing. But Broadway is..." She shrugged.

"Frivolous music," he repeated, and his dark eyes flashed with humor. "I'll have to remember that."

"While we're out, we need a few things to make supper," she said.

He smiled slowly. He loved working in the kitchen with her. "Okay."

She sighed as she finished her coffee. "You're so much fun to be with," she said without looking at him.

His big, beautiful hand reached across the table and caught hers in a warm clasp. "So are you, beautiful."

It was a moment out of time. She looked into his eyes and got lost. So did he. In the middle of the exchange of glances, a deep voice interrupted them.

"Cappuccino and sandwiches for lunch?"

They looked up. Dane Hunter, the US marshal who'd helped save Tony from a murder charge, grinned at them.

"Sit down and have some yourself," Tony invited.

"Not on my salary," he chuckled, pulling up a chair.

"My treat," Tony said.

Hunter glared at him. "I don't take bribes."

"I can see the headlines now," Tony mused. "US marshal bribed by former mob boss with panini and cappuccino…"

"You know what I mean," the other man chuckled.

"Yes, I do, sadly," Tony replied. "The media would have a field day."

"Back in my father's day, the media had real journalists who told the truth. Now truth is whatever doesn't hurt somebody's feelings."

"You're getting poetic," Tony accused.

He sighed. "I guess so."

"Is your dad still working security for Ritter Oil?"

He nodded. "He can't outrun the bad guys anymore, but he hires men who can," he chuckled. "Colby Lane's still there, too."

"Old man Ritter's a card."

He nodded. "His son isn't bad, either. There are rumors that he'll take over the company when his dad retires. He'll do a good job."

"Any feedback about James?" Tony asked, lowering his voice.

He nodded. "That sympathy card might not have been your best idea."

Tony grinned. "Come on. It was funny. Admit it."

"I guess it was," Hunter chuckled. "But it stoked the fires. He's got Peters out beating the bushes for ways to put the hurt on Tanner Everett."

Odalie's faint gasp was audible.

"Don't worry," Hunter told her gently. "He's got more security than the president right now. James would have to be insane to go after him. But you and your sister-in-law are easier targets."

"Covered," Tony said. "I put on extra people."

Hunter's dark eyes narrowed. "Background checks?"

He scowled. "Of course background checks. Ben hired an agency to… Okay, what the hell do you mean?" He'd put his coffee down with a thud and his eyes were intent and unblinking.

"One of the men your man was going to hire won't pass a background check. Peters gifted him a clean background, did a little computer work and sent him to Ben."

Tony was cursing in Italian under his breath.

"It's okay. Ben doesn't seem to trust anybody because he hired another agency to vet the agency he hired first." He chuckled and shook his head. "Damn, he's good. I wish he worked for me."

Tony was relaxing a little. "That's why he works for me."

"He was something as a wrestler, too. I sort of miss seeing him in the ring."

"Me, too."

Hunter chuckled, because Tony and Odalie spoke at the same time and then looked at each other and laughed.

"Don't tell me. You like wrestling."

She nodded enthusiastically. "I have an autographed photo of Ben from his wrestling days. My dad took me to Dallas to see a match when I was in school."

He just stared at her. "Rodeo, wrestling, couture and skeet shooting medals. Miss Everett, you are unique."

"Very, and kindly look in some other direction," Tony mused, although his eyes were twinkling.

He shrugged. "No need to worry about me. I'm off women for the next hundred years, at least." He got to his feet. "If I hear anything else, I'll let you know. Meanwhile, double-check everybody."

"You know it."

They watched him leave. As he had before, Tony dialed a number and related the meeting. He chuckled as he hung up.

"I'm just confirming it," he told Odalie. "There's no such thing as privacy in my line of work. I want everybody clued in that I'm no stool pigeon."

"Well, that's obvious," she replied with a smile. "No feathers," she whispered.

He chuckled.

Nights were getting harder to endure. Odalie hadn't hungered for a man in her whole life before Tony, because she had no idea what people were talking about when they mentioned passion. But now she did know, and she was starving to death for him.

But they cooked together, watched TV together and then went to bed separately, because Ben was always around. As Tony whispered to her one evening after supper, Ben had ears like a lynx.

However, the abstention was working on Tony as well. One afternoon after they'd gone walking in the park, they ended up at her apartment with the phones turned off and the doors locked while they indulged in several hours of the most intense passion either had ever known.

Tony groaned as he shuddered over her one last time, after a marathon of intimacy that left them both satiated and exhausted.

She sprawled half on his body and half off, shivering in the aftermath.

"It just gets better and better," she moaned, because every time she moved, it was like a little climax, she was so sensitized.

"And better," he agreed huskily. His big hand smoothed over her silky skin, pressing her body close on his. "I was starving to death."

"So was I." She sighed. "It really is like eating potato chips."

His hand tangled in her long hair as he fought to calm his heartbeat and his breathing. "And it's a good thing I'm sterile or you'd probably be very pregnant right now. Then where would your opera career be, Miss Everett?" he teased lightly.

She sighed. Her cheek moved against the soft hair over the hard muscle of his chest. "Babies are sweet," she said softly. "But I guess you're right."

His heart jumped. "You like kids?"

"Yes." She kissed his chest. "I like opera, too, though," she added so that he wouldn't feel that she was chiding him for his lack of fertility.

His eyes were quiet and sad as they studied the ceiling. "I would have loved kids," he said quietly. "It just wasn't in the books."

"Life gives us some things and takes others away. I think it evens out, though."

"Yeah."

She yawned. "And now I'm sleepy."

He laughed. "Me, too. At least we don't have to worry about Ben overhearing us."

"I never knew it would be like this," she confessed. "I mean, it's almost like an obsession. You get so hungry...!" She flushed and stopped the words.

"It is an obsession," he agreed. "The sweetest obsession in the world." He kissed the top of her head. "I don't know how I lived before you came along."

Her lips parted on a quick breath. Had she really heard him say that?

His arms drew her closer. "One day at a time—isn't that your mantra?" he teased. "It works for me, too. But I can't live on leftover passion," he added at her ear. "After all, we have to have something to look forward to." He rolled her over and kissed her hungrily. "Feast after famine," he whispered into her softly swollen mouth. "And I fear we've feasted too enthusiastically. Again."

She looked up at him with warm, loving eyes. "I don't care," she said huskily. "It's worth it."

He brushed the damp hair away from her face. "I don't like hurting you," he said seriously. "I have to learn to be less enthusiastic when we're together. I'm sorry. I should have stopped sooner."

"I didn't want to stop and you didn't hurt me," she denied, her arms wreathed around his neck. "I love being with you like this. I love it that you want me so much." She swallowed, hard, and lowered her eyes to his chest. "I want you… all the time," she confessed, her voice so soft that he had to strain to hear it.

He groaned as he bent to her mouth and kissed her with a tender intensity that made tears spring in her eyes. "It's like that with me, too," he whispered. "Even when you're not with me, you're still with me."

"Yes."

He wrapped her up tight and just held her for the longest time. He couldn't conceive of a life without her. But she had a unique talent, one that she'd spent her whole life nurturing so that she could sing at the Met. It wasn't fair to her to keep her here like this, with no commitment, to…use her.

He hated the way that sounded. He really wasn't using her. He adored her. She'd become as necessary to him as breathing. But he kept his feelings hidden, under control. He didn't want to influence her choices. She should be free to do what she wanted with her life.

Maybe one day he'd have a chance to keep her, somewhere down the line. But he couldn't force her to choose a life with him, not with all their differences. He felt guilty that he'd pushed it like this, that he hadn't been able to resist her.

He really hadn't. He'd ached for her, and not just for a few weeks. Ever since his first sight of her, he'd been obsessed with her. She was the icing on the cake, the angel on top of the Christmas tree. She was…the whole world.

But he couldn't tell her that. It wasn't fair. Right now, she was caught up in her first love affair, and she was saturated with hunger for him. It would wear off, as obsessions did.

Then where would they be? She had opera, which was her life's work.

He had…well, he had work, too. But his work would never make up for the lack of Odalie in his life.

Even if opera would make up for the lack of him in her life. It was something that had to be faced.

But not right now. Not today.

He rolled onto his side and curled her soft body into his. And they fell asleep, with nothing resolved.

14

And so, they rocked on for three weeks, while Mrs. Murdock's mother survived surgery and rehab, and while Tony and Odalie grew closer by the day. But it wasn't just a physical closeness. Odalie loved being with him. He was funny and full of stories about things that had happened to him, about the gallery and art that he'd purchased, about his travels. She listened to him by the hour, loving just his company.

Inevitably, they spent time in the bedroom, mostly at her apartment because of Ben's excellent hearing. But even as they grew closer, Tony slowly started them drifting apart. She had the audition upcoming, and he was as nervous as she was. He wanted her to have her shot at the Met. But he hated letting her go. His life would be empty. It was selfish, feeling like that, but he couldn't help it. She'd become the light in his darkness. How would he see when she left him?

The audition was less harrowing than she'd thought it

would be. She passed it with flying colors, and she was even given a part in the holiday production. It wasn't a big part, but it was a singing part.

The only thing was that she threw up when she got home, and had to take a tranquilizer as well. The thought of being onstage in a production, even in a minor role, was horrifying to her.

This was why she'd never really pushed herself. She'd done the visiting young artist programs back home, she'd sung in the church choir, but those performances weren't for the Met. They were, however, just as terrifying.

She'd talked to her therapist back home about her inability to cope with the reality of performing in front of people, that it never got easier, that the terror never left her. He'd suggested hypnotherapy, but she didn't want to mess with her mind. And then he'd suggested that she might just do operatic recordings, if she felt she really couldn't manage the overwhelming stage fright.

She'd spoken with her doctor as well. He'd advised her to think long and hard about applying that sort of continual stress to her life. If she was really that afraid of performing in front of a live audience, the rewards might not be worth the price she'd pay. He knew how well she sang; he was always encouraging her to use her voice. But he reminded her that a career should be something approached with joy, not stark terror. All the authorities said that stage fright could be controlled, even eliminated. There were case histories, however, of people who finally gave up their dreams of stardom just to lose the constant stress and upset.

Lastly, she spoke to her mother, finally, about the problem. Heather had never had stage fright. She loved performing. But she'd known singers who'd had to give it up because they became alcoholics or addicts, due to the enormous stress of doing something that frightened them constantly. It was an individual thing. Heather could advise, but it was going to be up to Odalie to decide if she wanted to spend the next decades of her life being terrified every time she walked onto a stage.

There was one last consideration as well, but she couldn't confide in anyone about it. She loved Tony. She'd never felt such a passion for any man alive, and she knew in her heart that she never would again. She was a one-man woman.

If it came to a choice between life with Tony and a career on the stage, Tony would win hands down, just as Cole Everett had when Heather'd had to make the same choice. It had been harder for Heather, too, because she was already well-known in her profession.

Odalie had already decided that if Tony asked her to stay with him, she'd agree. But he hadn't asked. If anything, he'd become more distant as the days went by. She knew he still wanted her, but he didn't come with her to her apartment alone anymore. And while he still kissed her, it was almost as if he did it for appearances more than because he wanted to. The incredible closeness they'd shared in the beginning was slipping away, like an unanchored ship being pulled out to sea. Odalie didn't know what to do, how to keep from losing Tony. And he wouldn't talk about their relationship. If she even tried to discuss it, he changed the subject. She was feeling less confident about the future.

As the first performance approached, Odalie was fitted for a costume. She told the folks back home when she'd be on-stage. They were all overjoyed for her, especially Heather, who'd once wanted a career in opera as well. But Heather had chosen love over career. She wasn't sorry.

Odalie had the same choice to make. Heather had heard from Stasia that things had really heated up between Tony and Odalie.

She wondered if her daughter was being tormented with the same choices that she'd faced when she was even younger than Odalie was now. It was a hard decision to make between love and a career. And it was a very private choice. She didn't interfere. She did wonder if Odalie would be happy without Tony if she decided on her career. Having seen the two of them together, she was convinced that neither would thrive if they went their separate ways. Even when they'd been at the ranch, they looked like two halves of a whole.

Besides that, there was Odalie's fear of going on the stage. It was much more than just stage fright, which could be conquered. It was an actual phobia that even years of therapy hadn't lessened. What sort of life would that be? Odalie had a beautiful voice. She did. But if she was going to spend her career being scared out of her mind night after night, that was no sort of life. Better she married Tony and sang in church on Sundays. Considering how Odalie spoke about Tony these days, her daughter wanted him much more than she wanted a career.

Mrs. Murdock was due home the next day, and Tony had become remote. He was the perfect host, welcoming and enjoying working in the kitchen with Odalie. But he'd stopped gathering her into his arms at every opportunity or even kissing her from time to time. He was more like a big brother now.

She didn't understand. Ben wasn't around all the time, so that wasn't an excuse, either. It was like Tony was having second thoughts.

"Do I have to go?" Odalie asked after they'd cleared away the supper dishes.

"You do," he said with a breezy smile. "Mrs. Murdock will be giving us hard looks. Not that Ben would give us away. But it would be awkward."

"Oh." She sighed, her sad eyes glancing off Tony's, while he pretended not to have a care in the world. "Well, then I guess…"

The doorbell rang.

"I'll get it," Tony said, because he knew who it was. He'd called her.

He'd done a lot of soul searching. He couldn't jeopardize Odalie's career because he wanted her. She had a voice that was a gift. What could he offer to balance the Met? He was older than she was, he had a cold and dangerous past, and he couldn't give her kids. He'd lived in dreams for the past few weeks, but it wasn't fair to her. He wanted the world for her. And she was never going to leave of her own accord. She thought she loved him, but that was just because she had nobody to compare him with. She'd meet men, nice men, as she progressed in opera. Young men who could give her kids, who could give her a good, clean character.

No, he couldn't be selfish, even if it was going to be like amputating a limb without anesthetic. He had to let her go. Make her go. And this was how he was going to do it.

He opened the door. "Mauve," he said, then caught her up in his arms and kissed her hungrily.

She kissed him back and then laughed and protested, patting her hair back into place.

Tony put an arm around her and led her into the living room, where a pale Odalie was standing like a young statue in her sweats.

"Odalie, this is Mauve," he said, introducing them. "*Cara*," he told Mauve, "you remember that I've mentioned my adopted daughter's best friend, Odalie? She's going to sing at the Met. Ben and I had her over for the night while we got some more protection at her apartment." His face hardened. "She had a peeping tom."

Nice lies, Tony, Odalie was thinking. She forced a smile. "It was kind of Mr. Garza to look out for me," she agreed, not missing the way Tony flinched when she said that. She smiled at Mauve. "Ben and one of his guys took care of my problem so I can go home now!"

Mauve laughed, apparently not noticing any undercurrents. "Ben can take care of most problems all by himself."

"Yes, he can. Well, I'll get my bag…" Odalie began.

"Ben, drive her home, and make sure you check around the place first, you hear me?" Tony added.

"You bet, boss!"

Tony sat down on the couch with Mauve. "So, tell me about the ballet you saw," he began.

Odalie didn't say a word all the way home. She just sat, like somebody in a trance. In one hour, her entire world had collapsed. She could hardly believe how quickly it happened. What had she done to make Tony turn his back on her so completely? Was he afraid that she was getting too attached to him? Did he have cold feet about the future?

She had no idea what was going on. And that woman. She knew who Mauve was. She was Tony's girlfriend.

They pulled up at Odalie's apartment. Ben was on his walkie-talkie as he opened the back door, talking to one of his men.

He walked Odalie to her door, carrying her bag. He put it down just inside the front door.

"If you hear anything, you call me, okay?" he asked quietly. "You've got my number on speed dial, yeah?"

"I do," she said. She forced a smile. "Thanks for bringing me home."

He shrugged. He grimaced. "You take care."

"You, too."

She smiled and closed the door behind him. She went into the bedroom and put on her gown, climbed under the covers and cried her eyes out.

It had been almost three weeks since Tony had invited Mauve over as Odalie was leaving his apartment. Odalie had gone home for Thanksgiving. Tony and Ben had planned to go with her originally, but Ben had called. In a subdued, reluctant voice, he said he was sorry, but the boss was spending the holiday with Mauve and Ben was going to Jersey to have dinner with Tony's cousin Connie and her family.

It broke Odalie's already shattered heart. But it was just one thing more to prove that Tony had put her out of his life.

She wished Ben a happy Thanksgiving and hung up, tears in her eyes. Even though she'd half expected Tony to back out, it was painful. She remembered lying in his arms, being kissed so hungrily that she thought her passion would set them both ablaze. She remembered sitting next to him while they watched movies, walking beside him as they went around town, looking at the holiday decorations that were already going up, holding hands in the nippy cold wind.

And here she was, on Thanksgiving, sitting back home with her family, pretending to enjoy herself. While inside, she was slowly being smothered by sweet memories of another time, another place. It was the most painful holiday she'd ever had. The Brannts came over to visit and she and

Maddie talked about the Met, but Odalie's heart wasn't really in it. It was almost a relief to get aboard the big jet and go back to New York.

Odalie was rushing around to get ready for her first performance, while her family lounged in her living room trying to help her keep her cool.

"Don't go loopy," Stasia laughed as Odalie picked up and discarded the same skirt twice. "Just put on anything. You'll have to change into a costume at the Met anyway!"

"I know. I'm just…" She looked at Stasia with eyes tormented with anguish.

Stasia understood more than Odalie realized, because she'd talked to Ben earlier. She drew her back into the bedroom while the others were talking.

"What happened?" she asked solemnly, because there had been little opportunity to talk at the ranch on Thanksgiving for all the visitors.

Odalie sighed. "I don't know. We were a couple, really a couple, for weeks, and then, all at once, he started distancing himself. Finally, he had Mauve come over and he kissed her in front of me and sent me home." She looked up at Stasia. "It's like whiplash, only worse. I don't know what I did wrong."

Stasia hugged her. "Men are hard to understand. Tony especially."

"He had second thoughts," Odalie said quietly. "That's not hard."

Stasia sighed. "Well, we aren't going to let it ruin your first performance, now are we?" she asked with a sympathetic smile. "Not after you've worked so hard for so long to get here."

Odalie looked at her with wide, wild eyes. "If I can just manage not to throw up onstage…!"

"Odalie, if this isn't what you want, you should tell them," she said softly, meaning the family.

"They've all sacrificed for it," she argued. "All the voice lessons, the travel, the expenses…!"

"They love you. So do I," Stasia replied. "None of us want you to do something that threatens your health. You know that."

She looked down at her feet. "It's all I have left," she said in a faint whisper. "I thought I had Tony…"

"You're going to go onstage and give a magnificent performance," Stasia assured her. "You're not going to even think about Tony. Not tonight. Got that?"

Odalie looked at her and managed a wan smile. "I'm not going to think about Tony," she agreed.

And the fates laughed.

Everyone was seated. Odalie was backstage in her costume and makeup, trembling with fear, almost in tears as she heard the murmur of the enormous crowd outside the curtains.

"Odalie!"

She actually jumped as she heard Stasia's urgent voice.

She went to her quickly, surprised. "Stasia, you can't…!"

"Tony's been shot." Stasia's face was white, and she'd been crying.

Odalie's gasp was audible. "When? How? Is he alive?!"

"I don't know. Ben said they took him to the nearest ER…"

"We have to go, right now…!!"

"But you're going onstage," Stasia protested.

Odalie was already running toward the stage manager. She was back in two minutes, headed for the dressing room. Stasia followed her, still crying, and waited while she got into her street clothes and grabbed her coat.

"But you'll lose your chance," Stasia sobbed as they started out the stage door.

"I don't care," Odalie said recklessly. "Where's Ben?"

"I'll call him…"

"He has to be alive," Odalie was whispering to herself. "Even if he ends up with someone else, he has to live. Please, God, he must live, he must…!" Her voice broke. In all her life, Odalie had never been so terrified, not even on the stage in front of hundreds of people. If Tony died, what would she do? How would she live?

Please let him live, even if I have to lose him to another woman, Odalie prayed silently. *Even if I have to do that. Just let him live!*

Stasia managed to text Heather while Ben was pulling up at the curb, saying only Tony had been shot and they were en route to the hospital and assured Heather that Ben would protect them both—there was no need for Tanner and Cole and John to come after them. Heather sent a reluctant Okay. Talk later.

The women dived in the back before Ben could even get out to open the door for them.

"Go!" Stasia called to him. "Where is he? How is he?"

"I don't know," Ben groaned. "All I got was a message from my guy that he was shot, and they took him to the nearest ER," he added, naming the hospital. "It's only a few blocks away. One of my guys is going to get his butt kicked for this!"

"I'll help," Stasia said, her voice breaking.

"Hey, now you calm down," Ben said gently. "You've got a baby to worry about."

Stasia's hand was on her belly. "I know. Who did this to Tony?!"

"That James man," Odalie said through her teeth.

"I don't think so," Ben replied.

"But he was out for blood," Odalie said, her own voice unsteady.

"Yeah, but he was after your people," he told her, "not the boss."

"There was that interloper that tried to finger Tony for a murder he didn't commit," Stasia said. "The New York bunch."

"Just what I was thinking," Ben said. "So, I called Teddy."

"Good." Stasia's voice was harsh. "There will be retribution. I just hope Tony's still…"

"Boss is tough," Ben said through his teeth.

"Yes," Stasia said.

She reached out and took Odalie's cold hand in hers. Odalie wasn't saying much, but her face was pasty white and her eyes were huge.

"We'll know something soon," Stasia assured her. "Just hold on."

Odalie nodded, too choked with fear to speak.

They piled out of the car at the emergency room entrance and hurried in past EMTs and police and civilians milling around.

They'd just turned the corner where the admission desk was located when they spotted Tony walking toward them, ruffled and with blood on the white shirt under his suit coat, but walking.

"Oh, thank God!" Odalie whispered.

"Yes!" Stasia said.

"Boss!" Ben called as the three of them surged toward him.

Tony looked at them and then at Odalie with horror on his face. "What the hell are you doing here?" he demanded.

"You're debuting at the Met tonight! Mauve and I were on the way there when someone started shooting near the subway entrance. He shot two of us before the police tackled him."

"It wasn't an attempted hit?" Ben asked under his breath.

"Not tonight," Tony replied. "What are you two doing here?" he asked again.

Stasia grimaced. "We thought you were killed," she groaned, and hugged him.

"Not hardly," he replied. He glared at Odalie. "You get right back over to Lincoln Center and get on the stage!"

Before Odalie could even speak, Mauve came out of the restroom, drawing her mink coat close. "Why do they keep it so cold in here? Oh, hello, how's your peeping tom?" she asked Odalie.

"No problems," Odalie managed to say with a wan smile.

"Peeping tom?" Stasia asked.

"It's a long story," Tony said. "Get going! You'll miss the curtain!"

"Yes, we…we should go," Odalie said, all at sea.

"We're glad you're okay," Stasia said.

"Yeah, boss, we was worried," Ben chuckled. "I'll get them back to the theater. Eddie will drive you two home," he added, motioning to a big, husky guy hanging around the waiting room. "I'll see you later."

Odalie didn't look back or she'd have noticed the expression on Tony's face. Odalie had spent her life training for her big debut at the Met, but she'd thrown it up to rush over here because she thought he was hurt. And he was hurt, that he'd treated her so badly, even if it was for her own good. He wanted her to succeed. He didn't want to be the reason that she lost her chance at a golden career.

But that look on her face, that stark terror that he was

wounded…he'd never forget it as long as he lived. It would humble him until he was an old man. Her career had been life itself to her. But it was obvious that Tony was more. His eyes closed on a silent groan of agony. She loved him. She truly loved him.

He was never going to forgive himself for hurting her so badly by turning to Mauve. Yes, it was for her own good. He wanted her to have what she'd spent her life studying for. He wanted her to sing at the Met.

But for himself? He'd have given anything in the world to have her walking beside him on lazy afternoons at the park, in his arms in the darkness loving him, laughing at his stories of the old days back home. He would have the memories at least. Sure. Cold comfort. Very cold.

"Well, at least you only had a flesh wound," Mauve said on a sigh, bringing him out of his thoughts. "Are we going on to the Met?"

"I'd rather go home," he said heavily.

"I guess so," she replied. She looked up at him and recognized the pain, the acceptance of loss, the anguish of what he felt for that pretty young blonde woman. She smiled sadly. He was a good man. She hoped he could compete with the Met and win. After all, she had other prospects. "Well, Tony, we had a good run, didn't we?"

He stared at her blankly.

"Are you really that ignorant?" she teased. "She threw up her debut at the Met because she was afraid for you."

His heart jumped. He hadn't really thought of it in words just yet. He drew in a breath. "Yeah."

"She's really pretty."

"She's pretty. She's also worked her whole life to go on the stage and sing opera. She's going to be a star," he replied quietly. "She has the voice of an angel."

"Is that what she wants, or what you want for her?" she asked gently.

He paused as they got to the street, and he shifted uncomfortably from one foot to the other. He wasn't enumerating his faults and shortcomings, but he was aware of every one of them. He had nothing to offer her. He was going to let her go. He cared too much to sacrifice her happiness for his own.

"Let's go," he said curtly, and motioned for his bodyguard to get them into the stretch limo pulling up at the curb, with one of his men driving it.

"Maybe we can get you back in time," Stasia was saying.

"I'm not going back," Odalie said quietly. She turned to her friend, noting that the window to the front seat was closed, so that Ben couldn't overhear what she said. "This is not what I want, Stasia. I'm not sure it ever was." She went over the misery of the past few years and the truth of her so-called great career.

"But you've had therapy," Stasia argued.

"And it didn't work" was the quiet reply. "I've gone through half a dozen therapists, I've tried all the steps except for hypnosis—and there's no way I'm risking that. Nothing has made it any easier. One of the doctors even said that considering some of my risk factors, the constant stress could even result in a heart attack."

"You never told me that!" Stasia exclaimed.

"I was afraid you'd tell Tanner. You guys don't keep secrets. And if Tanner mentioned it, Mom would worry herself sick." She didn't add that she'd had some fainting spells lately that had her concerned, and that was just because of the audition.

"I didn't realize it was that bad," Stasia said gently.

Odalie drew in a long breath. "I've been pretending. It was a lovely dream. But I can't bear going out on a stage night after night after night feeling this way. Especially now," she added softly. "I never knew what love was, before." She met Stasia's eyes. "Part of me wishes I'd never found out," she added with a laugh.

"What do you really want to do?" Stasia asked.

She looked at her sister-in-law. "Marry Tony and have half a dozen kids and sing in the choir on Sunday?" She shook her head. "That will never happen. I don't know what I want. But it isn't a career on the stage—I'm absolutely sure of that. My voice teacher suggested doing recordings. That's not a bad idea. Maybe I'll look into that. But right now, I just want to go home and put tonight behind me."

"You poor kid. You've got it bad for Tony," Stasia said.

"I love him, Stasia," she said softly. "I love him with all my heart. For a little while, I thought it was mutual. We were almost never apart. He seemed to be just as crazy about me as I was about him." She laughed harshly. "Then he invited Mauve over just before I left the apartment, and he kissed her half to death in front of me, to make sure I knew how little I meant to him."

Stasia flinched. "Odalie, I'm so sorry."

The other woman fought tears. She looked out at the bright lights dotting the darkness along the streets. "Life teaches hard lessons," she said sadly. "We learn them, sooner or later. I just need…a little time. I hope the family won't take it too hard."

"Don't be silly," Stasia said. "They love you. We all do. It will be all right."

And it was. They were all sympathy, especially Heather, who knew from personal experience how little a career mattered beside the love of a good man. Of course, she hadn't shared her own past turmoil of career versus love with her husband or either of her sons. It was Odalie's business.

Poor Odalie. She looked as if she'd lost the world. How odd that Tony would be so close to her and then suddenly develop a taste for his former girlfriend. It didn't really make sense.

Or perhaps it did, Heather thought as she read her daughter's drawn face. Odalie was like her mother. She was capable of loving only once, just once, with her very soul. She'd give up anything for that love, sacrifice anything. Maybe Tony already knew that. But he was making the decision for her. Probably he thought she'd be sacrificing a great career and he deliberately chased Odalie away. Could it be that simple? Maybe it was. Anybody with eyes could see how Tony felt when he looked at Odalie. It had been that way from the time they met.

A day would come when Odalie would want to talk. When the memory of tonight wasn't so raw, Heather could talk to Odalie about this and help her find a solution. Tonight, of course, was for tears. So the sooner the family went home and let her cry it out, the better things would be. They all hugged Odalie on the way out.

"You're sure Ben's got your back?" Tanner asked while he and Odalie were briefly alone at the stretch limo that would take the family to their plane at the airport.

"Ben's got everybody's back." Odalie teased, "Even yours, while you're up here."

"You trust him a lot," Tanner said gently.

"I do. He was a navy SEAL before he went into wrestling and then forged a career as a bodyguard. They don't come any tougher."

"Okay. I'll stop worrying," Tanner said.

"I'm tough enough, mostly." She grimaced. "Well, usually. There was this guy who tried to get into my apartment..."

"What?" Tanner exclaimed.

"Ben found out who he was and told Tony. Tony made a phone call..." She closed up. She hadn't meant to let that slip out.

"Who was the guy? Did Tony tell you?"

She nodded and grimaced. "He was a contract employee of that man who's been after you, Tanner."

"Phillip James," he said through his teeth.

"Yes." She studied her brother. "I didn't mention it earlier. I didn't want to worry you all, especially on the night I debuted at the Met." She laughed hollowly. "Some debut, huh?" She lifted her eyes. "What now?"

"Now we go on the attack," he said tautly. "I'm tired of giving him free shots at us. James is more dangerous now than ever before," he said. "I sent a photograph I'd taken of two of the victims in Iraq to a senator I know, who's high in the intelligence community. I thought he'd help, but he said he couldn't be sure the picture wasn't photoshopped." He looked absolutely disgusted. "So now I'm looking for somebody else in Congress who doesn't mind taking risks for a worthy cause."

Stasia, shamelessly eavesdropping, moved closer to the two of them while the others were talking to Ben.

"Tony said that a lot of people have things they want to hide, things that James knows and uses against them," she told Tanner. "It's not that people don't want to help. It's that they're afraid their pasts will come back to haunt them. Probably he's got something on that senator you know, and made threats."

Tanner sighed. "I've been around DC long enough to know

that's true," he confessed. He looked at Odalie and then back at Stasia. "You two are my softest targets," he said gently. "You have to be protected, all the time."

"I'm almost always with you," Stasia said, laying her head against his broad shoulder. "And Ben's got Odalie's back. We'll be fine. You go after that salamander and serve him up fried!"

"Exactly!" Odalie seconded, with a little jerk of her head.

Tanner chuckled. "If this was old days in the West, and I had to stand off bandits, you two would be my choice of companions. The bandits would run like hell."

"Absolutely," Stasia laughed.

Odalie seconded that opinion.

"So I'll see how much trouble I can stir up for James," Tanner said finally.

"With my blessing," Odalie replied, and kissed his tanned cheek. "You two be safe."

"We will," Tanner said.

"You be safe," Stasia said. She hugged Odalie. "And rethink that career business. There's no sense putting yourself through that torture for a job, even a dream of a job. You'll die young. Stress kills."

Odalie sighed. "Yes."

The family reunited at the curb, where the limo stood with its doors opened. Heather kissed Odalie. So did Cole and John.

"One day at a time, kid," Cole said with a grin.

"Yes, Daddy," Odalie said, and laughed, because it had been his favorite saying since she was a little girl following him around the cattle pens.

He chuckled. "Things work out if you just let them," he said a minute later, and his face was solemn. "Give it time."

She grimaced.

"You'll see," he added as they all climbed into the car.

Later, with her doors locked, Odalie sat down in her living room, in the warm silence that was like a comforting blanket.

Tony had been here. The room still held his imprint, the sound of his deep voice laughing, the scent of his spicy cologne in her nostrils, the warm, delicious hardness of his mouth grinding insistently into hers as his hands found soft flesh and touched it so very tenderly...

She groaned and got to her feet. And almost fell. She was having dizzy spells, and at night she barely had enough energy to fix food or wash dishes. She went to bed with the chickens. She got sick if she smelled potatoes cooking, and it was her favorite food. Mashed potatoes. Scalloped potatoes. Potato soup. She loved it all. And now it made her sick.

Something had to be wrong with her. She was usually very healthy. Could it be that even the stress of this little part in the Met holiday special had caused her problem? She'd had the dizziness and fatigue for a month or more...six weeks?

Her heart skipped rope. She counted the days since she and Tony had first been intimate. No! It couldn't be! He'd said he was sterile. He and his wife could never have children.

But was he sterile? They'd assumed he was, so neither had used any precautions. And now...morning sickness?

Her mind stopped working. That would certainly put paid to a career at the Met, if she was pregnant! Plus, it would be the greatest joy of her entire life. Tony's baby. A little boy, maybe, with wavy black hair. Or a little girl with long blond hair.

She shook herself. She was daydreaming. She just had some stupid virus. She went to bed.

But the next morning, she went to a drugstore and bought a pregnancy kit. They knew her in the store and the female clerk grinned. "A pregnancy kit?" she teased.

"For my outdoor cat," Odalie lied with magnificent indifference. "She's been stepping out. If we're in time, maybe we can stop at least one litter!"

"Heartless woman," the other clerk snorted. "Poor little mama cat!"

"She's had two litters in a year. That's enough," Odalie replied. "Cat food is expensive," she added, and because she was wearing sweats, as she usually did, they accepted that she was in the same income bracket as her companions.

"Tell me about it," one clerk moaned. "I've got a German shepherd. He's eating me out of house and home!"

"I've got two bull terriers, a golden retriever and three tabby cats," the other one sighed. "I work to feed them. Good thing I'm not having to support a baby as well!"

They all laughed.

Odalie went home and used the pregnancy test, then held her breath while she waited for the results.

She watched the field slowly, slowly change color. As it did, her face grew whiter and whiter.

She stood staring at the plastic thing in her hand, while her mind fought against science to refuse the conclusion.

"I am not pregnant," she told herself firmly. "I am absolutely not...pregnant...!"

She barely made it to the commode to throw up.

15

"You poor little thing," Odalie cooed to her still-flat stomach, "to have such a low-down, cold-blooded animal for a father!"

She'd actually phoned Tony, thinking she might as well tell him what was going on.

She didn't get a chance. The minute he heard her voice, he went on the attack.

"Why didn't you go back on the stage that night?" he asked angrily. "They said you actually went home!"

"Of course I went home! It was useless to go back when they'd already replaced me!"

"You can get your place back," he said stubbornly. "This is your big chance. Don't blow it!"

She felt her heart dying in her chest. She'd hoped that he might have missed her, that he might want her back. She'd hoped that Mauve had been nothing more than an impulse to push Odalie toward the Met.

But it was obvious that Tony's only interest in her was her voice. He didn't want her, so he was encouraging her to go back to the Met and get out of his life. At least, it felt that way to an unwed mother at a crossroads in her life. She'd thought that she had choices. But she didn't. Tony was telling her so.

"Listen, kid, you and I had fun for a few weeks," Tony said, and she couldn't see that he was grinding his teeth as he lied to her. "But we both know your future is on the stage. You have a beautiful voice. You'll go far." He drew in a breath. "I know you had a crush on me, but that was just physical. We burned out the passion, didn't we? Had a good time. Enjoyed each other. But now it's time to get back down to reality. We don't belong together. It's like oil and water. You'll realize that one day. Meanwhile, you go back to the Met and patch things up. I'll help. One day, you'll be a famous opera star, and I can say I knew you when you were just a nervous beginner... Hello? Odalie?"

She hung up. It was useless to talk to him. He'd had his fun with her, and now he only wanted to see her as someone he'd known on the way to fame. He didn't care. Probably he never had. He wanted her and she wanted him. So they had a few weeks to burn out the passion and now he was over it.

But she wasn't. She'd taken everything seriously. She'd been thinking of a future with him. He'd been enjoying a brief affair. It was likely that he'd had many of them since his wife died. He certainly knew his way around a woman's body.

So here was Odalie, pregnant and deserted and alone. She got up from the sofa and packed a bag. She wasn't calling Ben or Tony or anybody else. She was leaving town. She wanted to get away from everybody and everything and just...just get over the past miserable weeks. Then maybe when she came back she'd be able to cope. Maybe.

Tony was just finishing lunch when his cell phone rang. He answered it immediately when he saw the number, with his blood running cold.

"What's happened?" he asked Tanner without preamble.

"I just started the wheels turning to have Phillip James busted and his whole crew indicted for what happened in Iraq," Tanner said. "I found a representative who was actually there at the time and took pics, ones I didn't even know about. His photos were confiscated, but he remembered that I'd made waves at first, so he contacted me. We went on the attack in DC through his political contacts."

"Good for you!" Tony said. "But why call me...?"

"Odalie," he said at once. "You need to watch her like a hawk. She's the most vulnerable right now, and James will be out for revenge. This is going to cost him his career once we get it to the right people. He knows that."

"Oh, boy," Tony said heavily. "Okay. We're not exactly in contact right now, but I'll make sure Ben doubles her protection."

"Why aren't you in contact?" Tanner asked without thinking.

"I want her to get that career she's spent her life working for," he said tautly.

There was a pause. "So you made the choice for her," he guessed.

"Look," Tony said wearily, "I'm older than she is. I've got a background that no sensible woman would want to live with. Even without the career thing, she deserves better," he added flatly.

"Shades of my parents," Tanner said.

"What?"

"My mother was famous," he replied. "She had to choose between my father and a career. Given the choice, she didn't even hesitate."

"The circumstances were different," Tony said.

"Not that much," Tanner replied. He laughed softly. "Why don't you ask Odalie what she wants?"

"She's spent her life working…"

"Just ask her, Tony."

There was a smoldering pause.

"On that note, I'll hang up," Tanner said. "But please, double that scrutiny. James will be out for anybody's blood he can get. Don't let it be Odalie's."

"I'll take care of her," Tony promised.

At least, he thought when he hung up, she was somewhere that he could protect her. That was a blessing. Maybe he'd think about what Tanner said.

Phillip James was high on cocaine, but even higher when his top agent, Peters, gave him the news.

"I told you having a tail on her would pay off," James exclaimed. "Where is she going?"

"Nassau," Peters said. "If I leave now, I'll get there before she does."

"Get on the plane. Take her to some little motel, off the beaten track. Take two of the new agents with you," he added. "Tell them she's an industrial spy or something. Hold her there until I make arrangements," he added, his face flushed with delight.

"Boss, her dad's rich and he's got political ties."

"No threat at all," he scoffed. His face hardened. "Now I'll make Tanner Everett pay for what he's trying to do to me. I'll get his sister and then I'll go after his wife. I'll kill everyone I can get my hands on!"

Peters felt sick. The man was obviously out of his mind. Someone would pay for these bloody vendettas, and he was willing to bet it was himself James would throw under the bus for them. He was trapped. He'd have to do what he was told. But if he could find a way, he'd try to save Miss Everett. Pity to hurt such a pretty young woman.

"Get going!" James shot at him.

"Yes, sir. On my way."

"And don't you forget what I've got on you," James added in a soft, cold tone. "I can put you away for twenty years."

Peters took a long breath. "Yes. I know that." He went out and closed the door behind him.

"What the hell do you mean, you can't find her? You didn't have somebody watching?!" Tony raged.

Ben held out both hands, backing up a little, just in case. It had been a long time since he'd seen the boss this mad. "I did have people watching. I always have people watching. The guy went to the bathroom, that's all. She must have gone out while he was indisposed..."

"Indisposed." Tony ran a hand through his thick black hair. "James is out there just salivating at the thought of getting any one of the Everett women in his hands for revenge, and we've got one missing, and we can't find her!"

"I'm working on it," Ben said. "I'll have something any minute!"

Tony stared out the window. "She called me. I told her... I told her a lot of lies," he said to himself, his voice torn with pain. "I never should have done that. I was sorry the minute I said it, but she hung up. Now she won't answer her phone."

He turned to Ben. "What the hell are we going to do if James finds her first?!"

"He won't. I swear he won't," Ben assured him. "I've got men checking manifests for every train, bus and plane out of New York...!"

Tony's phone rang.

He saw the number, thanked God and answered it. "Where the hell are you?" he exclaimed.

"What do you care?" Odalie asked furiously. "You had your 'fun' with me, didn't you? So now it's off to somebody else for more 'fun'!"

She was standing in the shadows of the grand hotel near the wharf, among the tall palms a little out of sight. There were only a few passersby. One gave her a curious look, but then he smiled and nodded, turned around and walked back the way he'd come.

"I lied," he said. "I didn't mean a word of it! I was trying to...well, never mind. For God's sake, where are you? Don't you know that Phillip James has agents looking for you right now?!"

"He'll never look for me in Nassau," she said smugly. "And you won't find me, either! I have reservations at a place way out in the boonies as soon as I can get a cab to take me there."

"What are you doing in the Bahamas?" he demanded.

"I'm deciding whether or not to keep my baby," she almost yelled at him.

"Your...what? A baby?" Tony exclaimed with hushed wonder. His head started spinning. Joy bubbled up in him like an exploding volcano. "A baby? A baby!" There was such tenderness in his voice that it calmed her at once. "Oh, my God, a baby!! You're pregnant?!" he whispered, his voice choking with feeling.

He didn't sound as if he didn't want a baby. She paused, confused by the joy in his deep voice.

"You...you said you were sterile, didn't you? Well, guess what, you're not!" She looked around. That man who'd passed her was coming her way, with another man. She lowered her voice. "And now here I am with my whole life turned upside down while you carouse around with your mistress... Oh! Oh! Don't you dare...! What...what are you doing? Who are you...?!" Her voice faded out at once.

Tony's heart stopped.

Just a minute later, another voice came on the line. "Hey, Garza, that you?" a voice demanded.

"Yeah, it's me," he said icily. "Where is she?"

"You don't need to know that. We'll give her brother a call in a few days. Maybe we'll call today, just to let him know how bad things are going to get."

Tony took a slow breath. "You will pay a high price for this," he said, and his voice was as cold as a tomb.

"You wish." And the line went dead.

Odalie was bundled into the back seat of a car by a man she recognized as the agent who'd delivered Tanner's back-pack to her when he'd been presumed dead. Two other men jumped into the front seats and the car took off.

"What...?" Odalie cried out hoarsely.

"Just sit still and don't make a fuss," he told her. "We're going to take a little trip."

"Where to?" She wanted to know. Inside she was shivering because she knew who was responsible for this and its likely outcome.

"Just to DC," the man replied.

"Will I be alive when we get there?" she asked with false bravado.

"Of course."

"Your boss is a weasel," she said coldly.

He just sighed. He knew that already.

She was terrified and doing her best to hide it. It was highly unlikely that they were going to ask for ransom. She knew that Phillip James had scores to settle with her brother and that she was one of the two "soft targets" she'd been told about when her security had been tightened by Tony.

She prayed silently as she and the agent, Peters, got aboard a plane bound for the States. It was a private plane. Nobody else was on board except her companion, Peters, the pilot and copilot, and two other men who looked as if they could wrestle alligators. She prayed even more as she was taken to an office in a building inside the Beltway and locked in. They had her in handcuffs, and there she stayed, sitting in a chair, while they made preparations for whatever unspeakable act they were going to perform on her.

She closed her eyes, wishing that she'd stayed in New York, where she was protected. Nassau had been an impulse, a response to Tony's painful summary of their relationship. Here she sat, pregnant and about to die, and that worm had turned his back on her and their child. Except that she couldn't get past the sound of his deep voice soft with wonder as he'd acknowledged the baby. He'd sounded as if she'd offered him the world. He hadn't seemed angry or dismissive.

He knew how beautiful her voice was. He knew about her ambition and what she'd sacrificed for it. He'd only been furious when he knew that she'd left that first performance at the Met to rush to the hospital when she thought he'd been fatally injured. He'd wanted her to realize her dream. So, if that was the case, wasn't it possible that he'd deliberately brushed her off, thinking that he wasn't going to be the cause of her losing her one chance at singing in the Met?

That would be like him, she thought. He would want what was best for her, not what was best for himself. And only now, facing death, was when she'd realized it. She was going to die, and he'd blame himself forever as being the cause of it.

She wished she had some dark skill, like being able to pick locks, so that she could escape. But, although she was strong and she knew her way around ranch work, she couldn't get out of handcuffs. Even if she could, she had no idea where she was, or even where Tony was.

Oh, Tony, she thought miserably, *it's just not fair that it has to end like this!*

"You've got her? You've got her?!" Phillip James was high as a kite, but this took him even higher. His men hadn't let him down. He had a way to pay Tanner Everett back for all the misery the stupid man had caused him. And as a bonus, he got to torture Tony Garza, who liked the girl he'd had kidnapped. He laughed. He was on top of the world. He was going to play this like a perfect sonata. It would be beautiful.

It was good that Stasia had Tony's private number. Tanner punched in the numbers with fingers that didn't want to work. The past five minutes had been hell on earth.

It rang once. Twice. Three times. "Come on, damn it, Tony, answer the phone!" he muttered. Four rings...

"Garza" came the gruff reply.

"Tony, it's Tanner Everett..."

"Who called you?" Tony asked.

"A contact in Nassau. He says...!"

"Yeah," Tony said, confirming his worst fears. "Listen, your phone is going to ring soon. It will be James. Don't answer it. In fact, don't answer any phones until I get there. Do you understand? Tell me."

Tanner swallowed, hard, exchanging looks with the rest of the family. "I understand."

"They may think it's a ransom call. But it won't be. I think you know that already. He's set on revenge. He doesn't need money. If you answer the phone and he gets to tell you what he's planning, he won't call back, and that will be the end of any chance we have to save Odalie. You get me?"

"I do," Tanner said gruffly.

"I'll be there as soon as I can. Keep everybody in the house. Have eyes everywhere. Remember about the phone. No matter how tempting it is, do not answer it."

"We won't," Tanner said.

"I'll get there as quick as I can." He hung up.

Tanner turned to the rest of the family, scattered around the living room. "He said not to answer the phone under any circumstances."

"But it might be a ransom call," Heather said, fighting tears.

"Tony knows what he's doing," Tanner said. "We have to trust him."

Cole made a rough sound in his throat. "I don't like dealing with animals, either, but not answering the call might cost Odalie her life. If they want ransom, we'll pay it, no matter what it is!"

Tanner didn't want to say it in front of the women, but Cole was unpredictable, and he might grab for the phone if it rang.

"Okay, this is how it is," he said, then drew a deep breath. He met Cole's eyes. "He won't be asking for ransom."

Cole stared at him. "Then what does he want?"

"Vengeance," Tanner said simply. "I'm threatening his little empire. He doesn't like it. So he's going to…torment someone close to me as a warning to the others."

Cole's silver eyes flashed. "Revenge."

"Exactly," Tanner replied. "Cold and savage."

"The damned coward," John muttered.

"My poor Odalie," Stasia said, pressing close to Tanner for comfort.

"Oh, my poor baby," Heather whispered almost to herself.

Cole drew her close and held her. "We've been through storms before, honey. We'll weather this one, too. Through thick and thin…" he began.

Heather looked up at him and smiled through her tears. "And even thinner!"

They both smiled. It was a catchphrase from a TV show they'd both loved many years ago. They did that a lot, Tanner thought. They spoke in a private language of taglines, remembered dialogue from movies and TV, quotes from famous soldiers, lines from songs. The kids were amused by it, although none of them ever understood it. Perhaps they weren't meant to. Cole and Heather were so close that one of them was almost never seen separately. It was always the two of them, together.

Just as Tanner sat down, his cell phone rang. He looked at the number. He didn't recognize it. Heather looked at him with real pain. So did Cole and John, and Stasia. He drew in a long breath and just sat until the ringing stopped.

"What will Tony do, do you know?" John asked.

Stasia turned her head. "Whatever it takes to get her back safely," she said quietly. "Most of what he does these days is legitimate. But he can walk into a room back in Jersey even today, and the meanest man in the room will step aside."

"Some bad situations call for a bad man," Tanner told them.

"Fire with fire," Cole agreed. He sighed. "Tony may have been a bad man, but he saved my baby from a rattlesnake bite the last time he was here. He's okay in my book."

"Mine, too," Heather said, smiling.

The others smiled as well.

Meanwhile, a furious Tony was getting things done with methodical efficiency. He sent three men to a bar near a famous college in New England. He sent another man to the airport in Dallas. A fifth man walked into the room with an armful of burner phones.

"Here, take the damned things," the man said. "I think five cops followed me home! And I'm on the right side of the law!"

"Oh, stop bellyaching, Hunter," Ben chuckled. "You know you loved being mistaken for one of us."

Dane Hunter chuckled. "Maybe so." He studied Tony. "How sure are you that this agent can be turned?"

"Ninety percent," Tony said, pocketing two of the burner phones. He handed the rest to Ben. "He had a drunken escapade with severe results that his boss, Phillip James, was holding over his head. It might have meant a very long jail term. We, uh, sort of helped the evidence and the arrest reports get mislaid..."

Hunter had both fingers in his ears. "I'm not aiding and abetting. No more disclosures!"

Ben made chicken noises.

"You'd cover your ears if you had my boss," Hunter assured him. "Anyway, if you can turn this guy, we can put James away for a very long time."

"I'll do my best. If I can convince him, he'll call you when he leaves Dallas."

"Fair enough," Hunter said.

Tony turned to Ben. "Reimburse him for the phones. Then call Teddy and tell him it's the fed's birthday and we were giving him a cake." He glanced at Hunter with twinkling eyes. "Just so nobody thinks we're in cahoots with you."

Hunter chuckled. Ben rolled his eyes as he went to look in the petty cash drawer.

"I do envy you the people you keep around you," Hunter told Tony when he was ready to leave. "Loyalty these days is a rare commodity."

"It is." Tony shook hands with him. "Thanks for the help."

"I was already in the store looking for a new cell phone." He showed his. It was scarred, the screen was cracked and most of the protective case was gone.

"You should stop throwing it at walls," Tony advised.

Hunter shrugged. "I'm a troubled man."

Tony just laughed.

When Tony and Ben landed in the private jet at Big Spur, the whole family met them at the landing strip, in two vehicles.

"Truck or Jaguar, pick one," Stasia teased, hugging Tony.

"Truck," he said at once. "I very rarely even see one. I love trucks," he chuckled. They were trying to sound cheerful, but he could see behind the fake smiles. "Any calls yet?" he asked.

"One," Cole said as he and Tony climbed into the pickup truck. Ben vaulted into the bed. "But we let it ring."

"Hey, you could eat off this floor," Ben called through the back window.

Cole chuckled as he headed the truck toward the house. "I like to keep my vehicles clean and maintained. They last longer."

"They do." Tony looked out at the landscape. He worried

about Odalie. Were they hurting her? How much danger was she in? She could lose the baby if they roughed her up. The baby. His heart lifted like a helium balloon. He was going to marry her the minute he got her back, no matter how bad he was for her. At least he could protect her and his child.

"You're quiet," Cole remarked as they pulled up at the house.

"I've got a lot going on," he replied with a faint smile. "Now all I have to do is pull enough strings to get it together in time."

Cole just nodded.

They were all gathered in the living room. The grandfather clock was loud. Outside, a dog barked. Inside, you could hear a pin drop.

The sudden music blaring from Tanner's phone was enough to make people jump.

Tony held out his hand. Tanner gave him the phone.

Tony answered it only after the fourth ring. By that time, the family was chewing off their fingernails.

"Hello," Tony said.

There was a shocked pause. "Garza? Where's Tanner Everett? What are you doing with his phone?" James asked, his voice skipping a little at the unexpected voice.

"You'll be dealing with me," Tony said. He leaned back in the armchair and crossed his long legs. "Take down this number." He read it off the burner phone. "Call me back," he said, and he hung up.

There was a collective gasp.

"It's all right," he assured them gently. "Believe me, he's not about to hang up."

"Okay," Heather said, letting out a breath.

After a minute, the burner phone rang. And again, while

everyone fidgeted and bit nails, Tony waited until the fourth ring to answer.

"I'm here," he said.

"Well, I need to talk to Tanner Everett," James said, gaining authority in his voice.

Tony smiled. "You know, I could use a drink. There's a little bar about two blocks from here," he said, and named the college.

There was a stunned silence on the end of the line.

"Nice place," he added. "Small, cozy, dartboard on the wall. Sexy waitress with red hair…"

"How would you know about that?" James asked curtly.

"Picked up a package there earlier," he said, and his voice chilled. "The package is currently waiting in a room. You might want to call and have somebody check on that package, at the bar."

"You wouldn't…dare!"

"Call me back. You know the number." He hung up again.

They all stared at Tony. His face was like stone.

"It's not a real package, right?" Heather asked.

Tony nodded. "It's something our friend likes very much."

"Should we ask what it is?" John asked.

Tony smiled and shook his head. "We don't want too many accessories, now do we?"

John laughed.

The sound of the grandfather clock grew louder and louder. It was only a few minutes, but nerves were at breaking point.

Suddenly, the phone rang insistently. This time Tony let it ring five times before he answered it.

"Hello," he said.

"You give him back! You get him back…where you found

him…right now! I'll call in every damned agent east of Memphis…!"

"For a package?" Tony asked lazily. He toyed with the doily on the telephone table. "Why would you do that?"

"He's all I've got," the other man said through his teeth.

"Yeah. And she's all I've got," Tony said, and his voice chilled to the bone.

There was a long silence. "What do you want?"

"You get one of your boys to bring my package to the Dallas Fort Worth Airport," Tony said quietly. "When it arrives, I'll stay with it, and I'll call to have your package put back where it was found. I won't leave the airport until you've confirmed that your package is intact. Then your boy goes back to DC."

"So simple," James spat.

"One more thing," Tony said, and his voice softened and deepened. "If my package is damaged, in any way, your package will be delivered to you in a shoebox. Do you understand me? Say it!"

He could hear the other man swallow. "I understand," he said in a ghostly tone.

"Furthermore, if any of the Everetts are ever persecuted by you or any of your agents, ever, you will receive any number of shoeboxes with the same package, divided, inside." He paused. "And I'll be watching."

"I understand" came the defeated reply.

"We'll wait for the package at the international concourse in the airport. I assume you won't be stupid enough to send more than one agent on this assignment. I've told you the possible consequences."

"I'm sending one agent," James said heavily. "Just one." His voice shook. "He'll call you…when he gets there."

"Same number," Tony said. And he hung up.

"What was all that about packages?" Cole asked.

"If you say it's a person, all sorts of troublesome laws stand up and scream at you," Tony told him.

"As in kidnapping?"

"Bingo," Tony said.

"Well, I'm never playing poker with you," John chuckled. "Damn, what a bluff!"

Tony looked at him with an odd expression. "It wasn't."

"Wasn't what?"

"It wasn't a bluff," Tony told him. His dark eyes narrowed in a face like stone. "I never bluff." He noticed the curious faces. "Look, in my business, you never make a threat you can't back up. You never promise something you don't deliver. James knows my reputation. It's the only thing that got Odalie out of there alive tonight. He knew I'd do exactly what I told him I'd do. He only has one weakness, and I knew what it was." He smiled ruefully. "You don't promise to plant rose-bushes over somebody if you don't have any rosebushes," he added with sparkling dark eyes.

John chuckled. "Now I'm really not ever playing poker with you," he said, and everybody grinned.

Hours went by before Odalie heard voices outside the door. One was angry and very loud.

Phillip James was fuming. "I'll get him if it's the last thing I do in this life! He's already messed up too many of my plans. Listen, you make sure she's not harmed, not a scratch, you hear me?" he growled at Peters. "I won't risk my son even for revenge."

There was a pause and some murmuring. "Just don't mess up the wire. I might get something out of this, even if it isn't much. Hurry and get to the airport. I've got a plane waiting.

Damn Garza! He's always one step ahead! Well, don't just stand there. Get going!"

There was another brief bit of conversation. Footsteps died away. Then the door opened, and the familiar man came in. He unfastened the handcuffs and led her down the hall to a bathroom. "Be quick," he said gently, and looked ashamed and unsettled.

She thanked him. It had been a long time between bathroom breaks. It was a minor kindness, but one that had been unexpected. She was quick. She didn't know where she was going, but it sounded like they were giving her back to Tony. Her heart lifted like a bird in flight. She was alive and Phillip James had lost this evil game he was playing. She didn't know how Tony had done it, but he'd saved her life. And his child's.

Tony turned and looked at his watch. "We'd better get to the airport. We could grab a burger or something while we wait," he murmured absently. His mind was still on the baby. He wasn't going to tell the others just yet, but it was a delicious secret. And he couldn't wait to share it.

He'd been uncertain before about the future, but now it was as clear as polished glass. He knew exactly where he was going.

He and Odalie were never going to be apart again. The baby was a bonus, but he'd have married her if there could never be a baby. Despite his drawbacks, she loved him. And he loved her. Love would be enough to overcome all the obstacles. He'd never been more sure of anything.

Now all he had to do was save her...

Ben had vanished when they got to the airport, but he soon joined them at the burger stand. He nodded and smiled at Tony, who also nodded.

The others figured that something was going on, but they had no idea what. Anyway, the burgers were delicious.

The plane from DC was announced. They all moved to the international concourse to wait for Odalie.

She came into view slowly, her arm held by a familiar man. It was the agent who'd delivered the bloody backpack with photos of the family in it. Everyone assumed that it was Tanner's and that he was dead. This man had secretly advised them to look deeper, and they had. They'd found Tanner alive.

The agent, Brock Peters, let go of Odalie as they reached the family. She ran straight into Tony's arms, and was wrapped up tight, and held and rocked while he whispered to her as the others looked on.

"You're okay? You're sure?" Tony asked softly as he kissed her eyelids closed.

"I'm fine. I'm just tired and sleepy and hungry." Her eyes opened and she looked up into his. "Can I have a hamburger?"

He bent and kissed her nose. "You can have anything you want. And I mean anything," he whispered huskily.

She smiled at him and pressed close. "I'm so happy to see you. All of you," she added quickly as she turned to hug everyone else before she nestled back into Tony's arms.

"I have to make a call," Tony said, noting the agent's plaintive look.

He pulled out the burner phone and spoke in riddles to his men. They waited some more. The burner phone rang. Tony answered it, nodding and smiling. He told his men to leave the package where they'd found it, and they did.

Next, Tony had the agent, Peters, call Phillip James and tell him to check on his own package. He did, and reported to Tony that his package was fine, only a little inebriated.

"So now we're square, right?" James asked in a sullen but subdued tone.

There was a long pause. "For right now, yes. But if you're ever tempted to hassle the Everetts, remember this. I have people everywhere. If I don't, I know people who do. You have no idea at all how connected I really am. And if you're very lucky, you won't have to find out."

"I've still got enough on your senator friend to send his daughter up for twenty years," James said suddenly.

"So you said." There was a pause. "But we have some interesting news for you. There was an extra eyewitness in Iraq. And he was a professional photographer."

"You're lying!!" James burst out.

"You'll find out in a couple of weeks."

"The senator wouldn't dare…"

"You're right, he wouldn't. But this is a US representative, and he served in Iraq with a spec ops team." Tony smiled. "Just for the record, do you really think it was worth it for nothing more valuable than money and drugs?"

"That's power," James said curtly. "And it's the most valuable commodity on earth!"

"No," Tony said. "It's not." And he hung up.

With Odalie still clinging to him, he walked over to the agent, Brock Peters, with Ben.

"Give it to him," Tony told Ben.

He handed the agent an envelope.

The agent looked at Tony with surprise. "What's this?"

"A one-way ticket to New York City and ten thousand in cash," Tony said. "Here." He handed the agent a slip of paper. "That's Dane Hunter's private phone number. He's a US marshal. If you're willing to testify against James, he can get you in the witness protection program and you'll disappear."

The agent was torn. He looked at Tony with consternation.

"If you go back to DC tonight, you're a dead man," Tony said flatly. "James probably already has somebody ready to off you. Not only are you a witness to what he did overseas, you're a witness to a kidnapping." He indicated Odalie. "You'll take the fall for him."

Peters sighed. "Yeah. I'd already figured that out." He looked at the slip of paper. "This guy, Hunter. You trust him?"

Tony nodded.

"Okay. I'll see what he can do for me." He closed his eyes. "Boy, I'd like to know what it's like to sleep with both eyes closed."

"Hunter may have some ideas about that."

"You could have turned me in," Peters told him. "Made a lot of money."

"You can't take it with you," Tony said.

Peters laughed. "Well, no. I don't suppose you can." He glanced at Odalie. "Sorry for the less than gentle treatment, Miss Everett. It wasn't my idea."

She smiled. "I know that. Thanks for getting me here safely. And thanks for what you did when you brought Tanner's rucksack. Because of what you told us, we were able to find him alive."

"You're welcome." He shook hands with Tony. "I may see you around."

Tony chuckled. "You may not. Take care."

"Sure. You, too."

"One more thing," Tony added.

Peters's eyebrows arched.

"The wire...?"

Peters burst out laughing. "Damn, Tony, you don't miss

a trick. But I honestly forgot I had it on. It's been a stressful night."

He pulled off the wire and handed it to Tony, who stepped on it. Just to make sure.

They all waved Peters off as he headed toward the concourses.

Then Tony turned to Odalie. "We need to get you to a hospital and get you checked out."

"But I'm fine," she began.

He put his finger against her lips. "I'm scared," he said softly. "Humor me."

She sighed. She knew why he was worried, even though nobody else did. Not yet, anyway. She smiled. "Okay."

While she was being examined, the family stood outside the building so that the hopeless smokers could have a cigarette.

"We owe you more than we can ever repay," Cole told Tony.

"No, you don't," he said quietly. "The light in the world would go out if she left it. I would have done anything to keep her safe."

"Then could we ask why you sent her home alone at Thanksgiving and told her she was just a passing fancy?" John asked solemnly.

"Sure. Go ahead," Tony said.

John frowned. "Go ahead...?"

"Go ahead and ask. I said you could ask. I never said I'd answer you," Tony added with twinkling eyes.

John glared at him. "Now..." he began.

"She sings like an angel," Tony said quietly. "I'm almost thirty-eight years old. My background—well, you know about that. I may get arrested one day for some things I did when I was younger. I grew up poor, in a neighborhood where you

became either a cop or a criminal. And I think we had about
two cops total in our gang. She wanted to sing at the Met,
and I wanted that for her." He looked away. "I thought I was
the obstacle. So I removed it."

"So she could sing at the Met," Cole surmised.

"Yes."

Cole smiled. "Heather was a recording artist. She was famous. She sang like an angel, too, and she and her band played
gigs all over the country. But when it came to a choice between performing and me, I won hands down."

"You're saying something."

"I'm saying that there are things more important than fame
and fortune. And your background doesn't matter to a woman
who loves you." He indicated Odalie, walking toward them.
"Case in point. She doesn't even see anybody except you,"
he added with a smile.

It was true. Odalie went straight to Tony without deviat-
ing a single step.

"How are you?" he asked her softly.

She smiled. "I'm fine. And he even gave me something
for the nausea. Plus some high-powered vitamins. And the
name of a specialist."

He smiled back. "The baby's okay?"

She smiled with her whole heart. "The baby's okay."

"What baby?!" exploded in a chorus behind them.

16

"Oh, my God," Tony groaned as Stasia and Heather lit into him. He held up both hands. "I'm sorry…!"

"It's okay. I'll protect you," Odalie said, positioning herself in front of Tony. She flushed. "It was all my fault," she began.

"It was not," Tony protested. "And it's not a fault. It's a baby." He looked all dreamy, his dark eyes soft with wonder as he looked at Odalie.

"Whatever happened to 'I'm too old' and 'I'm a bad man'?" Stasia asked, tongue in cheek.

"When the baby's old enough to talk, he'll take my side," he promised.

"He?" Stasia asked.

He sighed, smiling at Odalie. "My dad had a brother, who had a son and both my grandfathers had sons. No daughters." He grimaced. "I'd love a little girl with long blond hair, but I'm more likely to get a tough little boy with black hair. And an attitude," he added. He grinned. "And he'll probably be born smoking a cigar, ordering the doctors around."

Everybody laughed.

Except Cole. He was staring at Tony with one eye narrowed. "They had a sale on ammunition at the gun shop yesterday," he began.

Tony held up both hands. "I don't even need persuading." He looked at Odalie with warm, soft eyes. "Every time I took her out, I had to fend off the competition. Wedding rings are a great deterrent," he added with a smug grin.

Odalie laughed and pressed close to him.

"We can get a license at the courthouse and get the judge to marry us," Tony said. "But later, I'd like us to get married in church," he added solemnly. "Just in case you ever want to get rid of me, I want to make it as hard as I can."

She laughed and punched him in the ribs. "As if!"

"What about the Met?" Tony asked, and he looked really upset.

"We'll have a nice long talk about stress," she promised.

He blinked. "About what?"

"You'll see."

"Can we go home now?" John asked. "I need to feed Precious."

Tony's eyebrows arched. "You got a dog?"

"Well, no," John said. "Actually, he's a…"

"Rattlesnake," the whole family voiced at once.

Tony's eyes almost popped out.

"Don't do that," John groaned. "He's got no teeth, poor old thing, and he doesn't even threaten to strike at people. I feed him freeze-dried things…"

"He lives in John's room," Heather said, shivering. "The maid won't even go in to change the sheets!"

"She will now, honest," John told his mother. "I put a sheet over the enclosure so she doesn't have to look at him. Hurts his feelings, of course," he muttered. "He can't help being a snake."

"Hurts his feelings." Cole was nodding. "One of my prospective buyers for that new lot of purebred calves was looking for the bathroom. He got loose and wandered into John's room instead."

"Oh, come on, Dad, it was just a little bit of plate glass…" John said defensively.

"A whole picture window," Cole translated, "plus a trip to the ER, a hospital bill and then therapy because the man has a snake phobia…!"

"I'll paint Precious green and tell everybody he's a tree boa," John said.

"I'll paint you green and tell people you're a leprechaun if you don't find other accommodations for your…pet!" Cole muttered. "It's unnatural to have a rattlesnake in the house!"

"The wedding," Heather interrupted. "The wedding?"

"We'll get the license first thing in the morning," Tony promised, pulling Odalie close with a sigh. "Please tell me there's a jewelry store in town?"

"Yes. It's a hundred years old," Heather laughed. "And he's got some beautiful antique sets," she added. "Old Mr. Scott says even the best jeweler in Dallas can't touch his inventory."

"We'll go ring shopping at the same time," Tony agreed. He looked at Cole and Heather. "I may have managed things badly," he said gently. "But nobody on earth will love your daughter more than I do or take better care of her and the baby than I will. And that's a promise."

Which caused Odalie to burst into tears, because Tony had

never said those words to her. She curled into him and held on for dear life.

Cole shook hands with him. Heather hugged him. So did Tanner and Stasia.

John shook hands, too. "You keep that promise. Just remember," he added with a smile and wiggled eyebrows, "I have worms."

Everybody broke out laughing.

Three days later, a radiant Odalie in a white designer silk sheath dress with a bouquet of snow lilies and white roses was married to Tony in the local circuit court's probate judge's office. A photographer had been hired to immortalize the couple for future generations.

"You look beautiful," Tony told his bride as he kissed her with breathless tenderness. "And I will love you until the stars burn out."

She smiled under his hard lips. "I'll love you just as long."

"That wasn't what you said on the phone just before James's men grabbed you," he said sternly.

"I was having morning and evening sickness and feeling faint at the time," she replied. "And you had thrown your girlfriend at me just before I went back to my apartment!"

"I was saving you," he said.

"From what?" she asked.

"From me, of course."

"I didn't want to be saved from you," she pointed out.

"Yes, well, you didn't make that clear, did you?"

"I made it perfectly clear. And come to think of it..."

"Ahem." Stasia moved between them. "We're here to get married," she murmured. "Not to start World War Three."

Tony frowned. "Is that why we're here?" he asked Odalie.

"Don't ask me. I just came in to get directions to the rest-room," she said with a straight face.

Stasia turned to the amused probate judge. "Could you go ahead and marry them? Then they can argue about why they're here without taking up your time."

The probate judge burst out laughing.

They had a huge spread at the ranch for anyone in the neighborhood who wanted to stop by to see the bride and groom.

There was a full house, too. Odalie had fun bouncing Cort and Maddie Brannt's little girl on her knee and anticipating her own child many months in the future.

Tony knelt beside her, smiling at the dark-haired, dark-eyed child. "She's a beautiful child," he mused, brushing his big hand over the child's thick head of hair.

"Ours will be beautiful, too," Odalie said, smiling at her husband.

"He will be if he looks like you," he teased.

"You're gorgeous yourself," she replied and kissed him gently. Her eyes brimmed over with love.

He touched her mouth with his fingertips. "I thought I had to give you up, for your own good," he said quietly. "It was the closest I've ever come to hell on earth."

"You thought I wanted a career, and all I really wanted was you," she said.

He brushed back her hair. "Are you sure you won't regret this?"

"Positive. No sane person will ever regret a baby," she whispered, smiling. "Or especially three or four of them. I like big families."

He chuckled. "I do, too. My own was pretty small, but I

cornered the market on distant relatives. That reminds me—
we're expected in Jersey next weekend for a big bash to cel-
ebrate the wedding."

"That will be fun," she said.

"You were a big hit with cousin Connie."

"I liked her. She's a firecracker."

"I like her, too. Especially now that she's all done match-
making," he added darkly.

She grinned at him.

He made a face.

It was too cold to sit on the porch after supper, so everybody sprawled around in the living room, where logs crack-
led and spit in the huge open fireplace.

"Have you thought about names yet?" Cole asked.

"I've only been pregnant a few weeks," Odalie pointed out.

Heather hit Cole with a magazine. "He started working
on names the minute we knew I was carrying Tanner," she
pointed out. "He carried baby books around in his pocket. That
was before cell phones," she reminded them with a chuckle.

"There were some great names," Cole mused.

"Murgatroyd. Rufus. Cornwallis." Heather was glaring at
him.

"Those were unusual names," he said.

"Very."

"Your mother has no sense of adventure," Cole informed
them.

"Alyson." Heather almost spat it at him.

"If you'd named me Alyson, I'd be carrying a big bat around
with me and I'd hit you with it twice a day," Tanner informed
his father.

"Your mother wanted to name you Merryweather," Cole pointed out.

Tanner glared at her. "Two bats. You'd get a turn also."

They all laughed.

But later, after the rest of the family turned in, when Odalie and Tony were sitting together on the sofa, he looked through one of the baby-name books Cole had left.

"You know, names really are important," he said, his voice deep and soft in the silence of the room, broken only by the snap and crackle of the wood burning in the fireplace.

"Well, we have several months to think about them," she reminded him.

He smoothed her head against his broad chest. "At least we have baby books online," he mused as he put the paper book down on the table.

She laughed. "Imagine dad being so wrapped up in names."

"Men get all gooey when we think about babies," he teased.

She looked up at him. "You really thought you were sterile?"

He nodded. "It was one reason I drew back from you. Well, that, and that beautiful voice." He grimaced. "I still feel guilty."

"That I'm not singing at the Met? I would have spent every night of my life throwing up."

He scowled.

"Stage fright," she said quietly. "I have it to an alarming degree. Years of therapy, years of hiding it from my family. I love singing. But I hate singing in front of people. It's why I didn't do the regional competitions. I knew I'd never make it through them. One day, I might do recordings, or something like that. But life is too short to spend it going crazy over fear of performing."

"You never told me."

"I never told anybody," she said. "People expected me to do great things." She grimaced. "The only great thing I wanted to do was live with you and have babies."

His face was a study in wonder. "Really?"

She nodded. "Really." She reached up and kissed him. "I'm like my mother. To me, family is the most important thing in the world."

"Next to names" came a drawl from the doorway. Cole was holding a dog-eared paperback. "Names are very important...!"

Heather had him by the arm. "You come right back here and leave them alone about names."

"Very important!" he called back as he was half dragged down the hallway to their bedroom, "Help!" he added.

They burst out laughing.

Eventually, when they were certain that no more attempts were going to be made against Odalie, they went on a two-week long honeymoon to Tangier.

"This is the most exotic place I've ever been," Odalie sighed as they lay recuperating in each other's arms after a long, sweet night of loving. "I don't think I'd ever get tired of it."

"Considering how good the food is, we might live here occasionally," he teased. "But I also have to take you to Sicily," he added. "I'd enjoy that myself, seeing where my family came from."

"That would be lovely," she said, nuzzling her face against his.

"I still feel bad about the Met," he murmured. "You might have really liked it."

"No, I wouldn't have." She lifted up on one elbow to look

at him. "Scared stiff all the time, sick at my stomach every day before I went onstage." She shook her head. "Most people can be cured of it. But I've spent most of my adult life trying to cope, and I never have. One doctor even told me that the kind of stress I experienced could lead eventually to a heart attack. I love singing. I do have a gift. But it's enough to share it in church or as an occasional guest artist at some venue. Just not all the time."

"I almost ruined everything," he said quietly. He ran his hand through her soft hair. "Almost lost you for good, and thought I was doing the right thing all along."

"I wanted you," she said quietly. "Only you. From the moment I met you. I fell hard."

He smiled gently. "So did I. And spent ages fighting it. I wanted somebody better for you."

"There isn't anybody better," she said simply.

He drew her down to him and kissed her with breathless tenderness. "I'll probably drive you nuts."

She smiled. "No, you won't."

He nuzzed his nose against hers and smiled. "Okay. If you're sure."

"Where do you want to get married?"

He stared at her. "We got married already." He showed her his wedding ring. "Remember your dad and his new box of ammo...?"

She hit him. "In church."

He laughed. "How about in Big Spur?"

She searched his eyes. "Where?"

"At your parents' church."

"But didn't you go to..." she began.

He put his fingers over her mouth. "Faith is faith. I never had much use for it when I was younger. But now, after some of the things I've seen, I believe in it more and more. When the kids are older, we'll find a church close to home up north. For now, let's do something that will make your dad happy. So he'll shut up about names," he muttered darkly.

She was diverted. "What do you mean, so he'll shut up...?"

He handed her his cell phone, opened to his messages. There, on consecutive days for at least two weeks, were suggestions for names.

She caught her breath. "I didn't actually believe my mother when she said Dad was obsessed." She looked up. "I'll have to apologize to her!"

He laughed as he put the phone away. He shook his head. "I guess we'd better start thinking about what we'd like so we can keep your father away from the birth certificate."

"Good thought," she agreed.

He pulled her close with a long sigh and they went back to sleep.

Tony had one last secret that he'd been keeping. But late one afternoon after Mrs. Murdock had gone shopping and Ben was working with his men, Odalie heard the opening strains of Puccini's "Nessun dorma" from the opera *Turandot*.

It was coming from Tony's study, where he kept his library of books and a desk. She walked toward it, entranced. The voice was pure honey, perfectly pitched, full of emotion. Beautiful. As the beautiful melody ended in its highest tone, and that was perfectly done as well, she pushed open the door and saw Tony as his voice lingered on that last, resounding tone.

Her mouth fell open. He grinned at her as he turned off the speaker. "You know my great-great-grandfather sang opera. But I didn't tell you that I inherited his voice."

"Wow," she said, spellbound, as she went into his arms. "You are incredibly talented! Why didn't you ever tell me?!"

"A man has to have a few secrets." He bent and kissed her tenderly. "So now we can sing duets in the shower," he whispered.

She laughed and kissed his chin. "I'll love that. So will the baby," she added gently. "We can sing lullabies to him."

"You said him!" he accused.

"Her," she corrected. Her eyes twinkled. "There's one set of twins on Mama's side of the family."

"My great-grandfather and his brother were twins," he said. "Do you think...?" His smile was radiant.

"We'll have to wait and see. But wouldn't it be awesome?" she exclaimed.

He kissed her hungrily. "Awesome," he whispered, and kissed her again.

Several weeks later, Tony and Odalie were having dessert and coffee at Tony's cousin's restaurant when Dane Hunter walked in.

He ordered cappuccino and joined them at their table.

"It's been an age," Tony chuckled, shaking hands.

"At least!" He smiled at Odalie. "And I believe double congratulations are in order?"

"Exactly," she said with a grin. "We're on the way to becoming parents!"

"Any word on what's happened over at Justice?" Tony asked.

"Just that Phillip James is trying every trick in the book to keep off the investigations roster."

"Is he having any luck?"

Hunter grinned. "Not so far."

"Good." He pursed his lips. "Any news on Agent Peters?"

Hunter stirred his cappuccino. "Now, how would I know about that?" he asked innocently.

"Just a wild thought. You do work for the US Marshal's

office. Although I sincerely hope he'll be willing to testify when James finally has to answer for Iraq."

"I have no knowledge," Hunter said. "However, I might be willing to bet that he will. If I were a betting man."

"How's your phone?"

Odalie glanced curiously from one to the other.

"Government salaries aren't what they should be," Hunter said sadly. He pulled out his phone with the battered case and the still-cracked screen.

"You should ask them for a replacement," Tony pointed out.

"If I did, they'd refer me to anger-management classes. I'm not going," he said belligerently. "I only threw it twice and I had ample justification."

"You could mention that."

"I could," Hunter said, his dark eyes twinkling. "Except that my boss was the reason I threw it. Both times." He put the phone away. "I'll just plug along until it wears out. Maybe by then I can retire and go fishing."

"Let me know when you retire," Tony chuckled. "I'll go with you."

Hunter raised his cup in a toast.

Later, Tony called Teddy to let him know that he'd been keeping company with the fed.

Odalie, holding hands with him, laughed softly as they walked down the sidewalk in the chilly air. "It's like being on probation."

He leaned down and kissed her. "Exactly."

"I like your friend the marshal."

"He's not so bad," he agreed. "But you can't mention that I said that around the family. Ever."

She wrinkled her nose at him and smiled. "I promise," she said.

"Listen, where are we having Christmas?"

She stopped sipping cappuccino and looked up at him. "Oh, dear."

"Oh, dear is right."

She bit her lower lip. "How about Christmas Eve at Connie's and Christmas Day at my folks'?"

He smiled. "You're good," he teased.

She laughed. "But when the babies come along, we have to spend Christmas Day at home."

"Agreed." He groaned. "Then we'll have to split things up again!"

"Don't rush your fences," she said softly. "We'll jump them as we come to them."

He smiled. "Okay."

She sighed, looking up at him. "I've never been so happy in my whole life," she said softly.

He traced her lips. "Neither have I."

"We started out so badly," she laughed.

"Self-defense on my part," he told her. "I wanted you the minute I saw you, and I spent the rest of the time telling myself you were my mortal enemy."

"Because I wanted to sing at the Met."

He shook his head. "Because I wanted you, even then."

"And here we are," she added, her voice soft with emotion.

He smiled slowly. "And here we are."

He pulled her close and kissed her, right there on the street. She reached up and slid her arms around his neck, and sighed, and smiled. So did he.

A neighborhood kid on a bicycle whistled loudly as he flew by them. But they didn't notice.

★ ★ ★ ★ ★

SPECIAL EXCERPT FROM

CANARY STREET PRESS

*A lone wolf meets his match in a heart-stopping
Long, Tall Texans romance*

Tanner Everett spends most of his time jet-setting around
the world. But that hasn't stopped Stasia Bolton, the
daughter of a neighboring rancher, from falling head
over heels for him. So Stasia is secretly thrilled when her
father proposes linking the properties in matrimony…
which means Tanner will be hers for good.

Despite his worldly ways, Tanner can't help but be enthralled by the quiet girl next door. But as the embers
between the two are fanned into flames, Tanner wonders
if he's found forever in the last place he ever expected.

*Read on for a sneak preview of
The Loner, Stasia and Tanner's story from
Diana Palmer's Long, Tall Texans series.*

ONE

Anastasia Bolton, nicknamed Stasia, was nineteen today. She looked at herself critically in her bedroom mirror, making a face at her lack of beauty. She had a pretty mouth and big, soft brown eyes. Her cheekbones were high, her ears small. She was only medium height, but her figure was perfect. She had elegant long legs, just right for riding horses, which she did, a lot. She'd done barrel racing when she was younger, but art had taken over her leisure hours. She painted beautifully.

She was named after a semi-fictional character in a movie her romantic late mother had loved, *Anastasia*, which starred Yul Brynner and Ingrid Bergman. Her mother had loved the movie and named her only child after the unforgettable heroine. Stasia lived with her father, Glenn Bolton, on a huge beef ranch in Branntville, Texas. Her last living grandparents, her dad's parents, had died of a deadly virus the summer before her graduation from high school. Her mother had died tragically when Stasia was only thirteen. There was no other family left, just Stasia and Dad. They were close. Glenn Bolton was only fifty years old, but he had a very bad heart and he was in the final stages of heart failure. It was treatable, but he hadn't shared that knowledge with Stasia. He was terrified of the open-heart surgery treatment would require. He and the doctor had spoken privately the week before, and afterward, Glenn had been quieter than usual and he'd contacted his attorney. That had been a private conversation as well. Stasia worried about what was being discussed. She didn't want to think about what her life would be like without him. She had no family except him.

Well, there were the Everetts, who lived next door to her father's ranch on their own enormous ranch, the Big Spur. They were sort of like family, after all, since Stasia had known them all her life. Cole Everett and his youngest son, John, were frequent visitors. Glenn had the only groundwater suitable for ranching in the small community of Branntville, Texas. A river ran like a silver ribbon through his entire property, so he wasn't dependent on wells for watering his cattle, as other ranchers were. He approved of Cole and John. He wanted more than anything to see his daughter settled with one of the Everett sons, but she was only in love with one of them—with Tanner, the eldest, who was the cookie-cutter design of the spoiled rich kid.

Cole hadn't spoiled Tanner. That had been his wife, Heather, a former singing star and current songwriter. Their firstborn had been the light of her life. He was twenty-five now, a strong, incredibly handsome young man with dark hair and pale blue eyes, almost silver like his father's, and a Hollywood sort of physique. He liked variety in his women, but for the past year he'd had a girlfriend who enjoyed the jet-setting lifestyle that he favored.

Cole had given Tanner a Santa Gertrudis stud ranch that he'd bought when the owner went into a nursing home, hoping to settle down his wild son. It was a good property, adjoining his and the Bolton properties, but the water situation there was dire. There had been drought in the past year, and they'd had to drill wells to get enough water just to keep the livestock watered. The Bolton place had a river running through it, and many small streams that ran over into the Everetts' holdings. However, that water didn't belong to them so they were unable to divert it for any agricultural purposes.

For a long time, Cole had toyed with the idea of a merger with Glenn Bolton, but Glenn wouldn't hear of it. He found all sorts of reasons for his stubborn attitude. Cole saw right through him. Stasia was still living at home, and she was in love with Tanner. The fly in the ointment was that Tanner didn't like Stasia. He liked experienced, sophisticated women like Julienne Harper, his girlfriend. Tanner could have made an empire out of the ranch Cole had given him, but he wasn't home enough. He and Julienne were always on the go somewhere. Skiing in Colorado, parties on somebody's yacht off Monaco, summers in Nice. And so it went.

Stasia knew about Julienne. Everybody in Branntville did. It was a small community where gossip flourished. It was mostly kind gossip, because the people who lived there had known each other's families for generations. Tanner was one of them. But Julienne, who was sarcastic and condescending, was an outsider, a city woman who'd alienated just about everyone she came into contact with.

Tanner had a couple, Juan and Minnie Martinez, who ran the house and managed the ranch for him while he played around the world. They'd just threatened to quit because of Julienne's last visit to Tanner's ranch. Cole had played peacemaker. The Martinezes were good at ranch management, and somebody had to keep the place going. Cole despaired of Tanner ever settling down to real work. He'd always had everything he wanted. Cole, who adored his wife of twenty-five years, hadn't had the heart to make her stop coddling Tanner, while there had still been time to knock some of the selfishness and snobby attitude out of him. Now, it was too late.

Stasia came into the living room where the men were talking with a tray of coffee and sliced pound cake. All three men stood up, an ancient custom in rural areas that still had the power to make her feel important. Her generation cared less about such things, as a rule, but Stasia was a throwback. Glenn had raised her the way his parents had raised him. She'd absorbed those conservative attitudes on the way of the modern world. She hated it. She hated it most because Tanner liked women who belonged to that sophisticated crowd.

John Everett looked like his mother, Heather, in coloring, at least. He was big and blond and drop-dead handsome, with his father's silver eyes. His young sister, Odalie, also looked like Heather, with pale blue eyes and blond hair. Tanner was the one who most resembled Cole, who was tall and still handsome. Tanner had the same thick, dark hair but with pale blue eyes that just missed being the silver of his father's.

John went forward and took the heavy tray from her. He grinned. "I love cake."

She laughed, a soft, breathy sound. "I know." She smiled at

him with warm affection. He was like a cuddly big brother to her. He knew that and hid his disappointment.

"How's the art going?" Cole asked with a smile.

"I sold a painting!" she exclaimed happily. "There was a man passing through, from someplace back East, and he saw the landscape I painted in the local art shop. He said it was far too cheap for something that lovely, so he gave Mr. Dill, the owner, three times my asking price. I was just astonished."

"You paint beautifully," John said, his eyes brimming with love that she tried not to see. He indicated the landscapes on the walls of the Bolton home; one with running horses in a thunderstorm was entrancing.

"Thanks," she said, flushing a little. "Mr. Dill said the man looked Italian. He was big and muscular and he had these two other big guys with him. He was passing through on the way to San Antonio on business."

"Sounds ominous," John teased.

She laughed as she poured coffee all around and offered cake on saucers with sparkling clean forks. "He told Mr. Dill I should be selling those paintings up in New Jersey, where he was from, or even New York City, where he owned an art gallery and museum. He said he was going to talk to some people about me! He even took down Mr. Dill's number so he could get in touch." She sighed. "It was probably just one of those offhand remarks people make and then forget, but it was nice of him to say so."

"You really do have the talent, Stasia," Cole told her. "It would be nice if he could put you in touch with some people in the art world back East. If that's what you want to do with your life," he added gently.

She smiled at him. "I like to paint." She grimaced. "I'd like to marry and have a family, though."

"No reason you couldn't do both," John said. "And if you had to fly back East to talk to people, well, we have a share in a corporate jet, you know. You could let us know when you had business there and I could go with you."

She smiled sedately. "Thanks, John, but it's early days yet."

"How's Tanner?" Glenn asked.

Cole's light eyes grew glittery. "Off on another trip. To Italy, this time. My daughter's studying opera in Rome. He thought he'd stop by and see her on the way to Greece."

"Odalie has a beautiful voice," Stasia replied, hiding disappointment. She'd hoped Tanner might show up with his brother and father. "Does she want to sing at the Met eventually?"

"She does," Cole replied. He drew in a long breath and sipped coffee. "I'll hate having her so far from home. But you have to let kids grow up." He glanced at John with affection. "At least this one doesn't have itchy feet yet!"

"I'm a homebody," John said easily. "I love cattle. I love ranching. I don't want to leave home," he added, with a covert glance at Stasia.

"Good thing," Cole chuckled. "I have to leave the ranch to somebody when I'm gone."

"You're not going anywhere for years," Glenn chided. "The Everetts are a long-lived bunch. Your grandfather lived to be ninety."

"Yes, but my father died before he was sixty, and my mother died before I married Heather," Cole replied. His face tautened as he relived those days, when a lie split him apart from Heather, whom he'd loved with all his heart. It had been a torment, those months apart before he discovered that a jealous rival had told him lies about Heather's parentage and made it sound as if he and Heather were actually related. They weren't, but it was heartbreaking just to think it. Heather had been singing in nightclubs in those days. Cole had been cruel to her because her feelings for him were all too visible and he thought nothing could ever be allowed to happen between them. When he found out the truth, Heather had already backed out of his life. It had taken a long time to win her back.

He glanced at Stasia. She reminded him of Heather in her youth. She wasn't as beautiful as his wife, but she was sweet and gentle and she'd make someone a good wife and mother. He knew that it wasn't going to be Tanner. The boy had mentioned weeks ago that he hated having to talk to her father at all because Stasia would sit and stare at him as if he were a tub of kittens needing a home. He found her juvenile and dull. John, on the other hand, adored her. Cole grimaced as he processed the thought, because Stasia so obviously thought of John as the brotherly type.

"Now, about what I mentioned on the phone," Cole began as he finished his coffee and put it and the cup and saucer back on the tray.

"I know what you're going to say," Glenn broke in, with a smile. "But I'll never give you permission to dam the streams."

Cole sighed. "Only one stream, the one nearest my south pasture. The cattle are going to suffer for that decision," he told the older man. "We've drilled every well we can."

"I know that," Glenn told him. "I've got things in motion that will solve your problem. Don't bother asking; won't tell," he chuckled. "But you're worrying over something that's already fixed. Just a matter of time. Short time, at that," he added with a faraway look in his eyes.

Cole started to argue, realized it would do no good and

just shrugged good-naturedly. "Okay. I'll rely on your conscience."

"Good place to put trust, since I do have one," Glenn replied. He scowled. "That boy of yours got himself into hot
water in France, they say. It was on the front page of the tabloid those Lombard people back East publish."

"It wasn't Tanner who started the trouble," Cole replied
curtly. "It was his…companion, Julienne Harper. She started
a row in a high-ticket French restaurant with another woman,
and her companion started cursing and threw a punch at
Tanner when he intervened. Tanner had some explaining to
do." He glanced at Glenn. "This time, I didn't interfere, and
I wouldn't let Heather do it, either. The boy's got to grow up
and take responsibility for his own actions."

"According to the tabloid, he made restitution for the victim's dress and paid the dentist to replace one of her date's
front teeth." Glenn shook his head. "Reminds me of you,
when you were that age," he added with twinkling eyes.
"Got arrested for a bar brawl when you got home from the
service, I believe…?"

Cole glared at him. "Some yahoo made a nasty joke about
what soldiers did overseas. I took exception. The guy wasn't
ever even in a good fight, what would he know about being
a soldier?"

"Well, your dad kept him from suing, at least," Glenn said,
and chuckled. "Most people around here were scared of your
father anyway. He was a real hell-raiser."

Cole smiled sadly. "He was, and he died far too young."

Glenn knew some stories about Cole's father that he wasn't
about to share. Some secrets, he reasoned, should be kept.
"Your son was in black ops when he went in the military,
wasn't he?" he asked suddenly.

Cole looked thunderous. "Yes, he was. I didn't find out until he was back home." He sighed. "I told him he had to get an education, so he joined the Army and got it that way. At least he finally decided that risking his life daily wasn't conducive to running a ranch. It's one reason I bought the old Banks property for him, to draw him back home." He leaned forward. "I thought if his income depended on ranching, he'd make better life decisions. At least he did get a degree in business, even if it was between assignments." He laughed shortly. "And then he met her." He shook his head.

Everybody knew what that meant. "Her." Julienne Harper. The fly in the ointment. She'd lured Tanner back into the jet-set lifestyle the military had purged him of, and now he was even less responsible than he'd been before.

"A bad woman can make a fool of a good man. And sometimes, the reverse," Glenn added. He didn't mention his late wife, but they all knew the tragic story. His wife had been suddenly and hopelessly attracted to a man straight out of prison who'd worked on the ranch. The tragic consequences were still being lived down, by Glenn and his daughter.

"She was a good woman," Glenn said stubbornly. "She was just impulsive and easily led."

"Which is how many good people end up in prison," John said sadly. "I'm hopeful that we can keep my big brother out of it."

Cole stood up with his son and clapped him on the back. "Something I'll never have to worry about with you," he said with obvious affection. "At least one of my kids turned out right."

He was referring to Odalie, who'd had a brush with the law in her teens, just as Tanner had—when going into the military was the only thing that saved him from serving time. Tanner had fallen in with a few ex-cons and gotten drunk with them. He passed out in the back seat just before they robbed a convenience store, but Cole had to get attorneys and pull a lot of strings to keep his son out of jail.

"Most kids turn out right eventually, even those who have a rough start," Glenn said with a smile.

"Yours turned out very well," Cole said, smiling gently at Stasia. "She reminds me of Heather at her age."

"And that's a compliment indeed," Glenn said, watching his daughter flush shyly.

"Well, we'd better get back home," Cole said. "We're getting ready for roundup. If you need any help over here, when you start, you know we'll do anything you need us for."

Glenn smiled and shook hands with both men. "Yes, I do know. I'll send my hands over if you need extras. We're waiting a week to start."

"We'd be grateful. No matter how many hands you have, a few more are always welcome."

"Done. Just say the word."

"I don't guess you'd like to take in a movie this weekend?" John asked Stasia on the way out the door.

She hesitated. She didn't want to hurt his feelings. She smiled gently. "I would, but I'm working on a landscape and I have a real incentive to finish it quickly now, just in case that nice man does give my name to somebody back East," she added with just the right touch of regret. She liked John, but she didn't want to encourage him. Nobody could replace Tanner in her heart.

"Okay," John said easily, hiding his disappointment. "Rain check?"

"Sure," she lied.

He grinned and they all went out onto the long, wide front porch to see the Everetts off.

Cole stared into the distance. "Good weather, for early spring," he said, admiring the grass that was just getting nice and green in the pastures beyond. "I hope it holds."

"So do I," Glenn replied.

"See you."

Glenn threw up a hand. Stasia waved.

The Everetts got into one of their top-of-the-line black ranch trucks and drove away.

"John's sweet on you," Glenn mentioned over supper that night.

"I know," she groaned. "I like him so much. He's like the brother I never had. But he wants more than I can give him, Dad. It wouldn't be right to encourage him."

Glenn nodded. "I agree." He cocked his head at her. "It's still Tanner, isn't it?"

She grimaced and nodded. "I can't help it. I've been crazy about him since I was fifteen, and he can't see me for dust. It's such a shame that I'm not beautiful and rich and sophisticated," she added heavily.

"A man who loves you won't care what you are or what you've got," he said gently.

"I guess not." She poked at her salad with a fork. "Julienne's really beautiful. Of course, she doesn't talk to the peasants. I saw them together in Branntville just before they left for overseas. She looked me up and down and just laughed." Her face burned at the memory. "So did he, in fact. He thinks I'm a kid."

Glenn had a faraway look in his eyes. "That could change," he said, almost to himself. He turned his green eyes toward her, the same green eyes that he'd hoped she might inherit.

But her brown ones were like his late wife's, he reflected, big and brown and beautiful. "You'll inherit this ranch," he added. "I hope you'll have the good sense to find a manager if you don't want the responsibility of running it yourself. And I hope you won't be taken in by any slick-talking young man who sees you as a meal ticket," he added worriedly, because she wasn't street-smart. "This property has been in our family for a hundred years. I'd hate to see it go to an amusement park for tourists."

She frowned. "Why would it go to someone like that?"

"Oh, this guy offered me a lot of money for the property just the other day, when I was at the bank renewing a couple of CDs. The bank president introduced us."

"You told him no, of course, right, Dad?" she asked.

He pursed his lips. He drew in a breath. "I told him I'd think about it." He didn't tell her that the ranch was mortgaged right up to the eaves of the house. His bad business decisions had led the place to ruin, something Cole Everett knew. It was why Cole was trying to get the ranch. But then, he'd have it soon, Glenn thought sadly. He couldn't let Stasia become a charity case, and the sale of the ranch wouldn't even cover the debts, as things stood.

"But it's right next door to the Everetts' new ranch, the one Tanner owns," she said worriedly. "Can you imagine how nervous purebred cattle would react to an amusement park next door?"

"I can," he said.

"Tanner could lose everything," she said. "His livelihood depends on the new ranch, especially since his dad has already split the inheritance at Big Spur between John and Odalie. He figured Tanner would have enough of a fortune with the Rocking C."

The Rocking C was the name of Tanner's ranch. The previous owner, an elderly Easterner, had called it his rocking chair spread. Hence the name.

"Well, Tanner might have to make a hard decision one day, when I'm gone," Glenn said, and smiled to himself.

"Are you plotting something, Dad?" she asked, worried.

"Me?" He contrived to look innocent. "Now, what would I have to be plotting about?" He chuckled. "How about some of that apple pie you made? This new heart medicine my doctor put me on makes me hungrier, for some reason."

"You never did tell me what he said when you went to him last week," she mentioned.

"Same old same old. Take it easy, take my meds, don't do any heavy lifting," he answered, lying through his teeth. He was due to speak to a cardiologist soon, who would decide if the open-heart surgery Glenn was frightened of was required to keep him alive. A quadruple bypass, the doctor had recommended, and soon. Too many fats, too much cholesterol—despite Stasia's efforts to make him eat healthy food—a history of heart problems and not recognizing his limitations had placed Glenn in a bind. Glenn hadn't shared that information with his daughter. No need to worry her. Besides, he felt fine.

A few days later, just after his cardiologist's office had phoned with an early appointment to see the intervention cardiologist, he started up the steps into the house and fell down dead.

Tanner Everett was cursing at the top of his lungs, so loudly that Cole had to call him down before Heather heard her son.

"Go ahead. Rage," Cole snapped. "But the will can't be

broken. Nobody in Branntville will agree that Glenn Bolton wasn't in his right mind when he made it."

"An amusement park! Next to my purebred herd!" Tanner whirled on his heel and glared at his parent. "And if I don't marry damned Stasia, that's my future."

Cole felt the resentment in the younger man. In his place, he'd have felt it as well. "It was a rotten thing to do," Cole agreed. "But we have to deal with what we've got, not what we wish we had."

"I'm twenty-five years old," Tanner raged. "I'm not ready to get married! Not for years yet!" He stared at his father. "You were older than me when you married Mother."

"Yes, I was. I played the field for years." He looked down at his boots. "I loved your mother. For a long time. But she had a rival who lied and said Heather and I were related by blood. She took years away from us."

Tanner knew the story. All the Everett kids did. It would have been a tragedy if Cole hadn't found out the truth in time.

"Heather was just about Stasia's age when I fell in love with her. She sang like a nightingale, just like Odalie does now. She was beautiful. She still is," he added softly.

Tanner, who'd never felt love for a woman, just stared at him without comprehension.

"There must be some way to dispute the will," Tanner said doggedly.

"Go ahead and look for one. But I'll tell you what our attorney told me: no way in hell. You marry Stasia or the property goes to the Blue Sky Management Properties. Stasia will get nothing."

"Bull! The ranch is worth millions," Tanner shot back.

"It was. Glenn was no rancher, even if his father was," Cole replied curtly. "The place is mortgaged to the hilt, and you can't tell Stasia that. She's got enough misery right now coping with her dad's death."

He grimaced. Even he was sorry for Stasia's situation. She couldn't help what she felt for him, he supposed. But he was never going to return it. She had to know that.

"Which leads to my suggestion. I'm giving you the Rocking Chair ranch, and merging Stasia's with Big Spur. We can pay off the debt by disposing of most of Glenn's beef cattle and replacing it with our purebred Santa Gerts. In other words," Cole added quietly, "either you make a go of your new ranch or you'll be out in the cold. I'm not changing my will, Tanner," he added firmly. "I'm sorry. But you could do worse. And it's about time you stayed home and managed your own damned ranch and stopped acting like some Eastern playboy."

"I hate dust and cattle," Tanner muttered. "You should have given this ranch to John. Then he could have married Stasia."

"She wouldn't have him," Cole said simply. "She doesn't love him."

He jammed his hands into his slacks pockets. "She doesn't love me, or she wouldn't have encouraged her father to do this to me!"

"I don't think she had anything to do with it. Glenn had a bad heart and she had no other family."

"You could have adopted her," Tanner said with a sarcastic bite in his voice.

Cole's silver eyes narrowed and started to glitter.

Tanner cut his losses. "All right, damn it!" he muttered. "I'll do what I have to. But I'm not settling down to aprons and babies and white picket fences! Not for any woman!"

"Nobody's asking you to." Cole felt sorry for Stasia. She loved Tanner. Maybe, maybe love on one side would be enough. But he was worried. Tanner was like a stallion with a new rope around his neck. This wasn't going to end well.

Stasia was in shock. She sat at the kitchen table and made the funeral arrangements, relying on the funeral home and her father's attorney for clarity. She was penniless. Worse, her father had forced his attorney to put a clause in the will. Tanner married Stasia, or her father's property went to the amusement park man, who would turn it into a loud, cluttered nightmare for Cole's horses and cattle.

She'd heard the terms of her father's will from their attorney, Mr. Bellamy. She was shocked and miserable, especially when she recalled what her father had told her only days before, about the offer from the amusement park man. She'd thought she'd get at least enough to live on from the deal, but it wasn't like that at all. Her father had kept so much from her. The ranch was worthless, mortgaged and debt-ridden. There was no way she could run it for a profit, or even hire someone to run it. And if the amusement park man got it, it would destroy Cole's ranch as well as Tanner's. Neither of them could afford to tear down existing stables and barns and rebuild them in a safer location. In fact, there would be no safer location, with that overlit nightmare of noise and light nearby. Not for one minute did she think Tanner would give in to her father's subdued blackmail and marry her. She was ashamed that he'd even put that clause into his will. Tanner would probably think it was her idea.

When she finished the preliminaries, she went to her father's closet to look for his one good suit and his best pair of wing-tip shoes. The sight of the suit set her off. She dropped down onto the spotless paisley duvet on her father's bed and bawled until her eyes were red and her throat hurt.

That was probably why she didn't hear the knock at the front screen door, which wasn't locked. It was also probably why she wasn't aware that Tanner had come into the room and was standing in the doorway, just watching her.

He knew she loved her father. He was the only family she had left. It hurt him to watch her cry. He'd had no real feelings for her, except irritation that she was infatuated with him and let it show too much. But she was really hurting. He'd never lost anyone in his family. Both sets of his grandparents had been dead when he was born. He didn't know death except as an observer.

"Stasia?" he called quietly.

She jumped, startled, and lifted a wet face with red-lined eyes to his. She swallowed down the pincushion that seemed stuck there and swiped at her eyes with the tail of the bright yellow T-shirt she was wearing.

"It wasn't my idea, what he put in the will," she said, as if he'd already accused her of engineering it. Angry brown eyes warred with his pale blue ones. "He said the amusement park man would pay him millions for the land and in the next breath he said it had been in our family for over a century and we should hold onto it." She swallowed, hard. "I didn't know we were bankrupt. I didn't even know how sick he was. He said he had new medicines and the doctor said he was...doing fine..."

Her voice trailed off. Tears fell like rain from her eyes. She averted them. She could feel the pity in him and she didn't want it. He didn't want her. She knew that without asking.

But he couldn't watch her cry. It touched something deep inside him that he didn't even know was there.

He moved closer, pulled her abruptly into his arms and

folded her up close. "Let it out," he said in the softest tone he'd ever used to her. "Go on."

She did. Her father had never been physically affectionate with her. Neither had anyone, except Tanner's mother. It was so nice to be held and cuddled and told that everything was all right. Nothing was all right. But Tanner was strong and warm and he smelled of deliciously expensive male cologne. She melted into him, letting the tears fall.

Finally, she regained control of herself and moved shyly away. "Thanks," she choked.

He shrugged. "I've never really lost anyone," he confessed. "Buddies, when I was in the service, and in black ops. But nobody close."

She looked up at him. "I guess not. I'm really sorry. About the will." She swallowed, hard, and turned away. "I'll find another buyer," she said softly. Then she remembered that she couldn't sell it herself. Besides, it was bankrupt. "There must be a way..."

"There's no way to break the will," he returned. "My father spoke to our attorneys about it. Your father was in his right mind all the way," he added tersely.

She grimaced. Her pale blond hair was loose around her tanned shoulders, disheveled and wavy. In the tight jeans and T-shirt she was very attractive. Tanner had never noticed how attractive before.

"Well, then, how about this?" she asked suddenly while he was still exploring her with new curiosity. "Suppose we get married and the next day we get it annulled?"

"No wedding night?" he asked with mock horror.

She just looked at him. "I don't want to sleep with you. I don't know where you've been," she said and forced a smile.

Humor flared in his pale blue eyes, despite his resentment at the situation they were in.

"Besides, I'm saving myself for my future husband," she added with faint hauteur.

"Most men like experience, not green girls, in bed," he returned.

"My husband will be an extraordinary man, with a good heart and brain, and he'll be grateful that I waited for him," she said.

"Of course. He'll be standing right next to the Easter Bunny, waiting."

She just stared at him. "Dad and I went to church every Sunday. My great-grandfather was a Methodist minister. He founded the church we go to. My great-grandmother had been a missionary in South America. You may live in the fast lane. Some of us still believe in fantastic things and we like a slower pace."

"Snail pace," he scoffed.

"Whatever." She turned away from him and pulled her father's suit and a clean, nicely pressed white shirt, and a tie, off the clothing rack. She picked up his immaculate black wing tips and put them beside the bed.

"What are you doing?"

"He has to have clothes to be...buried in." She almost faltered, but she took a deep breath and pulled a duffel bag out of her father's closet. "I'm going to take them to the funeral home and go over the arrangements with the director. Dad had insurance there that will pay for it all."

He was surprised at her efficiency, despite her obvious grief. He didn't know her well. In fact, he was convinced now that he'd never known her at all.

"Can I help?" he asked.

"Yes." She turned to look at him. "Go home."

Both eyebrows went up.

She cleared her throat. "I'm sorry. I don't mean to be snappy. I just want to be alone. I have to work through this by myself." Her eyes turned back up to his. "You never answered me. Can't we just get married long enough to fulfill the terms of the will and then get it annulled?" she asked.

"I honestly don't know," he replied. "But I can find out."

She nodded. "Then, would you do that?"

He stared at her with open curiosity. "You've followed me around like a puppy for years," he said absently, watching her flush. "For a woman with a monumental crush on me, you seem strangely reluctant to try and keep me."

"Most girls have crushes on totally unsuitable people," she said, fighting a scarlet blush. "They outgrow them."

"And you've outgrown yours?" he asked softly.

"Yes," she lied, averting her eyes. "Well, sort of. I mean, I just turned nineteen and I think I may have a future in art."

Sure she did, he thought to himself. She was talented, but a lot of women painted and never went past giving the canvases away as presents. His eyes went to a landscape on the wall of a windmill with a lone wolf sitting on a small grassy rise under a full moon. Beside it was a portrait of her father that was incredibly lifelike. He frowned. She really did have talent. Not that it would do her much good in this back-of-beyond place.

There was a knock at the front door. She stopped what she was doing, went around Tanner and went to the door. Two women from the church were there with casseroles and bags of food and even a cake.

"Oh, it's so kind," Stasia said, the tears returning as she hugged both women. "Thank you so much!"

"Your dad was a good man, honey," the eldest of the two said. "We all know where he'll end up."

"If you need anything at all, you just call. Or if you'd rather not be here alone at night…"

"I'll be fine," she said softly. "But thanks for the offer."

They said their goodbyes. She put up the food, aware that Tanner had come out of her father's room and was now lounging against the kitchen door.

"Small towns," he said, shaking his head. "And all the little idiosyncrasies that go with them, still amaze me. Nobody outside a rural community would bring food."

"It's a tradition here," she said quietly. "I've done my share of cooking to give to grieving families." She glanced at him. "But of course, that's not your style or Julienne's. You hate living here."

"I do. I've spent too much time in exotic places to settle for boring routine, even to please my father." He thought about Julienne with faint despair. She was great in bed. He'd never be able to replace her. She was already furious and threatening to leave him after being told about Bolton's will. "This isn't the lifestyle I want. The family ranch, a bunch of kids, a wife in the kitchen." He made a face. "I'd rather have Julienne in see-through black lace than all that put together."

"Fortunately for you, that's still possible. All we have to do is fulfill the conditions of my father's will and you can be off to the south of France, or Greece, or wherever you people go for fun."

He frowned. "What do you do for fun?"

Her eyebrows arched. "I paint."

"Besides that." He looked around. "It's just dirt and grass and mesquite and cattle."

"I like cattle. We have little white kittens in the barn," she said, and her face softened, like her brown eyes. "There's a family of rabbits out behind the barn. Dad had to fence them out of the kitchen garden." She stopped, swallowed hard, went back to storing away food. "I like to sit on the front porch in the evening, just at dusk, and listen to the dogs baying in the distance."

"God, how exciting!" he groaned.

She turned and looked at him. "You're older than me, but you don't know much about the way things really are, do you? You live in a fantasy world of artificial people and artificial places. I'd rather be who I am, where I am, doing what I'm doing."

"You'll rot here," he said shortly.

She just smiled. "Difference of opinion. I like my reality straight up. I don't need exotic stimulation to keep me going."

His eyes narrowed. "Meaning that I do?"

"You're not like your brother. John loves ranching," she said. "He doesn't even like to drive his Mercedes. He's more at home in a pickup truck or in the saddle. He's a realist, like me." She smiled sadly. "You're a dreamer. This is never going to be your kind of life." She said it with a hollow certainty that dulled her eyes. She loved him so much. But he didn't want her. He told her so with every word, every look. What he'd said about Julienne was like a knife through her poor heart.

"If I don't keep the ranch and make it pay, I'll lose everything and be stuck here in the mud like my brother," he said shortly.

"It's the end of the world as we know it!" she exclaimed in mock horror.

"What would you know about pretty clothes and party manners and sophisticated behavior?" he asked frankly, giving her a once-over with wise, sharp eyes. "I'd be embarrassed to take you anywhere in decent society."

"Did someone ask you to?" she asked reasonably and hid the pain that careless sentence dealt her pride.

"Just as well," he retorted. "Because if we can marry one day and annul it the next then, by God, we're doing it. I can't think of a worse fate than being tied to you for life."

"Thanks. I like you, too," she replied with a determined smile, mischief showing in her twinkling eyes. "You're sooooo sexy!" she breathed in her best femme fatale voice, puckering her lips at him.

Suddenly, it was just all too much for him. He was confused. She made him hungry, in a way even Julienne couldn't, and he was feeling trapped all over again. Damn her father!

He let out a rough curse and turned and walked out of the house. Only then did she give in to the misery she felt, when he could no longer see it.

TWO

Glenn Bolton was buried next to his wife and his parents in the big Bolton lot at the Branntville Methodist Church cemetery. The whole Everett family, except for Odalie, who was in Italy, attended. Just the same, Odalie sent a huge spray of flowers and called Stasia to tell her how sorry she was. Stasia and Odalie had been casual friends in school. In fact, Stasia was one of the few friends who stuck by her during all the problems Odalie had brought on herself back then. Despite being somewhat conceited and snobbish, Odalie felt close to Stasia. The feeling was mutual.

Tanner showed up at the ceremony, too. Julienne had reluctantly agreed to go, but Heather put her foot down. She was not sharing a pew with her son's call girl, as she put it. She ignored Tanner's outrage and Cole stepped in. He could do more with Tanner with a look than Heather could with outright indignation. Tanner went to the funeral with his parents and his brother. Without Julienne.

Stasia sat on the front pew and listened to the sermon, her face sad but resigned. Her father had been a good man. She would miss him terribly. But life did end. It was one of the absolutes that people just had to accept. Everybody died eventually.

She stopped on the way to the cemetery to speak to people she knew. At the cemetery there was a simple graveside service. Her father, a military veteran in his youth, had a flag and an honor escort from the local VFW post. It made her proud. When they handed her the flag that had covered his coffin, she couldn't hold back the tears.

"You're coming back home with us tonight," Heather told her when they were walking away from the cemetery. "You don't need to be alone."

"No, you don't," John agreed with a grin. "I'll show you my new calves!"

She smiled. "I'd like that."

Tanner glared at them all and went to his own car without a word and drove away.

"Tanner and I discussed Dad's will," Stasia told them later in their living room. "We're hoping that we can get married one day and have the marriage annulled the next," she added. "Then we'll both have what we want."

Cole ground his teeth together. He'd seen the will. He didn't want to tell her what he'd said to Tanner just two hours earlier. There was no room in the explicit language of the will for a loophole. They got married and they stayed married for at least a year. That was the deal. Stasia had been too upset to look at the will, but Cole and Tanner were allowed to see it, since it involved both Cole's ranch and the one he'd given Tanner. It was an airtight thing. Glenn must have anticipated

Tanner's approach to marriage. It was a shame. But there was nothing even their fine attorneys could do to combat it. At least, not immediately. They were still looking for that one tiny hole in Glenn Bolton's document that would give Tanner and Stasia a way out. It was a long shot, but not impossible. They were great attorneys.

Cole dreaded telling Stasia about the reality of the will. For the time being, he put it on hold. There would be time to talk tomorrow, after the trauma of the funeral today.

Julienne was pacing the living room of Tanner's ultramodern ranch when he got home. Her black hair curved in a pixie cut around her pretty face, but she was glaring for all she was worth.

"The Simpsons are waiting for us in Athens," she said angrily. "And we're stuck here while you nose around that stupid girl and her ranch!"

He stared at her with cold eyes. The only good thing about her was what she could do in bed. He'd never liked her. She was ice-cold with most people, and money was the only thing that mattered to her. She had no compassion for anyone.

"Not to mention your mother's attitude!" she went on. "What century does she think we're living in? I'm no call girl!"

"My parents and my siblings are conservative ranching people," he began.

"Well, I'm not hanging around here smothered in dust and smelly cattle. When can we leave?"

"My father and I went to see our attorneys this morning about the will. There's no provision to break it." He jerked off his tie and tossed it aside, dropping onto the couch. Nearby

was a grand piano. He played, his mother considered, mag-
nificently. She'd taught him from the age of three.

"What does that mean?" Julienne demanded.

"It means that if I don't marry Stasia, I lose the ranch."

"Oh, big deal, you can buy another one..."

"The ranch is where my inheritance is," he bit off. "No
ranch, no money, Julie."

She stopped dead. "You mean...?"

"I mean that if I don't marry Stasia, her ranch has to be sold
to the property developer and I'll have an amusement park for
a neighbor. I'll lose the cattle because of the constant noise.
No money. If I marry her, I keep the ranch, and the money."

"And what about me?" Julienne asked harshly.

"What about you?"

"You could marry me," she said, and smiled at him.

"The only money you have is mine. I'd be no better off,"
he pointed out. He got up and poured himself a stiff whiskey.
"And don't tell me you have scruples about sleeping with a
married man," he said coldly, staring at her. "You don't have
scruples."

She grimaced. He was right.

"So, what do we do?"

"You go to Greece. I'll marry Stasia and leave her here to
take care of things. I'll be along in a week or so."

"Oh." She brightened.

"Did you think I had putting down roots in mind?" he
asked, laughing. "Hell, I'm not family material, I never was. I
did black ops when I was in the service. You learn not to value
the things that normal people do." He finished the whiskey.
"This won't take long. I'll wrap it all up by next weekend.
Get us a hotel on the beach. Somewhere ritzy."

"I'll do that very thing," she purred.

★ ★ ★

Tanner went looking for Stasia two days later. She was sitting on the porch of his father's ranch house with a cat in her lap, one of the white kittens from her barn that she'd given to John, who loved cats. She was wearing her ever-present jeans with a yellow pullover sweater because it was a nippy spring evening. Her hair was loose around her shoulders. She looked very sad. And very young.

He was surprised at his lack of antagonism for her. He thought that she'd talked her father into inserting that clause in the will. But the Everett attorneys said that wasn't the case at all. The old man was afraid that Stasia would be thrown on the street when he died, because the ranch was in such debt. She'd have stability, at least, with Tanner. They told Cole and Tanner one other thing as well. Stasia didn't know that the will had a clause that required a year of marriage. She hadn't even looked at the will.

She glanced up and saw him. Her face colored, just slightly, a response that she couldn't help. She hated seeing the irritation in his eyes as he approached her. He was hating this, hating her, and there was nothing she could do.

"Well?" she asked in a world-weary tone. "Is there a loophole? Can we get married and have it annulled right after?"

He sighed. "No."

She averted her gaze to the kitten in her lap. "I loved my father, and I miss him. But if I died today, I'd be looking for him with a big iron skillet and I'd lay his head open for leaving us in this mess!"

He shoved his big, lean hands into his jean pockets. "Pity he didn't try to leave you to John. He'd be down in Dallas buying rings by now."

"I know." She grimaced. "John is such a nice man."

Nice. It told him all he needed to know about her opinion of his younger brother. It was a damned shame that she
couldn't love the other man.

"How long?" she asked, lifting her eyes to his.

Both dark brows lifted.

"How long do we have to stay married?" she asked, irritated.

He leaned against the railing of the porch steps. "A year."

She grimaced.

"Our attorneys couldn't find a single loophole that would
avoid it, either," he added quietly.

"I guess Julienne has broken every piece of crockery in
your house by now," she said idly.

"If she was over there, no doubt. She's gone to Athens. I'm
going, too, next week."

She looked up at him with fire in her eyes. "Oh, I see.
You're going to marry me so that you can keep your ranch,
and then you're flying off to Greece to commit adultery the
same day?"

His high cheekbones colored with anger. "I'm marrying
you to keep a damned amusement park off my south border,"
he said shortly. "It's not going to be a traditional marriage."

She stood up, putting the kitten down very gently. She felt
sick inside. She looked up at him. It was still a long way. "This
town is still talking about my mother and what she did to
Daddy," she said, trying to control her temper. "I've been the
subject of gossip my whole life because of it. And now you're
going to set the tongues wagging all over again by shaming
me in the eyes of every decent person for miles around?"

"It's a paper marriage, not a real one," he said, his voice
biting into her ears. "I don't want to marry you in the first
place," he added, eyes blazing with bridled fury. "You're a
little country hick with no sense of sophistication, you're

barely educated and you're still living in the Victorian age! I couldn't tie myself to a worse woman if I looked for years!"

Her brown eyes glittered with feeling. Her small, pretty hands curled by her side. "Careful, cowboy," she said very softly. "I don't have to marry you."

He choked back another insult as he realized what she was saying. Of course she didn't have to marry him. She could sell the ranch and he couldn't do a thing to stop her. She'd have no money, having cut off her nose to spite her face, but she'd be revenged. And he and Cole would have a good chance of losing their respective ranches because the noise the amusement park would make would play merry hell with those purebred herds of Santa Gertrudis cattle, not to mention the quarter horses Cole also bred for sale.

"Hell and damnation!" he burst out.

She cocked her head and studied him. The pain those insults caused her was carefully camouflaged. You didn't show weakness in front of the enemy, ever. She'd learned that from her father.

"Go ahead," she invited. "Turn the air blue. Raise hell. And see if it does you one glimmer of good." She looked him up and down with forced indifference. "Like I want to tie myself to a man who uses women like a handkerchief."

She turned and started to walk away.

He had her before she went one step, her slender body suddenly riveted to the length of his in an embrace that set every nerve she had tingling with helpless pleasure.

"Brave words," he whispered at her mouth. "Pity I don't believe a word of it."

"I mean…!"

His mouth cut off the angry remark. She was soft and warm and her mouth tasted of iced tea and mint. He'd managed for years to keep his hands off her, because he was attracted to her, however reluctantly. Now it was to his advantage to give in to those feelings. He needed her consent to the will's requirements as much as she needed him.

Heated, throbbing seconds later, he lifted his mouth just above hers. "Pure bravado, was it?" he asked, his deep voice husky with arousal.

"I don't want to kiss you," she lied, but she wasn't moving away.

He smiled as he bent again. "Liar," he whispered, and it sounded almost like an endearment.

She sank against him, helpless to resist a kiss she'd ached for since her fifteenth birthday, when he'd refused to come to the birthday party with John and Odalie and broken her heart. It was the closest to heaven she'd ever been. She couldn't afford to give in to him, to allow herself to be manipulated this way. But, oh, it was sweet, to feel his arms closing around her, to feel the expert, demanding pressure of his mouth on hers. He wanted her. She wasn't so naïve that she didn't know what the sudden hardness of his body meant. He might resent the will, he might even resent her, but he wanted her. At least, there was that.

The sound of a car pulling up in the driveway brought him to his senses. He was so lost in her that he'd forgotten the will, Julienne, all of it. He looked down into drowning brown eyes in a flushed, yielded face utterly beautiful with fascination, wonder.

Her mouth was softly swollen. She was trembling. His big, lean hands smoothed down her arms and he smiled.

"I'm not marrying you," she managed.

He only chuckled, deep in his throat. "Yes, you are. My

mother's already online looking at wedding gowns. You'll be prodded up to Neiman Marcus before you know it."

"I'm not playing second fiddle to your...!"

He bent and kissed her, very softly, enjoying the helpless response of her sweet little mouth. "I'll see you tomorrow. I have to go up to Dallas to see a man about a new stud bull." He kissed her one last time, smiling at her expression. She looked loved. Fascinated. He hated the pleasure her expression gave him. She was still a virgin, he knew that from things her father had let drop. He'd never been with an innocent. It would be an adventure. As for Julienne, well, what this little sunflower didn't know wouldn't hurt her. He could be discreet.

"I don't want to marry your son," Stasia muttered while she tried on the wedding gown Heather had coaxed her toward. "He's only doing it to save his ranch, because of Daddy's will."

"A lot of men marry for the wrong reasons, and things end beautifully," Heather said softly, her pale blue eyes smiling at the younger woman as she tugged a piece of lace into place. "I had a particularly rough time getting to the altar."

"I know," Stasia said softly and smiled. "But everything turned out very well for you and your husband."

"Eventually," Heather said. "I was independent by then and certain that I wanted a singing career. Cole was equally determined that he came first." She sighed. "So we compromised. I taught music locally and wrote songs for various singing groups, including Desperado," she replied, naming one of the more famous rock bands.

"Didn't you mind giving it up?"

"I loved him," Heather said simply. "A career would have meant spending my life on the road. I couldn't raise a family that way, and I wanted children, oh, so much!" she added.

"I wouldn't trade one second of my life for what I thought I wanted. And if I could live my whole life over, I wouldn't change a single thing."

Stasia smiled. "I love kids. I wouldn't mind having one of my own." She looked up at Heather. "Tanner doesn't love me, you know," she said abruptly. "His livelihood depends on keeping the ranch solvent. If Dad hadn't put that clause in the will, Tanner would never have considered me. He said I was an ignorant little country hick," she added, grimacing because the harsh words still stung.

"You aren't," Heather said quietly. "You're a talented artist. Very talented. Don't let him put you down."

"Oh, I don't," Stasia replied. She laughed. "I'm nobody's doormat. Not even his."

"No, you aren't," Heather agreed. "See that you remember that. He's always been stubborn and reckless. He and his father have gone head to head times without number because of it. He's too much like Cole."

"Was your husband like Tanner, when he was younger?"

"Exactly like him, doubled," Heather said flatly. "I'm still amazed that I didn't lay his head open with a baseball bat from time to time." She shook her head. "But he's like a rock when things get tough," she added. "I had a bad time giving birth to Tanner. I was in the hospital for over a week with complications, because they'd had to do a C-section. Cole never left me for a second. They put a cot in my room for him, and we stayed there, both of us, while I healed. Cole is an amazing person," she added softly.

Stasia smiled. "And you still love him, after twenty-five years of marriage," she marveled.

"Oh, yes," she agreed. "And you'll love Tanner just like that, after years of marriage and children."

"He doesn't want children," Stasia said sadly.

"Men don't know what they want," Heather said. "Give it time. He's been like a stallion all these years, free and wild. A bridle is a new thing to him."

"He said Julienne was in Athens waiting for him," Stasia confessed. "I told him that I'd had enough gossip in my life, without him rushing off to commit adultery on my wedding day."

"Well!" Heather exclaimed, and she hugged Stasia. "I was going to advise you, but I think you've got the situation well in hand."

Stasia hugged her back. "Thanks," she said, smiling. She looked at Heather with a sigh. "I'm only sorry it can't be John," she said softly. "I know how he feels, and it hurts me to see it. But I can't help what I feel for Tanner."

"John will find his own special woman one day," Heather said. "Pity is a sad excuse for a marriage."

Stasia nodded. "Yes, it is. But I wouldn't hurt John for the world."

"John will do just fine. Now. We need hose and shoes and a garter for you to toss!"

The wedding was the social event of Branntville. It had taken two weeks for the rushed preparations.

Julienne, sitting alone in Athens, had raged at Tanner over the phone, that it was just a paper marriage, so all the social things were unnecessary. To which Tanner had replied that Julienne could fly back and argue about them with his mother. Knowing how that lady felt about her, Julienne gave in with bad grace and hung up on him.

He mentioned the phone call to his father as he studied the new breeding bull in the barn at his ranch.

Cole gave him a steady glare. "You're being married by a minister," he pointed out.

He shrugged. "So?"

"So, marriage is a solemn vow," he replied. "You promise to be faithful to your partner."

"It's just words."

"Not to me," Cole said shortly. "Nor to your mother. We've been married for twenty-five years and I've never been tempted to stray. Neither has she."

Tanner eyed his father with surprise. "Never?"

Cole's silver eyes glittered. "Never. When I make a promise, I keep it."

"Well, it's different with me and Stasia," Tanner said curtly. "You got married voluntarily. I'm being forced to marry her."

"No, you're not," Cole said. "You can stop the wedding right now. Just go over to Stasia's place and tell her you're not going through with it."

Tanner grimaced. "Sure. And lose everything I own."

"For all the attention you pay to it, I can't imagine you'd miss it" came the surprising reply. "You're too busy hitting resorts all over the world with your professional escort."

Tanner's lips made a thin line. "You've been talking to Mom."

"You know how she feels about the woman."

"Julienne is my business."

"She'll be Stasia's business if you keep it up."

"I'll be discreet," Tanner told him. "But I'm not ready to settle down. Not even to keep an amusement park from moving in next door."

"Your choice," Cole said. He gave his son a steady look. "Don't disgrace the girl," he added in a soft, curt tone. "She's had enough of that."

He turned and walked off.

Tanner knew what he meant. Stasia and her dad had been forced to live down her mother's infamy, her affair, in a small community where everybody knew everybody else's business. It had been traumatic for Stasia, because she was still in school while it was going on. Worse, when her mother's paramour had suddenly turned his attention to a younger, richer woman, it had been Stasia who found her mother hanging on the back porch...

"Mr. Everett, there is a call for you," Minnie Martinez called from the back porch. Her voice was as cold as her demeanor. She didn't like her boss or his nasty girlfriend. Her husband was the full-time ranch manager. She kept the house immaculate and stood in for Tanner's secretary who worked two days a week in the office. Answering the phone was part of her responsibilities.

"Who is it?" he called back.

She made a face.

"Julienne?" He smiled as he turned and walked quickly up the steps and into the house, ignoring Minnie's angry glance.

"You should fire that stupid housekeeper," Julienne said, immediately going on the offensive. "She wouldn't call you to the phone because your father was with you. Is everybody afraid of him?"

"You've never seen him mad," he pointed out, "or you might have some sympathy for those of us who have."

"He's just a man," she scoffed.

"Sure." He sighed. "What do you want?"

"You! When are you coming over?"

"I'm getting married in two days."

"Then if you're not here in three days, I'm coming over

there to pry you away from your wife," she replied. "Honestly, you don't have to sleep with her, do you?"

"Of course not," he lied, because just thinking about Stasia
in his bed made him rigid with reluctant attraction.

"I'll make it worth your while," Julienne purred. "Do you
miss me?"

"Yes, I miss you," he said. "And yes, I'll be there in three
days."

"I'll hold you to that, lover," she said.

He went back outside to talk to Juan Martinez about the
new bull. It was spring, too late to put him on the heifers,
but he would be turned out with the other bulls in the fall,
to produce a new crop of purebred Santa Gertrudis bulls and
heifers next spring.

Stasia was getting dressed for her wedding with Odalie Everett helping in the bedroom of the Bolton home.

"I'll trip over my train and go headfirst into the minister,"
Stasia moaned as Odalie fastened the last button on top of her
wedding gown and twitched the fingertip veil carefully in
place on the upswept, artistic hairdo with its pearl hairpins.

"You won't," Odalie said, smiling. She was beautiful, as
Stasia wasn't. A lot of people didn't like her, because she could
be arrogant and cruel. But she was kind to Stasia because Stasia had been her staunch friend during Odalie's brush with
the law in high school. Odalie never forgot a favor, and she
was fond of Stasia even without their shared past. There was
one other reason for her affection: John loved Stasia and she
loved her brother. Odalie and Tanner didn't get along, except for brief periods. Like the rest of her family, Odalie had
no use for Julienne and said so, frequently.

"I wish I looked as good as you do," Stasia sighed, because

Odalie was a picture in blue chiffon, with her pale blond hair looped in braids on top of her head, her pale blue eyes in a face as beautiful as a fairy's.

"You look just fine," Odalie teased.

"And I wish I could sing like you. Honestly, you had me in tears when you sang 'Jerusalem' in church last Sunday!"

"I inherited that from Mom," Odalie said with a smile. "She could have been famous, but she just wanted to marry Dad and have kids."

"That's what I'd like to do. Have kids." Stasia made a face. "Fat chance. Tanner doesn't want kids. He's made that very clear. Which reminds me, I have to start taking a pill today."

"You didn't take the shot?" Odalie asked.

"I'm afraid of it. Some women get terrible weight gain. I like being slender. And how do you know about birth control?" she chided.

Odalie laughed. "Not for the reason you're thinking. I'm not shacking up with anybody until my wedding night. I've lived for a chance at the Metropolitan Opera all my life. But after I do that, if I can, I want the sort of marriage my parents have."

"I envy them," Stasia said.

"Me, too." She stood back and gave Stasia a nod. "You look super. And to allay your suspicions, I was having trouble with my periods, so my doctor put me on birth control just long enough to get them regulated again. Not for other purposes. As you might have noticed, my family doesn't move with the times."

"Well, most of it doesn't," Stasia corrected.

"Yes, I know, Tanner's private life is a trial to us all. Mom and Dad hate that woman he's with, but he won't give her up and he doesn't care what people say. Well, he will now, because Dad's made threats."

"He has?" Stasia was fascinated.

"You see," Odalie said as she started to put on the pretty wide-brimmed blue hat that went with her dress, because she was maid of honor, "Tanner doesn't actually own the ranch outright. Dad has controlling interest in it, along with a provision that allows him to buy back Tanner's interest in it any time he pleases."

"But he wouldn't do that," Stasia protested. "He'd leave Tanner penniless, especially since your dad has already split the Big Spur between you and John."

"Dad won't do it unless he's pushed," Odalie corrected, adjusting the tilt of her hat. She turned, smiling, a picture in her dressy outfit. "But Tanner won't push him. He's getting married today. And I expect Tanner will find marriage so sweet that he may never leave town again," she teased.

Stasia blushed. "On the other hand, he may light a shuck out of town immediately after the ceremony."

"Don't be silly. Okay, it's almost time. I'll leave you to drive over to the church with John."

Stasia hugged her. "Thanks, for everything."

"You're going to be my sister." She grinned. "I always wanted one. See you later."

Stasia watched her leave. Big, handsome John Everett, his brother's best man, paused in the doorway to look at Stasia with eyes that ate her from head to toe. He adored her. He knew that he'd never replace Tanner in her eyes, but he never gave up hope.

He towered over his father and his brother, a giant of a man with thick blond hair, and silver eyes like his father. In his fancy suit, he looked good enough to eat.

Stasia didn't love him, not the way she loved Tanner, but

she did adore him. She grinned at him. "Nice of you to give me a ride."

"No problem. Old Mr. Sartain, who's giving you away, can't drive anymore because he refuses to get his cataracts removed." He sighed. "I hope he won't walk you into the minister at the church."

She laughed. "I'll keep him pointed in the right direction. Shall we go?"

John put her in the car, very carefully because of her voluminous dress, and then climbed in beside her.

"The church is full," he remarked. "I didn't realize we knew so many people."

"Your mother said that a lot of them came from out of town."

"Yes, they did, including a friend of Tanner's from someplace called Jacobsville, down south of San Antonio." He leaned down. "They say he's a merc!"

Her eyes widened. "A professional soldier?"

"Worse. He owns an anti-terrorism school. He spent years in the profession himself. Now he trains younger men in anti-terrorism tactics. His name's Eb Scott."

"Tanner seems to know a lot of unorthodox people," she pointed out. "Remember what a stir he caused last year when one of his former black ops friends from England came to town? I thought Odalie was going to swoon, just to get his attention."

"Oh, he was off women," John replied drolly. "And he must have been a eunuch, to resist my sister." He shook his head. "Honestly, even if she is my sister, she's a dish!"

"Yes, she is," she agreed. "I didn't dare ask her, but is she still mourning your friend Cort?"

Cort Brannt was John's best friend, the son of King Brannt and his wife Shelby. They had a daughter as well, Morie, who was married to one of the Kirk brothers of ranching fame up in Wyoming.

"Not really," John said. "She didn't love him. She was only jealous when he started paying attention to his new wife, before she was his wife. And that's a story that ended with Odalie turning into the sweetheart she is now. Meanwhile she has those opera cravings. She wants to sing in the Met one day, so she's pressuring Mom and Dad to let her extend her studies in Italy. I think they'll give in. Mom could have done that, you know. She really has the voice for it."

"I know. Even Tanner is musical," she recalled. "He plays the piano with a gift."

"While the only thing I can play is the radio," John lamented as they pulled up in front of the church.

"And that's a fib," she teased. "You play classical guitar with a gift of your own."

"Mom gave up on me with the piano. I wanted to play baseball from morning to night, not sit at a piano." He glanced at her with a grin. "Guitars are portable. I could practice anywhere. And I was invited to. Anywhere *not* in the house," he added, and she laughed with him.

He parked his luxury car at the door of the sparkling white Methodist church with its towering steeple and went around to help Stasia out in the extravagant folds of her lovely wedding gown.

He paused and looked down at her with eyes that agonized, a look he quickly erased when she turned her gaze upward and smiled at him.

"Be happy," he said softly.

"Thanks."

He escorted her to the door, handed her over to Mr. Sartain, a family friend of hers and the Everetts' for many years, and took his place at the altar beside his irritated brother.

Tanner faced front, even when the music started and Stasia came down the aisle. For two cents, he told himself, he'd turn around and march past Stasia right out the front door. And what would that accomplish? He'd lose the ranch and his inheritance and be forced to work for a meager living for the rest of his life. Well, he'd have the legacy his grandmother had given Heather, which she'd given to him on his twenty-first birthday, and it would keep him for a while. But it wouldn't accommodate the jet-set lifestyle he and Julienne were accustomed to.

No, better to tough it out and do what he had to do. After all, Stasia meant nothing to him, really, and what he was doing would save the ranch. Stasia could stay here with her painting and he could go to Athens with Julienne. It was only for a year. A lot could happen in that length of time. Stasia might actually fall in love with his suffering brother John, divorce him and marry John. He frowned. Odd, how little that appealed to him, all at once.

The music was playing. The "Wedding March." He had the sheet music, in a book of similar compositions, but he'd never played it. The organist missed a note and he grimaced inwardly. But there was no time to process the thought.

Stasia was standing beside him, her head barely topping his shoulder. He looked down at her upturned face and almost caught his breath at her innocent beauty. He'd never really paid that much attention to her over the years. She was just Stasia, mostly a nuisance he had to put up with to see her father. But now...

"Dearly beloved," the minister began.

And Tanner took a deep breath.

THREE

The service seemed to fly by. Tanner slid a simple gold wedding ring onto Stasia's finger, and she put a similar one on his. The rings had already been purchased before she could pick out something she liked. He hadn't been forthcoming about an engagement ring and she'd been too proud to ask, especially after he'd bulldozed ahead with the wedding bands.

At least he'd gotten the size right, she thought, even if he hadn't asked what hers was. It was just one more indication that he had nothing invested in this wedding.

The reception was held at the church's fellowship hall, after the bride and groom had posed for wedding photographs. After noting Tanner's bored expression, Stasia was certain that she'd never want to look at them again. He made sure that everyone knew this was a forced marriage, that he had no interest in either it or his bride. He was doing it because

Stasia's father had made it a condition of his will. Everybody knew that, it being a small community.

It didn't help Stasia's lacerated feelings one bit, and she wished that she'd refused to go through with it. Her own weakness for Tanner had been her worst enemy. She loved him too much to refuse the marriage. But she should have refused. How was it going to be, with him off partying with another woman and the whole world knowing about it, guessing even if they weren't certain? Tanner Everett wasn't a man to be forced into anything. It would be like a bull yearling with his head in a noose and a cowboy on the other end. He'd fight, and keep on fighting, to throw it off.

She'd hoped against hope that he might give in, might actually learn to love her in time. But he was making it clear, without saying a word, that he didn't want Stasia. Looking around her, she noted the looks of sympathy she was getting from older people in the community. They knew. They all knew, and pitied her.

She cut the cake in the fellowship hall, Tanner's cool hand only briefly over hers as the photographer snapped his picture.

"And that's another one I'll never look at," she said under her breath as the photographer moved around the room.

"Excuse me?" Tanner asked, surprised.

She looked up at him with actual distaste. "The photographs. It must be like taking pictures at a wake. Nobody except your family is ever even going to see them."

He felt a surge of shame as she said that. He felt guilty for a lot of things. This was just the latest one. He was surprised at that, because shame was new to him.

He started to speak, but Stasia had already moved away, leaving her untouched cake behind, to speak to a friend of her father's.

★ ★ ★

It was a long afternoon, because the bride and groom weren't anxious to leave, and the gathering was a good excuse for some gossip and a lot of catching up on the part of local people. Stasia, standing with Heather Everett, watched it with interest.

"There's old Miss Barnes with old Mr. Jackson," she whispered to Heather, in a joyful undertone. "Both old, both single, and she's keen on him. He lost his wife last year and she's never been married!"

"Matchmaker," Heather chuckled as she sipped coffee.

"I like to see people happy," Stasia said simply, smiling.

"I wish you were, sweetheart," Heather said softly.

Stasia looked up at her with wide, resolved brown eyes. "I can still go stay at my own house when I like, your husband said so. It was nice of you both to offer to pay it off, much less keep it up."

"Everybody needs a place to go when they want some privacy," Heather said. "Besides, and I have to apologize for saying it, acquiring your father's ranch solves our water problems for many years to come."

"I did notice that," Stasia teased. She sipped her own coffee. "I'm just glad that it stays in the family, so to speak," she added. "It's been in our family for generations. It's home."

Heather touched her veil, pushed back over her pretty long, waving light blond hair since Tanner had lifted it and kissed her, quite coldly, during the ceremony. "The gown is beautiful. I noticed the photographer got a lot of candid shots."

"Oh, yes," Stasia said enthusiastically. "He got one of Tanner being bored during the ceremony, and one of Tanner being bored while cutting the cake. Look, there he is getting one of Tanner being bored drinking coffee...!" She stopped at the sight of Heather's expression. "Sorry. I got carried away."

"I'm sorry, that things have turned out like this," Heather replied. "You know you've always been my first choice of possible daughters-in-law."

"I do know that, and I'm sorry, too." She drew in a breath and looked toward John, who was sipping punch with a morose expression. "Why couldn't it have been John?" she wondered sadly.

"That's a question for the philosophers. And it's going on five o'clock. If you and Tanner stay here much longer, there's going to be even more gossip, I'm afraid."

"Good point. I'll turn in my coffee cup and announce it to him. He'll be thrilled. I'll have to alert the photographer," she added pertly.

Heather just shook her head.

Stasia put the coffee cup back on the table and thanked the caterers at the same time. Then she went in search of Tanner.

He was standing by a window, looking out, both hands in his pockets.

"Your mother says that if we don't leave soon, people will start to talk about us," she told him.

He seemed to brighten.

Stasia motioned to the photographer. "Quick," she said, "get a shot of him right now!"

The photographer, not in the know but obliging, took a quick picture of the two of them, Stasia with a sparkle in her eyes and a smile on her pretty mouth, and the surprised but amused look on Tanner's face.

"Be careful with that one," she told the photographer. "It's sure to be a family favorite."

He chuckled. "Yes, ma'am."

"We're about to leave," she added, "so you might get shots of the car that a few of the local boys have been…adorning."

"Yes, I, uh, did notice soap and cans and string…"

She grinned as he left.

"What did you mean, about the photo being a family fa-vorite?" Tanner asked.

"It's going to be the only one the man gets that shows you with anything except a bored expression, of course," she re-plied. "Don't mind my feelings, I don't have any. They've all been sheared off by the will and its aftermath. This isn't a day I want to remember, either, Tanner, in case you won-dered," she added, and she turned around. "Thank you all so much for coming!" she called to the people, most of whom she knew. "We're going home now."

There were some knowing looks and a few chuckles as she started toward the front of the fellowship hall with Tanner trailing behind. He stopped to talk to a tall man with blond-streaked brown hair, a little silver mixed in. He shook hands with him before rejoining Stasia. He didn't offer to intro-duce his visitor.

Stasia didn't care. She was tired and sick of the whole busi-ness. Seeing John standing to one side with agony in the eyes he averted, she felt even sicker.

She went to him, compassion forcing her actions. "You have to come and stand with the others, because I'm throw-ing the bouquet right to you," she teased.

He forced a smile. "Throw it to somebody who has a chance of getting married."

She wiggled her eyebrows. "I am!" She leaned up and kissed his tanned cheek and then went back to Tanner.

He was suddenly irritated, and it showed. "What was that all about?" he asked curtly.

"Nothing you need to know," she said with a cool smile. She turned and lifted the bouquet, with people lining the

sidewalk on both sides. "Okay. Here goes!" And she threw
the bouquet, just as she'd threatened, right into John's hands
with the accuracy she'd always managed when playing sand-
lot baseball with her friends as a child. Sadly, most of those
friends had moved to the city for better opportunities, or married. They kept in touch, but lightly. Small towns had little
to offer in the way of high-tech opportunities.

The chauffeur held the door to the limo open, with the
photographer hovering.

"We might as well make a traditional exit," Tanner muttered under his breath. Before Stasia could react, he pulled
her into his arms, bent, and kissed her as if he were going to
war on a sailing ship and would never see land again.

She went under like a drowning victim. She never could
resist him. She loved him too much. She stifled a moan as
the kiss deepened into layers of pleasure she hadn't dreamed
of. Just when she thought she might actually pass out from
it, he twirled her back up into a standing position and eased
her into the car.

"That should solve two dilemmas," he said shortly as the
chauffeur closed the back door.

"What...dilemmas?" she managed in a high-pitched, shiv-
ery tone.

"Your need for proper photos, and my brother's to keep his
hands off you."

She gaped at him.

He averted his eyes. That had popped out from nowhere.
It hadn't been on his mind. Or had it? He hadn't liked Stasia
kissing John, even on the cheek. That had made him angry.
And guilt had ridden him hard, because he'd cared nothing
for Stasia's feelings as he proceeded to turn a wedding into
a wake.

He was confused and mad and unsettled. It wasn't a normal condition. He'd stopped to thank Eb Scott for showing up, but he hadn't wanted to introduce his friend to Stasia. He didn't want any part of his life, past or present, to be entangled with hers. He wanted freedom. He wanted Julienne. Yes. He had to remember that. He wanted Julienne. Perhaps he could write it on his palm and refer to it often, because when he'd been kissing Stasia, Julienne had never existed. That was a surprise. His attraction to his new wife was an unwanted, unneeded obstacle. His life was planned. Stasia had no part in it, now or ever.

Before he'd settled that in his mind, they were at the ranch. He paid the chauffeur, thanked him and followed Stasia into his house.

The Martinezes were enthusing over her dress.

"Everything is prepared, just so," Minnie said quickly. "The master bedroom, and the food only needs to be heated. Most of it is cold cuts, too. There is wine and champagne in the refrigerator. And flowers everywhere!" she added, indicating vases full of them. One was filled with Stasia's favorite, sunflowers. She went close to sniff them, smiling.

"Those are from Mrs. Everett," Minnie said. "She loves them, too."

"It's my father's nickname for her," Tanner volunteered. "Sunflower."

"We must go. It is my brother's birthday, so Juan and I are leaving. If you need us, Señor Everett, you have our cell phone numbers," Minnie concluded.

"Sure. Have fun," he said.

Juan congratulated them also but avoided speaking directly to Tanner. He had only contempt for a man who kept mistresses. He was very conventional. Like Minnie.

"Are you hungry?" Stasia asked, looking in the fridge. "There's a whole tray of cold cuts, cheese and salami and even prosciutto!" she exclaimed. "And black olives, my favorite, Edam and Gouda and Havarti cheese…!"

Her enthusiasm made him smile. "Okay. It sounds good. Breakfast was a long time ago."

"Yes, it was, and I didn't have any. I was too nervous to eat anything," she confessed. "I'll just change…oh, my gosh!"

He laughed at her expression. "What's wrong now?"

"My clothes!" she said. "I don't have any!"

He gave her a long look. He was still fascinated with his reaction to her at the church, and churning inside with unexpected desire that hadn't lessened even a fraction since their arrival here. "I expect if you check the bedroom, my mother will have packed a suitcase for you."

She let out a sigh. "Of course. I didn't even think… I'll be right back!"

She went out of the room at a fast clip, her mind entirely on finding the suitcase. That was why she didn't notice that Tanner was close behind her. She moved into the master bedroom and it wasn't until she heard the door close, and then lock, that she realized she wasn't alone…

She turned around and he was moving toward her, his eyes blazing with hunger. She caught her breath.

"What, cold feet?" he chided. "When we both know how you feel about me."

"I'm hungry," she procrastinated, trying to move back. "We could have some cold cuts."

"While you work up an appetite?" he mused. His hands circled her tiny waist and his mouth went to her neck. "I already have one, thanks."

"Tanner, this isn't a good idea," she faltered, her breath

coming in tiny jerks as her cold hands rested on his broad, muscular chest.

"Why not?"

"I can think of a whole bunch of reasons," she said, but her eyes were closing, her body was arching toward him, her senses were exploding in sensuality.

"Me, too," he whispered at her mouth. "We can discuss them later."

And while his mouth covered hers, suddenly demanding, he carried her to the bed.

She knew about men and women. Her classes in school had been moderately shocking. But what Tanner did to her was completely out of her experience, even beyond what she'd read in the passionate romance novels she loved to read.

Well, some of it was like that. But reading wasn't like doing. When you were reading, you couldn't feel the soft abrasion of a man's skin sliding against yours, or feel the sensations his big, lean hands aroused when they slid to the inside of your thighs and around them, or the ache that came from feeling a man's mouth on your bare breasts.

Her short nails bit into his back as he moved on her, her wedding gown on the floor beside the bed, along with his suit, as one intimacy led to an even greater one. The window was open next to the bed, and the curtains blew back and forth, echoing the motion of the lean body moving on Stasia's.

The first quick thrust had first shocked and then caused a burning pain. But his mouth had erased the pain very efficiently as it moved to her breasts. His hands went between them and aroused a sudden stab of pleasure that made her eyes roll back in her head. She felt like flame, burning and reaching up even to the stars in a mad bubble of ecstasy that arched her tortured body and let out a shuddering, alien moan from her mouth until his covered it.

She went from one plateau to another, mindless and fluid, a prisoner of his desire and her ache to assuage it. She gloried in his own satisfaction when it finally came, feeling him shudder endlessly, hearing his tormented moan at her ear as he clutched the sheet on either side of her head and arched down into her in an agony of fulfillment.

She'd wanted to look, but she was too shy. She hid her red face in his neck and held on while they shivered and sweated in the lazy aftermath of an unexpected mutual satisfaction.

Stasia had read that virgins almost never enjoyed their first time, that it was embarrassing and painful. At least, that's what her girlfriends had told her. It hadn't been that way for her. Tanner was dynamite in bed. No wonder Julienne stayed with him so long.

Julienne. Her body cooled. She was a body in bed. Had he been thinking of Julienne during that long evening of pleasure? Had she been standing in for the woman? It was like a stab in the heart.

And there was something else. She hadn't taken the first of the pills that would prevent pregnancy. If she turned up with a child, she'd have to fight Tanner tooth and nail, because he'd demand a termination. In fact, he'd probably be standing over her in the morning with that pill they gave after the fact. If he knew. If. He. Knew.

She hated herself for the thought. She couldn't hide a pregnancy, much less a child. He'd know as soon as his family knew, and he'd hate her.

But this hadn't been her idea. She hadn't asked for it. Had she?

He moved away from her, aware of guilty pleasure and

shock. He hadn't meant that to happen. He'd been missing Julienne. No. That was a lie. He'd gone hungry for Stasia from the first time he'd kissed her. The hunger had only grown. Today, it had reached flash point. The issue was that one time hadn't satisfied him. He'd had her, how many times? Twice, three times? Well, at least she was on the pill. He didn't have that to worry about. He'd actually phoned the pharmacist, whom he knew, to make sure she'd picked up the prescription.

So what did they do now? He'd done something he couldn't take back. It was a low thing, to seduce a woman he didn't plan to stay married to, to give her false hope that he was beginning to care. He wasn't, of course. She was sweet and kind and good-natured, and surprisingly passionate in bed. Not that it mattered, when Julienne was waiting for him in Greece, of course.

He swung out of the bed without a word and walked, nude, down the hall to his own room. He pulled clean clothes out of his closet and went to take a shower. Maybe it would wash off the lingering scent of that light, floral perfume that Stasia favored.

Stasia lay where he'd left her, in a jumble of emotions, the foremost of which was exhausted pleasure. But she'd better not dwell on that. Of course he'd enjoyed her, he was a man. They could enjoy anything feminine, anytime, she knew that.

When he was gone, she got up and found her suitcase, hurriedly dragging out jeans and underthings and a T-shirt with a sunflower on it.

She rushed into the shower and soaped away the smell of her reluctant husband. She washed her hair as well. It was so baby-fine that it would air dry, and the waves would fall naturally into it.

When she was clean, she hung up her wedding finery and went off into the kitchen to fix lunch. She glanced at the clock and grimaced. Supper.

She had food on the table when Tanner came back. She avoided looking directly at him, but she couldn't help the scarlet blush.

"I didn't know what you wanted to drink. I made coffee, because that's what I usually have with supper."

"Dinner," he said, going to the refrigerator. "Supper is colloquial."

"Okay, go ahead, throw your exotic references at me to point out that I'm just a stupid country girl with no education," she said merrily. "I don't care." She lifted the glass of white wine she'd poured herself to her lips and took a big, long swallow.

He turned, not certain he'd heard her right.

She looked back at him with raised eyebrows. "Oh, shouldn't I have said that? You've started early, you know. Correcting my grammar. Next you'll be on about my accent, and then you'll start on my clothes."

He glared at her, looked back in the fridge and frowned. "I thought there was a bottle of Riesling in here."

She picked up the half-empty bottle and read the letters to him. "R.I.E.S.L.I.N.G. Is this it? If you want some of it, you'd better hurry." She showed him the bottle. "It's going fast."

He scowled at her as he closed the refrigerator. "You don't drink."

She held up her glass and sloshed it at him.

"You didn't drink," he corrected. He took the bottle from her and poured himself a large glass before putting the stopper back in it. "There was a nice merlot in there also."

"Was that the dark wine?" she asked, and he nodded. "I can't drink dark wine. It has tannin in it."

"So?" he asked.

"I get violent migraines from tannins."

He sipped his wine. "My mother has them. So does John."

"I know. Your mother talked to my doctor about a preventative. I take it. But I still get them sometimes."

"I never get headaches."

While they talked, they filled their plates.

"How do you know about prosciutto?" he wondered while they ate.

"Daddy took me to this really elegant restaurant in San Antonio once, so I'd know what they were like. We had all sorts of expensive dishes, including this lovely ham." She took a bite of it and closed her eyes with delight. "I could eat my weight in it."

He studied her under his eyelids. She was pretty, like that, with her hair curling down around her shoulders, no makeup on. She looked natural, real. Nothing like the over-painted women he'd spent most of his adult life around.

He looked back down at his plate.

"When do you leave?" she asked, and took another sip of wine.

He looked at her with his glass suspended between his mouth and his hand. "What?"

"It's a simple question. When do you leave for Greece?"

He scowled. "Why do you want to know?"

She sighed and finished her wine. "Because when you leave, I'm moving back home," she said simply. "I have a canvas to finish."

"The will says that you live here," he pointed out.

"Wills can't read," she retorted.

"People can, and it will be noted. Your father's attorney will be watching, Stasia," he added curtly. "So will the prospective buyer's attorney, who's still in town, hoping for a chance to get his hands on your ranch."

"Oh, bother," she muttered. "If my father hadn't interfered, I could have sold the ranch to your father, you could have your kept woman, and I could go home and finish my canvas!"

He stared at her with icy pale blue eyes. "My kept woman?"

She blinked, half-lit. "If she isn't independently wealthy, and you pay all her bills, that means you keep her, doesn't it?" she asked simply.

"You make it sound raunchy."

"I haven't given an opinion."

"My mother has. Several. Repeatedly," he muttered.

"Your mother is a conventional woman with a wonderful marriage."

"Conventional," he agreed, irritated. "Unlike your own mother, yes?" he added, hitting where he knew it would hurt.

She was too tipsy to care what he said. She just looked at him, with eyes as old as the earth in a face gone quiet and pale with misery.

"God, I'm sorry!" he said shortly. "I didn't mean that."

"Sure you did, Tanner," she replied, sitting back in her chair. "You're here under protest because my father forced you to marry me, and all you want is to be free. Well, be my guest," she said, waving a hand in the air. "I'll stay here and paint while you sail around the world with your..." She stopped and laughed drunkenly. "I was going to say, your kept woman, but you don't like that. So how about your dependent? No? Your harlot...oh, no, excuse me, that was a very low blow, wasn't it?" She burst out laughing as his face hardened. "We don't have harlots in the modern world. There is no right and wrong. Everything's good, no matter how sordid. The world's turned upside down, and I'm living on the wrong side." She sighed, reaching for the bottle again.

"No." He took it away from her, got up and filled two cups with coffee. He was vaguely ashamed of himself. He didn't like the feeling. But that was no excuse for savaging Stasia, who'd also been forced into marriage. She loved him. He ground down on that thought, because it hurt him even more.

He put the coffee in front of her. "Drink that," he said firmly.

"No," she said belligerently, and glared up at him. "I'm happy. If I drink that, I'll remember this day, and I'll be looking for a dagger to do myself in with!"

"Join the club," he muttered, sitting back down.

"I hate you!" she blurted out.

"That'll be the day," he said curtly.

"I wish I hated you," she corrected. She glared at him. "You didn't have to sleep with me!"

"We didn't sleep," he pointed out.

She flushed. "You know what I mean!"

He gave her a long, appraising look. "A marriage on paper isn't legally binding without consummation." It was the truth. And it wasn't. He could have left her innocent. But that kiss on John's cheek still rankled, for reasons he couldn't understand. He hadn't wanted to take a chance that John might poach on his preserves while he was off in Greece with Julienne.

Put that way, it sounded cruel. Attached to one woman, married to another. Adultery or bigamy? But then, he didn't want Julienne for keeps. She was too cold, too heartless. She was like him, he thought, surprised. He was cold and heartless, too, for putting money above compassion. He'd let himself be forced into marriage with Stasia, discounting her feelings for him, walking all over them, in fact. Her wedding day and he'd spoiled it for her. He'd taken the joy out of it. Likely she'd never marry again. This would be her only memory of what should have been a joyful occasion. As she'd said, even the photographs would be a sad memoir of a sad day.

"I'm leaving tonight," he said curtly, and got up.

She just looked at him, pleasantly drunk and uncaring. "Shall I pack for you?" she asked airily. "I read that in one of my books. It sounded so…married," she added, and laughed.

"You're drunk," he pointed out.

She grinned. "And you're lucky. Because if I wasn't drunk, I'd be looking for the biggest baseball bat I could find, and then I'd go looking for you."

She probably would have. He remembered her playing baseball with all of them and a few other ranching kids after they'd branded calves and were enjoying home-cooked barbeque outside the barn.

She'd been a scrawny little thing, but she had grit. She'd outrun half the boys and outfought them as well. She never gave up, never gave in. She was pretty, even if not in the same class with Julienne, and she was loyal to the people she cared about. She had many good qualities. They could leave out the drinking one. He laughed to himself as he packed. Even drunk, he couldn't sink her.

He was sorry for that remark he'd made about her mother. He remembered the harsh gossip she and her father had endured after her mother's suicide. She'd found her mother, hanging from a rope on the back porch, after she got home on the school bus. Glenn had been out of town for two days. So Stasia had made the discovery all alone. She'd phoned the Everett home in hysterics. It was Tanner who'd answered the phone, who'd left a trail of fire getting to her house to hold her and comfort her, and then to call for help.

How could he have forgotten that? He'd been home on leave from the military at the time. Stasia had been, how old then, six years ago? Thirteen. A scrawny, leggy thirteen, but with that odd vulnerability over a core of steel that still hallmarked her personality. She'd straightened up very quickly from the shock and gotten on with the nuts and bolts of notifying her father and helping him through the grief.

She was an odd person, he thought as he finished packing. Vulnerable and soft on the surface, pure rock underneath when she needed to be. And in bed, a sensual dream of perfection, he thought, and then smothered the thought. That was the way to hell, paved with his good intentions. He didn't want to be a ranching husband with a brood of children. That was Stasia's dream, and he hoped she'd find a man who shared her hunger. Just not his brother John, he amended, and then stopped and glared at himself in the mirror. Where the hell had that thought come from?

He walked back into the dining room to find Stasia almost comatose at the table, her hair all over the place, her head down on her hands.

"You're going to have the great-grandmother of headaches when you wake up in the morning," he assured her.

"Go away. I'm sleeping."

He sighed. He put down the suitcase, swung her up into his arms and started for the master bedroom.

"I can walk," she protested.

"I could let you prove that," he threatened.

She relaxed against him, provoking more unwanted and unwelcome sensations that made his feet tingle.

"Go away, then, I don't care," she murmured drowsily. "I'll just paint until you're a distant memory."

"Good luck with that."

She made a rude sound and sighed. "I hate you."

"You said that."

"Oh. Okay. Just so you know."

He put her down on the bed, grimacing as he recalled the pleasure they'd shared on it so recently. He took off her sandals and pulled the cover over her.

"You will hate yourself in the morning," he predicted.

"I hate myself now," she murmured.

"Good. If you can't hold your liquor, don't drink."

She made a sound and then fell asleep.

He stood looking at her for a long time before he finally turned away, closing the door behind him. He felt as if he'd just made a monumental mistake, but he didn't know why.

Don't miss
The Loner *by Diana Palmer,*
Available wherever Canary Street Press books and ebooks are sold.